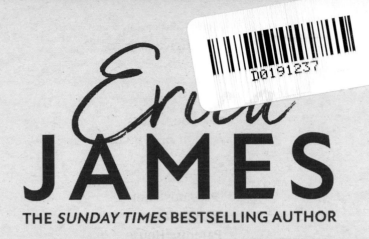

Erica JAMES

THE *SUNDAY TIMES* BESTSELLING AUTHOR

A SECRET GARDEN AFFAIR

ONE PLACE. MANY STORIES

HQ
An imprint of HarperCollins*Publishers* Ltd
1 London Bridge Street
London SE1 9GF

www.harpercollins.co.uk

HarperCollins Publishers
Macken House, 39/40 Mayor Street Upper,
Dublin 1, D01 C9W8

This paperback edition 2023

First published in Great Britain by
HQ, an imprint of HarperCollins*Publishers* Ltd 2023

ISBN: 9780008413781

For Samuel, and Edward and Ally, and
my grandest of grandchildren.

This book is also in memory of my dearest friend
Ray Allen who was the wittiest of men. He
not only made me laugh every time we spoke,
but millions of others too when he created the
character of Frank Spencer. God bless you, Ray.

Chapter One

July 1981
Larkspur House, Suffolk

Libby Mortimer was not the running-away sort, she really wasn't, but having been given the chance to escape London with all its cruel reminders of romantic fairy-tale weddings, she couldn't get away fast enough. If that made her a coward, so be it.

The city – and Marcus – was far behind her now and with the window down, and the warm air whipping at her hair, she willed the old VW campervan to make the journey to Suffolk. To break down on top of everything else would be the final straw. But then surely nothing could make life any worse than it already was?

In one of her typically flippant remarks, Mum had completely dismissed Marcus's infidelity and told Libby that she was over-reacting, that what he had done was what a lot of young men did, he'd been sowing his wild oats one last time before marrying.

'You know how it is,' Mum had gone on, as if explaining nothing more significant than a change in the weather, and quite oblivious to the pain she was inflicting, 'boys will be boys, they don't think about the consequences of their actions.'

'If that is meant to make me feel better about finding my fiancé cheating on me with my best friend three weeks before my wedding day,' Libby had replied, 'you couldn't be more wrong.'

'Darling, I'm just trying to make you realise that these things needn't be as . . . as calamitous as you seem to think they are.'

'Is that really all you can say?' Libby had asked in disbelief, her hand gripping the receiver. 'You'll be telling me next it's nothing but a storm in a teacup, or that I'm making a mountain out of a molehill!' It was fair to say that her mother had a heavy hand when it came to clichés and it was nothing short of a miracle that she hadn't peppered the exchange with more. So far, she'd notched up *boys will be boys*, but doubtless that was just an opening salvo.

'There's an awful lot more I could say,' she replied, 'but I can tell by the unpleasant shrillness of your tone that you're beyond listening to reason or taking well-intentioned advice. The only thing I will say is that you should find it in your heart to forgive Marcus his one error of judgement, and at the same time wonder what part your so-called best friend played in this. I wouldn't put it past that cunning girl to have led him on. I've never trusted her, if I'm honest.'

'So none of this is Marcus's fault?' Libby had said, her voice having risen yet further up the scale of what her mother would deem unpleasantly shrill.

'I didn't say that, but you mustn't fall into the trap of over-dramatising. Instead, think how disappointed the guests will be if you cancel the wedding. And your beautiful dress, surely you don't want to let that go to waste?'

'You can't be serious?'

'I am, darling, I'm perfectly serious. Are you really going to throw all that away, and the bright future you and Marcus could have together, because he had a silly fling? Just consider what you're prepared to lose. And let's face it, I doubt you'll be lucky enough to find yourself another man as eligible or as good a provider as—'

Her mother hadn't gone any further with her list of reasons

why Libby should think herself lucky to marry a cheat and a liar, because Libby had done the unthinkable, she had slammed down the phone on Nancy Mortimer. It was something that at the age of twenty-seven Libby had never done before, although there had been numerous times when she had been sorely tempted to do so.

Since that conversation Libby had done a number of other unthinkable things. She'd thrown the blue sapphire and diamond engagement ring Marcus had given her in his face – a ring very like the one Prince Charles had given Lady Diana – and then, and she wasn't proud of this, she'd gouged a groove along the side of his brand new Porsche with a screwdriver. It was a pathetically unoriginal thing to do, but she'd done it because she had known it would annoy him more than anything else she could do or say.

It was horribly petty of her, and she hadn't even felt a scrap of satisfaction for what she'd done. In fact, she'd felt ashamed of herself, thoroughly humiliated by resorting to such a childish act of malicious revenge. Which was precisely what Marcus accused her of, of acting like a child. That was after he'd begged her to forgive him for sleeping with Selina. He'd sworn that it had happened only the once, that it meant nothing, but when Libby confronted her friend, Selina had a different version of events. She claimed that she had lost count of how many times she and Marcus had had sex.

'How could you of all people do this to me?' Libby had demanded, fighting hard not to cry, wanting desperately to hang on to what was left of her dignity, to keep the avalanche of her emotions from crashing down the crumbling mountainside of her self-control. 'You knew better than anyone how much I loved Marcus. I just don't understand how you could have been so two-faced. One minute you're picking out your bridesmaid dress and helping me prepare for my wedding, and the next

you're in bed with Marcus. How could you have done that?'
She felt as hurt by her friend's betrayal as she did by Marcus's.

Her expression indifferent, Selina had shrugged. 'It wasn't
about you. It was about me and my feelings for Marcus.'

Libby had been shocked at the coldness in her friend, something she'd never seen before. 'Why don't you just go ahead and
tell me that all's fair in love and war?' she had said.

Her question had been met with another careless shrug. 'I don't
need to. But rather than attack me, you should ask yourself this:
if Marcus really loved you, why did he want to be with me?'

It was a good question and one Libby had failed to answer
in the last thirty-six hours since her life had been upended by
finding Marcus and Selina in bed together.

Or would it be more accurate to say it was a question she
couldn't bring herself to answer, not honestly at any rate?

Either way, the one thing she could be sure of was that she
was running away from what she'd thought was her future and
going back to her past at Larkspur House where, apart from one
of the saddest moments of her life, she had enjoyed some of the
happiest times. It was a truly wondrous place, a place of exquisite
enchantment and, according to Elfrida and Great-Aunt Bess, it
was a place where her broken heart would start to heal. Given
how awful she felt, that seemed a tall order but if anywhere
could restore her faith in love and mend the shattered pieces of
her heart, it was Larkspur House.

Entering the village of Finchley Green, and passing a row of
thatched cottages and their pretty gardens of hollyhocks, lupins,
lavender, climbing roses and lady's mantle, she spotted two neighbouring cottages that seemed to be in competition with each
other to see which could be the more patriotic with their red,
white and blue summer bedding plants in honour of the Royal
Wedding. Both houses were decorated with flags and bunting,

but one had a twee miniature wishing well in the middle of a circular bed and on its roof was a picture of Prince Charles and Lady Diana – it was the famous photo of the pair on the day they announced their engagement to the world back in February. It was a painfully taunting reminder of when Marcus proposed to Libby and she was suddenly seized with the desire to stop and do something unthinkable to that photograph.

Resisting the feeling, as strong as it was, she carried on through the village, passing the green and duck pond and the parade of shops, then down the hill, over the small bridge, taking the sharp bend to the right and then along Woodley Lane, the narrow track where frothy cow parsley brushed the sides of her recently painted campervan.

She and Selina had been running their catering business – buffet lunches mostly for corporate clients in the City – for eighteen months now and while Selina had been happy to continue using her car to deliver the trays of food to their clients, Libby had decided to trade in her Honda hatchback for a VW campervan. She'd had it resprayed and the words *From Our Pantry to Your Table* added. The van had proved to be a godsend and was perfect for transporting food around town, but it was a nerve-jangling bone-shaker for a longer journey such as this one.

What would happen to the business now was very low down on Libby's priorities. In preparation for her marrying Marcus, and so that she could focus on all the last-minute arrangements for the wedding, she had cleared her diary of work commitments, leaving Selina to carry out those that remained. She had kept her diary free for the dates of her honeymoon as well, so she had five to six weeks to reach a decision on what she was going to do next. Working with Selina was clearly not an option.

Before making her escape from London she had worked through a list of things she had to do, such as cancelling the wedding flowers and photographer and then informing the bridal shop that she wouldn't be needing the dress. The bills would still have to be paid, and no doubt her mother would complain endlessly about that, but it was unavoidable. There was the issue of wedding gifts being returned, but that would have to be dealt with in due course.

Something else she'd had to do was explain to her friends that the wedding was off. Once they'd recovered from their shock, they'd offered to do all they could to help, but really there wasn't anything they could do. This was something Libby had to come to terms with and hopefully, being back at Larkspur House with Bess and Elfrida, the process of healing would begin.

*

With a wheelbarrow now full of deadheaded offerings for the compost heap, together with weeds which had dared to set up home in the gravel of the drive, Elfrida Ambrose trundled her way round the side of Larkspur House, brushing against the beech hedge as she went. Then butting open the gate with the barrow, she continued towards the walled kitchen garden, traversing the herringbone path with care – a number of bricks had worked loose and had the cunning ability to take the unwary by surprise. She really should remember to remind Andrew to fix them. The trouble was, being her only gardener, he had so much to do as it was.

In the enclosed space of the kitchen garden, where the baking heat was trapped by the four sun-warmed brick walls, the scent of ripening peaches on the espaliered trees was heavy on the air. There was the sweet smell of strawberries too, shiny ruby-red jewels peeping out from their green foliage and the protective layer of straw she'd carefully wrapped around each plant. She would come back later to pick what they needed for supper that evening. Or maybe she would ask Libby to do it for her. The girl would need to be kept busy. Not that picking a bowl of strawberries was going to be the answer to Libby's problems.

Removing her gardening gloves, Elfrida took out her secateurs from the back pocket of her corduroy trousers and chose a selection of herbs – mint, chives, parsley and French tarragon.

Unable to resist it, she rubbed the tarragon leaves between her fingers and breathed in the strongly aromatic fragrance. Of all the herbs she grew, this one, with its summer-fresh smell of aniseed, was the most evocative; it had the power to transport her back to a time when she was young and falling in love. And a time when she was considered a great beauty.

As hard as it was to believe now, back when she had been celebrating her twenty-first birthday at the Ritz in London, photographs of her had appeared in *Tatler* and the gossip columns. She'd been referred to as *Elfrida Ambrose, the vibrantly beautiful daughter of Charles and Cecily Ambrose and younger sister of Mrs George Lassiter.* It was a description that had not gone down well with her sister who had taken offence at what she regarded as an implied insult, that only one of the sisters was beautiful. Prudence had grumbled about the slight for weeks, oblivious, or perhaps not caring, how pettily jealous she sounded. In the end it was George, her husband, who put her right. 'You're a married woman, Prudence, therefore your looks are of no interest to anyone but me.'

George, it had to be said, had not been the most charismatic of men, but then it wasn't his personality which had attracted Prudence. His appeal lay in the houses in Mayfair, Norfolk and the Highlands, all of which had added up to the kind of status Prudence had seen as her right. She always had been such a frightful social-climbing snob. It had been one of the many things that had made it so difficult for the two sisters to get on. Having such differing views on life, they were always pulling in opposite directions.

The appetising smell of baking greeted Elfrida when she passed through the cool of the scullery and pushed open the door to the kitchen. Bess was there, taking a tray of scones out of the old range. On the oak table was a plate of rock cakes and a Victoria sponge dusted with icing sugar, buttercream and jam dribbling down the side of the cake.

'You do realise Libby is visiting us on her own, don't you?' remarked Elfrida, going over to the Belfast sink to put the herbs she'd picked on the draining board. 'She's not bringing an army of hungry soldiers with her. Unless you've omitted to inform me of that small change of plan. Do we need to make up extra beds?'

Red-faced and perspiring, her hands inside a pair of oven gloves, Bess slid the scones onto a wire rack. 'Of course not,' she said, 'I just want to spoil the poor girl.'

'As you always do,' said Elfrida with a smile, thinking that there was nobody with a bigger heart than Bess Judd. She had been sixteen years old when she first came to work here. That had been fifty-nine years ago, and Elfrida could remember the day as though it were yesterday, mostly because Bess's arrival came after Elfrida had returned from time away in Italy where she had absconded from a finishing school, much to her sister's fury. On her return to England, Prudence, who was four years older than Elfrida and saw herself as being in *loco parentis*, since both their parents were dead, had been insistent that it wasn't fitting for Elfrida, who had only recently turned twenty-one, to live alone at Larkspur House. She wanted the house, which had been left to them by their parents, sold, and Elfrida installed at Tilbrook Hall in Norfolk where Prudence and George could keep a close eye on her. Elfrida had declared with equal vigour that she would do no such thing. 'Larkspur House will be sold over my dead body!' she'd remonstrated with her sister.

'That could be arranged,' Prudence had said darkly.

Elfrida had appealed to George and put it to him that the last thing he needed was an irksome sister-in-law cluttering up his life. The thought must have so appalled him, he squashed all counter-arguments from his wife and after promises and assurances from

Elfrida that she would conduct herself in a manner that would not bring shame raining down on them all, she was permitted to continue living at Larkspur House with the small retinue of staff, most of whom she'd known since she was a child. The hiring of a lady's maid was a stipulation laid down by Prudence, and one was duly sought.

Bess Harding (as she was called back then) arrived with a small, battered suitcase and the ready eagerness of a quick learner. She was a rosy-cheeked girl with a spirited nature who despite her youth had already worked as a young lady's maid, and of her own admission she was very organised and could sew like a proper seamstress. But they were the least of her talents as far as Elfrida was concerned. Loyalty and friendship and being totally trustworthy were the attributes that won Elfrida's admiration, and which, after all the extraordinary things they had gone on to share together, were still the qualities that meant more to her than anything else.

With Bess now standing at the Belfast sink, Elfrida moved over to the table and was just about to sneak a rock cake when Bess cocked her ear at the open window. 'She's here!' she cried. Then wiping her hands on her apron, she spun round. 'Now whatever you do, as I told you before, don't bombard the poor girl with a hundred questions about that wretched Marcus. Keep the conversation light.'

'Any other instructions?'

'Yes,' replied Bess as she went through to the hall, 'keep your grubby hands off those rock cakes while I help Libby in with her luggage.'

'You know, sometimes I can't help but wonder which one of us is the boss here.'

'No, you don't,' Bess called back to her. 'How else would you keep this show going if it wasn't for my superior management skills?'

'It was a rhetorical question!' shouted Elfrida, defiantly taking one of the rock cakes and biting into it.

'Libby, my dear, am I permitted to make the tiniest of observa-tions?' enquired Elfrida.

Poised to lift the teapot and replenish their cups, Bess glanced sharply across the white-clothed table and assembled plates of salmon and cucumber sandwiches, rock cakes, scones and sponge cake to where Elfrida was reclining in her wicker chair. She was dabbing the corners of her mouth with her napkin with as much refined delicacy as if she were dining at the Savoy dressed in her finest clothes.

They were actually sitting on the terrace in the shade of the rose-covered pergola, where every now and then a pale-pink rose petal floated slowly down from above their heads and landed on the table. Bess hoped it wouldn't put Libby in mind of wedding confetti. And far from wearing her best clothes, Elfrida was in her customary baggy old corduroy trousers, a man's collarless shirt with the sleeves rolled up and a bashed-about Panama hat rammed on her head. Her long silvery grey hair was plaited and lay to one side of her neck so that it curled over her shoulder and across her chest like a cat's tail. Bess half expected it to twitch as a sign that, like a cat, Elfrida was about to pounce. As she most assuredly was.

In a bid to remind Elfrida that she was supposed to be on her best behaviour, that under no circumstances was she to say anything to upset Libby any more than she already was, Bess cleared her throat warningly, but Elfrida merely tilted up her chin in a most infuriatingly pugnacious manner and held out her cup for a refill. Which Bess pointedly chose to ignore.

'Of course you can,' Libby said in response to Elfrida's question.

'You've lost weight,' Elfrida said. 'Much too much, in my opinion.'

Bess had thought the same when she'd first set eyes on Libby, in fact she'd been quite shocked by the change in the girl's appearance since she'd last seen her but had refrained from saying anything. Instead she'd made a mental note to feed the girl up during her stay.

'Most brides lose weight in the weeks before their wedding day,' Libby said mildly. 'Especially their aborted wedding day.'

'Yes, but you look positively gaunt, my dear, which is a most unappealing look. Unless, that is, you're an actress playing the part of a tragic heroine dying of consumption, then the half-starved look is *de rigueur*. You're not suffering from consumption, are you? Or perhaps you're anchoretic?'

Again, Bess gave Elfrida a warning rattle of her throat. There was bluntness and then there was downright battering-ram bluntness, which was Elfrida's special forte.

'Bess, you can do that all you want, making that ludicrous noise like a blasted rattlesnake, but I'd sooner you poured me some more tea and accepted that there is no point in us sitting here eating this fine spread you've laid on without us getting down to the nitty-gritty.'

'The nitty-gritty is that you're being your usual tactless self,' Bess fired back. 'And you can pour your own tea instead of sitting there like Lady flipping Bracknell!'

'Tactless! *Moi?*' Elfrida gave an exaggerated shudder of shocked outrage. 'Why, I'm the most discreet and judicious of people.'

'You couldn't be discreet if your life depended on it. You sit there blundering in without a care for anyone else's feelings, thinking only—' Bess's words ground to a sudden halt as she realised with horror that Libby was crying. Her chin tucked into her chest, her hands and napkin covering her face, her shoulders were heaving with terrible sobs.

'Oh, my darling girl,' Bess said, reaching across the table to her. 'I'm so sorry we've upset you.' She gave a *see what you've done now* look at the cause of the upset.

11

'Oh dear,' said Elfrida, 'have I misjudged matters?' She did at least have the grace to sound contrite. 'Take no notice of me, Libby, I'm nothing but a silly old woman who should know better.'

Very slowly, and lowering her hands, Libby raised her head. 'There's no need to apologise,' she said in a tight choking voice. 'I'm not crying, I'm laughing at you both. Honestly, you have no idea how good it is to hear you two bickering. It's the first normal thing that's happened to me since I found Marcus and Selina in bed together.'

'There you are, Bess!' declared Elfrida with a triumphant cry, 'I knew it was right not to treat her with kid gloves.'

'As if there's any other way with you.'

'Please stop, you two, or you'll set me off laughing again. And Elfrida, to put your mind at rest, I'm not anorexic. Or even *anchoretic* for that matter.'

'I'm very pleased to hear it. And to get to the nub of things, despite what a certain person sitting across the table from me thinks, can we take it that there's no chance of you resolving things with Marcus and making a go of it?'

'No chance whatsoever,' Libby said with sudden vehemence. 'I never want to see him again as long as I live.'

'Good girl, because in my view, for what it's worth, and no, Bess, I won't be quiet, not until I've said my piece; Libby, you're better off without him. He wasn't right for you. You're worth a hundred of his type. And I feel perfectly placed to say that.'

'Are you saying that because he cheated on me?'

'No,' Elfrida said emphatically. 'I thought it right from the start.'

Privately Bess agreed with what Elfrida had said, but it was always dangerous to start bad-mouthing someone at this stage when emotions were running so high, because if Libby did decide to forgive Marcus there would be no taking back the harsh words about him. Wanting to avoid that, Bess said, 'How about another sandwich, or another slice of cake?'

'Now you see, that's the difference between your great-aunt and me,' said Elfrida with a gay laugh. 'I employ the wrecking ball technique and come right out and tell you that you're as scrawny as a scarecrow, while Bess takes the softly, softly approach by thinking you won't notice that she's slyly fattening you up, cake-crumb by cake-crumb. She'll have you in a cage faster than you can say Hansel and Gretel!'

Bess tutted. 'You really can be quite absurd at times, can't you?'

'I aim to please.'

Libby smiled and helped herself to a sandwich. 'Both methods have their attractions. Although I'll pass on the cage option if it's all the same to you.'

'There's only one person who deserves to be put in a cage, and we both know who that is,' said Bess.

Elfrida rolled her eyes. 'This is what I have to put up with, Libby. She's become quite the bully in her old age.'

'Don't forget I'm five years younger than you,' Bess retorted.

Elfrida gave a coyly preening flick of her plait. 'Only just. Not that anyone would guess that.' She took a sip of her tea which she'd poured for herself, then pulled a disagreeable face. 'Cold tea, is there anything worse?'

Bess sighed. 'I'll go and make us a fresh pot.'

'Why don't you let me do it?' offered Libby. 'I'd like to make myself useful while I'm here.'

'Plenty of time for that,' said Elfrida, standing so abruptly she jolted the table. 'I shall do the honours.' She seized hold of the teapot and held it aloft as though it were a trophy she'd just won. 'Here I go, stately as a galleon,' she chorused.

When she'd disappeared inside the house, Bess turned to Libby. 'I'm afraid, unlike a fine wine, she doesn't improve with age. Lord knows I've tried my best with her.'

'I wouldn't want her, or you, any other way,' said Libby.

'But you must tell me if she crosses a line. She intends well, it's just that occasionally she could do with sugar-coating some of what she says.'

'I might be a bit bruised and battered from the events of the last few days, but I'm not made of glass.'

'I know. But the last thing I want is for your feelings to be trampled all over. You've just had your world tipped upside down, and no one has the right to make light of that. Not when you must be feeling so painfully raw.'

Libby pursed her lips, as if considering this description, picking up one of the rose petals on the table. 'Actually,' she said, 'right now it's mostly anger I feel and which I'm trying very hard to hold in.'

'It might be better if you didn't. Perhaps, just like a pressure cooker you should let it all out in one long angry burst.'

'That sounds quite appealing, but also,' Libby added with a small smile, 'quite dangerous. Think how it would horrify my mother. You know what she's like about hiding one's emotions.'

'Well, she need never know. Does she know you're staying here?'

'No, I'm afraid I couldn't bring myself to tell her, not when she thinks I should go ahead with the wedding. I swear all she cares about is what others think if I don't.'

Sadly, thought Bess, that was so often what Nancy ever cared about.

'Now then,' Elfrida's voice called out from across the terrace, 'I've had a change of plan. Forget about tea, what we need is champagne!'

Bess made to get to her feet to go and take the tray from Elfrida, but Libby was faster off the mark. 'Let me take that from you,' she said.

'That's what we need round here, a much younger pair of

hands,' said Elfrida. 'Any chance I can put you to work in the garden during your stay, Libby? There's always plenty to do and you're one of the few people who I trust to help me.'

'I'd be disappointed if you didn't ask me to pitch in.'

'Why the champagne?' asked Bess warily as she watched Elfrida peel away the foil and wire-work, then skilfully ease out the cork with her strong fingers before filling the coupe glasses without spilling a single drop of the golden liquid.

'We need to make a toast to Libby and her new life,' Elfrida answered. She passed the glasses round and, still standing, as though to give more emphasis to what she was about to say, she lifted up her glass. 'Libby,' she intoned, 'Marcus is just someone you used to know; you must chalk the bounder up to experience. And to quote dear old Oscar Wilde, experience is simply the name we give our mistakes.'

'Very nicely put,' said Bess with relief as they chinked their glasses together, wanting to add, *now sit down, dear, before you say anything to spoil the moment.*

But naturally Elfrida wasn't finished. Of course she wasn't.

'*Non, Je ne regrette rien!*' she began singing with full-throated gusto, so much so it caused a dove that had been gently cooing in a nearby tree to flap its wings and fly off in startled fear. As luck would have it, they were only treated to a couple of lines of the song and after ending with a beaming smile, Elfrida tossed back the contents of her glass in one effortless swallow. She then raised her arm and threw the glass against the wall of the house before disappearing back inside to fetch a replacement.

It had been a wildly dramatic gesture, and one Bess hadn't seen Elfrida make in many years. It conjured up myriad memories, of gloriously happier times, of being on the French Riviera and of watching Elfrida dance with the devastatingly handsome love of her life, Nikolai Demidov. He'd been a giant of a man and in his arms with her bewitchingly blithe spirit, Elfrida had looked like the prettiest of ringlet-haired dolls. They'd made such a dashingly glamorous couple.

It didn't take a genius to work out that Elfrida clearly associated Libby's broken heart with her own from all those years ago.

Relinquishing the hold that memory had on her, and all that followed, Bess offered Libby something else to eat. 'How about a scone? You'll need something to soak up all the champagne Elfrida has in mind for you to drink.'

'I can always say no to her.'

'True. But you know how persuasive she can be.'

*

From the sideboard in the dining room, Elfrida selected a glass from the remaining coupe glasses. They were all a little dusty from lack of use, but nothing a wipe with a tea towel wouldn't remedy. Despite what Bess might say.

There had been a time when every wine and sherry glass and whisky tumbler would have been in constant use and the silverware buffed to perfection. In what felt like another lifetime, Larkspur House had rarely been without a house party of some sort. Guests had loved to spend their weekends here, enjoying the beauty of the garden – sometimes even helping in it – but always, there had been an atmosphere of fun and gaiety. Sometimes the laughter might have been a little forced, but it had helped chase away the sadness.

So often that's what one had to do in life to get by, pretend that the pain wasn't there. It was what Libby was going to have to do. Just as both Elfrida and Bess had done. Sometimes there was nothing for it but to be the consummate actress in order to project the person you wanted everyone to believe you were. Elfrida had learnt that skill at a very young age.

Chapter Two

September 1923
The Côte d'Azur
Elfrida

It was September 1923 and I was twenty-two and brimming with confidence and *joie de vivre*. As I stood on the terrace of the charmingly dilapidated old villa that was nestled into the rocks halfway between Antibes and Cannes, I believed there was nothing the world could throw at me which I couldn't hurl back, and with added interest. Why wouldn't I believe this when I felt I had already lived at least three lifetimes over and was as worldly-wise as an ancient sage? After all, I had been running my own household for a year now and was entirely responsible for myself and the future of Larkspur House.

The source of my confidence, as strange as it might sound, was tragedy. Tragedy can do either of two things to a person; it can break you, or it can make you. In my case it had made me; I was stronger for all the heartbreaking grief I had experienced. My first loss happened when I was twelve years old and my beloved older brother, Bobby, killed himself, although I was under strict orders from Prudence always to refer to his death as a tragic accident. The word suicide was never to be mentioned, much less the reason he ended his life. Then two years later, in 1915, and when our parents were travelling home from yet another

17

of their plant-hunting expeditions, they perished on board the *Lusitania* when it was torpedoed by the Germans. With the Great War raging, it being the only way I knew how to assuage my grief, I threw myself into helping Mr Padget, our elderly head gardener. The under gardeners had gone to fight, so only Jimmy Padget and I were left to maintain the beautiful garden Mama and Papa had so lovingly created. It was my refuge and where I felt closest to my parents. It was also where I did most of my learning, much to the disgust of my governess, who despaired of ever refining me in the manner she thought fitting.

Two years after the war had ended, when my governess left to teach a more obliging student, Prudence insisted that I should go to a finishing school in Florence. It was the one she had attended, and she hoped it would transform me from a wilful ragamuffin with dirt constantly under my fingernails, into a dutiful and compliant young lady capable of attracting a wealthy husband, just as she had.

Needless to say, her plans for me went awry when after a month I escaped from the finishing school with a fellow inmate, an American girl called Dorothea Mickelberg. We took the train to Venice to stay with her parents who were renting a palazzo on the Giudecca. They invited me to go to the Côte d'Azur with them and in their company, I adopted a new air of sophisticated sangfroid, and although my allowance was not as generous as Dorothea's, the two of us went shopping for elegant clothes together. We had a ball, dancing until one in the morning and flirting outrageously with any number of handsome young men who took our fancy. It was, in so many ways, a happy reminder of the jolly house parties Mama and Papa hosted when I was a child. When they were home and not searching distant lands for rare plants, my parents loved to entertain and seldom was there a time when a guest wasn't staying at Larkspur House. Some stayed for weeks on end.

After Prudence threatened to come and fetch me home from the South of France, I reluctantly took my leave. I wasn't afraid to face the music which I knew awaited me, I could dance to any unpleasant tune my sister wished to play for my benefit.

It was during my journey home, on the train from Paris to Calais, that I met a man who was to change my life. A few years older than me, his name was Mallory Vaughan, and he was the grandson of the wealthy industrialist Thomas Vaughan. We hit it off straight away, teasing each other that we were disgustingly vulgar, coming as we did from 'common trade'. The Vaughan money was originally made from bricks and mortar back in the early nineteenth century, and mine from Ambrose Woollen Mills in Yorkshire. But unlike the Vaughan empire which had gone from strength to strength, the Ambrose finances had dwindled after the mills had been mismanaged and sold off to a competitor.

Our financial disparity aside, I adored Mallory instantly. How could I not, when he promised to lead me wildly and deliciously astray?

Which was how I ended up on the terrace of Villa Bellevue that September evening with my cup of confidence running over, along with the champagne in the glass I was holding which had just been jolted by Mallory in his clumsy haste to kiss my cheek.

'Freddie!' he yelled above the music that was being played by the band inside the villa and where guests were dancing the Charleston, a dance only very recently brought to the Riviera by the influx of American visitors. 'I've been looking for you for simply ages, where on earth have you been hiding yourself?' It was a typical exaggeration on Mallory's part as we'd spoken not an hour ago.

'I haven't been hiding,' I said, 'I've been dancing and then I came out here to catch my breath and enjoy a glass of champagne, which you have just slopped down my dress.' I was conscious as I was speaking that at Mallory's side stood a handsome, dark-haired man with eyes as dark as the sky above us. He was impeccably dressed in black coat and tails, the starched white wingtip collar of his dress shirt flawlessly pressed, and his white bow tie perfectly tied. Mallory always did have a fondness for a smartly turned out man, and this one was no exception.

'A thousand apologies,' cried Mallory, peering at my silk dress. 'I shall buy you a new one tomorrow!'

'There's no need,' I said, 'I'm sure Bess will be able to clean it for me. Aren't you going to introduce me to your friend?'

'Of course, that's why I was looking for you. I want you to meet—' But his words ran aground as at that moment another guest grabbed hold of him. She was a ravishing creature wearing a choker of diamonds and a shimmering beaded dress of silver chiffon that was far more daring than the frock I was wearing; and trust me, I thought I'd been daring. 'Introduce yourselves, darlings!' Mallory instructed as he was swept away.

The abandoned man's gaze briefly followed Mallory and the shimmering dress that we could both now see had an audaciously low back and revealed an expanse of milky white skin. Slowly he returned his attention to me and smiled, no more than a slight lifting of his generously wide mouth. It was a sardonic smile, I decided. For some reason he suddenly seemed a lot taller now that Mallory had gone, and a lot more substantial. Being a scant five feet and three inches tall myself, I was used to straining my neck to look up at men, but this one towered over me. I was also aware how pleasant he smelled, of soap with a tantalising hint of citrus, and maybe cedar. I knew that Mallory had his cologne specially made for him in Grasse; maybe this friend of his did too.

Not one to stand on ceremony, I proffered my hand. 'Elfrida Ambrose,' I said. 'Friend and co-conspirator of our much-loved host.'

'*Enchanté, mademoiselle,*' he said, raising my gloved hand all the way up to his lips and kissing it. 'I'm Nick, or Nicki, if you prefer.'

His English was just a little too studied to be his mother tongue, but there was no faulting his French in those two words – *enchanté, mademoiselle*. Yet, at the same time, I detected a hint of something else.

'Are you American?' I asked.

He stared at me; his eyes just fractionally narrowed as though perhaps wondering what had given him away. 'No,' he said. 'Try again.'

'Well,' I said ponderingly, 'I'm going to rule out French; you're much too tall.'

He tilted his head. 'I hate to correct such a charming inquisitor, but I'm afraid I must.'

'Oh, please, don't be afraid to correct me, I'm more than capable of accepting when I'm in the wrong. And of pushing back when I'm not,' I added.

'I'm sure you are,' he said. 'But thanks to my mother, I am half French.'

'And the rest of you?' And goodness, there really was an awful lot of him!

'Russian,' he answered.

Yes, of course, I thought. Europe was full of White Russians who had escaped the revolution. 'So where's home for you?'

'Here and there.'

'How marvellously mysterious you sound.'

His dark eyes glinted. 'It's my way of making myself sound more interesting than I really am.' He signalled to a passing waitress and exchanged my now empty champagne glass for a full one while helping himself to a glass.

'*À votre santé,*' he said.

'*À la votre,*' I murmured back at him.

I sipped my drink and observed his face and the perfectly

upright way he held himself and began to consider the possibility that I had this man wrong; he really didn't seem Mallory's sort at all, he was much too stiff and formal.

'How do you know Mallory?' I asked when I realised I'd been caught staring at him for just a little too long.

'I only met him last week, in Paris at a party held at the Ritz for a friend of mine.'

'And here you are now.'

'He thought the change of scene might do me good.'

'And has it?'

He eyed me over the rim of his glass. 'I'm starting to think it just might,' he said.

He then explained that he'd arrived that afternoon and was staying nearby in a villa owned by a cousin.

'Has Mallory told you what the locals have nicknamed this place after he rented it last season?' I asked.

'No.'

'*Maison Folie.*'

He cocked an eyebrow. '*Mad house*. And is it?'

'Good Lord yes! Mallory has a very eclectic circle of friends.'

'Will you be here for the entire season?'

I shook my head. 'Just for a few weeks.'

'And then where?'

'I shall go home.'

'Where is that?'

I told him about Larkspur House and the quiet village in Suffolk where I lived. Before I knew it, I'd told him about the garden and what it meant to me. All the while I spoke, his attention never wavered, his eyes of polished onyx never left mine. It was oddly alarming, and perhaps why I rattled on to the extent I did. When I finally fell quiet, he asked me a question that took me by surprise.

'And what do you intend to do with your life?'

I gave a trilling little laugh, deciding it was time to sound less earnest, and to apply some of the charm for which I was known. 'My intention is to do all I can to avoid marrying well, as my sister would have me do,' I said.

He frowned. 'Marriage doesn't appeal to you? I thought that's what all girls wanted.'

'It may have escaped your notice,' I said, the cynicism in my voice laced with coquettish challenge, 'but it's 1923 and the world has changed. These days there are more opportunities available to women.'

'I suspect the world must change a great deal more to accommodate you, *Mademoiselle*. But do these new opportunities of which you speak preclude a husband and children?'

'Not at all, but I have too much I want to do before I succumb to the needs of a demanding husband and a brood of cherubic-faced children.'

'I believe not all husbands are demanding.'

'Whoever told you that was lying!'

Once more he frowned. 'How sad to be so cynical at so young an age.'

'And how sweet of you to think I'm too young to be cynical. How old do you think I am?'

He drank his champagne and slowly ran his steady gaze over me as though peeling away not just my dress, but the sophisticated veneer I had so carefully applied to myself. The intensity of his scrutiny caused goosebumps to spring up on my bare arms and shoulders and I gave an involuntary shudder.

'You're cold,' he said. 'Here, hold my glass and I'll give you my tailcoat.'

'There's no need,' I said.

But he wasn't having any kind of refusal from me. I had the impression that he wasn't used to people saying no to him. His tailcoat was laughably too big for me, but despite not being cold,

23

the warmth of the fabric felt good, like slipping into a comfortingly warm and fragrant bath.

'You haven't answered my question,' I said then.

'It would be very ungallant of me to do so,' he answered. 'Besides, I know exactly how old you are, Mallory told me.'

'Did he, indeed? I shall have to have words with him. What else did the wretched man reveal about me?'

'That would be telling. But if I may be permitted to offer some advice, you sound like a young woman falling into the trap of seeking excitement but finding only trouble. I would urge you to be cautious.'

Irritated at his patronising tone and that he should dare to tell me what to do, I gave a careless laugh. 'Oh, there's plenty of time for caution when I'm in my dotage.'

'Something tells me that won't ever happen.'

'What? You think I won't live long enough to grow old?'

'No, *Mademoiselle*, you'll live for ever, but you won't ever be old, and I doubt you'll ever heed my advice to be careful.'

Before I had a chance to think of a suitable response to what he'd just said, as extraordinary as it was, he tossed back the last of his champagne. 'And now, *mademoiselle*,' he said, 'as much as I have enjoyed talking with you, I fear I must leave you, to avoid being accused of monopolising you in a manner that would be considered most inappropriate. I should not wish to keep you from the chance to dance.'

'You could always ask me to dance,' I said, amused at his excessively correct manner.

'I could do that, but I prefer a waltz to this new dance everyone is performing with such abandon.' He then gave me a courtly bow and strode away.

'Your coat!' I called out to his retreating figure.

'Keep it,' he replied over his shoulder. 'I have another.'

*

The next morning, I rose early, as did Mallory. We were two of a kind in that respect, no matter the lateness of the hour to bed or the strength of a hangover. While the rest of the guests who were staying slumbered on, we were served breakfast on the terrace amongst the large terracotta pots of lemon trees and with the view of the sun-drenched coastline and sparkling sea before us.

Once the maid had left us alone and I was pouring our coffee, Mallory leant forwards. 'Now, Freddie, I want you to tell me everything! What did you think of the delectable Nick?'

I gave an insouciant shrug. 'There's not much to tell. We chatted for a while and then he left. Frankly, I don't think he could get away fast enough.' I put the coffee pot down and gave Mallory a stern look. 'And I have a bone to pick with you. What have you told him about me, and for what purpose? Were you matchmaking? Because if so, I have to tell you that you have misjudged things.'

'In what way?'

'Are you sure he isn't more inclined to be a . . .' I chose my next words with care, adhering to the rules of our close friendship, that certain things were understood without ever being put into actual words. 'A *special* friend for you?' As the night had worn on, and the more champagne I had drunk, the more I convinced myself that my failure to secure the interest of the haughty Russian was because he wasn't interested in women.

'Sadly not, more's the pity,' Mallory replied. 'Count Nikolai Demidov is well beyond my reach.'

'*Count* Nikolai Demidov?' I repeated.

'Didn't he give you his full title when he introduced himself?'

'No. In fact, he shared very little about himself.' *Unlike me*, I thought, recalling how I had babbled on about Larkspur House and myself.

Mallory smiled. 'My dear girl, are you saying you failed to lasso him with your exquisite English rose beauty and wily charms? Haven't I taught you anything?'

'Drink your coffee and shut up.'

He ignored my reprimand. 'For what it's worth, I guarantee you haven't seen the last of him. He'll definitely want to see you again. How could he resist?'

I thought of the tailcoat which Bess, my maid who always travelled with me, had put on a hanger upstairs in my bedroom, and wondered if I was wrong and Mallory was right. Had leaving his coat with me been a deliberate ploy on the Count's part to arrange a further meeting?

I drank some coffee and nibbled on a delicious pastry that was stuffed with apricot and almonds. 'Why are you so keen for him to see me again, Mallory?'

'Because, my dear, I think it's high time you stopped playing your flirtatious games with eager young pups and fell in love.'

I gave a suitable huff of disapproval. 'How do you know I haven't already?'

'Because you would have told me, and more to the point I would have known by the sparkle in your eyes and the glow of your peaches and cream complexion.'

He was right, of course, I would have confided in him if I'd seriously fallen for anyone, because ever since we'd met on that train bound for Calais three years before, he had become my closest friend and confidant. He knew that for all my talk and apparent sophisticated worldliness, I was merely acting a part. In other words, I was a fraud.

But then so was Mallory. The real Mallory Vaughan had fought in the trenches in the Great War and had lost countless friends and witnessed terrible things. On his return home he'd been determined to put the horror behind him and devote himself to a life of pleasure and beauty, and to share what he had with as many people as he could. He was such a generous soul.

That generous spirit had led him to entrust me with creating a new garden for him at March Bank, his beautiful manor house in Oxfordshire. His knowledge of plants was almost as great as mine, and we could happily spend hours together choosing what to plant and where. Those were the times I most enjoyed with Mallory, when he was truly himself and not the flamboyant showman he was known for being.

I would have happily undertaken the job of redesigning his garden without being paid, but Mallory had insisted March Bank was to be my first official commission as a garden designer, and that I was to use it as a calling card to garner further work. As a consequence, when I had recently visited my sister in Norfolk, I had been approached by a number of guests staying for the weekend at Tilbrook Hall who had heard of my work for Mallory and requested my services to redesign their own gardens. Naturally Prudence was scandalised at the spectacle of her sister touting for business to support herself, but I did what I always do, I ignored her.

My thoughts returned to the man who had left me so abruptly last night and who had slighted my ego by turning down my suggestion that he should dance with me.

'Mallory,' I said, 'why are you so keen for me to have a grand passion with an aloof Russian count?'

'Oh, come on, Freddie. How can you not be attracted to the romance of a dashing aristocratic White Russian who fled his homeland during the Russian revolution? He's perfect for you!'

'Hmmm . . .' I said, and left it at that.

Three hours later, as I returned from my swim down in the bay, having negotiated the steep pathway cut into the rockface of the cliff, Mallory was waiting for me. His face was wreathed in the biggest of smiles.

'He's sent you flowers, and a card inviting you for dinner at his villa. If you're in agreement, he'll fetch you himself.'

I surveyed the extravagant bouquet Mallory held out for me. 'You opened the card?' I said, snatching it from him.

'Naturally! I wanted to be sure he's treating you the way he should.'

'Hmmm . . .' I said once again.

*

I spent the next hour or so swearing I would not bow to being jockeyed around in the way that Mallory was so determined I should be. There was something very peremptory too about the invitation, but perhaps that was just the way of a Russian count.

Curiosity, of course, had the better of me and I accepted the invitation and then spent an age wondering what to wear. Bess did her best to assure me that whichever dress I wore, I would be certain to dazzle.

'But I'm not sure I want to dazzle,' I told her. 'I'm not in the least bit concerned about impressing this man.'

She gave me one of her looks that indicated she knew that was a barefaced fib on my part. Having been in my employment now since last year, we had developed an easy rapport and I had come to value her opinion. Particularly when it came to selecting which dress I should wear. She also had a knack for doing my hair, which I was ashamed to say I could not master.

Unlike many women of my age, I had not had my hair cut into the boyishly short style of the moment. If I was vain about anything, it was my hair which was long and naturally wavy with a reddish tint to it, and as a result I had often been likened to a pre-Raphaelite beauty by amorous suitors. At Bess's suggestion, she had occasionally created a faux bob for me by gathering my hair into a tight chignon at the nape of my neck and put in extra waves to it at the front and sides. However, I still preferred the Mary Pickford look. Last night Bess had styled my hair by pinning it up so that I resembled, as she called it, a Greek goddess. This evening I had requested a slightly less dressy look as I was determined not to appear as though I were out to impress.

'As you wish, miss,' she'd said.

Mallory's guests from last night had all left now and when I went downstairs, I found him alone in the salon, cocktail shaker in hand.

'I'm making you a gimlet,' he said, 'something to sooth away the bad mood you've been in all afternoon.'

I tutted, but nonetheless accepted the cocktail and had just finished it when one of the maids appeared to say that Count Demidov was waiting for me outside.

'Can't even be bothered to get out of his motorcar to come and get me,' I muttered bad-humouredly, throwing a velvet stole around my bare shoulders and picking up my evening bag, as well as the borrowed tailcoat.

'Oh, do stop being such a crosspatch, Freddie. Go and have fun, that's an order. I shall wait up for you to hear all about it.'

When I stepped outside into the still warm twilight there was no sign of a motorcar, only the imposing silhouette of a man humming softly to himself. I couldn't say why exactly, but the sound of him humming was completely at odds with what I knew of him thus far. Humming seemed far too light-hearted for a man of his solemnity.

'Good evening, *mademoiselle*,' he said.

'Good evening, *Count* Demidov,' I said in return to his greeting, noting that he was casually dressed in cream trousers with a navy-blue sweater and a cravat at his neck. Then, looking around him as though to emphasise the fact that there didn't seem to be any sign of a motorcar, I added, 'Are we to walk to your villa for dinner?'

29

He shook his head. 'We can if you would like to, but my preference is to take you by boat to our destination.'

'Oh,' I said, more than a little surprised. 'What fun.'

He took his tailcoat from me, slung it over one of his broad shoulders and, offering his hand, said, 'Shall we?'

He assisted me down the rocky path even though I was quite familiar with it. It would have appeared rude to refuse his help and besides, the last thing I wanted was to make a fool of myself by missing my footing and stumbling into his arms. Even by my coquettish standards, when I so chose, that would be a cliché too far. There was no questioning the strength of the guiding hand and arm extended to me and I didn't doubt that a girlish swoon would have him sweeping me up as though I were as light as a feather.

He was silent all the way down to the beach, perhaps concentrating on his footing, which rendered me silent as well; an unusual occurrence, it has to be said.

Tied to the jetty was a sleek motorboat and after helping me aboard, he started up the engine and off we went, skimming across the gentle swell of the water.

'You can use my coat again if you're cold,' he said as the sea air whipped at my hair and undid the good work Bess had earlier put into it. Not that I minded. It felt good to feel the salty air rushing at my face and rippling the flimsy silk fabric of my dress. And when Count Demidov, one hand placed securely on the wheel of the boat to guide us to our destination, wherever that was, turned and smiled at me, I suddenly felt intensely alive. The blood fizzing through me like champagne, I felt exhilarated, as though I were embarking on a thrilling adventure, running away with a mysterious dark stranger!

Chapter Three

July 1981
Larkspur House, Suffolk

It was no surprise to Libby that she woke the following morning with a head that felt like it might explode. By Larkspur House standards her hangover wasn't too debilitating; she could at least stand upright and her eyes managed, just about, to tolerate the bright morning sunshine that was streaming in through the open window.

Out of bed, and resting her elbows on the cool stone sill, she looked down at the Long Border which was considered by many to be the crowning glory of the garden. Over the years it had appeared in any number of magazines and books and had even been featured as a perfect example of an English herbaceous border on *Gardeners' World*. That was an experience Elfrida swore she would never repeat. 'Oh, Percy was an absolute dear,' she said of the show's presenter at the time, 'but heavens, the whole rigmarole of the thing was such a tiresome bore, all that waiting for the light to be just right.'

The central sweep of lush green lawn was flanked by two borders about ten feet deep backed by high yew hedges, and at the furthest end was a precisely positioned focal point of a large stone urn. Never one to put in one plant when half a dozen would do, Elfrida had crammed the borders full of roses, thalictrum,

31

salvias, penstemon, lupins, dahlias, hummocks of lavender and santolina. Tall wrought-iron obelisks stood like sentries at regular intervals the length of the two borders to add extra height to the planting scheme, and were smothered in a variety of clematis, their saucer-sized flowers every shade of pink, purple and white. It was a vibrant eruption of colour and reflected perfectly the woman who had created it and who was currently occupied with deadheading one of the many rose bushes. Her footsteps, as well as the marks the wheelbarrow had made, were tracked in the dewy wet grass.

It was a scene Libby had witnessed for as long as she could remember. As a young child she had thought Larkspur House to be the most magical place in the world and on this sunny July morning, she thought the same thing; it was a balm to the soul. Here, in this beautiful sanctuary, this enchanted place as Elfrida had always called it, she could almost believe that she had escaped to a parallel universe where Marcus and his brutal betrayal couldn't touch her.

Of course, eventually she would have to return to that other world, because she could only hide for so long. She would have to return to London and face Marcus in order to disentangle their lives. But really, what was there to disentangle? It wasn't as if they had to go through the aggravation of divorce, thank goodness. Nor was there a jointly owned property to deal with; buying a house together was something they had planned to do once they were married. Until two days ago she had been dividing her time between her own flat, which she shared with Selina, and Marcus's which she would have moved into when they returned from their honeymoon.

So why shouldn't she let him deal with the fallout of his actions? Why shouldn't he be the one to inform the guests who didn't yet know that there would be no wedding and that any presents they had bought for the happy couple should be returned? This problem was not of her making, was it?

There again, how satisfying would it be to send a curt note of apology to the guests explaining that the wedding was off, owing to the groom sleeping with the bride's closest friend? Thinking how horrified her mother would be if Libby did just that, it was a dangerous temptation, particularly after the dismissive way Mum had spoken to her,

But then more charitably she thought how hard her mother made life for herself. She was so tightly wound she just couldn't appreciate what she had. It wasn't even as though she'd had a tough life: anything but. She had been brought up by parents who loved her; she'd married a man who had loved her in his undemonstrative way, and she had wanted for nothing. Dad's death sixteen years ago had left her more than adequately provided for, yet somehow, even when Dad had been alive, none of it had ever been enough to make Nancy Mortimer truly happy; there was a bitterness that ran through her that Libby couldn't fathom.

Something else she had never been able to understand fully was her mother's coldness towards Elfrida and Bess who was, after all, Mum's only aunt. Mum's own mother, Grandma Joan, had displayed the same coolness to Bess and Elfrida and Libby could only assume there had been a falling out at some point. It was what often happened in families, the slightest of disagreements that escalated to the point of no return. Elfrida also had a less than cordial relationship with her own sister.

Whatever had caused the rift, and over the years Libby had tried and failed to discover what it was, it had left Mum and Grandma Joan displaying all the signs of jealous resentment. On one occasion, when Libby had raised the matter with Elfrida, she had laughed and said something about provincial folk and their distaste for anyone who led a life that didn't conform to what they considered the norm. At the time, Libby hadn't really understood the remark; she'd been too young. But she hadn't been too young to realise that when she returned home after one of her idyllic holidays spent at Larkspur House, it was better if she didn't go on too much about the wonderful time she'd had, just in case her mother put a stop to her visits. Given how both Nancy and Grandma Joan had felt about Elfrida and Bess, it was a wonder Libby had been allowed to visit them at all.

From a young age Libby had discerned the art of compartmentalising things. There was time spent at home, time spent away at school, time spent with her grandparents and then best of all, time spent at Larkspur House where she had the freedom to do more or less as she pleased. She could go for long walks on her own, climb trees, lie on her back in the long grass in the orchard staring up at the sky through the leafy branches listening to the birds, and stay up late to go with Elfrida to hear the nightingales singing. Not once would she be chided for messing up her clothes or frittering precious time away.

But what she'd loved to do best of all was help Elfrida in the garden and listen in awe as the older woman named all the plants in Latin. She'd learnt more Latin that way than she ever did at school. And when Libby wasn't in the garden with Elfrida, she was in the kitchen with Bess. After one visit she announced to her mother that when she was old enough she wanted to study horticulture and design gardens just like Elfrida had. Her mother had told her that she would do no such thing, it was out of the question, grubbing around in the soil was no job for a proper young lady. There was quite a scene about it, with Libby unable to understand why her mother thought it was such a bad idea; but to keep the peace, Libby had backed down and instead pursued her other interest, which was cooking. For some reason her mother thought that much more acceptable and appropriate for a young woman.

She had never forgotten the pride she'd felt when she was not yet eleven and had presented Elfrida and Bess with an entire meal which she had cooked herself, by carefully following the recipes in

Bess's well-used cookery books. She had set the table in the dining room with the best silver and glassware, filled a vase with flowers from the garden, lit the candles in the silver candelabra and even opened a bottle of wine.

The thought of wine now seemed to set off a renewed thumping in her head, reminding Libby of the champagne she had consumed yesterday, followed by an assortment of lethal cocktails Elfrida had mixed. She had a vague recollection of climbing the stairs up to her bedroom, but it was a blank from then on. She must have undressed herself, because she was now in her nightdress with her clothes from yesterday lying in puddled heaps on the floor beside the bed.

The sight of them evoked the memory of finding Marcus in bed with Selina – their discarded clothes had laid a trail to his bedroom.

Laughably, Libby's first thought when she'd seen Marcus's trousers lying on the floor was to tut at his untidiness and bend down to pick them up. But then she'd spotted a pair of shoes and a dress which she knew didn't belong to her, followed by the unmistakable sound of gasps and ecstatic cries coming from the bedroom.

The most painful part of replaying that scene in her mind was trying to remember the last time she and Marcus had had sex that way, swept up in a messy wave of greedy passion and ripping their clothes off before they made it to the bedroom, then afterwards lying in a tangle of limbs slick with sweat. It had been like that in the beginning, but somewhere along the line sex had become more routine, something they did after cleaning their teeth and switching off the bedside light.

How had the fizz gone out of that side of things so quickly, or was that just how things were between two people who had been in a relationship for more than a year? Or had Selina been the reason for things going off the boil? Had Marcus been busy finding his satisfaction with her and not Libby?

She felt the heat of angry betrayal rising in her chest, pressing against her ribs and sucking the air out of her. The pain added to the throbbing in her head and she had to clamp down hard on the emotion before it had the better of her.

Think positive thoughts, she told herself, fixing her gaze on Elfrida – such a slight, insubstantial figure at this distance – who was now, mallet in hand, hammering wooden stakes into the ground to support an exuberantly flowering dahlia. Thinking that she'd be a dangerous woman right now with a mallet in her hand, Libby smiled.

In the last few days her mind had been a spinning-top of angry regrets and being at Larkspur House made her realise she had another regret, that she hadn't visited Bess and Elfrida more in the last year. She'd been too wrapped up in Marcus, as well as embarking on her new catering business, and she had neglected the two women who had always been there for her. She wouldn't allow that to happen again. Especially not when time was marching on for them both. Although old age and infirmity hardly seemed possible, looking at Elfrida as she swung the mallet and drove home another wooden stake. At seventy-nine years of age, the woman was quite exceptional; a true one-off.

In many ways it was the house itself that seemed suddenly to have aged. With its faded wallpaper, peeling paintwork, scarred wooden floors, knocked-about edges and general chaotic clutter, it was definitely looking a little shabbier and more neglected than when Libby was last here. She knew that Bess did her best to keep on top of it all, along with some help from a woman in the village who came in to clean, but really the place needed a thorough sorting out. Perhaps that was something Libby could do while she was here. Maybe she could even have a go at some redecorating; she was good at that. She had single-handedly redecorated her flat and had really enjoyed doing it.

Well, if she was going to do anything useful while here, she had better have a shower and then dress.

It was half past ten when Libby eventually made it downstairs to the kitchen where she was greeted with the smell of freshly brewing coffee and sizzling bacon.

'I thought you might need a good breakfast to set you up for the day after the excesses of last night,' Bess said. 'Now sit down and I'll pour you some coffee. Do you think a spoonful of sugar added to it might be in order?'

Libby smiled. 'To help the medicine go down, you mean? No, I think black and strong will do the trick. But you really shouldn't be waiting on me like this.'

'Nonsense. You know I love to make a fuss of you when I have the chance.'

'And you know how much I appreciate it. Now tell me the truth, did I say or do anything hideously embarrassing last night?'

'You were a little weepy at one point,' said Bess, placing a mug of coffee on the table in front of her, then going back over to the frying pan on the range hotplate.

'I'm sorry.'

'Don't be. If you can't indulge in a few tears at a time like this, when can you, I should like to know?'

When Bess put the plate of fried bread, egg, bacon and tomatoes in front of her, Libby tackled it with surprisingly hungry relish.

While she ate, and while Bess had her back to her as she put the frying pan in the sink and ran the tap on it, Libby took the opportunity to assess the state of the kitchen. She tried to do it with an objective eye, rather than with an eye of familiarity and fond affection.

The bulky old refrigerator was making its usual humming noise over in the corner, only it seemed louder now, and there was a crust of rust forming on the cream paintwork at the bottom of the door. The blackened old range which dominated the room looked like something out of a museum, although Bess swore by it, and occasionally at it. Many years ago, she had nicknamed it The Beast, and Libby knew from experience how true that moniker was when the oven chose not to work. Above it was an old-fashioned clothes dryer where Bess dried herbs from the garden, but several of the wooden slats were broken and something was amiss with the pulley system as the airer was positioned at a peculiar angle, one end almost touching the ceiling, and the other end just inches from the shelf where Bess kept the pans she used most often. On the wall opposite The Beast was an enormous cream-painted dresser which was home to a plethora of crockery and junk. One of the drawer knobs had come off and presumably it was no longer possible to open the drawer.

On the floor, in front of the range and where Bess was standing at the sink, there were worn patches in the green linoleum through which the original stone floor was showing. Apparently, well before Libby was born, Bess had insisted that she have something warm under her feet in the kitchen as well as a surface that was easier to keep clean. Elfrida hated to have anything changed or updated in the house, but she had reluctantly given in to Bess's request that time. Libby could sympathise; Larkspur House was no ordinary house and deserved to be revered for its Arts and Crafts heritage, but there again she could see things from Bess's point of view. Anything that helped to make life easier at this stage in their lives had to be worth considering.

After Bess had dealt with the frying pan, she poured herself a cup of coffee and joined Libby at the table. It was then, when Libby took in the serious expression on her face, that she knew Bess had something to tell her, and it wouldn't be good.

'What is it?' Libby asked.

'It's your mother. While you were upstairs, she rang to speak to you.'

'Did you tell her I was here?'

'Not straight away, but when she threatened to come here to look for you herself, I gave in.'

'Why was she so sure I'd be here?'

'She claimed Larkspur House was the obvious place you'd come running to and that we'd welcome you with open arms, if only to defy her.'

'How preposterous! And why does she always have to make out she's the victim?'

'Because you know your mother as well as I do – she can't help but feel she's been wronged or hard done by.'

'What else did she say?'

'Well, after a good deal of haranguing, she insisted I persuaded you to return to London and your senses. Which obviously I won't do. As I told her, only you can decide what you do next.'

'Do you think she'll come here anyway?'

'Probably. But I think she's going to do something far worse.'

Libby put down her knife and fork and took a fortifying sip of coffee. 'She wouldn't, would she?'

'I hate to say it, but I'd be surprised if she hasn't done it already.'

*

Bess proved herself right later that morning while Libby was helping Elfrida in the garden.

She was listening to Jimmy Young on the wireless and scrubbing potatoes when the telephone in the hall rang for the second time that morning. Bess debated whether to leave it to ring or go and give the caller a piece of her mind. Libby had given very clear instructions that should Marcus telephone this number, Nancy having said she would tell him to do so, she didn't want to speak to him.

When the ringing finally stopped, Bess carried on scrubbing the potatoes, but within seconds it resumed and this time, though she knew she was imagining it, it sounded even more demanding and persistent.

Wiping her hands on her apron, and convinced it was Marcus, she breathed in deeply, ready to give him a few home truths.

It *was* Marcus.

'No, you can't speak to Libby,' Bess told him when he'd made his request.

'Come on, Bess, I know you're cross with me, and I've been very stupid, but please let me speak to her.'

Bess heard the familiar charm of his voice coming at her down the line. 'But she doesn't want to speak to you,' she said firmly.

'She'll have to sooner or later, she can't hide with you forever. So please, will you just fetch her, as there are things she and I need to resolve.'

'Young man, Libby is not a dog to be fetched. And correct me if I'm wrong, but I believe you have resolved matters by sleeping with her best friend and putting paid to there being anything more to be said on the subject.'

There was a pause before Marcus said, 'As her great-aunt I'm sure you mean well, Bess, but really, this is none of your business.'

'Is that so? Then I have no business in asking Libby to come to the telephone, which, I might add, she told me very precisely she would not do. She doesn't want to speak to you, Marcus, and I can't say I blame her.'

And with that, Bess hung up and went back to the kitchen. She hadn't exactly given Marcus a piece of her mind, but she'd made Libby's wishes all too clear. Just as she had with Nancy.

'Don't force my hand,' Bess had warned her earlier.

After an intake of breath, Nancy had said, 'You wouldn't dare!'

'Why wouldn't I?'

'Because you promised.'

'Then don't make me break that promise.' In a softer tone, Bess had said, 'Please, Nancy, this is not about you, and it's not about me, it's about Libby. For once, can't you put aside your animosity? Would that really be so difficult for you?'

'If you have to ask that, then you're more selfish and insensitive than I thought you were.'

'Are you never going to put the past behind you, Nancy?'

'How can I when I live every day with the past hanging over me?'

'The answer is to let it go. Otherwise, you'll end up a lonely and bitter old woman and risk losing the love of your only child.'

'Don't you dare presume to lecture me on how to be a mother when you don't know the first thing about it!'

The acrimony in Nancy's voice was hard to bear. 'I know about caring for people,' Bess said quietly.

'No, you don't! All you know about is putting yourself first. Elfrida's the same. And if anyone lives in the past, it's you. Why else have you stayed in that ghastly house and continued working like a drudge for that woman?'

'*That* woman,' Bess had said evenly, 'has given me an extraordinary life.'

'Well, that's all right then, so long as you've had an *extraordinary* life.'

The sarcasm that had come down the line at Bess had been like a poison-tipped arrow fired directly into her heart, and in response she'd felt a pain in her chest and a quickening of her pulse. Rather than let Nancy upset her further, she had ended the call.

Now, as she continued with scrubbing the potatoes, she thought of what she had said to Nancy about Elfrida having given her an extraordinary life. It was no exaggeration. In return for Bess's loyal service, and her devotion as a friend, Elfrida had given her

41

more than she could have ever dreamt of. But there had been terrible times that had gone hand in hand with the good.

It was suffering those bad times that had ultimately bound them together in the most profound of ways, and for that Bess would forever be in Elfrida's debt.

Chapter Four

August 1923
Larkspur House, Suffolk; Tilbrook Hall, Norfolk; the Côte d'Azur
Bess

'Bess, we're off on our travels again.'

'Where to, miss?'

'To my sister's in Norfolk for a weekend house party, an invitation I didn't plan on accepting, but since it's her husband's birthday I thought I'd better show willing. Otherwise I'll probably never hear the last of it.'

'Very well, miss. Is there anything specific you'd like me to pack?'

Elfrida looked up from what she was doing, which was watering a row of tomato plants. We were in the glasshouse and with the afternoon sun flooding in I could feel myself perspiring beneath my uniform. For some reason Elfrida never seemed to be bothered by the heat. But then she was wearing a simple ivory frock and a large-brimmed straw hat while I was wearing my maid's black dress that was absorbing the sun's rays and practically cooking me alive.

Turning to regard me, she smiled. She had such a sweet, almost childlike face – wide cheekbones, large doe eyes and a tiny pointed chin just like a little fairy. But there was nothing of the child about her. Or fairy come to that. In the months I had been working here at Larkspur House as her lady's maid, I knew my employer was as tough as they came. She was not what some would describe as a lady in the conventional sense, she was too independent and rebellious to be pinned down by such a description. She was full of fun and was the most quick-witted person I knew, and while she could be kind and generous and endlessly patient, she could also blaze with biting scorn if provoked. She was never cruel, but she could be sharp, especially if she was mimicking her sister. But there was no one I admired more, and I would have gone to the ends of the earth to please her.

'Bess,' she said in answer to my question, 'you know my taste well enough by now to know what's best. Just so long as you pack dresses that will turn a few heads and send my sister off into a fit of the vapours.'

'I know just the ones,' I said.

'I knew you would.' With that she returned her attention to the watering can in her hand and I was about to turn and leave, when she said, 'Oh, and by the way, two days after we come home from Norfolk, you're coming to the South of France with me.'

I stared at her. 'You want *me* to go with you?' I couldn't keep the astonishment out of my voice. I was used to travelling up to Scotland with her, or down to Hampshire, or Oxfordshire, Kent or Shropshire, but a trip abroad was a different matter altogether.

As if reading my mind, she said, 'How else will I manage if you don't come? It's your own fault,' she added, 'you've made yourself completely indispensable to me.'

'But I've never been abroad before.'

'Even more reason for you to come. You'll be quite safe; the natives won't eat you. I can't vouch for some of Mallory's chums though, they can be a bit of a wild bunch, but I promise to bring you home in one perfectly unharmed piece.'

'How long will we be away for?'

'A few weeks. Perhaps longer. These things are never carved in stone with Mallory. Or with me, for that matter.'

Escaping the heat of the glasshouse, I left her to her watering and made my way back to the house.

Compared to my previous place of work, Larkspur House was quite modest in size, but it was a much happier household. That was because there was a refreshing lack of servant hierarchy; there was no snooty butler or stuck-up housekeeper looking down their noses at everyone else.

From the first day I started work here I knew it was going to be different to any kind of domestic service I had done before, and I'd been doing it since I was fourteen. Whereas previously I had worked for large families with an army of servants, at Larkspur House there was just Miss Elfrida Ambrose and a small retinue of devoted staff.

There was Mrs Ridley the cook (Riddles as Elfrida called her), Iris the housemaid, and a woman called Peggy who came twice a week to do the laundry. My job as a lady's maid was to take care of anything of a personal nature for our employer. It was a step up from my last employment and I'd been glad of the chance to better myself. There was also Jimmy Padget the head gardener, and Victor the under gardener, a sorry scrap of a lad who'd fought in the war and returned home to Finchley Green a shadow of his former self. In confidence, Elfrida told me that he'd suffered a mustard gas attack in the trenches and although he wasn't capable of working in the way he once had, she couldn't not give him his old job back.

It quickly became clear to me that the mistress of the household was no ordinary young woman. She spent most days out in the garden, either working alongside Jimmy and Victor, or on her own. Many a time I had to go and find her to remind her that guests were due any minute, or that they had already arrived. If guests were staying, they were often roped in to help their hostess in the garden; but only those who showed any aptitude for it, which was quite a number of them. A shared love of horticulture, so Elfrida told me, was the basis of the majority of her friendships.

And then there were the parties Elfrida liked to throw. Fancy dress parties were her favourite way to entertain her guests. I was assigned the task of creating costumes for her based on sketches she would provide. In the time I had been here, her wardrobe of fancy dress outfits was considerable. Joan of Arc, Napoleon's Josephine and Marie Antoinette were some of the costumes I was most proud of.

Mrs Ridley had worked at Larkspur House since Elfrida was a small child and said the house parties were reminiscent of what had gone on when Elfrida's parents were still alive.

There was one room in the house, on the second floor, which no guest was ever allowed to stay in. It had belonged to Robert Ambrose, Elfrida's brother, who had died when she was twelve. Officially his death was referred to as a tragic accident, but from the snippets of gossip I had got wind of, it seemed that he had committed suicide by throwing himself out of his bedroom window. Elfrida never spoke of it and I didn't dare raise it with her. Though the room wasn't to be used, the door wasn't locked, and I had several times stepped inside when the housemaid was dusting or opening the windows to let in fresh air. It wasn't exactly a morbid shrine, with everything left just as it had once been, but it was undoubtedly kept separate from the rest of the house, as a means to honour the dead brother Elfrida must have adored.

*

Elfrida drove us to Norfolk. Until I had come to work for her, I had never so much as sat in a motorcar, never mind been driven anywhere by a woman. The first time I travelled with her in the

46

Austin 7 I had clung onto my seat for dear life, convinced I was about to meet my death. Elfrida had laughed at me and made the death trap go even faster, causing me to squeeze my eyes shut and pray that when the end came, it would be quick and painless.

But before too long I came to look forward to our journeys together, relishing the wind in my hair, if the top was down, and the exhilaration the speed of the little motorcar gave me. I did ask on one occasion if my mistress wouldn't prefer to have a chauffeur and her response was to snort in a very unladylike manner: 'What, and deprive myself of the thrill of driving? You should try it and then you'll understand what I mean.'

There were, I came to know, certain economies to be made and a chauffeur was considered an unnecessary extravagance. On several occasions I had overheard Elfrida discussing with her friends that since she didn't have a bottomless pit of money like they had, she would have to find a way to pay for the upkeep of Larkspur House as she would rather die than be forced to sell her beloved home. It was either that or find herself a wealthy husband, as her sister said she should.

It turned out that Prudence had lined up several potential husbands for her younger sister to meet at Tilbrook Hall that weekend in Norfolk.

I was helping Elfrida dress for dinner the first night of our visit when she confided in me that she very much feared, thanks to Prudence, that there were two nincompoops downstairs waiting to propose to her.

'Only two, miss?' I said, picking up the silver-backed brush from the dressing table and starting work on her beautiful mane of chestnut hair. 'I find that hard to believe.'

She smiled at me in the mirror. 'I suppose I should be flattered, but I know all too well that the man my sister would consider a good choice for me would be wholly at odds with the man with whom I would want to spend the rest of my life. If indeed such a man exists, and I'm not at all sure he does.'

Leaning forwards, she opened the jewellery box in front of her on the dressing table and pulled out a long rope of pearls and a pair of pearl earrings. She then caught my eye in the mirror again. 'You have a sister, don't you?'

'Yes, miss.'

'Is she older or younger than you?'

'Older.'

'Does she boss you around?'

I shook my head. 'Not at all. Ever since our parents died from that awful Spanish flu and it was just the two of us, we've always been close. Being older, she was both mother and sister to me and there isn't anything I wouldn't do for her.'

'You're very lucky. Is she in service too?'

'She was, but she's married now, and she just does a bit of laundry and sewing work. Her husband didn't want her working all hours. He's what you'd call a proud man.'

'By *proud*, do you mean stubborn, in that everything has to be done his way?'

'Isn't that what marriage is like, miss? A wife doing as her husband says?'

'Sadly yes, which is why, if you and I have any sense, we shan't rush into it.'

'No chance of me doing that, miss.'

'I'm very happy to hear it. And between you and me, the reason I accepted my sister's invitation to spend this weekend here is because I plan to make good use of her, her wealthy friends too. She'll be absolutely livid, but I don't care, needs must.'

It wasn't my place to enquire what she had in mind to do, and since she didn't elaborate, I added the final pin to her hair and said, 'There, that's your hair done, miss. I hope it's to your satisfaction.'

She inspected herself in the mirror, turning her head to the right, and then to the left. 'As always, you've done a marvellous job, Bess. How could I trust anybody else to do my hair ever again? You see now why you must come to the Riviera with me – I need you to make sure I look my best at all times.'

I felt my cheeks flush at her praise. 'Shall I help you with those pearls now?'

'Good Lord no, I can manage that perfectly well on my own, I'm not entirely useless, despite what you might think.'

My cheeks flushed even more, worried that I'd offended her. 'I'm sorry, I didn't mean you weren't capable of—'

'No need to apologise, I know exactly what you meant and please don't think for a minute I don't appreciate your help.' She clipped on her pearl drop earrings, lifted the pearl necklace over her head, wound it twice around her slender neck and then rose elegantly to her feet and slipped on her oyster-grey satin shoes. The colour matched her fringed dress which stopped an inch or two below her knees. I passed her evening gloves to her and she pulled them on.

'Wish me luck with the nincompoops, Bess,' she said. 'And don't bother to wait up for me, I'll sort myself out.'

'Unless, of course, you've eloped with one of the nincompoops,' I said, keeping my face as serious as I could, at the same time hoping I hadn't overstepped the mark.

My comment made her laugh out loud. 'Imagine Prudence's face if I did that!'

Tilbrook Hall was a much grander place than Larkspur House and below stairs in the servants' hall there was the usual pecking order with the butler and housekeeper presiding over everybody else around the supper table. Because it was a house-party weekend there were plenty of other visiting servants just like me. Some of them I'd met before during previous visits and I knew them to be natural gossips. There was a degree of one-upmanship amongst a few of them, a game I had no intention of playing.

As soon as I'd finished eating, I escaped to my room, which was up a narrow flight of steep stairs at the top of the house and where it was as hot as a bread oven with the August sun on it all day. With the last of the evening light now gone, I lit the candle I'd brought up with me and sat down to write a letter to my sister.

As regular as clockwork, every week Joan and I exchanged letters. She loved hearing about Elfrida and those I worked with. She said that I wrote about them so well, she felt as though she knew them personally. However, I was also discreet, not just because I knew it would be wrong to gossip about my employer and her friends, but because I would never dream of being disloyal.

My sister said that in comparison to her life, mine was so much more interesting than hers. I didn't know if that was actually true, but what I did know was that I wouldn't swap places with her. I had no intention of being tied to a husband for a long time yet as I knew that if I did marry, I wouldn't be able to continue working for Elfrida. And I certainly wouldn't be able to go to the South of France.

*

Those first few days at Villa Bellevue were the most remarkable of my life.

I had seen the sea before with my sister, we'd gone to Margate for the day one summer, but the sea in France was so different. It was actually blue. A brilliant turquoise blue that dazzled my eyes. The sand in the curving bay on the beach below the villa was so clean and pale it was as if somebody spent all night cleaning it. In a way I suppose that was true; that when the tide crept in with its crystal-clear water, the beach really was washed clean.

The sun shone every day, and the air was filled with the scent of sun-warmed lavender, pine, lemon, and eucalyptus trees. No wonder people behaved differently here, as though every single day was laid on solely for their benefit and had to be made the most of, no matter the consequences.

There were things that went on at the villa that shocked me, but I knew it was none of my business what people got up to in the privacy of their bedrooms, or even outside in the shrubbery. I just hoped Elfrida wouldn't do anything too scandalous. I'd have hated for her to come to harm.

Naïvely I had originally thought that she and Mr Vaughan were romantically involved, they seemed so happy and at ease together, but I soon realised my mistake. Elfrida was effectively his chaperone, a decoy to cover up where his real affections lay. I knew, of course, such men existed, I wasn't that green, but I had never actually come across one before. Whatever preconceived ideas I'd had, they were abandoned because I knew what a dear friend Mr Vaughan was to Elfrida; there was a deep bond between them. I often wondered, especially during those first weeks we were in France, if he reminded her of her adored brother in some way.

It was during the third week of our stay at Villa Bellevue that everything changed. I had noticed that Elfrida was showing signs of restlessness, which I took as an indication that she was ready to return home.

But then Count Nikolai Demidov showed up.

Chapter Five

July 1981
Larkspur House, Suffolk

Last night banks of clouds had rolled in from the east while they'd been eating supper in the garden. The air had been sultry, thick as treacle and teeming with gnats. The first languid roll of thunder had rumbled overhead several hours later when Libby had been getting ready for bed. But if a thunderstorm had raged throughout the night, she had been oblivious to it as she'd slept like the proverbial baby, until awoken early by the sound of rain pattering against the window, which she'd had the foresight to close before turning out the light.

It was the first decent night's sleep she'd had since her world had imploded. It was too soon to say she was feeling less shocked, let alone coming to terms with the loss of the life she and Marcus were going to share together, but since coming here to Larkspur House and being with Bess and Elfrida, there were definitely moments when he didn't dominate her thoughts. But then, from nowhere, there he would be in her head, a reminder of something they'd shared; a joke, or a kiss, or maybe nothing more than a fleeting glance, or a look of love. But had it been love? How could it have been, on his part? She was even beginning to doubt that what she had felt for Marcus had been real.

If it had been true love, why was it possible for her to feel the opposite of that emotion: hate? A few days ago, she had been so happy to be marrying the man who she had believed was the love of her life: now she was repulsed by him. She hated everything about him! She especially hated how humiliated and powerless he had made her feel with his betrayal.

Yet even as she felt the now familiar tremor of anger building within her, the memory of when she'd first met Marcus played like a film inside her head. She had been serving a buffet lunch at the investment bank in the City where he worked, and on her arrival he'd been kind enough to hold the door open for her when she'd been carrying trays of food into the meeting room where a retirement lunch was to be held. Selina was supposed to have been with her, but she'd gone down with a cold the day before, so Libby had to do the function alone. Several times during the lunch the attractive man who had helped her, and who was about her age, commented on how good the food was, particularly the filo pastry parcels which she'd filled with a mix of prawns and creamy smoked haddock.

She was used to people enjoying her cooking, but there was something about this handsome man's appreciation, and the charming way he smiled at her, that made butterflies spring to life in her stomach. All the time she was moving inconspicuously around the room serving people, she'd been conscious of his eyes following her and at the end, when she was preparing to leave, he approached and asked if she had a business card as he'd like to arrange a small private party. But when he telephoned her later that evening, it wasn't to request her services as a caterer, but to ask her to have dinner with him.

After several months of dating, he joked that the old adage was true, that the way to a man's heart was most assuredly through his stomach. 'I was yours from the moment I first tasted your filo pastry parcels,' he said. 'It was love at first bite!' It became their joke and one that she never tired of hearing.

Looking back on it, with his effortless charm and good looks, Marcus made it so easy for her to fall in love with him. He showered her with compliments, was never jealous or possessive and was always appreciative of anything she did for him. Her friends, including Selina, all thought he was great, especially the way he fitted in so well with her life, and they regularly told her how lucky she was to have hit the jackpot with him. No one was saying that now.

As early as it was, being just after six-thirty, it wasn't early enough to make it downstairs before Elfrida and Bess. There they both were, fully dressed and sitting at the kitchen table, finishing off their breakfast of porridge.

'Don't you two ever sleep?' she asked them.

'The early bird always catches the worm,' said Elfrida, up on her feet and going over to the back door to put on her wellington boots.

'You're surely not going out to the garden in this weather?' The rain was now coming down in stair rods.

'Those tomato plants in the glasshouse won't water themselves.'

'Why don't I do it for you?'

Elfrida gave her a baleful look. 'Are you implying what I think you are, that I'm too much of an old duffer to cope with a few drops of rain?'

Libby laughed. 'I wouldn't dream of it.'

'There's never any point in trying to make life easier for her,' said Bess when Elfrida had gone.

'What about you?' said Libby, going over to fill the kettle to make herself some tea before Bess rose from her chair to do it. 'Will you accept my help?'

'What kind of help would that be?'

'Why not let me cook while I'm here? And perhaps I could do some of the cleaning? I'd sooner be busy than idle.'

'I hope you're not suggesting I've let things slide?'

Libby pulled out a chair and sat opposite her great-aunt. 'Of course not. But it's a big house and you can't be expected to do it all on your own. It's simply too much.'

'I do have some help.' There was a hint of indignation in Bess's voice.

Libby warned herself to proceed with care. 'But an extra pair of hands wouldn't go amiss, would it?' she said. 'And I don't just mean while I'm here, but when I've left.'

Bess sighed. 'Finding help these days isn't so easy. We're lucky to have the woman who comes in as it is, and she isn't keen to do any more hours. There's no one else in the village who is prepared to work here. Why would they when they can earn more working behind the bar in the local pub, or in any of the shops? And don't forget, Elfrida isn't always the most straightforward of people to be around.'

Libby smiled. 'You've managed well enough all these years.'

'That's different. I'm not scared of her.'

'What about Andrew who helps in the garden? Is he scared of her?'

'Oh, Elfrida's as sweet as pie to him; after all, she knows which side her bread is buttered.'

'Personally, I've always found her bark to be a lot worse than her bite,' said Libby.

'But then you've never done anything to annoy her.'

'I wish that were true when it comes to my mother; I seem to annoy her constantly. Do you suppose we ought to plug the phone back in now? Lord knows we don't want her descending on us because she couldn't get through on the telephone.'

'But if you speak to her, she'll only make you feel worse. The same goes for Marcus if you answer the phone to him.'

'Dear sweet Bess, you've always tried to protect me, haven't you?' She smiled and added, 'Even unplugging the telephone so Mum and Marcus couldn't pester me.'

'And why wouldn't I? Somebody has to look out for you. If your grandmother was still alive, she'd be doing her best to defend you, wouldn't she?'

Libby wasn't so sure that was altogether true. Grandma Joan had always taken Mum's side in any argument or difference of opinion. Dad used to say that letting Mum have her own way was the best course of action to keep the peace.

'I'm going to have to speak to Mum and Marcus sometime, so better to get it over and done with. I'm not having anyone accuse me of cowardice. That's one thing I won't ever let happen.'

'You sound full of fighting talk this morning.'

Libby laughed. 'That's because I'm not suffering a monumental hangover.'

With the kettle now boiling, she went over to make a pot of tea. Noticing there wasn't much tea left in the caddy, she made a mental note to check what else Bess was running low on and maybe suggest they go shopping together. That was surely something her great-aunt would let her do? Suggesting that she could redecorate parts of the house to spruce things up might be more of a challenge.

And what of the idea that had come to her last night when she was getting ready for bed, how would that be greeted? Personally, she thought it was a flash of inspiration on her part and was amazed that it hadn't been done before now.

'Tea?' she asked.

'Go on then,' said Bess. 'Pour me a mug and then I'll make you some breakfast.'

'No, you won't. I'm quite capable of making myself some toast.'

She found some milk in the vibrating fridge that sounded like it was about to take off like a jet plane, gave the tea a stir in the pot, poured it, and then joined Bess at the table again.

'So,' she said, 'given how bad the weather is, what shall we do today?'

Bess eyed her warily. 'That sounds awfully like you already have something in mind.'

'As I said before, I want to be useful while I'm here. And so as well as giving you a hand, I wondered if I could do something which I think Elfrida might appreciate. It was actually Elfrida who sowed the seed of an idea last night when we were having supper.'

'What was that?'

'It was when she was referring to some of the gardens she's created and that in the attic there are box-loads of photographs and old letters referring to those gardens, including Larkspur House. So, I thought I could go through everything and put it into some sort of order. I bet those boxes contain a fascinating story, and who knows, if we could find a publisher, it could be a great source of information for future generations of garden designers.'

Bess frowned and shook her head. 'I can guarantee Elfrida won't see it that way. She's been approached in the past to have her work documented, but she flatly refused to agree to it. She believes that garden designers should look forwards, not backwards for inspiration.'

'But wouldn't she enjoy seeing her life's work carefully pieced together so she could relive it?'

'Elfrida might forget which day of the week it is, but I think you'll find she can remember every detail of every garden she's ever created without the aid of a photograph to jog her memory.'

It was on the tip of Libby's tongue to say that might not always be the case, but instead she said, 'But you could persuade her to let me do it, perhaps?'

Bess slowly put down her mug of tea and gave Libby a long hard look. 'Why are you so keen to do this?'

'I . . . I need a diversion, something that will distract me from thinking about Marcus. Exploring someone else's life strikes me as the ideal way to stop dwelling on what a failure my own is.'

Until Libby had actually said the words out loud, she hadn't realised just how true this was. It was excruciatingly painful to acknowledge just how spectacularly she felt she had failed.

An hour later, when Elfrida hadn't returned from watering the tomato plants, and at Bess's request, Libby went to look for her.

With the hood pulled up on the old gardening coat she'd grabbed from the hook in the scullery and a pair of spare boots on her feet, she made a dash in the direction of the glasshouse. Pushing open the door, she went inside but there was no sign of Elfrida, just the rich earthy smell of damp compost and the more pungent, heady smell of ripening tomatoes.

Back out in the rain, she pondered where Elfrida might have gone. But where to start, when there were three acres of garden to search? And what would she be doing out here in this down-pour anyway? What would any gardener be doing in such heavy rain? Libby asked herself. She recalled Elfrida hammering in stakes to support the dahlias yesterday. Was she doing that again to stop her precious plants from being battered by the deluge?

She set off for the Long Border, but there was no sign of Elfrida. From there, Libby went to the Lime Walk where there was a wrought-iron gazebo at its furthest point; maybe Elfrida was sheltering in there.

That also drew a blank. Next, she hurried on through the archway in the yew hedge to the Topiary Garden and entered the circular Hydrangea Haven. But all she found there were large blousy flowers drooping under the weight of so much rainwater.

Libby knew that this area of the garden meant the world to Elfrida; it was a poignant connection to her parents. Many of the planting expeditions her parents had undertaken to China and Japan were to discover rare Hortensia species to bring back to England, and it was while returning from one of these trips that they'd met with their deaths.

The loss of their parents had a devastating effect on Elfrida and her sister, but while Elfrida threw herself into maintaining the garden here to cope with her grief, Prudence's sorrow turned to anger at what she regarded as their parents' selfishness and their apparent desire to put their plant obsession before their children. So distraught with rage was she that she took a pair of shears to every hydrangea in the garden and then doused the roots with whatever chemicals she could lay hands on from the head gardener's shed.

It had taken Elfrida years to undo the harm her sister had caused, and she'd vowed that there would always be hydrangeas at Larkspur House. In fact, they became one of her trademark feature plants in every garden she ever designed. Each one, so Bess told Libby, was a memorial to her parents, whom she had dearly loved.

Libby tried the Rose Garden next, followed by the barn where the mower and all the gardening tools were kept, but still there was no sign of Elfrida. Deciding that she must have done the sensible thing and gone back up to the house, Libby did the same. But it was when she was approaching the herringbone brickwork path that she saw what looked like an abandoned heap of sodden clothes lying on the ground up ahead.

It was Elfrida.

*

'Oh, for heaven's sake, what a lot of fuss and bother everyone is making!'

'And rightly so,' said Libby.

'And we're not taking any argument from you,' said Bess. 'You're to do as you're told.'

Elfrida looked to the young man standing at the side of the bed and offered up one of her most appealing smiles. 'Tell them,' she said in her sweetest and meekest voice, 'that I'm absolutely fine. I'm built to last. A little tumble isn't going to finish me off.'

The doctor returned her gaze with a steady one of his own and put away the device he'd just used to test her blood pressure. He had lovely eyes, she thought, an unusual shade of amber with flecks of hazel which were surrounded by thick eyelashes. They were just the sort of eyes to turn a girl's heart over.

'Miss Ambrose,' he said, 'you may well be built to outlast the rest of us mere mortals, but your *little tumble* has resulted in a sprained ankle and a nasty bump to your head, so I would deem it a great honour if you would take my advice. I'd sooner you went to hospital for an X-ray to make sure all is well, but I can see I'd have more chance of flying you to the moon than you agreeing to that. Which is why you're going to take my advice.'

Elfrida viewed him sceptically. 'Which is?'

He took out a torch from his medical case and switched it on. 'That total bed rest is an order,' he said, shining the beam of light into her eyes, first her left, then her right, 'and if you start to feel sick, you're to go straight to hospital. Ignore my advice at your peril.' He added, straightening up, 'Speaking as your doctor, that is.' He gave her what appeared to be a challenging look, as though daring her to disagree.

'But you're not my real doctor, are you?' she said. 'You're far too young, for a start.'

Bess issued a warning rattle in her throat. 'Elfrida, don't be so rude.'

The doctor merely smiled and replaced the torch in the case. 'I'm filling in for Dr Wilcox following his retirement.'

'Retirement?' repeated Elfrida. 'When did that happen?'

'Five months ago. I'm covering here in Finchley Green until a replacement can be found.'

'Well, I call that a pretty poor show. After all those years as my doctor, and the many intimacies we shared, and the man leaves without so much as a word. How rude!'

'I expect he couldn't take the heartbreak of saying goodbye.'

Elfrida laughed at that. 'What did you say your name was?'

'Dr Matthews. And to put your mind at rest, I have been qualified for five years, and that means I'm not some fresh-out-of-medical-school doctor who can be wrapped around your little finger, as charming as that might be.'

'Clearly your reputation goes before you, Elfrida,' said Libby.

'Yes,' joined in Bess, 'it's probably written all over your notes that you're a particularly troublesome patient.'

Elfrida tutted. 'In that case, since you're all ganging up against me, I think I should like you to leave now, I'm tired.'

And with that, the doctor said he'd call in tomorrow to check on her during his rounds.

When they'd done as she asked, and had shut the door behind them, Elfrida sank back into the welcoming softness of the pillows and closed her eyes. She would never have admitted it to Bess or Libby, or that young doctor, but she felt wretched. To have been honest with them might well have landed her up in hospital and once someone of her age was admitted to hospital, who knew when you would be able to escape.

So she'd made light of the thumping headache she had and how painful her ankle was. Libby and Bess had wanted to call for an ambulance, but Elfrida had overruled that and compromised by saying that they could call the surgery for a doctor if that would make them feel better. She had hoped they would climb down, but Libby hadn't and an hour later that young whippersnapper of a quack had shown up.

And all because she'd missed her footing on the blasted brick path which she'd been meaning to have fixed for some weeks.

Now here she was lying on Bobby's old bed which Libby and Bess had somehow managed to bring down from upstairs. She had argued with them that she could sleep in her own bed, if they would just help her up the stairs, but they'd vetoed her wishes, claiming, no matter how vociferous her objections, that it would be better all round to bring down the single bed and make her comfortable in the drawing room.

Many a time after Bobby had died, Elfrida had secretly crept into his room late at night and slept in his bed; it had been her way of feeling closer to him. Years later, whenever she felt in need of comfort, that was where she would sleep. At the time of his death, it had broken her heart that he hadn't felt able to go on living, or that her love and adoration for him hadn't been enough to dissuade him from ending his life. He'd been the dearest of brothers, such a sweet and sensitive boy.

Sadly, too sensitive for the world back then.

Had he lived, and despite him being older, Elfrida knew that she would have been the one to take care of him and keep him safe. As a young child she had made him promise that the two of them would always live together at Larkspur House, that they would never be parted. Oh, how she wished he had kept his side of the bargain. But then how often did any of them keep the promises they made? She was just as guilty as the next person when it came to failing to keep her word.

Her eyelids growing heavy with tiredness, she had the sensation of being on a boat at sea, and as the feeling grew, she saw herself skimming across the waves, the setting sun on her face, and her heart racing with an emotion she hadn't felt before.

Chapter Six

September 1923
The Côte d'Azur
Elfrida

When the imposing colossus at the wheel of the boat swung it round in a wide sweeping arc and brought it to a stop alongside a wooden jetty, the smouldering setting sun was now so low that it was no more than a faint ember-glow in the sky that was tinted with a wash of pale lavender.

Once he had the boat secured, and in what seemed a continuation of the studied silence he'd adopted during our brief journey, Count Nikolai offered his hand without a word and helped me to step onto the jetty.

'Had I known the means of transport provided, I would have worn something a little more appropriate,' I said, as the lower part of my dress rose audaciously to reveal my knees.

Keeping his gaze of polished onyx firmly above the hem of my dress, he gave me what I now recognised as one of his typically measured looks. 'And deny me the pleasure of seeing you so beautifully attired?' he said. 'What a shame that would have been.'

He indicated the steps we should take that were carved into the cliff face. Compared to the path for Villa Bellevue, this was far superior; the steps were evenly spaced, as evenly as nature would allow, and we covered the distance to the top in no time at all.

Having already surprised me with our mode of transport, Count Nikolai did so again with where we were to eat. Awaiting us inside a stone-built gazebo with a pantile roof was a white-clothed table set for two. A man almost as powerfully built as the Count, though not quite as tall, and whom I took to be his personal valet-cum-butler, was standing over the table as if guarding it with his life. He was introduced to me as Ivan and with his black hair, thick eyebrows and bearded face an image of a Cossack in a red tunic and black breeches and boots sprang into my mind.

'Ivan is indispensable to me,' claimed the Count, which drew a discernible tut from the man who had now set about lighting the candles in the silver candelabra, and then a couple of storm lanterns hanging from chains set into the roof of the gazebo. As he carried out the task, I was struck by the strong fragrance of aniseed that filled the air around us. Bending down, I ran my hand through the aromatic leaves of a sprawling patch of French tarragon planted to one side of the gazebo. It was one of my favourite herbs.

While I was breathing in the scent of the tarragon, the two men exchanged a few words in what I took to be Russian, and then my host, while opening a bottle of champagne, asked if I would like to freshen up before we ate. I supposed that in his polite way he was giving me the chance to tidy my hair after our boat ride, but I refused the offer. For all I knew I looked as wild as the snake-haired Medusa, but I was determined to show myself above caring about anything so trivial as a few loose wind-blown locks.

When Ivan had retreated and we both had a full glass in our hands, I said, 'I need to know what to call you.'

'I told you last night, Nick, or Nicki.'

I shook my head. 'Those names seem much too informal for a man like you.'

'What kind of a man do you think I am?'

I sipped my champagne, which was delightfully dry and crisp and a cut well above that which had been served last night at Mallory's party. 'A solemn and very correct and formal man,' I replied. 'A man who is reserved to the point of aloofness.'

His dark eyes fixed ever more intently on me. 'That makes me sound very poor company, and I wonder at your acceptance of my invitation to join me for dinner this evening.'

'I very nearly didn't accept.'

He didn't seem at all put out by my candour. 'What tipped the balance in my favour?' he asked.

'Curiosity.'

'No,' he said with a shake of his head, 'I don't believe that. I think you're here because you were bored with the company you've been keeping.'

I bridled at that. 'I do hope that's not a criticism of my friendship with Mallory, because if it is, I'm afraid you and I can never be friends.'

'I admire your loyalty. It's a trait that is close to my heart, but it wasn't Mallory I was thinking of.'

'Good. But I have to say, if you think I'm here out of boredom, that's an awfully big assumption on your part.'

'As great an assumption on your part to think that I am reserved to the point of being aloof.'

'*Touché*,' I conceded with a smile.

He leant forwards to clink his glass against mine. 'To many more assumptions between us,' he said, with a smile that instantly altered the rigid set of his face and made him look much younger than I had previously imagined. I had put him in his mid thirties, but now I reviewed that estimate. It was possible he was not yet thirty.

'To many more assumptions,' I echoed, 'which we may or may not prove to be justly made.' I drank some more of the champagne and stared out at the beautiful view. The gazebo must have been perfectly placed to enjoy the best view of the sea and the coastline. I wondered if, with a powerful telescope, it was possible to see Villa Bellevue with its terracotta roof tiles and duck-egg blue shutters nestled amongst the pine trees on the headland to the left of us.

My thoughts turned to what my host had just accused me of, of being bored. Boredom was anathema to me. I hated to be idle and twenty-four hours ago I had indeed been mulling over the possibility of returning home earlier than planned. I never tired of Mallory's company, but some of his friends – or scrounging hangers-on – were not to my taste and I had grown weary of their leech-like presence at Villa Bellevue.

'You haven't answered my question,' I said eventually, noting that the man sitting a few feet from me had been in no hurry to fill the silence between us. 'What shall I call you?'

'You are determined to recreate me, is that your wish?'

'Yes,' I said with a teasing smile. 'That is my sole purpose in life, to create things as I think they should be.' The words tripped off my tongue without me really thinking what I was saying, but when I thought about it, I realised it was true. This was exactly how I approached the garden at Larkspur House, I was perpetually finding fault with it and improving upon it, continually adding new and what I considered better creative touches. It was what I planned to do professionally now that the weekend at my sister's in Norfolk had gone so well – not her plans to find me a husband, but my own to find some potential clients.

'In that case, you may decide what to call me.'

'Then I shall call you by your proper name,' I said. 'Nikolai. It suits you perfectly.'

'My mama would be very pleased to hear that, since it was her choice for me.'

Ivan reappeared with a tray and after placing it on the table, he removed a large silver dome to reveal a glass dish of shiny caviar and a plate of blinis. There was a plate of lemons cut into quarters and a pot of what I guessed was sour cream between two finger bowls. Everything was neatly laid out before us and once again we were left alone.

'I took the liberty of assuming you liked caviar,' Nikolai said.

'You assumed correctly. But is there no vodka to go with it?'

'We'll move on to that later. For now, you're drinking Russian champagne. Do you approve of it?'

Ah, so not French, I thought. That explained why it didn't taste like the usual stuff I drank with Mallory. 'I'd go so far as to say I could easily acquire a taste for it,' I said. 'It's delicious.'

'Sadly, I would have to advise you not to grow too fond of it as this bottle is quite rare. You see, my cousin keeps an impressive cellar of wine here and I'm guilty of having plundered it for this special bottle for us to enjoy this evening. It was produced before the Revolution by Prince Lev Golitsyn on his Novyi Svet estate. But unfortunately, following the revolution, nothing that has been produced in my country since matches the quality of what we're drinking. Perhaps one day that will change.'

I took another appreciative sip, feeling guilty that we were squandering something so prized. But I was also extremely flattered that I had been considered worthy to drink it. 'I hope your cousin won't be too cross with you,' I said.

'I'm sure he'll forgive me when he knows it was for a good cause.'

I raised my gaze to meet his. 'What precisely would that good cause be?'

'To find out more about you,' he replied. 'What else?'

I deliberately left his question hanging and helped myself to a scoop of caviar, the black beads glistening in the candlelight. It proved to match perfectly the excellent quality of the champagne we were drinking and I savoured every delectable morsel.

Dabbing his mouth with his napkin, my dining companion topped up our glasses before returning the bottle to the ice bucket.

'Now it is my turn to ask you about your name,' he said. 'Why docs Mallory call you Freddie? How can he do that when you bear no resemblance whatsoever to a boy?'

I laughed. 'It's just a nickname; a diminutive of Elfrida. He's the only one who does it.'

'Why is that?'

'It's because we're so close. Not as lovers, you understand, there's never been anything like that between us.'

'Of course not,' he said. 'I understand completely.'

Did he? Did he know where Mallory's interests truly lay? Whether he did or not, it was not something I was prepared to discuss. 'Mallory is like a brother to me,' I explained.

When Nikolai didn't respond to this, I found myself saying, 'I had an older brother. I loved him dearly and maybe that's why I love Mallory the way I do; he reminds me of my dearest Bobby.'

'You said *had* a brother, does that mean he's dead?'

'Yes. He died when I was twelve years old. I was the one who found his body.' This was an admission I rarely shared with anyone and I had to wonder why I had just now.

In the flickering candlelight, Nikolai's expression became solemn. It was then I realised how dark the sky had become and how it was now studded with diamond-bright stars.

'At so young an age that must have been dreadful for you,' he said, the timbre of his voice low, almost reverent. 'But please forgive me for using a word that will hardly describe the pain and sadness you must have felt.'

'The word *dreadful* will suffice,' I murmured, pondering why the devil I was talking about my dead brother when by rights

I should be dallying disgracefully with this handsome man who had gone to the trouble to filch a rare bottle of wine from his cousin's cellar in order to seduce me in extravagant style.

Yet if seduction was on the menu that evening – if that was the 'cause' – it wasn't immediately apparent. But perhaps Russian counts went about things differently to other men.

'Do you ever use your title?' I asked.

'Do you mean, do I insist on using my title to elevate my aristocratic credentials above those less privileged?'

'No one would blame you if you did; after all, it's what you were born into, a sense of entitlement, of being born to rule.'

He tutted. 'I see it as an irrelevance these days, the world has changed, just as you said last night. But . . .' he hesitated before adding, 'I have found it has the ability to open doors which might otherwise remain shut against me. Especially in America.'

'Yes, I would imagine it would.'

'Originally those who wanted the revolution, for life to be fairer for all, had my sympathies, but as is the way of mankind, progressive thinking and good intentions soon drowned in the rivers of blood that were shed.'

I winced at the imagery his words conjured. 'Do you still have family and friends in Russia?' I enquired.

He shook his head, 'Those who didn't leave St Petersburg in time, or Petrograd as it is now, perished in the slaughter.'

I thought of the Tsar and his family, and how shocked the world had been at the reports of their deaths. It had been unthinkable that such a thing could happen. Was it any surprise the man with whom I was dining had such a serious demeanour? *How frivolous I must seem to him,* I suddenly thought. No wonder he took the approach he did with me, questioning the superficiality of my life.

'I take it that Mallory told you of my full name and title,' he said, 'perhaps in the hope it would pique your interest after my making such a poor impression on you last night.'

'Who says you did make a poor impression?'

'You did, when you said earlier that you were disinclined to accept my invitation to have dinner with me.'

'Actually, that was more of an act of rebellion on my part at what Mallory was up to. I rather think he likes the idea of the Count and the Pauper – he's such an old-fashioned romantic.'

Nikolai frowned. 'You are hardly a pauper, *mademoiselle*.'

'I am compared to the people with whom I generally mix.'

'Then I would propose you don't mix with them or their kind, and then you will feel so much the richer.'

I laughed. 'How simple you make the world seem.'

'It's as complicated as you want it to be.'

'Says the man staying in his cousin's villa overlooking the Mediterranean and drinking a rare bottle of vintage champagne.'

I could see he was holding back a smile, which I chalked up as a point to me.

Our main course was sole meunière with brown butter sauce and creamed spinach and sautéed potatoes. Every mouthful was heavenly.

'Whoever your cook is, you're a very lucky man,' I remarked.

'I shall inform Ivan of that.'

'Goodness, he really is indispensable to you, isn't he? Has he been with you for long?'

'He worked on the family estate and we were together when we fought in the war. Afterwards, he worked with me on a more personal level.'

'And fled Russia with you and your family?'

Nikolai nodded. 'At my urging. I feared he might be murdered by association if he remained.'

'Will you tell me about your family and how you ended up in America?' I asked, conscious that once again the conversation had taken a sombre turn. But very likely that was this man's natural default setting.

'It's a common enough story,' he began. 'The Demidov wealth, which matched nearly that of the Tsars, was made from metal mining in the eighteenth and nineteenth centuries. As you can imagine, we lived in considerable style and luxury, nothing was beyond our reach. Down the years we wielded power and influence and were much admired and respected, all qualities that warranted our execution in the eyes of our new masters. I could have stayed and fought back with my fellow White Russians, but I chose the coward's way out and fled.'

'That was hardly the act of a coward,' I said, surprised at the admission and the critical tone of his voice. It was loaded with regret.

'I suspect I shall always regard it that way. I know my father views what we did as a betrayal. He hates the thought that after secretly sending money abroad we were reduced to sewing jewels into the lining of our clothes and then crawling away like beaten dogs on our bellies. In my father's eyes it was a shameful act of disloyalty to the country that had given us so much. It was our home and our birthright and we willingly handed it over to a bloodthirsty mob who will surely destroy it.'

'You did what you did to survive,' I suggested, wondering how I would have reacted if I had been in Nikolai's shoes. Larkspur House was effectively my very own Motherland and I knew I was determined to do all that I could to keep it. But if a marauding mob was at the door threatening to kill me, would I stay and fight, or would I flee with as many possessions as I could carry?

Instead of responding to my comment, Nikolai changed the subject and asked what I planned to do with my life, given that last night I had informed him that I had ruled out marriage.

'Well,' I said with a smile, aware that it was time to lighten the mood, 'having tasted his cooking, I'm now considering marrying Ivan. But I fear you've deliberately misquoted me.

71

What I actually said last night was that I was in no rush to marry, not that I had ruled it out.'

'So what do you intend to do with your life before you've decided you're ready to marry? What will you do with yourself? Because in my experience, one can only drift for so long. One needs purpose, a reason to get up of a morning.'

Irritation flared within me. 'You doubt that I have that? I had hoped for more from you.'

'Forgive me,' he said. 'My intention was not to cause offence, but to warn you of the danger of not having a clear sense of direction in life, of being a lotus-eater. It is such a shallow existence.'

'Oh, I have plenty of purpose for myself, I assure you. More than you could ever imagine.'

'Tell me then. I would like to know.'

I did. And perhaps because I wanted to prove that there was more substance to me than he imagined, I told him about the woman I so admired. Her name was Norah Lindsay and I badly wanted to follow her example and be a garden designer just like her. I spoke of Gertrude Jekyll too, how she had transformed the way many viewed horticulture and garden design. I was so carried away with assuring him that I was no lotus-eater and never would be, that I started waxing lyrical. It might have been the champagne, or the intoxicating warmth of the scented night air, or more probably it was my sheer determination to prove myself, but once I'd begun, I couldn't stop the flow of my words.

'We are created to be creators,' I went on. 'Creativity is at the heart of every person, if only we knew it. When I see something that looks like it can't be done in my garden, or something that is out of kilter with nature, I see it not so much as a challenge or a battle to make it bend to my will, but as an invitation to dance in time with nature and to create something truly beautiful.'

Finally, I fell quiet to draw breath and Nikolai smiled. 'That, *mademoiselle*, sounds not so much a purpose, but a mission, or a crusade, and I don't doubt for a moment that you will achieve your ambition. I suspected last night that I was in the presence of someone who not only knew her own mind, but was uniquely special, and this evening you have confirmed that. I would deem it a great honour if during the time you have remaining here on the Riviera, you would agree to see me again.'

How could I resist such a courtly request? Or the unexpected praise he'd just lavished on me.

But had there ever been any doubt that I would want to see him again?

Over the following days Mallory hardly saw me as I spent all the time I could with Nikolai.

With the weather still warm and balmy, we explored the pine-scented coast in his cousin's boat, puttering from one secluded bay of golden sand to another. We swam from the boat and Nikolai was surprised at my proficiency, that I could seemingly swim and swim and never tire. With my long wet hair trailing down my back, he called me his beautiful little mermaid. We lay on straw mats on the sand in the shade of a parasol and sometimes in no shade at all, my wilful nature recklessly overriding the warnings of my sister and governess who had said that a lady must never let her skin be anything but the colour of milk.

The exercise of swimming gave us a good appetite and sometimes we ate a picnic lunch in a quiet spot – the nearby and unspoilt beach at Juan-les-Pins was a particular favourite – and other times we ate in splendour at the Grand-Hôtel in Cap-Ferrat, where Nikolai knew the new owners, Henry Dehouve and André Voyenne. Dinner was always under a starlit sky in the gazebo with the scent of tarragon wafting on the night air. We played bezique to the sound of the gramophone, the two of us taking it in turns to wind it. We drank copious amounts of vodka together and he taught me to make a toast in Russian and hurl my empty glass against the nearest hard surface.

Being the curious sort, I had asked for a tour of his cousin's villa, which he was happy to give me. I couldn't say the extravagant furnishings were to my taste, I preferred the understated simplicity of the Arts and Crafts style, but the Persian rugs were exquisite, and the gilt-framed portraits that lined the walls fascinated me. Nikolai explained who the aristocratic men and women were as they stared back at me with haughty grandeur in their finery of silks, jewels and furs. They were all members of the Demidov family and charted Nikolai's pedigree as far back as the seventeenth century. He explained that his cousin, Anatoly Demidov, had departed Russia long before the rest of the family had, taking with him most of his wealth to live in Paris. It had been Anatoly who had subsequently helped Nikolai and his parents escape to America, where Nikolai and his father had set themselves up in business as hoteliers, catering primarily for their fellow White Russian émigrés.

And yes, of course, Nikolai had taken me to his bed, which was a stately four-poster affair draped in heavy burgundy brocade and fringed with gold tassels. How could we not end up in bed together when every minute we spent in each other's company a strong current of electricity kept sparking between us? For my own part, a brush of his hand against my arm as he let me take the wheel of the boat, or a hand to my elbow as he guided me to a chair or through a doorway, had been enough to make me believe it was possible for a human being to self-combust.

It had been a relief the first time we kissed because I had known it was a prelude to what we both wanted and which we had both known was inevitable. I had no fear about giving myself to Nikolai and afterwards he confessed that he had been scared of hurting me. Lying in his bed, as he cradled me in his strong arms, he assured me that it would be better the next time. I asked him to prove it and burying his face into my neck and kissing me, his lips travelling down to my breasts, he set about doing just that.

For my last night before I departed for home, Mallory insisted on throwing a farewell party for me. Nikolai was, of course, invited. The truth was we would have preferred a night on our own, but Mallory wouldn't hear of it.

Bess knew all about Nikolai, in as much as she knew what I had shared with her, coupled with the evidence of my unused bed. In readiness for the party that evening, she spent an age on doing my hair to guarantee I would look my best. I wanted to tell her that Nikolai had seen me with wet hair dripping down my back like seaweed when we'd been swimming, and also, of course, when I hadn't had a stitch of clothing on.

As with all Mallory's parties, there were plenty of guests and plenty to eat and drink as well as a band hired to play for the evening. It was a night of excess and boisterous fun but for me it was overshadowed by knowing that in the morning I would be saying goodbye to Nikolai. He seemed to be in the same frame of mind as I was but then, as he frequently said, nobody did melancholy better than a Russian. Having previously disparaged any form of modern dancing, he requested the band play something of his own choosing, which was a Russian waltz. It was, I later discovered, the tune he had been humming the evening he'd come to fetch me in his boat to take me to his cousin's villa for dinner.

'Is this our farewell dance?' I asked him as we became as one within the warmth of his embrace and the music washed over us and tugged at my heartstrings.

'It's whatever you want it to be,' he said.

It wasn't the answer I wanted to hear, but before I could say anything, he said, 'Go back to England, Elfrida, and embark on your magnificent crusade to make the world a more beautiful place, then when you've done that, I shall come and ask you if you're ready.'

'Ready for what?'

His response was to kiss me.

We ended the night by hurling glasses against the wall of Villa Bellevue before retiring upstairs to bed. When I woke after a few hours of deep sleep, the other side of the bed was empty.

Nikolai was gone.

He had said he hated goodbyes, but I thought his departure while I slept was far from noble. Even so, when Bess and I climbed into Mallory's motorcar, our luggage already having been taken on ahead to the station at Antibes where we would board the Blue Train bound for Paris and then Calais, I clung to the hope that Nikolai would magically materialise to wish me a *bon voyage*.

But he didn't come. Not to the villa or to the station.

It was four months later that I learned that he had deceived me. The discovery shattered my heart into a thousand pieces.

Chapter Seven

July 1981
Larkspur House, Suffolk

Libby put the supper tray on the writing desk in front of the window where the late afternoon sun was streaming in. She'd just opened the French doors to let in some fresh air when Elfrida stirred.

'How are you feeling?' Libby asked her.

Her expression dulled by sleep, Elfrida looked about her as though trying to work out why she was in bed in the drawing room. Ignoring Libby's question and putting a hand to the side of her head, she said, 'What time is it?'

'It's nearly six o'clock.'

'But that means I've been asleep for hours.'

'We thought it best to leave you. Dr Matthews made it clear that you needed to rest.'

'Hmmm . . . we'll see about that. What's on the tray?'

'I've made you some tomato and basil soup with croutons and a cheese scone. How does that sound to you?'

'It sounds like you're treating me as if I'm a half-wit. It also sounds like you might have a mutiny on your hands with Bess if you commandeer her kitchen too much. How did you seize control, lock her in the pantry?'

'I sweet-talked her into letting me help,' Libby said.

Elfrida manoeuvred herself into an upright position, grimacing as she did so, but when Libby offered to help, she waved her away, telling her not to fuss.

'I think you'll have no choice but to accept a degree of fussing for the next few days,' Libby said patiently.

'Is that so?'

To all intents and purposes, it was business as usual with Elfrida, in that she seemed determined to disregard any advice or concern. Yet for all her show of indomitable spirit and cavalier attitude, there was no escaping the evidence of Libby's own eyes that Elfrida's complexion, normally glowing with good health from spending so much time outdoors, was drained of colour. She looked older too, the lines on her face just a little more pronounced, her lips drawn and pale. Her appearance was not helped by the state of her dishevelled hair. Libby also noticed that the joints of Elfrida's fingers were enlarged from a lifetime of gardening and for the first time she thought that, like the house, Elfrida was showing signs of wear and tear.

The thought brought home the realisation to Libby that both Elfrida and Bess were reaching a stage in their lives when they might need help, whether they wanted to believe it or not.

'If you don't rest, I could always ring Dr Matthews and tell him you've taken a turn for the worse,' Libby said to Elfrida. 'He'd have you admitted to hospital faster than you could say pass me that bedpan.'

Elfrida contemplated her with a steady gaze. 'Or I could tell Dr Matthews that you had only bothered him because you were in need of having your broken heart mended. I must say, he'd be a very pleasant distraction for you.'

Libby was astonished at the way Elfrida's thought process worked. 'Carry on like that and I'll have to assume you're concussed and babbling. Now drink your soup while it's hot.'

'But you did notice how attractive Dr Dishy is, didn't you?' Elfrida persisted.

'Well, you certainly seem to have,' Libby muttered. *Dr Dishy indeed!* And determined to scotch any meddling Elfrida might have in mind, she helped herself to a crouton from the dish on the tray and said, 'So who's Nikolai?'

Elfrida looked at her over the rim of the mug of soup in her hands, the sleepiness instantly gone from her eyes. They were now as sharp and as bright as they ever were. 'Why do you want to know?'

'I heard you saying the name in your sleep when I came in.'

'Were you eavesdropping on me while I was having a private conversation with myself?'

Libby laughed. 'Put like that, I suppose I was. Who is he?'

'Just someone.'

'Someone special?'

'All my friends were special.'

'He was definitely a friend, then?'

'What is this, a test to check my cognitive powers after a bump on the head? You'll be asking me next what day of the week it is.'

'Nonsense. I'm merely being unashamedly nosy. Would you like me to cut that scone in half and butter it for you?'

'Yes, if it will stop you interrogating me!'

Relieved to have put a stop to any more mention of Dr Matthews – and yes, of course she had noted how attractive he was, she'd been cheated on by her fiancé, not had her brain removed! – Libby decided to broach what she wanted to discuss with Elfrida.

While putting forward her idea, that she wanted to create some kind of archive to record and celebrate Elfrida's achievements as a garden designer, she mentally crossed her fingers for a positive reaction.

But infuriatingly Elfrida seemed in no hurry to respond to Libby's request, concentrating instead on eating the buttered scone, followed by a sip of soup, and then another.

'So what do you think?' prompted Libby. 'It might be a fun

project for us to do together. Bess could help as well. It would be like doing a jigsaw, slotting together the pieces of your life through the gardens you created.'

Elfrida continued to chew on another mouthful of scone, before raising the mug of soup to her lips once more. 'For what purpose?' she finally asked, her eyes fixed firmly on Libby's.

'To produce a historical document.'

'History be damned, I've never heard so much twaddle in all my life! The gardens I helped create speak for themselves, some of which have already been featured in magazines and a number of books. And frankly if they don't speak for themselves in their own right, then I didn't do my job properly.'

'But wouldn't you like to complete the job by documenting them all? Think how happy the owners would be.'

'Don't be ridiculous, most of the owners who paid me to work on their gardens are dead and buried.'

'That's even more reason to document what you did; the new owners would love to know the story behind their gardens. I know I would.'

'I doubt they'd give a damn.'

Libby wasn't ready to give up. 'Wouldn't you enjoy the process of documenting what you've achieved?' she tried.

Elfrida tapped the side of her head lightly – the opposite side to where she had an egg-sized lump. 'I have it all up here. That's all the documentation I need.'

'But what happens when you're no longer around? Who will tell the story then?' Too late she realised the clumsy insensitivity of the question.

Elfrida paid it no heed though. 'Who's to say there's any story to tell?'

'How can there not be a story? For instance, just the story behind the garden here is worth recording for posterity, isn't it?'

The next morning, and after Libby and Bess had helped Elfrida dress and assisted her to the cloakroom, a battle of wills ensued, with Elfrida wanting to eat breakfast in the kitchen 'as any normal civilised human being should', as she put it. Once she'd eaten, she then declared she would only return to rest in the drawing room if she could do so on the couch. Nothing would induce her to spend any more time in bed. Beds, she said, were for sleeping in and she wasn't the slightest bit tired. Libby let her have her way. If there was one thing she had learnt from her relationship with her mother, it was to know which battles were worth losing in order to win the war.

After the rain of yesterday, today shone bright and clear and so once they had Elfrida installed on the couch, Libby opened the French doors. She then promised Elfrida that she would inspect the garden for damage from the heavy downpour and do her best to put things right.

'You could at least let me sit outside in the garden,' Elfrida complained.

'Nice try,' said Libby, 'but I wouldn't trust you to stay put for a single second.'

'Who would have ever believed you could be such a tyrant,' Elfrida muttered waspishly. 'You obviously take after your mother more than I ever thought.'

'That's a harsh blow, Elfrida, especially as I'm only trying to look after you.'

'In my experience, that's the trouble with tyrants, their true colours only emerge once they have a taste of power.'

'Then you'd better watch yourself,' said Libby good-humouredly.

As it turned out, there was no need for Libby to go and check on the garden as Andrew, the gardener, arrived. Rattling off her numerous edicts, Elfrida could not have sounded more imperious had she been sitting on a throne dressed in a black crinoline with a crown perched on her head. But Andrew took it all in his stride and ambled away to do her bidding.

With Bess keeping Elfrida company in the drawing room, Libby seized her moment to venture up into the attic. Before going to bed last night, she had been given permission, albeit reluctantly, to fetch down whatever garden-related letters, documents and photographs she could find.

Now, and with a sense of embarking on a mission, she climbed the stairs to the top floor of the house. From there she took the narrow staircase that was at the far end of the landing and where she had already placed a pair of wooden stepladders beneath the loft access.

It took Libby a while to find what she was looking for after sorting through a plethora of cobwebby junk with only the light from a flickering torch to guide her. The old steamer trunk which Elfrida had told her to look for had been covered with a collection of rolled-up rugs. Once she had it free of the rugs, she opened it and found what had to be more than a dozen box files. She opened one at random and looked inside. Just as she'd hoped, here was her first stash of old black and white photographs. Again, at random, she picked out a photo and held it closer to the wavering light from the torch and looked at an elegant couple in what she guessed was Edwardian attire.

The woman was wearing a high-necked floor-length dress cinched in at the waist with a sash and on her head was a large hat decorated with flowers. The handsome man at her side wore a morning suit and top hat and with his head turned towards the woman, there was no mistaking the look of adoration on his whiskered face. Libby flipped the photograph over and in a child's sloping hand, possibly Elfrida's, were written the words *Mama and Papa*, followed by the date of 1910.

Delighted with her discovery, and not doubting that the rest of the boxes contained more of the same, Libby turned her thoughts to how she would lug the treasure trove down from the attic.

She was just mulling over her options when from downstairs she heard the front doorbell. Seconds later she heard footsteps, which had to belong to Bess, and then the sound of a man's voice.

From nowhere came the thought that it might be Marcus. But why? Why would he come here? To beg forgiveness in the hope that the wedding would go ahead? If so, what would she say to him? More importantly, what if she believed him? What if he was genuinely contrite and convinced her he still loved her and wanted to be with her?

Every one of these questions made her stomach churn as she remembered how it used to be with Marcus, how very much in love she had been with him. Could she forgive him if it meant she could feel the depth of that happiness once more?

But then she felt sick with shock that she could entertain such an idea. How could she think of forgiving him? What he had done was beyond forgiveness. Never would she think so little of herself that she could imagine being with him again. *Never!*

So fired up did she feel, she dragged the trunk towards the loft access, and, leaving sufficient space for her to reach the stepladders, she stood on the top rung and grasping the handle on the trunk, pulled it towards her. Bracing herself, she bore its weight and step by step, she slid it slowly down the ladder.

She'd just reached the bottom and had the trunk safely on the floor when there was an ominous creaking sound followed by a sprinkling of dust falling on top of her. It took her no more than a split second to realise what was happening, but her feet didn't move quickly enough to get out of the way in time.

*

It was difficult to know which was more chilling, the scream or the crash.

The young doctor who Bess had just shown in to see Elfrida, and who had brought with him a pair of crutches, darted out of the drawing room and charged up the stairs, taking them two at a time. Bess went after him, dreading to think what they might find. Why had she let Libby go up in the attic on her own? Why hadn't she insisted they do the job together?

By the time she reached the landing on the top floor she was out of breath and her heart was beating hard inside her chest, which suddenly felt as tight as a drum. Her heart almost stopped when she saw the enormous gaping hole in the ceiling with its exposed timber joists, but then her body was flooded with relief when she saw Libby. The girl was standing the other side of the wreckage, which included the tipped-over stepladders and a large trunk, but as smothered as she was in dust and chunks of heaven knows what, she was, thank God, very much alive.

Dr Matthews had just extended a hand towards Libby when above their heads came the sound of yet more of the ceiling about to give way.

'Get back!' he shouted to Bess, pulling Libby out of harm's way just in time before an avalanche of plaster and an assortment of junk from the attic fell on the space where Libby had been standing.

Covering her mouth as the powdery dust filled the air, Bess was rooted to the spot, frightened that the slightest movement from her might set off another landslide of rubble. On the other side of the landing, the young doctor was moving towards the safety of the staircase with Libby. He urged Bess to follow and after giving the ceiling a momentary fearful glance, she did as he said.

They had reached the landing below when Bess heard Elfrida shouting up to them from the hall on the ground floor. The only words Bess caught were those asking if Libby was all right.

'Tell her I'm fine,' croaked Libby with a spluttering cough. Her eyes looked startlingly wide and bright against the powdery alabaster complexion she now had from all the dust. Even her eyelashes had been whitened. 'But I think she's going to be terribly cross with me when she sees the mess I've made,' she added. 'It's going to take more than a dustpan and brush to tidy it up.'

'At the very least a large broom,' suggested the doctor. 'Are you sure you're all right?'

'I'm fine. Really.'

'In that case,' he said, 'Mrs Judd, maybe you'd like to go downstairs and assure Miss Ambrose that no harm has come to her granddaughter.'

'I'm not her granddaughter,' Libby said.

'Aren't you? And there was me thinking the two of you were cut from the same cloth.'

'What cloth would that be?'

'The stoic kind.'

'Well, this stoic wants nothing more than to have a shower right now.'

'Fair enough.' Then turning to Bess, he said, 'Sorry for not realising you were Libby's grandmother.'

Wiping the dust from her face, Libby shook her head at him. 'Wrong again,' she said, 'Bess is my great-aunt.'

'Thank goodness we've sorted that out,' he said with a laugh. 'Anyone else here who I can accuse of being your grandmother?'

'Only Andrew the gardener.'

He smiled. 'In that case, why don't you have your shower and I'll go downstairs and check on my patient, then I'll find something useful to help me make a start on clearing up the mess.'

'There's really no need for you to go to all that trouble,' said Bess. 'Don't you have more house calls to make?'

'No, Miss Ambrose was the last on my list. I now have a few

free hours before I need to be back at the surgery. If you're interested, I know someone who's a builder. I could give him a ring to see about making the loft safe again.'

'That sounds expensive!' shouted a voice from below them.

They all peered over the banister, down to where Elfrida, leaning on the crutches Dr Matthews had brought, was staring back up at them. 'I'll ask Andrew to take a look,' she said. 'I'm sure he can put it right.'

'With all due respect, Miss Ambrose, unless he's a proper builder, I'd advise caution. You don't want a badly done job that might cause another accident.'

'With all due respect, Dr Matthews, your expertise lies in medical matters and not my finances.'

'Take no notice,' said Bess, 'she's as tight as they come when it comes to spending money on the house.'

'I heard that, Bess!'

'You were meant to!'

'If I were you, Dr Matthews, I'd get out quick,' said Libby, 'while you still have your sanity.'

'Sound advice, I'm sure, but I quite like the idea of hanging around to see what else you three get up to; this seems like a house where anything can happen.'

'And, Bess, since accidents always happen in threes,' shouted Elfrida, 'I'd say you'd better watch your step.'

'Why? Are you planning to put marbles on the stairs for me to lose my footing on?'

'I wouldn't dream of doing anything so prosaic. I'd think of something far more ingenious if I had a mind to incapacitate you.'

'They're devoted to one another really,' said Libby.

Dr Matthews smiled. 'I can see that.'

'I wouldn't count on it,' muttered Bess, before turning to Libby and saying, 'Shower time for you, my girl. And Dr Matthews, if you could telephone that builder you know to give us a quote for the necessary work, I'd be most obliged.'

'Consider it done.'

*

The plumbing wasn't exactly state of the art at Larkspur House, but Libby welcomed the feeble jets of hot water from the shower on her body. She took her time washing away the grimy film of dust that had reached into her every pore, as well as coating every strand of her hair. She was conscious that she'd had a lucky escape. *Another lucky escape*, she thought. The first from marrying Marcus, and now from nearly getting herself killed. An exaggeration possibly, but if she'd stayed in the loft a few seconds longer who knew what might have happened?

Tipping her head back, she let the jets of water gently wash her face. Her eyes felt gritty and she wondered if there were any eyedrops in the house. If there were, they'd probably be hopelessly out of date. Just as so much of what was stored in the pantry was well past its sell-by date.

Yesterday she'd found a tin of Bird's custard powder that was dated 1974, and another tin which contained rock solid Bisto powder that was so old it may well have travelled with Noah on board his ark. On another shelf and tucked behind a box of empty glass jars, she'd found a store of home-made chutney and jam that, according to the labels on the pots, ranged in age from 1969 to 1978. Wartime rationing, so Bess had informed Libby after she'd pointed out the vintage produce in the pantry, had taught them never to waste anything.

'And that means eating food that should be labelled as a toxic hazard?' Libby had queried.

'We've survived all these years without a problem,' Bess had countered, 'so don't go thinking you can throw anything away while my back is turned.'

When Libby emerged from the bathroom, a towel wrapped around her head and another around her body, she found Bess waiting for her. Laid out on the bed was a selection of clean clothes.

'He's a very handy man to have around,' Bess said.

'Which man would that be?' asked Libby, all smiling insouciance. As if she couldn't guess.

'The delightful Dr Matthews.'

'Is he *delightful?*'

'I would say so.'

'What, just because he offered to help clear up the mess I made?'

'Not just that, it's his manner I like. He's very amenable.'

'That might well be true, but please don't start getting any silly ideas about him.'

'Such as?'

'Only last night Elfrida suggested that he would be a good way to heal a broken heart.'

'She said that?'

'She did. And now you're effectively thinking the same thing, aren't you? But you mustn't. The last thing I need is a rebound relationship, especially so soon. Until a few days ago I was on the verge of marrying; I can't just switch my emotions on and off as you and Elfrida seem to think I should be able to.'

'But a new friend might be nice for you while you're staying with us?'

Libby smiled. 'You know absolutely nothing about him. He could be married with a family.'

'He's not wearing a wedding ring.'

'That means nothing. And aren't you forgetting, a doctor can't get involved with one of his patients, can he?'

'But you're not one of his patients, are you?'

'Oh, I give up!'

Bess smiled.

*

Downstairs in the drawing room, Dr Matthews having left some minutes ago after he and Andrew had brought the trunk down from upstairs, Elfrida was sitting on a footstool next to it.

She had cautiously lifted its lid, half expecting the ghosts from the past to fly out at her. But what she found was a muddled mess of photographs and papers which had tumbled out of the box files. Thinking it would take an age to sort it all out, she leant forwards and helped herself to a handful of photographs.

The first photograph she looked at was of her at Lambert Chase in Northamptonshire. With her was dear Atticus and his lovely wife, Leonora. It had been Elfrida's thirty-third birthday. She could remember thinking how old and wise she was at that age, and how perfectly in control of her life she was. How wrong she'd been!

Chapter Eight

October 1934
Lambert Chase, Northamptonshire
Elfrida

My muddy gumboots sucking at the sodden earth, I stepped nimbly back onto the equally sodden lawn where I took stock of the progress I'd made that day. Or, more particularly, I gauged how much more work I still had to do while taking the opportunity to pour myself a cup of hot chocolate from my trusty thermos flask.

Since half past nine that damp autumnal morning I'd focused my attention on the avenue of pleached hornbeam trees. I was underplanting the trees with Erysimum to provide a lovely pink and mauve froth through which tulips with their waxing white goblets would poke through in the spring. The gardeners here at Lambert Chase had dug out the two long beds according to my specific instructions following my previous visit two weeks ago. I'd returned late yesterday afternoon, just in time to make use of the ebbing light to check that the layout of the new beds was as it should be. Too often I had a battle on my hands with clients' gardeners in that they were too quick to dismiss me, or my ideas. It was such a relief when I did encounter a head gardener who was open-minded enough to consider doing things differently or could accept that a woman might actually know what she was talking about.

At Lambert Chase, Frank Colefax had only been employed as head gardener eighteen months ago and was not much older than me, which meant he wasn't irreversibly set in his ways. We worked well together and with his help I was sure that I would create the best garden I possibly could for Atticus and Leonora Whittaker. As friends of Mallory, they had seen what I had achieved for him at March Bank in Oxfordshire, as well as the transformations I had wrought at Gillingham Court in Kent, Strickland Hall in Buckinghamshire and Chelmsley Manor in Hertfordshire. All of these gardens now opened their gates to the viewing public as part of the National Garden Scheme which had started seven years ago as a way to raise money for charity. I had opened Larkspur House as well, reluctantly so at first, but I soon realised it was an ideal way to showcase my design work.

The way I liked to go about things was to accept commissions on the basis that I would be put on a retainer which would cover an unlimited number of visits to the client's garden to discuss plans and to check on work carried out. On top of this were the invoices I submitted for plants, bulbs and seeds and miscellaneous expenses. Occasionally a client would query the bills I submitted, but I never backed down, that was my cast-iron rule. Never would I undervalue myself.

Originally when I started out my clients had been friends or acquaintances but then my name as a garden designer had spread more widely, thanks to an article about my work in *House & Garden* magazine. Mallory's garden at March Bank and the one at Tilbrook Hall I had created for my sister had both featured in the article, which had pleased Prudence no end. Her pride at what was written about her garden had produced a satisfying about-face in her attitude towards the way I had chosen to support myself.

She had initially been appalled at my suggestion that I should redesign the garden at Tilbrook Hall for her and George. It had been bad enough that I had already inveigled myself into her circle of friends and gained some of them as clients – this, she believed, was a disgusting act of shameless exploitation on my part – but to consider myself sufficiently qualified or experienced enough to tackle the grounds at Tilbrook Hall, and expect to be paid for the work, was to exploit her goodwill as well.

If shameless exploitation was what would enable me to keep Larkspur House, then I had no hesitation in using whatever advantage I could. To that end I had a trump card up my sleeve: Norah Lindsay.

Not only was Norah a well-connected socialite, but she was a much-in-demand garden designer, a celebrated designer at that. She moved in the kind of social circles to which Prudence aspired. If I had to name one person who had inspired and influenced me in my work, then it was Norah with her wonderfully intuitive style. I don't think I admired anyone more.

I had met Norah quite a few times over the years, but the first time had been when I'd been a child and she'd been a guest at Larkspur House during one of my parents' house parties. At the time, I had thought her to be the most beautiful woman I had ever set eyes on and had watched how effortlessly she charmed everybody to whom she spoke. She had the ability to light up a room and I was not so much in awe of her, as in love with her.

'I want to be just like you when I grow up,' I whispered to her one day when she took my hand and asked me to show her my favourite part of the garden at Larkspur House. Smiling, she'd bent down and said, 'No, no, Elfrida, you must be the gloriously unique person you are destined to be. Never ever be afraid to be yourself.'

So, using Norah Lindsay as my trump card, and claiming that I could be as well respected as she was, if given the right chance, I convinced my sister and her husband to let me loose on their garden. It was not an easy commission; Prudence queried every plan I produced for her and did the same with the invoices I submitted for payment. As annoying as her attitude was, it taught me the need to be extremely thorough when it came to bills and accounts. It was a chore I hated doing, but as luck would have it, Bess proved herself to be a dab hand when it came to keeping accounts and I happily passed the job over to her.

Seven years ago, and to my very great consternation, I nearly lost Bess. She came to me one morning to hand in her notice. Her sister, she said, was pregnant and confined to bed and needed Bess's help. Selfishly, I didn't want to be without her and asked why her sister's husband couldn't take care of his wife. Apparently, he had his hands full with work and even if he could spare the time, he wouldn't be of any real use. Determined that I shouldn't lose Bess, I struck a deal with her – I would let her have the necessary months away, but she was to return to me just as soon as she could. In the meantime, I would hire a girl to fill in for her. I'm afraid to say her temporary replacement had lacked initiative and a willingness to go above and beyond the usual demands of the job, and it made me appreciate Bess's company and usefulness even more.

When the day finally came for her to return and I went to collect her from the station, I'd surprised her, myself too, by hugging her. She'd instantly burst into tears and sobbed how good it was to be home. 'I've missed you and Larkspur House so much, miss,' she'd wailed.

'Then you must take great pains never to leave me again,' I'd said with a laugh, touched by her devotion.

'I won't leave again, miss. Not when you've been so kind in keeping my job open for me. It isn't everyone who would do that.'

'But then as you well know, I like to do things differently. And anyway, I find I really can't manage without you.'

For some reason, instead of cheering her as I'd hoped, my words had set her off crying again. So I distracted her as I drove us home with all my latest news, namely the gardens I'd been working on, and the changes I'd made at Larkspur House.

Happily, most of the commissions I undertook were enormous fun and gave me the opportunity to spend time with good friends, as well as enjoy the comforts a quality country home offered, such as roaring log fires, splendid meals, hot baths and stimulating company. That was certainly true of my visits to Lambert Chase where Atticus and Leonora were wonderful hosts.

I had been working on their garden for nearly two years and I was glad of the regular income the commission gave me. More than once during the years following the financial crash and when I'd had to have the roof mended, or pay a landslide of unexpected bills, I had been tempted to throw in the towel and marry a man who would help finance Larkspur House for me. But I had met no one with whom I could imagine myself truly happy, or even moderately happy for longer than a few months.

Naturally, given that I was now thirty-three and officially an old maid, Prudence despaired of my ever finding a husband. My friends, including Mallory, still hung on to the hope that one day I would fall wildly in love, but I had my doubts.

It pained me to admit it, but my trust in love had been shaken by what Nikolai Demidov had done to me all those years ago. Naïvely I had allowed myself to make the mistake of falling in love with him, and what a fall it had been! It had taken no more than a few days for me to lose my heart to him, and my wits. But when I came to my senses, I saw that the dream I'd believed in had been nothing but a fragile fantasy spun from glass which had shattered and pierced my heart painfully with its lethal shards. I was determined that should never happen to me again. Never again would I let a man betray me in the way Nikolai had.

In the months that passed after I'd returned from the Riviera that year in 1923, I waited for some form of communication from Nikolai. Surely a letter would come from him, a few lines to say he was thinking of me? But nothing came. Then four months almost to the day since I'd left Villa Bellevue, a letter arrived from Dorothea, my old friend from my less than enjoyable time at the finishing school in Florence. I hadn't seen her in a very long time, although we'd kept up an intermittent correspondence, and in this latest letter from her she wrote to say that she was over from America and would be in London for a few days.

We arranged to meet for lunch at the Ritz and it was when we had just finished our dessert that Dorothea dropped her bombshell. Of course, she had no idea it was a bombshell, and I did my best not to give myself away; the humiliation would have been too much to bear. The nub of it was, Dorothea had been in Paris the previous month staying at the George V Hotel and had run into an acquaintance she knew from back home. It was none other than Count Nikolai Demidov who was in Paris enjoying his honeymoon.

I trilled along with her about it being a small world and, to test my strength and acting skills, I said that that was quite extraordinary because I had bumped into him a few months ago while staying on the Riviera.

'He sure gets about,' said Dorothea with a laugh before launching into another tale about her travels in Europe and giving me time to reflect on what a fool I'd been. A stupid little fool who had lapped up his every lie. I'd been pathetically gullible to believe in him. He'd spotted my vanity and self-delusion a mile off and had played his hand perfectly, letting me think I was the one in control. Thereafter, and to get him out of my system, I threw myself into my work and a series of meaningless relationships.

But that was then, this was now. And now, I had another two barrow loads of tulip bulbs and wallflowers to plant. I could have let Frank Colefax and Amos, one of the under gardeners, do the planting, but I had set them to work in the woodland garden where they were planting aconites, as well as digging up the dahlias in another border. Besides, I loved nothing better than to immerse myself in the one thing I loved doing most. If I hadn't actually done at least half of the planting myself for a client, I didn't consider I had done a good job. It was also, as Bess would be the first to say, because I didn't trust others to do the job as well as I could do it.

That evening, Atticus and Leonora were giving a party. They loved to entertain and did it on a grand scale, warming the house with log fires in the hall, drawing room, library, dining room as well as the guest bedrooms, and filling the house with fragrant flowers which were either grown in the heated glasshouse or specially delivered from London.

Obviously, I never saw what went on below stairs, but Bess informed me that the servants' hall would be a hive of activity with everyone putting a shoulder to the wheel. Never one to shirk, Bess would join in and help if an extra pair of hands was required. She was good like that, always prepared to go the extra mile. Just as she had with my hair this evening before I descended the wide staircase and joined everyone in the drawing room for a cocktail.

I still hadn't had my hair cut into a fashionably short style and relied heavily on Bess to style it in the way that had become synonymous with what was regarded as my signature look. When I was working, I had my uniform of men's trousers and a collarless shirt with a waistcoat and a jacket if the weather was particularly cold. On my feet I wore a pair of stout leather boots and my hair was securely pinned up under a cloth cap. Many a time while working in a client's garden, and because I wasn't overly tall, I had been mistaken for a young lad, which always amused me. Especially when that same person later encountered me over dinner in a silk dress and with my hair up, looking the epitome of feminine charm and elegance. It amused me too that people had been so shocked by the photographs recently printed in the newspapers and magazines of Marlene Dietrich wearing a man's suit, complete with tie. I'd been wearing trousers for years now.

But this evening I was dressed to the nines in a new satin dress cut on the bias and which dropped to the floor, flowing over my body like the lightest of summer breezes. It was silver in colour and around my shoulders I had my favourite silver-fox fur stole. I had scrubbed the dirt from my fingernails and as I surveyed my reflection in the mirror, I derived a sense of pride from the fact that thanks to all the physical work I did, I still had the same slight figure I'd had in my twenties. Unlike my sister who had grown distinctly matronly with the passing of the years, but then she had spawned a couple of sprogs.

Confident that I was looking my best, I sallied forth into the *grand salon* where everybody was glass in hand and chattering away merrily, but then at the sight of me a sudden cheer went up, followed by: 'Happy Birthday, Elfrida!'

I was astonished that anyone knew it was my birthday, as I most definitely hadn't mentioned it, but then I spotted Mallory coming towards me. 'Don't be cross, darling Freddie,' he said, 'but of course I had to tell them it was your birthday when they invited me for the weekend.'

'You didn't say you would be here, you sneaky devil!' I chided him.

'And spoil a delicious surprise? Not on your life, sweetheart!'

It turned out that the party was entirely for my benefit and the guests had all been in on the secret. Bess too.

I was onto my second cocktail and on the verge of forgiving Atticus and Leonora for their deviousness when the next surprise, or more accurately, the next shock of the evening presented itself. At the sight of Nikolai Demidov coming into the room the glass I was drinking from dropped clean out of my hand.

'What a dreadful waste of a good drink,' I heard Mallory say.

For the next hour I made a conscious effort to ignore Nikolai. I danced with anyone who asked me and flirted accordingly. Every now and then I stole a glance in Nikolai's direction, checking to see if he was watching me. I so badly wanted to make him jealous, to make him realise what he had missed out on. I was also trying to see if he'd brought his wife with him, but as far as I could tell, he was alone. He clearly had no intention of talking to me. Which suited me perfectly.

I was just wondering what he was doing here, what his connection was to Atticus and Leonora, when I found myself being swept back to the dance floor by Mallory. 'I have a confession,' he said, 'which I know is going to annoy you. The thing is, I'm responsible for Nikolai being here. I asked Leonora and Atticus to include him in your birthday celebrations.'

Furious at his admission, I tried to wriggle out of his grasp, but Mallory held me all the more firmly. 'No running away, Elfrida,' he said, 'cowardice is not in your nature.'

'But why?' I demanded. 'You know how I feel about him after what he did to me.'

Then before he could answer my question, I felt the weight of a hand on my shoulder and suddenly every one of my senses was on a state of alert. I didn't need to turn around to see who it was, but I did so all the same. And there was Nikolai. Up close, he was just as tall, just as intensely sultry-eyed, just as damnably attractive, and just as if the last ten years had never happened. 'We need to talk,' he said. 'In private.'

Chapter Nine

July 1981
Larkspur House, Suffolk

In the kitchen, and while Libby was upstairs dressing, Bess was lost in thought as she waited for the kettle to boil.

One way or another, she had a lot on her mind, and it had her in a state of discombobulation. It was not a word she often applied to herself. But what with Elfrida's accident in the garden yesterday, which admittedly had resulted in nothing worse than a sprained ankle and a bump to her head, and then the attic floor giving way above Libby, it was all adding up to make her feel decidedly on edge. But what really concerned her was what might be lurking inside that large trunk that was now in the drawing room.

The surprise to Bess was that Elfrida had not only kept so much stuff, but that she had consigned it to the attic and never once told her about it.

Another surprise was that Libby's request to delve into the past hadn't been met with a firm refusal, but for some reason Elfrida had given the girl not exactly her blessing, but the green light to go ahead with the project.

'Are you sure it's a good idea?' Bess had asked Elfrida last night. 'What if she finds something that—'

'Oh, I doubt that very much,' Elfrida interrupted in a careless tone.

'But how can you be so sure?'

For answer, Elfrida had given an infuriating shrug of her shoulders and said, 'I just am. Now stop worrying.'

But Bess had good cause to worry.

With a cloud of steam now billowing up from the kettle on the range, she made the tea. She fetched a bottle of milk from the refrigerator and filled a jug, and then added cups and saucers to the tray, all the while muttering to herself that Elfrida was playing with fire. But then she always had.

Although, to be fair, Bess had had her moments when she'd been far from the cautious woman she was these days. Which was, of course, what worried her most. Because what if there was a photograph or a letter in that trunk that could lead to her being revealed for the woman she really was?

Elfrida said she was overreacting, that the worst that could happen was that Bess might end up breaking the promise she had made all those years ago.

'Don't you think it's time that happened anyway?' Elfrida had asked. 'Maybe then the past could be put right.'

Bess had disagreed. She didn't think the past could be put right as easily as Elfrida made out. As far as Bess could see, any attempt to do so could only lead to a lot of pain and distress.

At the thought of the ugliest of truths ever becoming known, her heart began to beat faster and her mouth went dry. She took several deep steadying breaths and then picked up the tray to take through to the drawing room.

She was greeted by Elfrida sitting on a footstool and waving a black and white photograph at her.

'Come and see what I've found, Bess!' she cried. 'It's a photograph of Amos when he was an under gardener at Lambert Chase. I remember taking the picture, lining up all the gardeners in front of the house and telling Amos not to look as if I were about to shoot him!'

Bess leant in for a better look at the photograph. 'More likely he was contemplating how soon it would be before he was tempted to shoot you,' she said, remembering with great fondness her long since passed husband.

Chapter Ten

October 1934
Lambert Chase, Northamptonshire
Bess

'What d'yer say, Bess Harding, shall we make things official and get ourselves wed so I can make a respectable woman of you?'

'What makes you think I'm not a respectable woman already, Amos Judd?' I bristled.

We were sitting on the wooden bench in the courtyard just off from the servants' hall of Lambert Chase. The chilly autumn night air was not conducive to being outside for long, but Amos had been unusually insistent that he wanted to talk to me, and alone. I should have guessed what he was up to, but I didn't.

Normally he would go home when he'd finished work in the garden, but today he'd hung around and eaten his supper with the rest of us. It was when everything had been tidied away and we were listening to the band playing upstairs for Elfrida's surprise birthday party that he had approached and said he had something he wanted to discuss with me. No sooner had we stepped outside into the darkness than I'd heard the others laughing in the kitchen behind us and somebody saying, 'You behave, Amos Judd!' Another voice had said, 'Don't do anything I wouldn't do!'

'Now don't you be taking on like that,' Amos said with a laugh in reply to my question, 'it's just a turn of phrase. I know all too well there's no more respectable a woman than my Bess.'

'Just so long as you remember that and don't think you can start taking any liberties with me,' I said, wondering when I had become *my Bess* to him.

He laughed some more. 'So is that a yes, then? Will you marry me?'

'I had no idea you felt this way,' I said. It was an outright lie; I'd had a strong suspicion that his feelings for me had been growing ever since he'd started shyly to present me with little posies of flowers whenever I arrived here with Elfrida for one of our visits. He'd even asked if he could write to me.

We had exchanged letters, but mine were always brief and little more than day-to-day accounts of life at Larkspur House, or about wherever I had recently travelled. In contrast, Amos's letters betrayed his eagerness for the next time he would see me. I never let on to Elfrida what was passing between the two of us, but if she had guessed that something was going on, she didn't say anything.

'How can you say that you had no idea how I felt about you when we've been . . .' Amos's words trailed off and he suddenly looked so very earnest and uncertain, and not at all his customary self. 'Do you feel nothing for me, Bess?' he asked, his shoulders slumped and his eyes barely meeting mine.

'Of course I do. It's just that you've sprung this on me. Marriage is such a big step.'

'I know that. But I thought I'd grab my chance while I could. I've been trying to pluck up the courage for ages now. I very nearly asked you the last time you were here. But after you pushed me away when I tried to kiss you, I lost my nerve.'

I remembered the moment all too well. It had haunted me ever since. I'd felt so sorry for him, yet at the same time I'd been rigid with fear and unable to apologise or even make light of my treatment of him.

'Amos,' I said with as much kindness as I could put into my voice, 'will you give me time to think about this? I need to speak to Miss Elfrida.'

Although it was dark, with only a weak light coming from the coach lamp on the opposite wall to where we were sitting, I could see the frown on his face as he leant away from me. 'Why?' he said. 'To ask her permission?'

'Not exactly, but there are important things we have to consider. For instance, where would you and I live?'

'Here, of course, in the village, this is where I work. My cottage is only small, but it's crying out for a woman's touch.'

'But I live and work in Suffolk and Miss Elfrida needs me.'

'But I need you, and you could find work hereabouts, maybe here at Lambert Chase.'

'I doubt Mrs Whittaker needs a new lady's maid,' I said.

'You're clever and adaptable, you could do some other type of work. And you really are the woman I want to spend the rest of my life with.'

I studied his face, a face I had come to know so well during the many visits I had made here with Elfrida. I could see the tender love in his expression. He wasn't what you'd call handsome, but the more I had got to know him, the more I had appreciated his strong angular features and gangly body that always gave me the urge to feed him up. But as much as I had enjoyed his company, I had been adamant there would be no intimacy between us.

That one and only time he'd tried to kiss me, I'd panicked and shoved him away. I knew he was offended, but how could I tell him that I was scared of being touched, that the very act of intimacy filled me with bone-deep dread? It was my own fault; I should never have allowed him to think we could ever be more than friends. But then so much was my own fault.

There had been a time when I would have written to my sister Joan about Amos, but now I didn't feel able to. Motherhood had changed Joan; her world revolved around Nancy, whom she absolutely doted on, and it seemed there was no room in her life for me anymore.

Joan's husband, Dudley, had changed too, and if I didn't know better I'd say they both looked down on me now. In their determination to give their daughter everything they believed she deserved, Dudley worked all hours. They had moved to a new house in a completely new area shortly before they'd become a family and they now lived in Tunbridge Wells, where Dudley had set up his own business selling second-hand motorcars. The last I heard, he was doing so well he was in the process of buying a second garage. In the few letters I received from Joan, there was a lot of emphasis on their making something of their lives, as though they were ashamed of where they'd come from and who they'd once been.

I didn't blame them for wanting to better themselves; I had felt the same way when I first started work at Larkspur House, but that didn't mean I turned my back on those to whom I'd always been close.

As for Nancy, she was nearly six years old now and it pained me to admit it, but the child was showing signs of being thoroughly spoilt, which would serve her ill in years to come if it wasn't nipped in the bud. But if ever I said something to my sister about it, I was told not to interfere. It hurt to hear Joan speak that way to me, but I let it go; after all, as Joan would remind me, I was only the child's aunt. I would never have dreamt that she would behave so coldly towards me.

So no, I wouldn't write to my sister to ask for her advice on whether I should marry Amos. The only person to whom I felt I could unburden myself was Elfrida, but she was the very person I would be abandoning if I did agree to become Amos's wife.

Working for Elfrida brought me so much joy. She might be eccentric at times, like dressing in men's clothes, or throwing herself into affairs with men who weren't worthy of her, but she could also be incredibly kind and generous. She was a woman who acted on instinct, but sadly just occasionally it failed her. Not that my own instinct hadn't failed me as well.

Then there was the happiness living at Larkspur House gave me and working alongside people whom I regarded as my family. Did I want to give that up, along with all the travelling I did with Elfrida?

I cared for Amos, I really did. He was a good and decent man, but he hadn't experienced life in the way I had since working for Elfrida. He hadn't had his horizons broadened by travel. He was old-fashioned and staid and that probably meant he was reliable. Sometimes that was what counted in life, wasn't it? Dependability surely laid down the strongest of foundations between two people. But would dependability be fun? Would life as Mrs Amos Judd be exciting?

Perhaps the real question I should be asking myself was did I love Amos, or could I come to love him?

Or did I want to end up as a lonely old maid, just as Elfrida joked was her future? Not that she would ever be lonely. Not Elfrida. She was too witty and vivacious and too much fun ever to be miserable and alone. If Amos was my only chance to marry, then perhaps I owed it to myself to say yes to this kind man sitting beside me who was patiently waiting for the answer he hoped to hear.

But instead of doing that, I suggested we should go for a walk in the garden. After a moment's hesitation, he agreed, and led the way across the cobbled courtyard.

'Perhaps we should have a lantern to guide us?' I remarked as we moved away from the light provided by the solitary coach lamp.

'No need,' he said, offering me his hand. 'I can find my way round the garden with my eyes shut. You just have to trust me.'

With it being such a cloudy night, the stars and sliver of new moon were barely visible in the velvet sky, and so I had no choice but to put my faith in Amos and hold his hand.

In silence we ambled along the Rose Avenue, then through an archway in the beech hedge to the Knot Garden, then turning right, with my eyes gradually growing used to the dark, I could make out the shadowy forms of the Topiary Walk. All this, and so much more of the garden, had been designed and created by Elfrida and I couldn't help but be proud of her, with what she had achieved in so short a space of time.

'Let's go inside the glasshouse,' Amos said, 'it'll be warmer in there.'

Warmer for what? I thought with a tremor of alarm.

He must have felt the tremble in my hand for he suddenly stopped walking and pivoted round to face me. 'Bess,' he said, 'please don't think I'm about to rob you of your virtue, I know how precious it is to you. It is for me too. I believe in saving oneself for marriage. Does that put your mind at rest?'

All I could do was nod nervously.

'Good,' he said, before setting off again for our destination.

He had just pushed open the door of the glasshouse and stepped aside to let me go in first, when I felt another tremor, coupled with a sixth sense that I should not under any circumstances take another step forward.

My instinct was right. At the far end of the glasshouse, I saw that we weren't the only ones to have come here in search of somewhere private. I could only see the back of the woman, but I recognised the dress that was hitched up around her thighs and stocking tops. It was only when the man, perhaps sensing they were no longer alone, opened his eyes and glanced over the top of Elfrida's head towards the doorway where I stood, that I registered who it was.

It was Count Nikolai Demidov.

*

Loyalty to Elfrida made me push Amos back before he saw what I had seen. I couldn't have borne the thought of Elfrida losing his respect, or him gossiping about her to the rest of the household staff at Lambert Chase. I dragged him away, pretending I hadn't recognised who we'd nearly interrupted in a secret tryst, and when we were back in the Topiary Walk, to stem the flow of his questions as to who it might have been in the glasshouse, I silenced him by planting a daring kiss on his lips. I had meant it purely as a distraction, and it was certainly that, because he must have been so taken aback by my mouth bumping ineptly against his that our teeth clashed. He immediately claimed the fault as his own and apologised for being so clumsy.

'Shall we try again?' he asked.

Overcome with awkwardness, I forced myself to say yes.

*

The next morning when I had taken Elfrida her breakfast, she asked me, and seemingly without a shred of discomfiture, what I'd seen last night. 'I know you were there,' she added, 'Nikolai told me.'

'I hardly saw anything,' I said, setting the tray on the bed where Elfrida was sitting up and looking as fresh as a daisy, and just as innocent.

'But enough to shock you and Mr Judd, I would imagine,' she said.

Pulling the curtains back, I replied, 'How do you know he was with me?'

'Why else would you be lurking in the garden so late at night?'

'I wasn't lurking,' I said, my cheeks suddenly flaming.

'I'm teasing you, Bess. But I'm sorry if I've embarrassed you. Was Mr Judd very shocked?'

'I made sure he didn't see anything, miss.'

'That was very thoughtful of you, as I know that kind of thing can be viewed quite poorly below stairs. Now, why don't you sit down and tell me about you and Mr Judd.'

Just as the colour had cooled from my cheeks, they flamed once more. 'Why do you think there's anything to tell?'

'Bess, this is me you're talking to, I've seen the way he hovers around you with that dreamy look in his eyes. Has he asked you to marry him yet?'

'Yes,' I admitted, 'he asked me last night and I don't know what to do.'

She stirred a spoonful of sugar into her coffee, then looked up at me. 'If you loved him, you'd know exactly what to do.'

'Is that how it is with you and the Count?'

Elfrida dismissed the question, an audacious question at that, with an unladylike snort. 'We're talking about you and Mr Judd, not me. How have you left things with him?'

'I told him I had to talk to you.'

'As indeed you are.' She sipped her coffee, then lowered the cup to its saucer. 'If you say yes to him, I presume that means you'll be handing in your notice, again,' she added.

'That's the problem, miss, I don't want to leave you. I like working for you and being at Larkspur House.'

'In that case, I may have the perfect solution for you, if Mr Judd is agreeable.'

Four months later not only were Amos and I married, but he was working at Larkspur House with a view to taking over from Jimmy Padget, the head gardener, when he retired. Home for us was a two-up, two-down cottage in the centre of the village of Finchley Green. It had no electricity, and the lavatory was in the garden next to the coal shed, but it was our home, and we grew to love it.

Just as I came to love Amos.

Chapter Eleven

July 1981
Larkspur House, Suffolk

With her cardigan on, a hat jammed onto her head and her handbag and a bunch of sweet peas from the garden placed carefully into the wicker basket attached to the handlebars, Bess set off for church on her ancient bicycle. It was a creaking and clanking contraption that had certainly seen better days. Much like the car in the garage.

Elfrida had bought the old Wolseley back in 1960 and Bess had never taken to driving it; but Elfrida had driven it like a maniac, thundering around the quiet country lanes without a care in the world. It had failed its last MOT and Elfrida hadn't done anything about having it put right, not after the man at the garage had said that she'd be better off getting rid of it and that he knew someone who'd pay a nominal amount for the vehicle in order to break it up for spare parts. Since then, the car had remained in the garage gathering dust and cobwebs, unused and unloved. Elfrida had decided they didn't need a car as they didn't go anywhere and the local shops delivered all they needed. And, of course, Bess could always cycle to the village if need be.

Bess's parting words to Elfrida before setting off had been to tell her not to do anything silly while she was out. Words which, naturally, had fallen on deaf ears as Elfrida was adamant her ankle was almost as good as new now, and she planned to potter in the garden as well as sleep in her own bed tonight.

Thankfully Libby had promised she would keep an eye on Elfrida in Bess's absence.

From the end of the drive, it was exactly two and a half miles to St Jude's but after less than a mile of pedalling at her customary brisk pace along the leafy tunnel of Woodley Lane, Bess felt a squeezing sensation in her chest, as well as what felt like a rush of blood pounding in her ears. She stilled her feet on the pedals and using the speed she'd generated, she coasted along the narrow lane.

Something similar had happened to her last Sunday when she'd cycled to church but she had filed it under 'just one of those things'. Until now she had forgotten all about it. Now it was very much in her mind. But what did it mean?

It means you're getting older, you daft old fool, she told herself.

Probably it was something to do with her blood pressure. All that worrying about what might be unearthed from that wretched trunk.

She had gone to bed early last night in something of a poor mood, having left Elfrida and Libby to stay up late rootling through the topsy-turvy contents of the trunk. Bess couldn't bring herself to join in with what they'd both found so fascinating. It had been like a game of Russian roulette for her, as with each photograph Elfrida plucked out and reminisced over, Bess had feared it could in some way possess the potential to bring down their carefully constructed house of cards.

What really concerned Bess were the notebooks that Elfrida had stored away, and which apparently she had forgotten all about. They were mostly full of notes made about the gardens she had created, with the addition of detailed plant lists and roughly drawn sketches and plans. But some pages were of a rather more personal nature – observations about parties attended, people met, love affairs concluded, and with no shortage of witty or barbed comments. Had Elfrida written anything in those notebooks which she really shouldn't have?

Now that the squeezing sensation in her chest had passed, Bess pedalled on, but at a slower speed. *No point in tempting fate*, she thought. And no harm in being sensible and reminding herself that despite a lifetime of good health, there was bound to come a time when her body would start to complain. The same was true for Elfrida, and though the infuriatingly stubborn woman would never admit it, her tumble in the garden the other day had been a warning to her that she wasn't invincible. Neither of them were.

As much as they bickered, Bess would be heartbroken if she lost the best friend she'd ever had. Undeniably they had what could only be described as an odd relationship. If somebody had told Bess when she first started work at Larkspur House, back in the days when she wouldn't say boo to a goose, that she would one day dare to speak to Elfrida in the way she did now, she would have declared that person quite mad. But what with everything they had experienced together, there had been a shift not so much in the balance of power, but a shift in the strength of their dependency on one another. It meant there was a special bond between them that could never be broken. There was nobody who had been kinder or more generous to her than Elfrida. In years gone by, whenever Bess had tried to explain this to her sister, Joan had refused to believe her.

'Whatever she's given you is no more than her way of buying your devotion,' Joan asserted. 'It's so that she'll have you at her constant beck and call.'

Nancy had pitched in too. 'Don't fool yourself that she really cares about you,' she had said. 'All you are to her is a servant to do her bidding. You've given your life to that woman, and for what? What do you have to show for your loyalty?'

But what did anyone have to show for their life when the end came? Had Joan, with her sanctimonious certainty that she was better than Bess, died happier because she had lived in a comfortable detached house in a smart cul de sac in Tunbridge Wells and her husband had owned a string of garages in Kent?

The way Joan and Nancy had spoken about loyalty it was as if it was a bad thing. For Bess it meant everything. To Elfrida as well. Had they not been so loyal to each other, it really didn't bear thinking what might have become of them.

St Jude's was at the opposite end of the village and after cycling past the pond and shops, Bess passed the cottage where she and Amos had started their married life. It had been extended several times since then and was now almost unrecognisable. The two cottages further along were decorated in honour of the Royal Wedding and Bess had to smile at the excessive amount of bunting which had been put to use. She knew from church that the owners of these neighbouring cottages were on the committee for arranging the village street party on the day of the wedding. It was to be held on the green and would doubtless be well attended; but not by anyone at Larkspur House. The last thing Libby would want to do would be to take part in a wedding celebration.

At St Jude's, Bess leant her bicycle against the buttress wall of the eastern side of the church, and taking her handbag and flowers, she followed the path round to Amos's grave.

Today would have been his seventy-fifth birthday, which was why she had brought sweet peas for him. He used to love growing them at Larkspur House as well as in the garden of their cottage and had regularly won prizes at the village show for his blooms. Taking the vase that she kept on his grave over to the tap, she filled it with water and arranged the flowers in it. Back at the grave, she wished Amos a happy birthday and tried, as she so often did, to think what life might have been like if he hadn't died when he had. Would they have stayed here in Finchley Green, or would he have eventually persuaded her to leave Elfrida so they could live out their retirement years together someplace else? Would they have continued to be happy, or would they have grown tired of each other?

She never had an answer to any of her questions, and the same was true today.

Inside St Jude's, it was the standard small congregation that attended Morning Service, the younger members of the village preferring the Family Service at ten-thirty. Bess held the dubious honour of being the longest-serving member of the congregation, having begun her attendance back in 1927.

Acknowledging the others with a polite smile and a nod, Bess took her customary seat in a pew on her own. She liked to keep herself to herself, not because she was unsociable, but because this was her sanctuary, her place where she could be alone with her thoughts. It was where she repeatedly asked for forgiveness. The sad truth was, as Elfrida had once said, God may well have forgiven her, but Bess hadn't been able to forgive herself. She doubted she ever would.

As the service got under way and she joined in with the familiar responses, she felt the weight of the last week gradually lifting from her shoulders. It had been there since Libby had telephoned with the news that Marcus had cheated on her and had increased every day since. Bess loved the girl so dearly, she would happily take her pain and suffer it herself if she could.

Today marked the fifth day of Libby's stay and superficially she appeared to be coping well with the distractions Larkspur House was providing, but Bess knew better than anyone the effort it took to put on a brave face. Without a doubt it would be far worse for Libby when the time came for her to return to London and resume her life there, where she would be immersed in constant reminders of what should have been. For now, though, and for as long as Libby remained with them, Bess would wrap the girl in a protective shield of love.

She was halfway home when once more her chest felt as though it was being squeezed. She pedalled on into the leafy tunnel of Woodley Lane, persuading herself that it would pass, just as it had before. But this time, it didn't. The slight squeeze suddenly became a vice-like grip and she struggled to catch her breath. Of their own volition her feet slipped away from the pedals and the next thing, she was in danger of falling off the bicycle. Somehow, she managed to dismount without disgracing herself and, with her legs feeling like wet cotton wool, she wobbled to the side of the road where she let the bike crash to the tarmac and then sat down on the dusty dry ground, her back resting against the trunk of an oak tree.

It's nothing to worry about, she told herself. Nothing that a visit to the doctor's surgery couldn't put right. Blood pressure. That's what it would be. She just needed a tablet or two and she'd be as right as rain.

As if persuaded of her own diagnosis, that there was nothing seriously wrong with her, the muscles in her chest relaxed and once more she was able to breathe properly. Relief spread through her like a comforting warm embrace and rather than rush to stand up, she closed her eyes and let the feeling spread to every inch of her body.

When she opened her eyes, there was a red squirrel on the other side of the narrow lane staring back at her. She couldn't remember the last time she'd seen one and for a split second she wondered if she had fallen asleep and was dreaming.

It was no dream, she told herself when the squirrel scampered off into the undergrowth.

'Time for me to scamper away too,' she murmured.

Rising cautiously to her feet and finding that the strength in her legs had returned and, more importantly, she could breathe perfectly normally, she dusted herself down and climbed onto her bicycle and slowly, very slowly, pedalled for home.

Best not to mention any of this to Elfrida or Libby, she thought when she turned into the driveway of Larkspur House, the tyres crunching over the gravel. Libby in particular would worry and the poor girl had enough to deal with as it was.

Ahead of her, and parked to one side of Libby's campervan in front of the garage, was a builder's van with a ladder fixed to a rack on the roof. Alongside that was another car which Bess recognised as belonging to Dr Matthews.

Putting her bicycle away, she went round to the back of the house to let herself in, but hearing laughter coming from the garden, she followed the path that led to the terrace. It was there, in the dappled shade of the rose pergola, that she found Elfrida holding court and plainly enjoying herself. As soon as Libby saw Bess, she stood up.

'Bess,' she said, 'come and join us.'

'Yes do,' added Elfrida. 'Come and say hello to Mr Benson who has very kindly spared us some of his precious time on a Sunday to assess the damage to the attic. Wasn't that generous of him? And kind too of Dr Matthews for twisting his friend's arm to come to the rescue of we three damsels in distress. What's more, and because he says I've made a miraculous recovery and am now fighting fit, the two of them despatched that old bed to its rightful place.'

'That wasn't exactly what I said,' Dr Matthews said, up on his feet alongside Libby. 'I cautioned you to take care and not overdo it if I remember correctly.'

Elfrida gave a trilling laugh. But Bess stayed where she was. Since when had Elfrida ever described herself as a damsel in distress?

'Here, Mrs Judd,' Dr Matthews said, offering her his chair, 'have mine.' Next to him Mr Benson was out of his chair as well. Sporting a tan-coloured pair of cowboy boots, he was a stockily built man with a mop of curly blond hair. Smiling politely at her, he looked an affable sort of chap.

But Bess wasn't feeling particularly affable herself. She felt almost as if she were intruding. Clutching her handbag, and with her hat still on, she felt stiff and awkwardly out of place dressed as she was in her Sunday best, or what Elfrida called her 'prim and proper'. In contrast, the doctor and builder were in jeans and T-shirts, as was Libby. Elfrida, of course, was in her usual gardening clothes and fitted in perfectly.

And because she felt so out of place, she said, 'That's all right, I'll go and make a start on lunch.'

'No need,' said Libby, 'I've already prepared the vegetables and taken the beef out of the fridge. I just have the Yorkshire pudding batter to make.'

Bess was about to reply when Elfrida said, 'Dr Matthews has been telling us how as a medical student, and to supplement his grant, he used to work in a bar as a cocktail waiter. I've made him promise that one day he'll mix us a concoction that will knock our socks off!' She laughed gaily before adding, 'And it transpires that Mr Benson knows a thing or two about Arts and Crafts properties, so I have high hopes that we're in safe hands with him.'

Had Elfrida been at the cooking sherry? Bess wondered. Under normal circumstances, and rather than invite them to sit down with her, Elfrida would sooner pull up the drawbridge and pour hot boiling oil onto approaching tradesmen, whom she viewed as nothing more than money-grabbing swindlers. Yet here she was dispensing mercurial charm by the bucketful. Was it all an act in the hope that her hospitality would win over the builder, and he'd do the job at a cut-price deal? Or was it a case of the wily old bird trying her hand at playing Cupid with the good doctor and Libby?

Excusing herself on the pretext of needing to take an aspirin for a headache, Bess went inside the house and her hand resting heavily on the oak banister rail, she took the stairs slowly up to her bedroom. Kicking off her shoes and removing her hat, she lay on the bed, suddenly feeling drained of all energy.

She had only been lying there a few minutes when there was a light knock at the door, followed by Libby peering in at her.

'Everything all right?' she asked.

Bess sat up and swung her legs off the bed. 'I'm fine,' she said.

'Have you taken something for your headache?'

'Yes,' she said. That was the trouble with lies, you told one and all too often it led to another.

'Why don't you rest properly? Lie down again. Shall I make you a cup of tea? You do look a bit washed out.'

Seeing the concern on Libby's face, Bess said, 'Oh, it's nothing, I just didn't sleep very well last night. Now tell me what on earth Elfrida is up to.'

Libby smiled. 'As if we couldn't guess.'

'Subtlety has never been her forte.'

Still smiling, Libby went on to explain how Dr Matthews had telephoned to ask if it would be convenient for his builder friend to visit that morning and if so, he would come as well in order to show Mr Benson where the house actually was, with it being so off the beaten track.

'So here they both are and Elfrida is pulling out all the stops for them,' remarked Bess. 'And for your benefit.'

'Don't worry about that, I know what she's up to and if he has any sense, Dr Matthews does too.'

'I must say I'm surprised he's prepared to socialise with a patient when it's frowned upon these days. Mind you, it never used to be a problem, people didn't worry about that kind of thing years ago.'

'Apparently, as of Friday next week he won't be a locum at the Finchley Green surgery anymore, so I suppose it's not that clear or hard a line that he's crossing, is it?'

'Or he's prepared to do so because he—'

'Don't say it.'

Bess smiled and patted Libby's hands. 'I'm just teasing you.'

'So long as that's all it is. Now how about that cup of tea?'

'I'll come down with you.'

'Are you sure? You wouldn't prefer to rest until your head is feeling better?'

'It's better already, thank you.' Which was another lie because there had never been anything wrong with her head, but she did feel slightly better than when she'd come up to her bedroom, so perhaps it was only a tiny white fib. Her mood had certainly improved, thanks to Libby's company.

After Libby had made her a mug of tea and put the beef in the oven, the two of them went out to the garden and found that Mr Benson and his cowboy boots had taken their leave and Elfrida was insisting on giving Dr Matthews a tour of the garden.

'And by the way,' she said to Bess and Libby, 'I've invited our young doctor friend to join us for lunch.'

'It's very kind of you, Miss Ambrose,' Dr Matthews said, looking every inch like a man who had been backed into a corner, 'but I really should be making tracks, I only came to show Steve where—'

'No, no,' cut in Elfrida, 'I won't hear another word of refusal from you. Not after you admitted that all you had waiting for you at home was a paltry ham sandwich. That's not what a hardworking young man like you should be eating for his Sunday lunch.'

*

They ate lunch in the orchard, Libby having laid a red and white gingham cloth on the old wooden table beneath the sprawling branches of an apple tree. Around them the meadow grass, speckled with daisies, buttercups and clover, was long and where they had crushed it underfoot, its milky fragrance filled the warm soporific summer air that was vibrating with the hum of bees and birdsong. A ponderous silence hung over the four of them as they sat back replete and wrapped in a gilded haze of contentment.

Libby had cooked the meal herself, banning Bess from so much as picking up a wooden spoon, and privately she thought it had been pretty near perfect. The Yorkshire puddings had risen beautifully, the mix of herbs and mustard which she'd rubbed over the beef before putting it in the oven had formed a deliciously crisp outer layer, while the inside of the sirloin joint was succulent and pink, just as it should be, and the new potatoes, peas and carrots, all from the garden, had been full of the taste of summer.

Tilting her head to take in the expanse of cornflower-blue sky, she thought how lucky she was to have had the chance since she was a child to enjoy this enchanted place. One day, when the time was right, she would leave London and create her own little piece of paradise.

But why wait for *one day* and some so-called right time? What was to keep her there now that she was no longer marrying Marcus? Yes, London had been her home for some years, but only because that was where she had been expected to go when she'd completed her time at secretarial college. It was what girls of her type did – well-brought-up middle-class girls who were not quite cut out for university.

As the dutiful daughter her mother expected her to be, she had gone to secretarial college in Oxford and learnt to type and do shorthand as well as bookkeeping and filing. It hadn't been as dull as she'd feared; living in Oxford had been fun, and that's where she'd met Selina when they'd shared a flat on the Banbury Road.

Her mother's plan had been for Libby to follow in her very exacting footsteps – to be a first-rate secretary and then marry the boss and live comfortably ever after. Except Libby had hated working as a secretary. The tedium of typing boring letter after boring letter and basically being a dogsbody for a man who couldn't find time to collect his own dry cleaning because he was too busy seeing his mistress was not for her.

Selina had reached the same conclusion about her own career as a secretary and together they had retrained at a cookery school in Marylebone. Private catering was never going to make them rich, but Libby had enjoyed the creative element of what they did. She loved nothing better than trying out new recipes or devising new ones of her own.

Of course, her mother hadn't thought much of this career change, but Libby hadn't cared. She was doing something she had chosen to do rather than going along with somebody else's wishes.

And now that she wasn't marrying, she could do more or less what she wanted. She could retrain again if she wanted to, and live wherever she wanted to live. She could actually reinvent herself: she could be whoever she wanted to be. Anything was possible! She could travel. She could travel the world as a private cook. There were any number of avenues that could open up to her if she chose to live a completely different life. But what appealed to her most was the thought of retraining and doing something new. Now that would be a real reinvention of herself.

Spurred on by an imagination set free by the intoxicating mix of a perfectly beautiful summer's day and several glasses of Merlot, she suddenly realised she was getting so carried away with the idea of this new person she could be, even a wholly imperfect version of her, she hadn't noticed that, either side of her, Bess and Elfrida had both fallen asleep. At the sound of the two women gently snoring in unison, she looked across the table to see their lunch guest with a half smile on his face.

She smiled back at him and wondered if he was trying to work out how on earth he had ended up here this afternoon. He was, she decided, difficult to read. On the one hand he was incredibly helpful and easy to have around, and on the other he was as closed as a clam shell, giving little away about himself. Was he trying to keep his professional distance? But then why accept Elfrida's invitation? Was he lonely perhaps? He didn't seem the lonely sort. But then who did? It was something most people kept hidden from others because it was an admission of failure, to admit you didn't have somebody in your life who made you feel whole and complete.

Earlier, while he had helped her carry the dishes of food out here to the orchard, she had asked him about his builder pal and how they knew each other, and he'd said they'd been at school together in Ely. 'Steve really is a superb builder and very reliable,' he'd explained. 'I wouldn't have recommended him if I didn't know he'd do a good job for Miss Ambrose.'

'I'm thinking of having a go at doing some redecorating here,' Libby had said. 'Do you think your friend would advise me on the best place to buy the necessary paint and equipment?'

'Of course he would. He'll probably get it at trade price for you.'

'That would be great. Thank you.'

Throughout lunch, and despite Elfrida's attempts to interrogate him, Dr Matthews had given hardly anything away about himself. He'd been far happier encouraging her to regale them with one amusing story after another. Elfrida was a natural raconteur and had perfect timing when it came to a punchline. She also loved an audience. In return he'd told them a few funny stories of his time as a medical student, of dressing a skeleton – not a real one, but one used for anatomical study – in a suit and then placing it behind the wheel of a car and leaving it to be discovered. Then there was the prank of drinking what looked like a urine sample, but which was actually apple juice. 'All pretty juvenile,' he'd finished by saying, 'but it passed for fun back then.'

'It was very kind of Miss Ambrose to invite me to join you for lunch,' he said now, his voice hushed and breaking the drowsy silence between them.

'Consider yourself honoured,' Libby replied just as quietly. 'It's not something that often happens.' Then because if they were going to continue talking, she didn't want to wake Bess and Elfrida, she suggested they went for a walk.

At the sound of Libby and the young doctor rising from their wicker chairs, Elfrida's eyelids fluttered open and she watched them wander off through the orchard.

Smiling to herself, she closed her eyes and slipped back into the dream she'd been having before the creak of chairs had woken her.

Chapter Twelve

October 1934
Lambert Chase, Northamptonshire
Elfrida

'Elfrida, you have to let me explain.'

'I don't have to do anything you ask of me. Now remove your hand from my arm. Your wife might appreciate you riding roughshod over her, but I do not.'

Nikolai released his hold of me but as we stood on the semi-illuminated terrace, he fastened the powerful strength of his obsidian gaze on mine. Turning my back on him, and resting my hands on the stone balustrade, I stared out at the indistinct shapes of the garden in the shadowy darkness to gather my reeling senses. From the moment he had appeared I had experienced the sensation of endlessly tumbling from a great height, at the same time bracing myself for the inevitable impact, actually *wanting* it to happen. After all, I had waited an age for this moment, to tell Count Nikolai Demidov exactly what I thought of him.

'Please,' he said, 'just spare me a few minutes. I'm not asking for forgiveness, God knows I don't deserve that, but I want you to know the truth.'

I twisted round to face him. 'The truth is you weren't honest with me and I behaved like a pathetic little fool, drinking in your lies as you fed them to me!' I flinched, realising that I sounded crosser with myself than him. As well I might.

'I didn't lie to you at the time,' he said, looming over me and resurrecting the memory of how the sheer size of him used to send a thrill racing through my body. 'What passed between us all those years ago was real,' he continued, his voice low. 'I fell in love with you and I believe you fell in love with me. Do you deny that now?'

'Your arrogance is breathtaking!'

He shook his head. 'As is your beauty,' he murmured.

I stared at him, the wind suddenly knocked clean out of my sails, puffed up as I was on a swell of angry outrage and painful regret. 'Don't think you can distract me with a few words of misplaced flattery,' I said. 'It won't work. I'm not the silly girl I once was.'

'You were never silly. Never. But my words are not misplaced; it's the truth. You are even more beautiful than I remembered. But then I should have known your beauty would only intensify with the passing of each year.'

'Oh, for heaven's sake do be quiet and have some self-respect.'

His face darkened. 'I lost that a long time ago. Now please, will you let me explain why I disappeared from your life the way I did?'

'You don't need to explain anything. You told me you would wait for me while I went about the business of changing the world. And the biggest laugh is, I believed you. I trusted you. Then when I learnt from a friend that she'd bumped into you while you were enjoying your honeymoon, I had to accept that you hadn't meant a word of what you'd said and once I woke up to that, I put you out of my mind. Overnight you no longer existed. You were just someone I once knew.'

'Then why are you so angry with me? And why, in a attempt to make me jealous, were you deliberately flirting with those

127

men in there?' He inclined his head towards the house and the *grand salon* where I'd been dancing. 'None of whom is worthy so much as to look at you, never mind kiss you.'

I raised an eyebrow. 'It clearly worked because you strong-armed me away from them and here we are.'

'I had to. I couldn't stand by and watch another minute of you ignoring me. It was too painful.'

A burst of laughter had us both turning to see a group of revellers from the party spilling out onto the terrace. Seeing the fiercely stern look on Nikolai's face, they instantly fell quiet and moved off further along its balustraded expanse. 'For the love of God,' Nikolai muttered, 'is there nowhere private we can talk?'

I should have left him there on the terrace stewing in his own furiously dark mood, but I didn't. Instead, I told him to follow me. Knowing the garden at Lambert Chase as well as I did, I had no trouble finding my way down to the glasshouse where I knew we'd be alone. I was, I confess, curious to hear what story Nikolai was going to give for his not having told me about the girlfriend he married only a few weeks after plying me with his cousin's champagne and taking me to his bed. Although I could not pretend that I hadn't played my part, since I had been totally willing in all respects. I could not now imagine otherwise to suit my own narrative. But had I known he was on the verge of marrying I would have steered clear of him.

Once inside the glasshouse I shut the door and turned to face him, and God forgive me, but there it was, the electrifying desire I had felt for him before. Was it down to the humid enclosed space that we now occupied? Or the knowledge that we were entirely alone? Whatever it was, I was determined not to let it get the better of me and told him tersely to get on with his explanation.

In the silence, his shoes cracking like gunfire across the tiled floor of the glasshouse, he started pacing, his hands pushed deep into the pockets of his dress suit trousers.

'I didn't lie to you,' he began. 'When we met I was a free man. I had just broken off my engagement to a girl called Olga. The relationship, if you could call it that, was of our parents making. Our two families, both émigrés from St Petersburg, wanted to make the match between us. I cannot speak for Olga, but as far as I was concerned, I was prepared to marry her to please my parents. It seemed like something that would make them happy after everything they had suffered in fleeing their home and losing so many loved ones in the revolution.'

'So you were just being the dutiful son?'

'Is that so very hard to believe?'

I ignored his question and the hurt in his voice. 'Go on,' I said, 'tell me the rest.'

'I don't know why, but once Olga and I were officially engaged and our families were planning our wedding, things began to go wrong between us. We found we had hardly anything in common and we didn't seem able to agree on anything. Olga wanted to be out every night at some party or other, if not with me, then with her friends. We couldn't even agree where we should live. I wanted to be in New York where I was helping my father run the hotel business. He wanted me there too. But Olga wanted to be in Washington with her family and flatly refused to consider moving away. With no agreement in sight, I began to see a different side to her. When she couldn't get her own way, she would behave like a child, she would either scream and shout, or sulk and refuse to speak to me. I couldn't see a future with anyone so self-absorbed or so intransigent. I'm not proud of myself, reneging on a promise, but I didn't think it would be fair to either of us to marry.'

'And yet you did?'

He came to a stop and turned to face me. 'Yes. A few days after I'd said goodbye to you—'

'As I recall you didn't say goodbye,' I interrupted him. 'You slunk away while I slept.'

129

He swallowed. 'Yes,' he murmured, 'that was cowardly of me.'

'I'll say.'

'I'm sorry, but I couldn't face a full-blown farewell. And anyway, I thought I'd be seeing you again when I planned to be in London later that month.'

'Why didn't you?'

'I received a telegram insisting I fly home straight away where I was greeted with the news from Olga that she was pregnant. She had told her parents before telling me and so there was no question of our not marrying, I knew what I had to do. I convinced myself that a child might be the making of us as a couple.'

'A happy ending all round then,' I said. The sarcasm in my voice was as heavy as the muggy air enveloping us.

He shook his head. 'Far from it. After a difficult birth, the baby . . . a boy . . . was stillborn. We both grieved in our different ways, but Olga was left devastated. Understandably she looked for something, or some*one*, to blame and that was me.'

At the anguish in Nikolai's face, all my anger drained out of me. 'I'm sorry,' I said, and meaning it.

'Ever since then, mentally as well as physically, Olga has been fragile. I thought in time that another child might help, but that side of our relationship was not to be. Since then, my wife has been in and out of various clinics in America and here in Europe.'

'Is she here in England with you?'

'No, she's in a clinic in Switzerland.'

'Why did you never write to tell me the truth?'

'Would you have believed me?'

I hesitated, recalling how furious I'd been when my friend Dorothea had so blithely told me about bumping into Nikolai while he was on his honeymoon. 'I don't know,' I murmured. 'Perhaps not.'

I suddenly felt so petty, accepting that like Olga I had wanted someone to blame for my heartache, which was nothing compared to what he and Olga must have suffered at the loss of their child.

'Now what?' I asked in the silence.

'Now I return you to the party which was held in your honour to celebrate your birthday and I say goodbye,' he said.

'Just like that?' I blurted out. 'After all these years you simply walk away?'

'What would you have me do?'

My head told me to say goodbye and go back to dancing and flirting in the *grand salon*, except there was no point now in making Nikolai jealous. I wasn't even in the mood to dance because my treacherous heart was beating out the equivalent of an SOS signal for him to take me in his strong arms and kiss me one last time.

Trying to ignore both my heart and my head, I said, 'Did Mallory know of your broken engagement with Olga when we met?'

'No. Why would you think he did?'

'I remember him telling me that he invited you to that party at his villa because he felt you needed cheering up.'

'That's true, in as much as when I met him in Paris I was upset that I'd disappointed my parents by ending things with Olga. I was in Europe for a change of scene and to meet up with friends and some of my other relatives.'

'Such as your cousin whose champagne we drank with such enjoyment?'

He nodded before stepping towards me.

'But Mallory knows now?' I asked.

'Yes. We ran into each other in London a few days ago and after he took me to task for hurting you, I told him what I've just told you.'

'And he suggested you came here to kiss and make up with me, did he?'

'He seemed to think an apology from me would—'

'Would what? Have me falling into your arms, eager to take up where we left off all those years ago?'

'I wouldn't insult you with such an idea.'

'Good! Because it's a terrible idea and so typical of Mallory, him being such an incurable romantic.'

'I couldn't agree more. After all, we're not the people we were eleven years ago.'

'No,' I said, 'too much water has flowed under the bridge.'

'Turning back the clock never works.'

'It's a recipe for disaster.'

'Of course,' he murmured, 'everyone knows that some things are best left to the past. And yet . . .'

'Yes?'

'We might be the exception to the rule.'

'Well, I've always been that.'

He smiled and somehow the gap between us no longer existed, and I was staring up into his face. A face I swore I'd slap if I ever encountered it again, but nothing could have been further from my mind in that instance as I put a hand gently to the back of his neck and pulled him down to me so I could kiss him.

We kissed and kissed, our mouths and hands instinctively seeking out the familiarity of what we had once known. In the decade that had passed since our brief affair I had kissed any number of men, but not one had made me feel the way Nikolai had.

I was so lost in the moment, giving myself to him and greedily taking what I wanted, that I had no knowledge of the glasshouse door being opened. Not until Nikolai, who had hitched up my dress and lifted me onto him, abruptly stopped what he was doing and groaned. 'We've just been seen,' he said hoarsely.

I peered through the glass into the darkness and knew exactly who had seen us. Knowing that Bess would never say anything,

I couldn't be so sure about the man with whom she was now scurrying away.

'I'm sorry if I've put you in a compromising situation,' Nikolai said, pulling my dress down to make me decent, and then buttoning his trousers.

'You haven't. This was of my doing as much as yours,' I said.

He pulled me back into his embrace. 'Can I see you again?'

'You're seeing me now.'

'It's not enough. I want to speak to you properly. I want to know everything you've done since I last saw you.'

'Hasn't Mallory told you everything?'

'He told me you hadn't married. Is there a reason for that?'

'Several reasons. None of which has anything to do with you, so please don't jump to the arrogant conclusion that I couldn't find a man who lived up to you.'

He smiled. 'The same old Elfrida, always so ready to put me in my place by puncturing my inflated ego!'

I smiled too. 'Only for the sake of clarity. I would hate for you to think that I have spent the last decade yearning for you to walk back into my life.'

'It's what I've done,' he said. 'I swear, never has a day gone by when I haven't thought of you and wished that things had been different.'

In the days that followed, and after I had finished my work at Lambert Chase for Atticus and Leonora, I sent Bess home and joined Nikolai in London for the remainder of his stay. We stayed at the Ritz and to maintain an air of discretion we occupied two rooms with a connecting door. We barely left them, ordering in room service when we wanted to eat. It was the hardest thing to let him go, but I knew I had to. He had to return to Switzerland to collect his wife who, so he was told, was showing signs of progress, and take her home to America on board the SS *Normandie*.

We had both known our time together in London was limited, that there was no point in making plans for the future. Nikolai would never divorce his wife, not when she was so fragile. I wouldn't ask that of him, not when he told me that Olga had already tried to kill herself when he had raised the subject of ending their marriage.

For all his duplicitous behaviour in having an affair with me while his wife was in a Swiss clinic, I knew him to be an essentially honourable man. And besides, his life was in New York, and my life was here in England, so it was futile to think of the future. The here and now, living in the moment – and never thinking of the consequences – was enough for me. It was to become the mantra by which I would live the rest of my life.

If that meant I was bound for hell, then so be it. For what it was worth, I knew that Bess was praying hard for me, so I was happy to take my chances.

'Posterity my foot! And sorry to repeat myself, but for whose benefit would I be doing all this?'

'What about for my benefit? Would that be enough to twist your arm to let me fetch down the photos and letters you say you've stashed in the attic?' Pressing what she suddenly saw as her advantage, Libby added, 'If you hadn't wanted some kind of record of what you'd achieved, you wouldn't have kept what you have. You would have thrown everything away. After all, as you frequently say, you're not in the least bit sentimental, are you? So why have you kept what you have?'

'My, my, what a sly cat you are. Have you discussed this with Bess?'

'Yes.'

'And?'

'She warned me that you wouldn't be at all keen on the idea.'

'Yet here you are convinced of your powers of persuasion.'

'I wouldn't put it exactly like that.'

'However you view things, I just don't see much point in the exercise. Why would you want to go rummaging around in my past when you should be looking to the future?'

'But I don't have a future at the moment.'

Elfrida looked at her, her expression suddenly tender. 'Oh, my dear girl, that's one of the saddest things I've ever heard.'

Startled by what she'd admitted, Libby said, 'I'm sorry, that sounded horribly like I was wallowing in self-pity and looking for sympathy. Which I'm not.'

'Listen to me. You're allowed to feel sorry for yourself right now, but you're going to have to learn that when it comes to Marcus and your friend with whom he slept, you need to lock the pair away in a box and forget all about them.'

'I have a feeling that's not the current mode of thinking. We're not supposed to sweep anything under the carpet, or shove things in a box these days, it's got to be out in the open, every jot and tittle fully analysed and explored.'

Elfrida scoffed at that. 'I can't think of anything more futile. What is there to analyse about Marcus cheating on you?'

'Maybe knowing why he did it would help me to get over his betrayal.'

'For heaven's sake, we all know why he did it! He's a pathetic man who can't be trusted to keep it in his trousers. What more do you need to understand?'

'Well, did I do something wrong? Could I have been better—'

'Stop, stop, *STOP!* This is exactly the kind of gibberish with which you young folk fill your heads in your quest to find answers to questions that don't need to be asked. Just accept that Marcus is a very foolish young man. And I'm being quite objective when I say that. I have no particular axe to grind with him, other than wanting to give him a damned good shaking for causing you so much distress. But you should be grateful you've had a lucky escape.'

'How simple you make it sound.'

Elfrida tilted her head to one side. 'Life is as complicated or as simple as one makes it, as somebody once said to me.'

'That sounds easier said than done.'

'True, but it's a rule by which I've tried to live. It's less painful that way.'

'Is that why you're so reluctant to revisit what's in those boxes in the attic – is it too painful for you?'

'Good Lord no! Why on earth would you think such a thing?'

'I just wondered if shoving the past away in the attic was your way of avoiding thinking about any painful or difficult episodes in your life.'

Elfrida tutted at that.

*

Chapter Thirteen

July 1981
Larkspur House, Suffolk

'It really is an idyllic spot here, amazingly unspoilt, and the ideal haven to escape the troubles of the world. In the circumstances I can see why you came here.'

Libby had just told the man standing next to her all about Marcus and her aborted wedding day. There was no real reason why she should have shared with him something that was so personal, or painful, but it had been a natural progression of their conversation since leaving Bess and Elfrida sleeping in the orchard. While she didn't want to become defined by what Marcus and Selina had done to her, Libby knew that for some time to come it would have a bearing on almost every aspect of her life. It would affect her every thought and her every decision. How could it not?

Looking out over the parched meadow and sun-bleached fields beyond, a soft silky breeze caressing her bare arms, she leant against the wooden fence and rested her elbows on the rail.

'I scarcely know your great-aunt and Miss Ambrose,' he went on, 'but they seem to have an interesting relationship.'

'They certainly do,' said Libby with a small laugh, 'but there's nothing they wouldn't do for one another.'

'I guessed that while Miss Ambrose was showing me round

135

the garden earlier. She was telling me how long she and your great-aunt have been together. They share quite a history, don't they?'

'Yes,' agreed Libby, thinking of the photographs she had been looking at late last night. They'd been mostly garden related, but the ones that had intrigued her the most were of Elfrida and Bess, a few of which had been taken in some wonderfully glamorous locations, such as the South of France and Lake Como, and even New York. A number of the photographs showed Elfrida wearing some fabulous flapper dresses and looking as beautiful as a silent movie star.

A flicker of movement in the flawlessly clear sky caught Libby's eye and she watched a skylark soaring vertically upwards, its unmistakable song with its high-pitched ringing tone full of the sound of summer.

'It's funny, isn't it?' she remarked.

He turned to look at her, the late afternoon sun burnishing his hair with a coppery glow and emphasising his hazel eyes that were flecked with gold and amber. Libby couldn't help but think that Mother Nature had dealt him a generously fair hand of cards. Over lunch Elfrida had teased him that he must have any number of young female patients fall in love with him. 'Not at all, it's the much older ladies who are the real danger,' he'd said with a perfectly straight face, 'especially those who invite me for lunch.' Elfrida had laughed gaily at that.

'What's funny?' he asked.

'Us chatting like this,' Libby said, 'and I don't really know what to call you, unless you want to stick to the formalities, and I go on calling you Dr Matthews.'

'I think in this situation we can safely dispense with the formalities. My name's Daniel.'

She smiled. 'And as you know already, I'm Libby.' She held out her hand. 'Pleased to meet you, Daniel.'

'Likewise,' he said with a pleasantly engaging smile, while giving her hand a firm squeeze. 'I'm sorry we've met during what must be a very difficult time for you.'

'It is what it is,' she said with a shrug. 'But there's something you need to know. Elfrida is a sly old thing and I fear she might have ideas about you and me and I'd just like to make it clear that I'm definitely not—'

'That you're not interested,' he cut in. 'I understand completely, so please don't worry on that score. I'm in much the same boat myself.'

'You are?'

He nodded. 'My wife left me last year and we're currently going through the business of divorce. Which is partly why I took the locum job at the surgery here in Finchley Green; I needed a change of scene.'

'Is it working for you, the change of scene?'

'In many ways yes. It's given me time and space to come to terms with the painful fact that I messed up spectacularly.'

'In what way?'

'I didn't have an affair behind my wife's back, if that's what you're thinking.'

Which was precisely what Libby had thought.

'It was more banal than that,' he continued. 'I put my job first. I was working in a busy Cambridge practice and didn't have my priorities in the right order. I was putting the needs of my patients before those of my wife, and I paid the price when she found somebody else who was prepared to give her the time she deserved. I have no one to blame but myself.'

'It must be a difficult balance, particularly so for a doctor who really cares about his patients.'

'Yes, and I'm not sure how one goes about getting the balance right. I hope it comes with experience, or I'll be destined to mess up again.'

Me too, thought Libby. What if sometime in the future, when she allowed herself to fall in love once more, she chose another Marcus and had her heart broken all over again?

'Do you still love your wife?' she asked.

'No,' he said after a lengthy pause. 'But that's not to say I don't still care about her. If there's such a thing as an on/off switch for one's emotions, I've yet to discover it.'

'I know just what you mean.'

'Can I count on you not to repeat what I've told you, please? It was said in confidence.'

'Of course, I wouldn't dream of telling anyone. Where will you go when your time here in the village ends next Friday? Will you go back to Cambridge?'

'No, there's a surgery in a nearby village that needs a GP to cover for a period of maternity leave. It's quite handy as I can stay on here in the cottage I've been renting for the last five months.'

'Are you in the centre of the village?'

'Yes, I'm opposite that pair of cottages where the owners have gone a bit crazy with Royal Wedding décor and memorabilia. Every morning I pull back the curtains I'm face to face with Charles and Diana.'

Libby smiled. 'At least you won't have to put up with it for much longer. Once they're married it'll all disappear, as will the current frenzy for anything to do with Lady Di.'

'I wouldn't count on it.'

'For her sake I hope it does; it can't have been easy these last months having her every move and every word scrutinised in the press.'

'Comes with the territory when you marry a prince, and the future king of England.'

'I suppose it does, but I can't help but pity the girl. I hope she knows what she's getting into.'

Daniel nodded. 'Do any of us, when we fall in love?'

'Good point,' she said, recalling the interview Charles and Diana had given on the announcement of their engagement in February, and when the interviewer commented how very much in love they looked. Diana, all doe-eyed and demure, had replied, *'Oh, yes. Absolutely.'* Charles had then said, *'Whatever in love means.'* Libby had watched the interview with Marcus and remarked to him that it seemed an odd thing to say.

'What else do you expect the man to say?' Marcus had said. 'The poor devil was put on the spot to say something embarrassingly slushy and he wasn't having it. I'd have done the same thing myself.'

'Really?' Libby had said. 'Why?'

'Because it's what men do: we hate to talk about love and romance; it makes us look weak.'

'And yet some of the most romantic poems ever written were written by men,' she'd countered.

Marcus had laughed. 'Give me a Len Deighton thriller over a soppy poem any day of the week!'

She'd laughed too and playfully thrown a cushion at him. 'You're such a philistine,' she'd told him.

'But a philistine you love all the same.'

The memory brought her up short and pushing it from her mind, Libby moved the conversation onto safe ground. 'All credit to you, Daniel, that you don't seem at all fazed by Elfrida; it's not everyone who can handle her forthright manner.'

'I'm quite used to patients like her,' he said. 'Plus, she reminds me of my grandmother, a formidable woman who drove an ambulance during the First World War in Flanders. Right up until her death a few years ago she was still regularly playing tennis and compiling crosswords for her parish magazine.'

'I think your grandmother and Elfrida would have got on well,' she observed.

'Either that or they would have driven one another mad trying to out-fox the other.'

Libby laughed. 'You've just described an average day here with Bess and Elfrida. Scoring points off each other is what keeps them going.'

'But in one thing they're completely united,' he said.

'What's that?'

'You. They're obviously very fond of you and enjoy having you around.'

'Yes, I'm lucky in that respect. My great-aunt has always had a soft spot for me, as do I for her.'

'Is that why you came here when you discovered what your fiancé was getting up to? Most daughters would have gone home to their parents.'

Libby rolled her eyes. 'Most daughters don't have a mother like mine. She's not what you'd call the sympathetic sort.'

'And your father?'

'He died when I was a child. You'd think his death would have brought my mother and me closer, but it didn't. If anything, it made things worse; the gap became a chasm and ever since has just kept on widening.'

'Grief can do that; it can have the effect of shutting down the emotions as an act of self-preservation.'

'That's very true, but I don't think my mother has ever been very good at expressing her emotions, other than her anger or disappointment.'

Changing the subject again, she said, 'You were brave to accept the invitation to join us for lunch today. Or do you make a habit of accepting invitations from your patients?'

'Absolutely not. Strictly speaking it's frowned upon, professional distance and all that, but there's something about this place that—'

'That makes the real world and all its rules disappear,' she finished for him with a smile.

He smiled back at her. 'Something like that.'

'Elfrida has always called it her enchanted place, and I don't think there's a better way to describe it.'

For a moment they both turned and faced the view of the meadow, where the clover was alive with the drone of bumble-bees and somewhere in the distance an industrious woodpecker could be heard hard at work.

Then, just as a tortoiseshell butterfly fluttered around them before landing on the wooden rail of the fence, Daniel said, 'As much as I'd like to loiter here for the rest of the day, I've imposed on you all long enough and I really ought to be going. But before I leave, I ought to help with the washing up by way of thanks.'

'There's no need, you were our guest. And you somehow convinced Elfrida to have a proper builder in to fix the mess I created, for which I know Bess will be very grateful. As am I.'

'By the way, what was in that enormous trunk that you fetched down from the attic?'

Libby explained about the contents and how she was determined to compile a record of all that Elfrida had accomplished as a renowned garden designer.

'I'm surprised she hasn't been approached already to do that,' he said.

'She has, but refused to do it. It took some wheedling on my part to convince her it was something I could do.'

'Well, if you want to go back up to the attic to look for anything else, please don't, not until Steve has put things right.'

'Is that you speaking with your official doctor's hat on?'

He laughed. 'It's me speaking as a friend.' He hesitated before adding, 'I'd like to think we could be friends, Libby, if that's all right with you?'

'It is,' she replied.

They had just made it back to the orchard where both Bess and Elfrida were still asleep when Libby heard a voice destroying the peaceful and languorous warmth of the afternoon. There was no mistaking the owner of the demanding voice. Or the man with her.

'She certainly doesn't give the impression of a girl nursing a broken heart,' said Nancy, staring out of the window to where Libby was talking to Marcus in the garden.

'Since you don't have a heart, just a stone where one should be, how would you know what someone with a broken heart looks like?' responded Elfrida, not caring how adversarial she sounded. She'd stopped giving a damn what Nancy thought of her a long time ago.

They were in the drawing room, Nancy having insisted on taking refuge from the heat of the day inside the house where it was so much cooler. Her arrival had woken Elfrida with a jolt; the same was true for Bess who was now in the kitchen making a drink for their visitors. Daniel had made himself scarce at the first possible opportunity but not before Nancy had pointedly given him the third degree, demanding to know who he was and what he was doing here.

'I might have known you'd take pleasure in interfering and making matters worse instead of better,' sniped Nancy. 'But then it's what you've always done, isn't it, Elfrida? You're nothing but a malicious old woman who can't help but stick your oar in and cause trouble.'

'I had no idea you had such a high opinion of me,' said Elfrida, 'and there was I thinking you didn't like me. Just goes to show how wrong one can be.'

'Oh, for goodness' sake, just be quiet and keep out of a family matter that has absolutely nothing to do with you.'

'I beg to differ. I care very much about Libby so therefore her happiness is of enormous importance to me.'

'As it is to me,' asserted Nancy.

'Then why come here to force her into a marriage that will make her miserable and ultimately end in an acrimonious divorce?'

'I'm not forcing her to do anything of the sort. But it's only right that she and Marcus sit down together and talk. He's freely admitted that he made a mistake and has promised that it would never happen again.'

'And you believe him? Why would you put any store in that young man being able to keep a promise when he's already proved himself a lying cheat?'

'He should at least be allowed a chance to defend himself. That's why I've come here with him today. Isn't everyone allowed a second chance?'

Elfrida stared at her. 'I might ask you the very same question.'

Nancy blinked. 'You don't know me at all,' she said. 'You think you do, but you don't. You've never walked in my shoes, never once thought what it must be like to be me.'

'But this isn't about you, Nancy, it's about Libby and her happiness.'

'Which, as I said before, is *my* concern and not yours.'

Elfrida gave up, there was no talking to Nancy. There never was. She turned away to see Bess coming into the room with the tea tray. But instead of coming all the way in, she came to a stop. And then, as if it were happening in agonisingly slow motion, her body appeared, bit by bit, to slacken and her hands no longer seemed to be aware of the tray in their grasp and it dropped to the floor with a deafening clatter, cups and saucers and sugar cubes rolling across the rug, milk splashing like white paint and lastly the teapot landing with a terrible crash.

But worst of all, Bess, poor dear precious Bess, resembling a puppet with its strings cut, fell to the floor with a dreadful gargled noise that was half gasp, half cry.

*

'I came here in good faith to apologise and what do I find but you enjoying yourself with another man. I suppose that's you getting back at me, isn't it? I'm in no position to complain, I know, but really, there's no need for petty tit-for-tat behaviour. We have to be more grown up than that.'

Libby couldn't believe what she was hearing. Nor could she believe the self-righteous expression on Marcus's face. It was as if he actually believed what he'd just said.

'Do you have any idea just how offensive you sound?' she said. 'What on earth makes you think I would sink to your level and even if I did throw myself into a new relationship, which I have no intention of doing, what business is it of yours? We're no longer a couple. We are no longer engaged. We are no longer getting married. In fact, I don't even understand why you're here.'

'I came because your mother and I thought that if you and I could just sit down and talk there was still time to put this behind us and go ahead with the wedding.'

'You're here not because *you*, all on your own, thought we should talk, then?'

He shifted in his seat and pushed a hand through the floppy fringe of his hair. 'You're twisting my words.'

'And with so little effort on my part.'

He shook his head. 'Please, just for a moment, put aside your anger and be reasonable. We can still marry. The church is still booked and—'

'You mean you haven't cancelled the church? What about

the guests, have you told them the wedding's off? Have you told your parents?'

'No, I haven't. I was waiting for you to calm down so we could put things right between us.'

'My God, are you actually serious?'

'One hundred per cent serious. I know that we can put this behind us and get on with our lives just as we planned to.'

'Why? Why would you want to be with me when your affair with Selina proves that you never really loved me? Why not marry her?'

'I don't want to marry Selina. With her it was just sex. With you it was so much more.'

'What, exactly?'

'We were a couple. A real couple.'

'But what does that mean to you?'

'It means something true and lasting. It means stability and starting a family. You and I were planning a future together. A proper home and children. Isn't that what you wanted? What you still want?'

'What about love? You haven't once mentioned that you love me.'

'Of course I love you.'

Those words of Prince Charles echoed in Libby's head: *Whatever in love means . . .*

'So what were you doing with Selina?' she asked. 'And don't say it was just sex with her, or lie by saying it was a one-off. She told me it happened so many times between the two of you, she'd lost count.'

He frowned at that. 'I don't know what Selina has told you, or what game she's playing, but I want you to know that – and I'm not proud of my behaviour, but in my defence she as good as laid it out for me. She made it so easy. And I'm only flesh and blood. I'd defy any man not to give in to that kind of temptation.'

He raised his hand to stop Libby from interrupting. 'I shouldn't have done it, but I did and I'm sorry for the way you found out.'

'You mean there would have been a better way for me to find out you were sleeping with my best friend?'

'Please don't be facetious, Libby, it's not helpful.'

Helpful, she thought, a lava flow of red-hot anger suddenly coursing through her. She'd give him helpful! She banged her fists on the table and jumped to her feet. 'I'll be as facetious as I bloody well want!'

He looked startled at her outburst, and well he might. She rarely lost her temper. Even when she'd first found out about his deceit, she had held it together and barely raised her voice. Yes, she had keyed his car, but she had done it quietly and efficiently, perfectly in control. But right now, some fiery inner force she didn't know she was capable of feeling had driven away years of self-control. Good old Libby – even-tempered, kind-hearted, easy-going, sweet-natured, ever-dutiful Libby – was no more. She was a wronged woman. An angry wronged woman, a woman scorned who wanted to let rip and exact her revenge. She was Nemesis hell-bent on retribution!

'What a truly pathetic man you are!' she said, her voice so loud it strained her throat. 'Is it merely stupidity on your part or sheer arrogance that makes you think that a few pathetic platitudes and laying the blame on Selina is going to make me forgive you?'

The expression on his face had now turned to incomprehension. He was probably thinking, *Who is this woman shouting at me?* She was beginning to wonder herself.

'I thought you'd had time to cool off,' he said. 'I thought by now you would at least be rational enough so we could—'

'*Rational!*' she yelled, 'Why the hell should I be rational? And as for cooling off, what you really mean is that you'd hoped I'd had time to kid myself that you weren't the bastard I discovered you really are. And you know what, I might have had more respect for you if you'd come on your own initiative and not because my mother thought it was a good idea.'

'It *was* my idea. I discussed it last night on the phone with your mother and we both agreed it was worth a try. Your mother didn't hold out much hope, she told me that Bess and Elfrida would have influenced your thinking and turned you against me. I know they've never really approved of me. I've known it for a long time.'

'If they don't approve of you then it's of your own doing. This might surprise you, but I'm perfectly capable of making my own decisions without being influenced by anyone else.'

On his feet now, the look on his face had changed again and his bluey-grey eyes had lost all the softness she had once loved. They were sharp and full of something she had never seen before: vicious intent. Gone too was any attempt at contrition; now he was on the attack and instinct warned her that he was about to inflict yet more pain on her.

'If you really want to know the truth,' he said, 'sex with you was mediocre at best, that was why it was so tempting for me to go to bed with Selina. She offered far more than you ever did. If you're laying blame on anyone, try looking at yourself.'

Libby swallowed back the cruel bite of his accusation, knowing that she would later taunt herself with it by replaying it in her head. 'If that's true, why did you bother to come today?' she asked. 'Why pretend you still want to go through with the wedding?'

The coldness in his eyes had now turned Arctic. 'Because nobody walks out on me. And nobody makes me look a fool. I'm not having my friends, work colleagues and family thinking I've been dumped.'

'So coming here was to protect your poor little ego, was it? Has any of what passed between us ever been real?'

'I did love you, Libby. I loved you because you were different to the usual girls I'd dated. You were so practical and sweet and full of kindness. It's just a shame you weren't more open-minded.'

Never had being kind sounded more of a humiliating fault to Libby. Hardly daring to think what he meant by being more open-minded, she stared at him and saw a stranger opposite her. She tried to see the man she had loved, but he was gone. Whatever had existed between them, it hadn't been real. None of it had. And it came as a relief to realise that he had just handed her the on/off switch to her emotions which Daniel had earlier referred to. Where once there had been love, there was now nothing but loathing and contempt.

'Well then,' she said in an unnaturally calm voice, 'I believe we've said all we need to say and can both be thankful that we've had a lucky escape.'

She turned and walked away, only to see Elfrida standing at the open French windows of the drawing room, waving with some urgency for her to come in.

*

Bess was aware of being moved, of voices, loud and insistent. She felt too weak to make sense of what was happening, it was easier to go with the sensation of falling. It reminded her of another time, a very long time ago, when she'd experienced something similar . . .

Chapter Fourteen

September 1938
Villa Lucia, Lake Como
Bess

Being married to Amos turned out to be so much better than I'd been afraid it would. We were happy together, each prepared to compromise when necessary and equally prepared to admit when we were wrong. We were, we came to know, both prone to digging in our heels over what we perceived as a point of principle, but common sense always overruled stubbornness for stubbornness' sake. It was only after a few years of married life that I realised I was subconsciously mirroring the manner in which my mother had conducted herself as a wife, which was to say I knew which battles to fight and which ones to withdraw from. And more importantly, which secrets to keep.

In many ways, marriage hadn't changed my life all that much in that I still spent most of my time at Larkspur House, as did Amos. He had now taken over as head gardener, old Jimmy having retired. Victor had also left due to ill-health; he never really recovered from his experiences in the trenches during the Great War. For the last year Amos had been training up a new under gardener who was barely fourteen and called Alfie. He was a good lad who was willing to learn as much as he could, and sometimes I think Amos treated him as the son he would have liked to have.

We'd been married now for nigh on four years and had come to the conclusion that we would not have any children of our own. Amos said that not having a family didn't bother him, but I knew deep down there was a small part of him that longed to be a father. Secretly I was relieved; a child would have meant that I had to give up working and I didn't want to do that. That sounds selfish of me, I know, but it was the truth. Being tied to home with the demands of a small child would have stopped me from travelling with Elfrida and I loved our times away.

Elfrida had by now made quite a name for herself as a garden designer and she was stretched to breaking point at times with the Herculean workload she undertook. But she never once complained, not even when she ached so much from a day of hard physical labour that she could barely climb the stairs to bed. More than once I had almost to carry her up to her bedroom. It was as well she was so slightly built as otherwise I wouldn't have been able to manage it. I tried telling her that she needed to be more sensible and acknowledge that maybe she should say no to some of the commissions that came her way, but she would have none of it.

Earning enough money to keep Larkspur House was an obsession for her and if I'm honest I would have been heartbroken if she'd been forced to sell her home – her enchanted place. Amos had come to love it too and did all that he could to maintain the garden to Elfrida's high standards. Just occasionally he would have a run-in with her over some new bed she wanted to create, or how to plant something, but they would always find a way to resolve matters, even if that did sometimes mean that he spent the evening grumbling to me how impossible Elfrida was being.

'How have you put up with her for as long as you have?' he asked me one evening over supper, after a particularly trying day spent with Elfrida when she and I had returned from a trip away to work on a client's garden at Marlingham Hall in Hertfordshire.

Apparently Elfrida had changed her mind about the bed Amos had dug and planted in her absence. He was a patient man, perhaps the most patient man I knew, but in this instance Elfrida had pushed him too far.

'I suppose it's because I feel sorry for her at times,' I told him. He'd looked at me as though I were mad. 'Why?'

'She's the way she is because it's her way of protecting herself. To use a gardening term, she wears a tough outer shell to protect the vulnerable seed inside.'

'You mean she's a nutcase?' he'd quipped.

Whatever Amos thought of my description, I truly believed that the loss of her brother and then her parents soon after had affected Elfrida profoundly, and a lot more than she would ever care to admit. To confess how she felt would mean showing weakness and that was something she never did.

But then nor did I. We were two of a kind in that respect; we'd both lost our parents at a young age, but whereas I'd been lucky to have the support of a loving sister to help me through that time, Elfrida's sister, Prudence, had been no such thing. There again, she too had suffered the same loss and had no one to turn to.

It pained me greatly that the closeness I'd once treasured with my sister Joan was now a thing of the past. Oh, she was polite enough when she wanted to be, but there was no getting away from the fact that she looked down on me these days. The last time I saw her was a few months ago to celebrate Nancy's eleventh birthday party. It had been an extravagant affair in their local church hall where no expense had been spared, with an abundance of party food and paper decorations and balloons. There had even been a magician who had kept the children enthralled. At the centre of it all was Nancy, dressed in a party frock of white lace which sadly could not have suited her less. She tended to plumpness and the dress, a silly concoction of frills and bows, accentuated the size of her.

'She loves her food,' Joan would say proudly of Nancy's appetite, as though it was a wonderfully clever accomplishment. I hated to think it, but as far as I could see whatever Nancy wanted, whether it was riding lessons, tennis lessons or another slice of cake, she was given it. Neither of her parents ever said no to her. And now that Dudley's second-hand car business was such a success, they could afford to send her to an expensive girls' school in Tunbridge Wells. They had, in Joan's own words, really gone up in the world.

Amos had taken an instant dislike to Joan and Dudley the day of our wedding. He and Elfrida had overheard Joan saying that it was such a shame that not only was I shackled to a life of servitude, I had thrown in my lot with a mere gardener, a man who would never make anything of himself. 'You'd think she'd want to be more like me and marry a man with ambition,' Amos and Elfrida heard Joan say.

Amos didn't tell me what had been said, but Elfrida did. She wanted to know if I did feel I was shackled to her.

'Absolutely not!' I'd assured her. 'If I didn't love my job, I wouldn't do it. There's nothing I'd rather be doing. You've given me so much for which I'm enormously grateful.'

I later confronted Joan about her remarks and tried to explain to her that service was something you gave without expecting anything in return, that it was a way of life to be proud of. She was embarrassed to have been caught out, but defiant in her opinion that I could do better for myself than slaving for a woman who had a dubious reputation when it came to men, and for making do with Amos. 'Have you seen the state of his fingernails?' she'd said, as though this was the worst crime a man could commit.

When I'd told Elfrida this she'd laughed as though fit to burst. 'My dear Bess,' she said, 'if there's one thing I can't abide, it's a snob and I'm afraid your sister, like my sister Prudence, though they be worlds apart, have that ghastly trait in common. If I ever start showing the same character flaw you have my full permission to shoot me. Is that understood? And I'm sure there have been days when I've been at my worst and you'd have gladly pulled the trigger.'

It was conversations like this that made me love Elfrida all the more. She knew she wasn't perfect, that she could be demanding and erratic, and behave with reckless abandon, but I wasn't alone in being devoted to her. Mrs Ridley – Riddles, the cook – wouldn't have a word said against her and nor would the girls who came in from the village to clean. Every Christmas she would lavish gifts on us all and she never forgot a birthday. That was actually my job to remind her that a member of the household staff had a birthday approaching and she would immediately send off to London for a suitable gift – a pair of gloves, a box of prettily embroidered handkerchiefs, or a hat. For Amos she would buy him his favourite brand of tobacco, and for young Alfie, knowing that his family barely had two brass farthings to rub together, she would treat him to a new pair of boots, or a much-needed shirt or coat.

'I'll be glad when that boy has stopped growing,' she once said to me, 'he's costing me a fortune!' She didn't mean it, of course. Not for a second did she begrudge a single penny she spent on those who worked for her. It was why we held her in such high regard.

Amos might grumble now and then to me about Elfrida, but he would never speak badly of her to anyone else. Especially not at the Crown in the village where every Friday night he enjoyed a glass or two of ale, and where the conversation might turn to an exchange of gossip.

Elfrida was a natural target for tittle-tattle, and too often her name appeared in the gossip columns of the newspapers and magazines, along with a photograph of her wrapped in the arms of a handsome man coming out of a ritzy club in London.

What the people who snapped those photographs, and those

who wrote about Elfrida, didn't know was that it was all a front, a very convincing front at that. Elfrida had eyes for one man only, and that was Count Nikolai.

Which was why we were once more away from Larkspur House and currently staying in Italy, following a brief stay on the Riviera at the villa owned by the Count's cousin. Two years ago, and after a visit to Lake Como where he had fallen in love with it, Mallory bought a property here. He had immediately asked Elfrida to create a garden for him, and naturally wherever she went, I went too.

This was our fifth visit to Villa Lucia, and I didn't think I would ever tire of its beautiful location. Situated within a woodland setting with panoramic views of the lake, the house had been built at the turn of the century with privacy in mind. The original owner, an elderly English aristocrat who had kept his Italian mistress here, and in considerable style, had bought the land surrounding the house and garden, thereby ensuring there was no danger of being overlooked. Curious passers-by were non-existent due to the long and meandering road up the hillside to the villa, and if an intrepid nosy-parker made it that far they would be confronted with wrought-iron gates that were guarded at all times. The aristocrat had died three years ago, the mistress sent packing by the family, and the unwanted house with its six acres of lush parkland put up for sale.

Every morning when I opened the shutters of my room and marvelled at the view, I had to pinch myself that I wasn't dreaming. Looking at the smooth-as-glass water and the pretty town of Bellagio on the other side of the lake with its jumble of closely packed dwellings, with Varenna to the left, and the mountains beyond, I would count my blessings at my extraordinarily good fortune in being here. This was what my sister didn't understand about my life, that I had these glorious moments of unimaginable beauty to cherish. Whatever sacrifices I'd made in my loyal service to Elfrida, this was one of the things that made it all worthwhile.

This morning, and after I'd pushed back the shutters and watched a traditional fishing boat – a *batel* – crossing the lake, I dressed and went downstairs to Elfrida's room to lay out the clothes she needed for the day. Her bed, as it had been for the last week, had not been slept in. Which was how it always was when we came here because our visits were not just for the benefit of carrying out more work on Mallory's garden, but for Elfrida and Count Nikolai to spend precious time together.

Their affair, which had begun four years ago after the night of Elfrida's birthday party at Lambert Chase, was conducted in the strictest secrecy. The only staff present at the villa being myself, the Count's valet, Ivan, and Mallory's devoted valet, George Lee. A local woman came in to clean every other day, along with her husband and son who worked in the garden, and from what I understood, they were paid handsomely for their discretion. No doubt just as the staff employed by the previous owner had been.

Ivan was in charge of cooking and I was allowed to work alongside him in the kitchen. Initially I was quite scared of Ivan, he seemed so severe and fierce, but I soon learnt that he had a heart of gold and just as I was devoted to Elfrida, so was he to Count Nikolai. When I had grown used to his austere manner, I would often tease him that he was wasted as a valet, that he should be a chef running his own restaurant.

Following each visit to Villa Lucia, I would try out some of Ivan's recipes on Amos when I returned home, with varying degrees of success. Amos certainly wasn't a fan of borscht, or the small tin of caviar Ivan pressed upon me to give to my husband.

Much of what went on at Villa Lucia I kept from Amos. He wasn't as liberal-minded as I was, and he would have been shocked to know that Elfrida was sleeping with a married man. As with so much in life, the less said the better.

But as careful and discreet as Elfrida and Nikolai were, I worried constantly that the secret might become known and Elfrida's reputation would be shot. Or worse, that her heart would be broken. In an ideal world I'd have preferred her not to risk herself the way she did, but whenever I saw her with Nikolai, when I saw them talking and laughing together, or dancing alone on the terrace in the moonlight when they thought nobody was looking, I could see just how happy they were. I once asked Elfrida why Nikolai couldn't divorce his wife, but it seemed he wouldn't do that because her mental state wasn't strong enough to cope with the trauma. I suspected that even if Nikolai was a free man, Elfrida might not rush to marry him. Yes, she loved him, but how and where would they live? She would never be parted from Larkspur House, not even for a man like Nikolai.

Ivan confided in me that the Count's wife had tried on two different occasions to kill herself. The first attempt had been to take a cocktail of pills, and the second time she had used a razor on a wrist. As a result, she was constantly in and out of clinics in the hope that she could be made well again. Ivan said it was all as a result of the baby she and Nikolai had lost.

As soon as breakfast had been eaten, Elfrida left Nikolai and Mallory to attend to whatever business concerns they had to deal with that day and went off to work in the garden with the gardeners, Giovani and his son Giacomo. My job that morning was to go shopping with Ivan at the local market in Menaggio. We could have had everything delivered to the villa, but Ivan liked to select the produce himself.

It also gave him the opportunity to buy a newspaper and enjoy a *caffè corretto* – an espresso coffee with a drop of grappa added.

I had tried the drink myself at his suggestion and at first found it not at all to my liking. But Ivan urged me to try it again and before too long I was drinking it like a local just as he did. It was something else I had to keep from Amos. He would be horrified to know that his wife was sitting at a table outside a bar in the *piazza* at eleven o'clock in the morning drinking coffee laced with alcohol.

On this particular morning, I left Ivan to his newspaper – he had taught himself Italian and was reading the latest about Mussolini and his Fascist Blackshirts. Ever since Mussolini and Hitler had formed an alliance in October 1936, Amos had grown increasingly worried about the threat of war. He wasn't alone, especially since Hitler had marched into Austria and was threatening to do the same now to Czechoslovakia.

Amos hadn't been at all keen on my coming to Italy this time with Elfrida, not with 'that conceited peacock of a man strutting about with his Fascist Blackshirts stirring up trouble,' as he'd referred to Mussolini. This morning Ivan had just called him a lot worse while reading the front page of that day's copy of *Corriere Della Sera*.

Being here in such beautiful surroundings, where apartment balconies around the *piazza* spilled over with colourful flowers and laughing children chased one another in the bright sunshine while their indulgent mothers looked on happily, and smartly dressed tourists posed for photographs and admired the view of the lake and the passing boats, another war just didn't seem possible. Why would anyone want to go to war again and risk losing all this?

Leaving Ivan to his newspaper, I went to the tobacconist's shop to buy some picture postcards. Elfrida thought it was silly that I went to the bother of sending cards home, but I ignored her teasing, knowing that Mrs Ridley back at Larkspur House liked to receive one, as did Amos. I didn't know if my sister liked reading the cards I sent her, but I did it anyway. I also sent one to Nancy, hoping that she would appreciate me thinking of her.

I had just paid for the postcards, along with some stamps, when I turned around and saw a figure passing the entrance to the shop. I recognised him straight away and a feeling of sick dread swept through me and my skin crawled. Yet at the same time I refused to believe the evidence of my eyes. Surely it was no more than a passing similarity?

But as I tried hard to convince myself I was mistaken, I knew I wasn't. It was definitely him.

But what on earth was he doing here?

Holding my breath, I stood very still, hoping I wouldn't be seen, that I could make myself invisible.

When I was sure he had gone, I let out my breath and hurriedly retraced my steps to the *piazza* and Ivan. 'We should go,' I said.

He looked up at me, shielding his eyes from the brightness of the sun. 'So soon?' he asked.

'Yes, straight away.'

'But I haven't finished reading—'

'*Now!*' I said with such force he regarded me more closely.

'What is it?' he enquired. 'Are you feeling unwell?'

'Yes,' I said, grabbing at the excuse he'd unwittingly given me.

His brow furrowed, he quickly folded his newspaper and stood up, and just as he'd put a solicitous hand to my arm to assist me, I heard my name being called.

Once again, I stood as still as a statue, hoping that if I didn't react, the man would think he'd made a mistake and go away.

But he didn't go away. He came right over and, blocking out the sun so that he resembled a large black silhouette, he said, 'Well, bless my soul if it isn't really you, Bess!'

My chest squeezing tight, my heart beating so fast I feared it might burst, I suddenly felt as though I couldn't breathe.

'Aren't you going to say hello, then?' he asked.

His words, in that sickeningly honey-coated voice which I had never forgotten, gripped at my throat and I couldn't speak. I tried to, but I was lightheaded with the menace of his presence and then, as I experienced the sensation of the blood draining away from me, the ground beneath me gave way and I felt myself falling.

Chapter Fifteen

Elfrida didn't like hospitals. In fact, she hated them. The last time she had visited one it had been to see Mallory shortly before he died. He'd known that his death was imminent and had tried to console her by saying that she knew as well as he did that to be human was a continuous surrendering to loss and she must take his passing as no more than the inevitable circle of life.

Not wanting to dwell on the painful memory of losing Mallory, Elfrida pushed it from her thoughts and instead told herself that Bess would be fine. That's what the doctor had said, that there was no real cause for alarm, but they were just running a series of tests on Bess. 'There's nothing to worry about,' he had assured her.

Well, if that was true, Elfrida had wanted to say, why were they spending so much time on tests? But for once in her life she'd kept her mouth shut and come out here to the small hospital garden to be alone. She couldn't stay cooped up inside a moment longer. Libby had said she would come and find her if there was anything new to report.

Back at the house, Libby had behaved with admirable presence of mind. She had taken command of the situation with calm efficiency and in no time, there had been an ambulance roaring to a stop on the drive. She had told her mother to shut up at one point. Elfrida couldn't recall exactly why, but Nancy had indeed kept quiet after that. As had Marcus, who then took it as his cue to ring for a taxi to take him to the station in order to return to London.

None of which was important right now. All that mattered was that the doctor had been speaking the truth earlier and Bess would soon be home where she belonged.

With her ankle beginning to protest, and annoyance flaring that Dr Matthews had been right about her not overdoing it, she found a bench and sat down heavily. She needed to think. Her mind was a muddle of thoughts and regrets and things she had feared she might not be able to put right if the worst had happened to her dearest friend.

If there was one thing she wanted to say to Bess, it was to apologise yet again for that time when she had behaved so absurdly high-handedly and upset Bess in such a way that she'd never seen before. Incandescent with anger, Bess had reminded Elfrida how loyal she had always been to her and in return Elfrida had betrayed her. It hadn't been Elfrida's intention, but a moment's loss of patience and the need to right a wrong had caused her to break a promise and profoundly hurt Bess.

Elfrida sighed. Promises and secrets. They were the keepers of each other's secrets that were sewn into the fabric of their long friendship. There were some secrets that were like caged birds and they needed to be set free; but others that were just too awful ever to be released.

She was thinking in particular of a time long ago when they had been staying at Villa Lucia on Lake Como. A day for which poor Bess had never been able to forgive herself.

Chapter Sixteen

October 1938
Villa Lucia, Lake Como
Elfrida

It was early. Much earlier than I usually woke but lying here in my bed – not Nikolai's – I had something on my mind and I could never sleep well when I was worried.

For a while now I had tried to ignore what my treacherous body was telling me, refusing point blank to accept it was even possible. For pity's sake, I was thirty-seven years of age; I was too old for this to happen! Moreover, I had been convinced it wasn't something that nature had intended for me; it was why Nikolai and I hadn't always been as careful as maybe we should have been. Such was the extent of my conviction I had ignored what now seemed very obvious warning signs – the tenderness in my breasts, the slight nausea and the tiredness. The latter I had merely put down to the long hours I was devoting to Mallory's garden here at Villa Lucia and the late nights spent making love with Nikolai. Denial was a powerful form of defence and I had proved myself supremely adroit at employing it.

Until now.

Now with Nikolai gone – he left yesterday morning with Ivan to see his wife in the clinic over the border in Lugano – and with Mallory, accompanied by his valet, in Milan for a few days and then on to Verona, there was a danger I would have too much time on my own to think. It was a parlous state of affairs and one I was determined to evade for as long as I could, possibly in the hope that I was either mistaken or the problem would resolve itself. I had never before considered myself a coward, quite the reverse, but I was rapidly reviewing that opinion.

Throwing off the bed covers, I slipped out of bed and went over to open the full-length windows and push back the shutters. It was too early for the day to have gained any warmth and shivering at the coolness of the air, I grabbed my silk dressing gown from the back of the chaise longue and put it on. I then stepped onto the spacious balcony where there was a cast-iron table and two chairs. I stood in front of the stone balustrade and scarcely giving the panoramic view of the lake and the pearly dawn light a second glance, I gave hard scrutiny to the garden and all that I had achieved here, and still yet planned to do. A garden was a life-long project and one like this, which offered so much potential, would constantly change, especially with Mallory as its owner.

Since Bess and I had arrived here nearly seven weeks ago, the days had passed blissfully through September to October. The weather had been glorious for the duration of our stay, apart from some occasional evenings of dramatic storms that had produced spectacular displays of lightning, rending the sky apart along with thunder crashing and booming as it became trapped within the mountains.

In the distance I could hear the clang of church bells ringing out from around the hillside. It was a melodious sound I took pleasure in listening to. Continental bells always sounded so different to our own back at home. Registering that it was a Sunday and that the bells were a call to the faithful for an early morning service, I recalled how surprised Nikolai had been at my lack of belief in an Almighty. But then I was equally surprised by his certainty that there was a god. He was steeped in Russian Orthodoxy, it turned out, and always travelled with a small antique silver icon which had been in his family for several generations. His grandmother had given him the sacred image portraying the Holy Trinity when he was a boy, and it was clearly something he treasured.

He once said to me while we were swimming in the lake, 'How can you not believe in God when you are surrounded by all this?' We were floating on our backs and he was indicating the beauty of the lush hillside that rose smoothly upwards to the cerulean sky above us.

'I find it easier to believe in Mother Nature,' I told him. 'Mother Nature plays a fairer hand.'

The word *mother* caused me to flinch now and I quickly returned my attention to my handiwork, in particular the formal area of the garden directly in front of me. It was still in the early stages of growth, but I had created a gravelled parterre of box hedging that was punctuated with cypress trees at each corner and at the centre was a circular pond with a statue of Eros in the middle. Mallory had found the statue in Rome and arranged for it to be delivered to the villa. In each segment of the parterre, I had planted ten 'Pompon Blanc Parfait' Alba roses. It had been an easy choice to make as the rose has an upright growth with near-thornless stems, and a lovely fragrance. Also, the blush white of the cupped rosettes would glow in the dying light of the day and particularly so in the moonlight.

With regular watering I was hopeful the roses would settle in well enough after Bess and I had departed for England. I would leave Giovani, the gardener, very specific instructions on what was to be done in my absence. I had already given him instructions for underplanting the roses with some springtime colour. When Mallory arrived here in April next year, I wanted him to be greeted by an army of tulips – 'Couleur Cardinal' – standing tall and proud, their stems thrusting through a froth of forget-me-nots.

For the last few days my task had been to finish work on the hydrangea walk. I would have preferred to plant when the weather was cooler and damper, but I had to return home to begin work on a garden design for the owners of Beechwood Court in Oxfordshire, just a few miles from Mallory's house. My plans had already been approved and the nurseries supplying the plants had everything ready for me. Having been put on a retainer, I was looking forward to making a start on an extensive project that would help to keep me financially afloat for quite some time.

But that was ahead of me. This morning I had a delivery of *Hydrangea macrophylla* to plant. They were all 'Beauté Vendômoise', a favourite of mine, and of my parents. They had been good friends with Emile Mouillère who had bred the variety back in 1908 and so I always felt a special connection to Mama and Papa when I included it in a garden design. It was extremely floriferous and produced the most beautiful lacecap flowers that were white with a lovely blush of pink. I had chosen the perfect spot for them, where they would flourish in the dappled shade provided by the overhanging branches of a row of white-stemmed birches.

'But what if all your plans are about to come unstuck?' a small voice niggled inside my head.

Followed by another voice that sounded uncannily like Bess. *'So, miss, what are we going to do?'*

I sighed. It was a good question.

It was absurd that Bess still referred to me as 'miss', but old habits were hard to break, as I knew all too well.

Not once had Bess judged me in my affair with a married man, but then she wasn't the judgemental sort. Just as I wasn't. Now and then I felt guilty about what Nikolai and I were doing, but mostly I tried not to think of his unstable wife. I felt sorry for her, as much as I did for Nikolai, trapped as they both were in a fraught and loveless marriage. He had married her out of a sense of duty because she was pregnant and while that was very laudable, the noble act of a stoic, it had resulted in years of misery for the pair of them.

History was not going to repeat itself. Of that I was adamant. I was not going to put Nikolai in the exact same position. Where that left me, I couldn't say.

Later, when Bess called me up to the terrace for lunch – we usually took our meals together when it was just the two of us – I made a decision to talk to her.

Despite my own concerns I had noticed a change in Bess in the last week or so. She seemed distracted and was oddly reluctant to leave the villa. Not even to go out to the shops with Ivan as she'd done so many times before. It was possible that she was simply homesick and missing her husband. Even so, I decided to get to the bottom of whatever it was that was bothering her. After all, sorting out somebody else's problems would take my mind off mine.

'Now then, Bess, are you going to tell me what's troubling you?' I asked without preamble once we were seated.

'I don't know what you mean,' she replied.

'Are you homesick? Is that it?'

She hesitated and then, as if deciding I'd hit the nail directly on the head, she said, 'Yes. Yes, I am.'

The speed of her reply instantly made me suspicious that she wasn't being honest. 'Well, you only have another week to endure this dreadful place before we set off for home.' I cast my gaze around the garden meaningfully.

'Now you're making fun of me, miss, and that's not fair.'

'You're right, it isn't. But I'm afraid I don't believe that you're homesick. If I had to put my finger on when you started acting differently, I'd say it was after your last trip into Menaggio with Ivan. It's not anything to do with him, is it? You're not in love with Ivan and—'

'Good Lord, miss, what a vivid imagination you have, of course, I'm not in love with Ivan! How could you suggest such a terrible thing, as if I'd cheat on Amos. As if I'd ever be that kind of a woman who—' She clapped a hand over her mouth. 'I'm sorry, miss, that came out all wrong.'

'Indeed,' I said, taking a sip of the refreshingly cold beer she had poured for me. 'Having established that you're not an immoral whore of Babylon like me, are you unwell, is that the problem?'

'You're not an immoral whore, miss. That's not what I meant at all.'

'I've always believed in straight talking, Bess, so if a spade is a spade, especially in my hands, then that's what it should be called.'

I took a bite of the slice of crusty bread on my plate, followed by another sip of beer, deciding that if Bess wasn't prepared to open up to me, I would share my own problem with her. Furthermore, while gardening I had come up with an idea that might just get me out of the predicament in which I found myself.

'In the spirit of plain speaking,' I began, 'and as woman to woman, I have something I need to get off my chest in the hope that you might be able to help me. I think it's highly likely, and to put it as delicately as possible for your tender ears, that I'm with child.'

Bess gasped. 'Oh miss! Are you sure?'

I nodded. 'Not one hundred per cent, but unless I'm going through an early change of life, I believe I am.'

'Does the Count know?'

'No, and he must never know. This must remain strictly between you and me.'

'What about Mr Vaughan, haven't you confided in him?'

'Certainly not. He'd make a hoo-ha about Nikolai doing the decent thing by divorcing his wife and marrying me. And that must never happen.'

'But why? You love each other, so why not?'

'Because I do not want to be the cause of that poor wife of his making another attempt on her sorry life. I will not have that on my conscience. Or on Nikolai's.'

'How many weeks gone are you?'

'I'm assuming I must have conceived when we were staying on the Riviera with Nikolai at his cousin's villa before travelling on here.'

'Which would make you about eight weeks pregnant?'

'Yes,' I said.

'So how can I help you?'

'As I see it, I have several options. Have the baby in secret and give it up for adoption, keep the baby and not give a hoot about what people think of me, or—'

'Don't say it, miss. Don't say you'd get rid of it by doing, well, doing *that* awful thing.'

I shook my head. 'Fear not, that is not an option I'm prepared to pursue, even though it would solve everything.'

'It wouldn't, miss, it really wouldn't, you'd be—'

I held up a hand to stop her. 'Please don't say I would then be bound for hell and Satan's toasting forks. Spare me that.'

'I was going to say it's not legal and it would be putting your life in too much danger and I couldn't stand by and let you do that. Not for anything.'

'How sweet of you. But if you'll let me finish, the third option I'd come up with and perhaps the best one of all, is this. What if I had the baby in secret and then gave it to you and your husband to raise as your own? You've hinted in the past that Amos would like to be a father, but it hasn't happened for the two of you.'

Whatever reaction I'd anticipated from Bess, it was not the one with which I was suddenly confronted. She stared at me, her eyes wide, and then she suddenly burst into tears and proceeded to sob as if her heart would break.

Mystified at what I had unleashed, I went to her and crouching down on the ground beside her chair, I put my arms around her. But she would not be soothed and so with nothing else for it, I accepted that the answer was to let her cry until the river of tears had dried up.

It took a time, but eventually she fell quiet and with a final shudder and sniff, she said, 'I'm so sorry, miss, I don't know what came over me.'

'There's no need to apologise, Bess, but I believe you do know what came over you. Won't you tell me what it was? Does it have something to do with why you've been so out of sorts recently?'

For a moment she looked as if she might start sobbing all over again. 'You'll be shocked, miss,' she said, her lower lip trembling. 'You'll think I've let you down. You'll think I—'

'Good heavens, what on earth could shock me after what I've just shared with you? Now take a deep breath and tell me.'

'I don't know where to start.'

'The beginning is usually the best place.'

'No,' she cried with a catch in her throat, 'that's the worst bit!'

'All right, then start with the easy bit.'

'Do you promise you won't be cross with me?'

'I promise. Now get on with it before I'm so far along with this pregnancy I'm in danger of giving birth.'

My remark brought forth another sob and in a flash of realisation it dawned on me what the source of Bess's distress was. But how could I have been so stupid? Why had I never guessed?

'Oh, Bess,' I said, taking her hands in mine, 'is Nancy yours?'

She looked at me, aghast that I'd guessed. She nodded.

'Why did you never tell me?'

'I was too ashamed,' she said, 'and I thought you wouldn't let me work for you anymore. And anyway, how could I have worked for you and look after a child at the same time? I so badly wanted to keep on working for you, you'd been so good to me. I owed you so much I couldn't let you down.'

'So you gave your baby to your sister?'

'Yes. Joan and her husband had been trying for ages for a baby and then from nowhere I was pregnant. Giving her my child was the perfect answer; an answer to a prayer for us all. But it was the hardest thing I've ever done, and I've had to live with that ever since. I've had to stand back and see Joan spoil the poor girl and turn her into something she should never have been. But what could I have given her on my own? What advantages could I have given her?'

'And the father?'

'No, miss, don't make me tell you. Please don't.'

'Is it somebody I know?' I asked, ignoring her pleas.

She shook her head.

'But it was a man you loved but couldn't marry? Or a man who refused to marry you?'

'Oh, miss, love and marriage never came into it.'

'A fling, then? Just one of those things?'

Bess hung her head and began weeping again, silent tears full of anguish, and once again the awful truth dawned on me.

'My God, Bess, did the swine force himself on you? Is that what happened?'

For answer she began to shake and her sobs rose in volume. I held her as tightly as I could, vowing that if I ever knew the name of the monster who had done this terrible thing to her, he'd have me to answer to.

Chapter Seventeen

July 1981

Larkspur House, Suffolk

Libby had spent most of the night awake and worrying about her great-aunt.

Bess had been kept in overnight at the hospital, the medical staff of the opinion that they wanted to err on the side of caution. 'There's nothing to worry about,' the doctor had assured them, 'this is just a formality.'

A formality to him maybe, but for Libby his glib assurance only made her think that he was missing something, and that what Bess had experienced yesterday when she'd collapsed was more than a mere angina attack.

Now, with the first rays of light dissolving the darkness of early morning, Libby was downstairs in the kitchen filling the kettle. It was much too early to ring the hospital for the latest on Bess. Too early even for Elfrida to be up and about.

While she waited for the kettle to boil, and with a restless energy, Libby paced around the kitchen until she came to a stop in front of the dresser with its cluttered shelves. In dire need of something to do, to keep her from dwelling on Bess, and not caring about the furore her efforts to bring order to the chaos might cause, she began tidying the shelves. In no time, from amongst the precariously stacked mismatched crockery and recipe books, including some of Libby's favourites by Elizabeth David, she had removed three old gardening gloves, all for the left hand, a pair of rusting secateurs, a pile of old shopping lists and out-of-date money-off vouchers, several old lightbulbs, a tin of rusting nails and paperclips and balls of string, another tin crammed with seed packets that were hopelessly out of date, a shrivelled-up tube of glue inside a partially mended cream jug, a bundle of biros, none of which actually worked, held together by a rubber band, and a torch which also didn't work as the battery had corroded. Libby dumped the lot into the kitchen bin and with the kettle now whistling, she took it off the hot plate of the range and made a pot of tea. Leaving it to brew, she put the dusty crockery from the dresser next to the sink to wash.

While she drank her tea, having put a slice of bread into the toaster, she planned her next move which was to deal with the pantry and give it a good clean. Then she would tackle that mountain of ironing she had found in the laundry room. If the last twenty-four hours had taught her anything, it was that more help was required here. Bess could not take on the lion's share of running the house anymore. Whatever the woman who came in from the village to clean – and who was currently on holiday – actually did, it wasn't enough.

Libby might have her work cut out convincing Elfrida that she would have to dig deeper into her pockets to pay for more efficient and regular help in the house, but it would have to be done. In the meantime, Libby would take on the job. It was one of the many thoughts that had chased around inside her head while she was in bed and sleep eluded her.

She had heard Elfrida moving around in the night, no doubt fretting about Bess. Yesterday at the hospital a dragon of a ward sister had insisted they should all leave while her patient rested. Elfrida had plonked herself down in a chair in the waiting room with the defiant intention of spending the night there. As scruffily attired as she was in her gardening clothes and as slight as she was, Elfrida could still put her imperious voice to good use and wasn't afraid to do so, even with a nurse who looked like she had won many a battle in her time. In the end Libby had intervened and suggested that what they all needed was something to eat and a stiff drink, neither of which could be obtained where they were.

Whether it was Libby's reasoned approach or the temptation of several double whiskies that did the trick, Elfrida caved in. But not before she'd made it clear to the nurse that she wanted to be informed the second there was a change in Bess's condition. Perhaps unable to resist it, the nurse had the last word by informing her that family would, of course, be notified straight away. The significance of those words was that Elfrida wasn't family; that honour fell to Nancy as Mrs Judd's niece, and Libby as her great-niece. Which begged the question, what did family actually mean? Libby's mother might be blood-related to Bess, but Nancy had never shown the slightest hint of familial love towards her.

Buttering her slice of toast and then spreading a dollop of marmalade onto it, Libby glanced at the kitchen clock – it was five forty-five – and wondered if she dare telephone Dr Matthews – *Daniel* – later that morning. She wanted to believe that Bess was receiving the best possible care at the cottage hospital, but a second opinion wouldn't hurt, would it? Before going to bed last night, Elfrida had made Libby promise that she would ring the local surgery and speak to Daniel. Having originally declared him to be too young to know what he was doing, Elfrida now claimed that he was the only doctor she was prepared to trust.

'It's one of those things that happens over time when it comes to angina,' the doctor who'd examined Bess had explained at the hospital. 'There can be a gradual and partial blocking of the coronary arteries which could lead to just mild discomfort in the chest, or a feeling similar to indigestion. It can also resemble a heart attack, which can be very frightening.' He'd stressed that from all the tests they'd run, Bess was at the safer end of the spectrum, and that with the right medication, all would be well.

'Had Mrs Judd been overdoing things shortly before the attack,' the doctor had asked them, 'or endured a particularly stressful situation?'

Elfrida had thrown a furious look at Libby's mother. 'This is your doing,' she'd hissed. 'If you hadn't turned up out of the blue the way you did, this wouldn't have happened to Bess!'

'How dare you blame me!' Nancy had retaliated. 'This is your fault for making her your skivvy all her life!'

'She's never been my skivvy!'

'Stop it, you two!' Libby had intervened sternly, as the doctor had looked on awkwardly, probably making a mental note to keep these two angry women well away from his patient. When they'd arrived back at Larkspur House, Libby had rounded on them for their shameful behaviour.

Elfrida had hung her head and mumbled an apology but Mum, typical Mum, had taken umbrage and said she wasn't going to stay a moment longer if that was the kind of treatment to which she was going to be subjected. 'Frankly, Libby,' she'd said, 'I don't know who you are these days. Your father would be turning in his grave to hear you being so rude to me.'

And why do you always have to make it about you? Libby had thought sadly when she'd watched the glowing red of her mother's car's tail-lights disappear down the drive.

'You're up early.'

Her toast now finished, Libby turned round at the sound of Elfrida's voice. 'Not surprisingly, I couldn't sleep. How about you?'

'Off and on,' she muttered.

The question had been unnecessary, just as Elfrida's answer was because Libby could see for herself that what sleep Elfrida might have managed, it had been of little benefit to her. As Bess would say, the woman looked as creased and rumpled as an unmade bed.

174

She hadn't bothered to dress and wearing her slippers, nightdress and dressing gown that was fraying at the cuffs, with her hair having worked loose from its plait, she looked as though she had quite literally come apart at the seams. It showed just how much she loved Bess.

'Sit down and I'll pour you some tea; there's plenty in the pot.'

Elfrida shuffled over to the table and pulled out her usual Windsor-back chair. 'Bess will be all right, won't she?' she said when Libby had placed a mug of tea in front of her.

'From everything we've been told, I'm inclined to believe so,' Libby replied with more confidence than she felt.

Taking a sip of her tea, Elfrida said, 'I can't tell you how much I regret saying, even in jest, that Bess had better be careful as accidents always came in threes. It was tempting fate.'

'That's not like you to resort to superstition, Elfrida.'

'Extreme situations have that effect on us all when push comes to shove. I'm no different to anybody else. Or,' she added with a small shrug of her shoulders, 'as infallible as I like to believe I am.'

'We none of us are,' said Libby. 'But in this instance, I think we can dispense with blaming what's happened to Bess on fate. What we need to do is make sure it doesn't happen again.'

Elfrida nodded. 'You're not saying anything with which I haven't tortured myself for most of the night.'

'So you agree that you need to pay for more help around the house?'

'Of course I do. But Bess will hate the idea.'

'Tough!'

'Gracious, you've become quite bullish, young lady.'

'You'd better get used to it,' Libby said, 'this is the new me. Now, what would you like for breakfast?'

'Nothing.'

'Rubbish. You barely ate a thing last night and starving yourself will not help Bess. I'll make you some porridge.'

'Hmm . . .' said Elfrida. 'And what exactly have you done to the dresser? I hope you haven't got rid of anything.'

'I'm making myself useful while waiting for it to be a reasonable time to ring the hospital. And yes, I most certainly have thrown away a load of useless old junk and found the knob for the drawer.'

Elfrida eyed her warily, but perhaps it was a measure of her concern for Bess that instead of questioning Libby on what constituted junk, she said, 'I don't see why we can't telephone the hospital now. It's not as though they keep nine-to-five hours.'

'True, but I suggest we hang fire and avoid making a nuisance of ourselves.'

'I've never made a nuisance of myself in my entire life,' protested Elfrida.

'Then let's keep it that way, shall we?'

*

Bess had never spent any time in hospital before and with all the strange noises that went on she had found it impossible to sleep. She had been told that if the doctor was satisfied with her this morning, she would be discharged later in the day. Mentally she had everything crossed that that would happen.

The breakfast trolley was being wheeled around the ward at what seemed breakneck speed, crashing and clanking as it went from bed to bed. On the tray in front of her was an unappetising slice of flabby underdone toast and an unappealing poached egg that was cold. A mouthful of each was enough and despite feeling ungratefully rude for not eating more, she pushed the plate to one side and settled on making do with the cup of tea. The cup had a chip on the rim and the tea was too milky for her taste, but she forced it down and cast her gaze around the ward and the other occupants of the beds, most of whom seemed to be enjoying their breakfast.

Putting the now empty chipped teacup back in its saucer, she thought of her sister. Joan had died of a heart attack just a few years ago and really Bess should have considered the possibility that she too might be similarly affected with heart problems. But she hadn't. Stupidly she had taken it for granted that she didn't have anything to worry about, that because she was permanently on the go, she was healthier than Joan who, in contrast, had led a very sedentary life. Her sister had also gained a lot of weight as she'd aged, especially so after she was widowed, and Bess had always assumed the combination of those two things had led directly to Joan's heart attack and death.

Had Joan ignored the warning signs that something was wrong, just as Bess had tried to dismiss the moments of breathlessness? Even making light of what had happened to her while cycling home from church yesterday morning. It seemed absurd now to Bess that she had stuck her head in the sand and blithely carried on as though she were indestructible. But then she and Elfrida had been doing that for years, taking each day as it came with barely a thought for tomorrow. Was that because they spent too much time wrapped in the past?

Poor Elfrida, she had looked so worried and upset when she had finally been allowed to see Bess. Libby too had looked fraught with worry, and even Nancy, hovering awkwardly behind them, had worn an expression of concern. Bess had tried to convince them that she wasn't feeling as bad as they clearly thought she was. They'd only exchanged a few words before they were told to leave, that visiting hours were over.

The orderly was back with the trolley, crashing and banging as she went from bed to bed collecting the breakfast trays.

'Not to your liking, then?' the woman commented to Bess at the sight of her barely touched meal.

'Sorry,' Bess replied politely, 'I don't seem to be hungry this morning.'

'No need to apologise to me, love, I didn't cook it.'

Watching her push the trolley to the next bed and then leave the ward, Bess wished she could do the same, that she could slip out of bed and simply walk away. And at the same time, turn back the clock.

But to when?

To yesterday afternoon when they were happily enjoying lunch in the garden and before Nancy and Marcus had arrived?

Or much further back in time? To that first day she went to work for Elfrida and her life began? And if that were possible, was there anything she would change about her life?

She wanted to say yes, there was one very important moment that she wished had never happened. But to erase it would mean to lose out on loving a truly special person: Libby.

Chapter Eighteen

October 1926
Tilbrook Hall, Norfolk
Bess

He had been so charming and so handsome and always with a twinkle in his eye, and I'd felt so very flattered when he'd go out of his way to talk to me. Especially when so few of the servants at Tilbrook Hall did. They were an insular bunch who treated me, despite my regular visits, as an outsider of whom they disapproved. But their disapproval was mostly aimed at Elfrida for being, as they saw her, a lowly itinerant gardener. They said it was no position for a proper lady to put herself in. Well, I wasn't having that!

'Miss Elfrida Ambrose is the epitome of a proper lady,' I told them, 'and she's not just a gardener, she's a highly respected garden *designer* with a talent for creating something beautiful and lasting. Which is more than some folk around here will ever do in their lives!'

My heated defence of Elfrida did not win me any friends in the servants' hall, but I didn't care. I would not have anyone – not even the prissy housekeeper Miss Martin and the stuck-up butler, Mr Rogers – bad-mouthing the woman I so admired and to whom I was devoted.

I suppose that was when Michael O'Halligan made his move

179

and saw his chance to befriend me, to appear my one and only ally. He was relatively new to Tilbrook Hall, having only recently started work there as a footman. He was a good-looking man with short dark curly hair and thickly arched eyebrows that gave him a roguish air.

'Don't you be taking any notice of what they say about Miss Ambrose,' he said after my angry outburst. 'Just ignore them.'

'I can't,' I told him, 'because to ignore is to condone.'

'Why, that's very profound of you,' he said.

'It's the truth and a shame more people can't live by the same standard,' I replied.

'For what it's worth I agree with you,' he said, adding with a wink, 'We're kindred spirits, you and me. We don't really fit in here, do we?'

In the days that followed, he made a point of seeking me out for a chat. Since rarely did anyone else bother to do that, I welcomed his company and often found myself laughing at his tales of where he'd grown up in Ireland.

Then one day, he said, 'Now don't you be taking any notice what the others might be saying about me.'

'Why, what do the others say about you, Mr O'Halligan?' I asked.

'Oh, you know, that I've kissed the Blarney Stone and have a devilish way about me when it comes to the girls.'

'And do you?'

'I couldn't possibly say,' he said. 'But I make it my business only to be nice to the pretty ones like you. Now please, why don't you call me Michael?'

I was foolish enough to do just that and once that small step had been taken, I allowed him to turn my head with his smiles and winks and honeyed words of flattery.

In believing his interest in me was genuine, I was also foolish enough to think that I knew what I was doing. But I soon came to realise I was nothing but a naïve idiot who fell for the oldest trick in the book. Even when a small warning voice in my head whispered that I should be careful I was too taken in by him to heed the warning. Nothing bad was going to happen, I kept telling myself, for the simple reason I wasn't that sort of girl.

How wrong I was! I was exactly the kind of girl a man like Michael O'Halligan targeted, a plain girl who wasn't used to male attention and who was so wrapped up in my misguided certainty it made me hopelessly gullible.

I trusted him when he said he meant me no harm, that he just wanted to spend time in my company, that there was something so sincere and refreshingly honest about me that he couldn't help but hold me in the greatest of esteem. Oh, I lapped up his compliments, suddenly seeing myself in a whole new light. As ludicrous as it sounds, I felt I was now an attractive woman and that self-knowledge made me walk a little taller with my shoulders back and my head held high.

Our visit to Tilbrook Hall that autumn while Elfrida worked on creating a garden for her demanding sister was only meant to be for a week, but Prudence kept changing her mind about the design and planting choices and our departure was continually delayed. Had we left as originally planned, I'm convinced I would not have got myself into the mess I did.

One evening when supper was over in the servants' hall, I excused myself on the grounds that I had a niggling headache which an early night would hopefully put right. Taking a candle, I made my way up the narrow flight of stairs to my room. I had just changed into my nightclothes and was about to snuff out the candle on the bedside table when there was a soft tap-tap at the door. Wondering if it was Elfrida, and if she needed my help with something, I slipped out of bed and opened the door.

But it wasn't Elfrida, it was Michael O'Halligan. Mortified at the impropriety of him seeing me in my cotton nightdress and my hair untied and resting on my shoulders, I tried to close the door so he would only see my face in the gap, but there was something in the way. It was his foot.

'Now don't be acting all silly on me, Bess,' he whispered in the flickering light of the candle in his left hand while holding a cup and saucer in the other. 'I've brought you some hot milk with a dash of something in it to help ease your headache. It's my patent remedy and it never fails.'

His lilting Irish accent was so persuasive and despite knowing it was wrong to let him into my room, I did just that. I reasoned that it was better that we spoke inside my room and not out on the corridor where he might be seen.

Once he was in and I had taken the precautionary measure of closing the door so we couldn't be heard, he put the candle holder and cup and saucer on the chest of drawers and turned to look at me. Such was the intensity of his gaze as it moved from the top of my head to my toes and then back up again, I experienced a frisson of alarm and moved further away from him.

He smiled. 'Don't look so startled, we both know why I'm here. And it has nothing to do with warmed milk and everything to do with your desire for me.' His smile widened. 'I must say, that was a clever ruse on your part to say you had a headache and needed an early night. I caught the look you gave me and knew then that you wanted me to wait a few minutes before following you up here.'

'No!' I exclaimed in horror. 'That's not true!'

He chuckled and began unbuttoning the collar of his starched shirt. 'Don't be tiresome, Bess. We're both adults and free to have some fun. You know deep down that's what you've been longing to do, isn't it?'

I could smell alcohol on his breath and suddenly felt so scared I was worried my legs might give way. Summoning as much firmness to my voice as I could muster, I said, 'Mr O'Halligan, I think you'd better go.'

He shook his head. 'Not before I've had what I came for.'

'Lay one hand on me and I shall scream,' I said.

'No you won't, for the simple reason you don't want anyone to know that I'm here.'

'I'll say you barged in, just as you did.'

'And I shall say you invited me in, that you had been begging me to come to your room for days and I had resisted until I finally gave in to your pleas.'

'But you'll risk losing your job,' I said desperately.

He laughed and stepped towards me, his intent only too obvious. 'What do I care?' he said as I tried to step away from him. 'This was only ever a stopgap before going on to something better. I never hang around for long in one place. I'm an ambitious man, Bess, and have great plans for myself. Now stop being a spoilsport and take off your nightdress.'

There was no distance between us now and with panic rising in me, I tried appealing to his conscience, praying that he had one. 'Please,' I begged him, 'don't do this. I've . . . I've never been with a man before.'

My admission only seemed to amuse and inflame him, and he began fumbling to unbutton his trousers. Filled with terror at what he was about to do, I pushed as hard as I could against him and caught off guard, he stumbled backwards. Seizing my chance, I reached for the candle he'd put on the chest of drawers and thrust it right into his face, not caring that the hot molten wax splashed onto my hand. Letting out a yelp, he staggered once again, but my plan backfired as he then fell against me and I landed with a winded gasp on the bed with him falling heavily on top of me.

'You really shouldn't have done that,' he said. 'Now I won't be so nice to you. You have only yourself to blame.'

The memory of what he did next would never leave me. He was like an animal and didn't care how much he hurt me. In fact, I think he took a sick pleasure in knowing that I was in pain and was powerless to stop him.

The repulsive smell of his sweating and disgustingly aroused body was on me long after he'd gone. It was there in the morning too and no matter how much I tried to wash it away, it remained stubbornly on my skin, making me want to retch. It was, I accepted, destined to be an indelible stain that would be with me forever more.

After I'd taken her breakfast tray to Elfrida's room – she never ate breakfast downstairs with her sister in the dining room if she could help it – she told me that we would be returning to Larkspur House after lunch that day.

Not looking directly at her for fear of her seeing my dirty shame, I said, 'I'll see to your packing straight away, miss.' I left her room with a breathless wave of relief flooding through me that I wouldn't have to face Michael O'Halligan again. There had been no sign of him in the servants' hall earlier and I hoped he was hiding because I'd managed to burn his face with the hot wax from the candle last night. Or perhaps he was hiding because he was worried I would tell somebody what he'd done to me?

But I never would, for fear of him carrying out the threat he'd made before leaving my room: that if I ever told anyone what he'd done, he would find me wherever I was in the world and do it again. I believed him. I truly believed he was cruel enough to do just that. I also believed that this wasn't the first time he had forced himself on a gullible girl. Hadn't he said that he liked to move on from one job to another, as he tired of being in one place for too long? Now I wondered whether, rather than risk striking twice in one place, he moved around to satisfy his lust for a new victim. I would never know the truth, not for sure, but I was left feeling sickened by how easily I had fallen into his trap.

I did my best to put the horror of that night behind me, to concentrate on my work and behave as normally as possible. It worked until I began to suspect that I was pregnant. When I could ignore the suspicion no more, I had to take action and devised a plan. A plan that involved my sister.

Requesting a couple of days off, I went to see Joan and her husband in their terraced house in Bromley. Speaking to my sister on her own, I explained my situation, twisting the truth to give a more acceptable story and one that she would find less shocking. I told her that I had been let down by a man I thought had loved me. I said it was out of the question for me to keep the baby as an unmarried woman and planned to give the child up for adoption. Unless . . .

'Unless what?' she'd asked.

I saw the eagerness in her expression, her ready swiftness to put two and two together. It was devious of me, I know, for I knew how badly she and her husband wanted to have a child of their own and it just hadn't happened for them. Now here I was offering them what I hoped was the next best thing.

'Unless you would want to have the baby and raise it as your own?' I answered.

Our conversation ended with us both in tears – relief for me, and happiness for Joan that she was finally going to be a mother. But we had yet to put the proposition to her husband. Without his agreement, I would be forced to think again.

Dudley insisted on having a lot more information before he reached a decision. Did the father of the baby know about it? Was he a decent type? If he ever knew of the child's existence would he be the sort to cause trouble?

I fed Dudley a pack of lies, even hinting that the man who had got me pregnant was the son of a well-to-do family for whom Elfrida had carried out a gardening commission. I lied so fluently I almost came to believe the deception myself.

It was easily apparent that the thought of a baby with good breeding, even if only partial good breeding, appealed to both Joan and Dudley and I believe that was what clinched things in the end. What they were most worried about was that I might renege on the arrangement, that I would one day demand to have the child returned to me. To ensure that could never happen, Dudley insisted that we draw up an agreement, but not one overseen by a solicitor; we didn't want another party involved, our secret had to remain between the three of us.

The agreement stated very clearly that I gave up any right ever to call the child my own and that I would always be known as Aunt Bess. I had no idea if we were breaking the law, if it was actual fraud we were committing, but my name would not appear on the birth certificate and I would have no say in the way he or she would be brought up. Also, I must never tell the child the truth of its birth.

Dudley proved to be a stickler for the rules by which we would proceed and between us we came up with a detailed plan to cover our subterfuge. Firstly, when there was a danger that my pregnancy might begin to show, I would have to leave Larkspur House to go and help my unwell sister through her 'pregnancy'. While staying with Joan and Dudley I was not to go out; the risk of anyone seeing I was pregnant was to be avoided at all costs.

Meanwhile, Joan would have to improvise and fake her own pregnancy. A crucial part of the plan in the final weeks of pregnancy would be Dudley and Joan moving away from Bromley and setting up home somewhere completely new, where they wouldn't be known; and then when the time came, and this was the riskiest part, Joan and I would deliver the baby ourselves.

That was the one part of the story we'd concocted that truly frightened me, but I refused to dwell on it. All that mattered was that I would be free of the shameful and unwanted baby that was growing inside me as a result of the ordeal Michael O'Halligan had put me through. I kept telling myself that once the child was born, I could start to live my life again, free of the consequences of that dreadful night.

But as the months of my pregnancy went by and my body blossomed and swelled and I could feel the first stirrings of life inside me, and as Joan fussed around me looking forward with happy anticipation to motherhood, I felt an attachment developing to the baby. So deep did the attachment become I feared I might not be able to go through with the plan and part with the child.

Yet I knew I had to. I could not be a mother and continue my life working for Elfrida who had so generously insisted on keeping my job open for me while I was supposedly taking care of my sister. And what greater gift could I give my loving sister than the child she and Dudley had always wanted?

There could be no going back. The dice had been rolled and this was the sacrifice I had to make.

Chapter Nineteen

July 1981
Larkspur House, Suffolk

Bess had been home now for a week after being discharged from hospital and despite her protests that she didn't feel ill, Libby was taking no nonsense from her – she was to rest as much as possible and take her medication as instructed. Following Daniel's advice, Libby had written down how, when and why Bess was to use the medication. 'It's to avoid any mix-ups or misunderstandings,' she'd told Bess and Elfrida. Which had not gone down well with them.

'Goodness, I wonder how we ever managed without you before now,' Elfrida had muttered.

Undeterred, Libby had emphasised the importance of each drug that had been prescribed for Bess, particularly stressing the difference between the digoxin which she had to take every day and the glyceryl trinitrate tablet which she had to place under her tongue if she was short of breath and felt an attack coming on. 'You don't want to mix those two up, do you?' she said. There was also warfarin which Bess had to take to thin her blood, and that meant she had to avoid aspirin and be careful not to bruise or cut herself as even a small cut would bleed copiously. It was a lot to take in. Thankfully there had only been the one occasion since coming home when Bess had had to take one of the glyceryl trinitrate tablets. So that was an encouraging sign.

Certainly, looking at Bess this morning as they enjoyed the beautiful weather while sitting on the terrace with their cups of coffee, she did indeed seem the picture of good health. She was shelling peas – a task that even Libby could hardly call arduous – and next to her Elfrida was sharpening several pairs of secateurs with a whetstone before oiling them.

An hour ago, Dr Winscombe from the surgery in the village had paid a visit to check on Bess and all three of them had agreed that he wasn't a patch on Daniel. He'd been disagreeably terse, giving the impression he had far better things to do than pay a house call. Probably he was one of those doctors who preferred being on the golf course than treating sick people. If that was the best the Finchley Green surgery could do in finding a new permanent doctor, then heaven help the poor patients in the village.

Gathering up their empty coffee cups, Libby left Bess and Elfrida on the terrace and went inside to get ready to go shopping.

In charge of cooking now, she was also in charge of choosing what they ate which gave her the chance to make some healthy changes to Bess and Elfrida's diet. A little less dairy and red meat would be a step in the right direction, although she would have to be careful how she went about things. Subtlety would be the name of the game.

Subtlety was not a word that could be applied to Tina, who was currently ramming the ancient Hoover against the oak skirting boards in the hall. What she lacked in thoroughness, she made up for in cheerful enthusiasm and her ability to talk non-stop while drinking coffee laden with an astonishing six teaspoons of sugar.

Wearing tight flared jeans and a skin-tight leopard print halter-neck top that left little to the imagination, her wrists bedecked with an array of noisy bangles and her frizz-permed hair tied up with a brightly coloured chiffon scarf, she wasn't at all what Libby had expected.

'They're such a nice pair of old ducks,' she'd said of Elfrida and

Bess after Libby had introduced herself a few days ago when Tina showed up for work after her holiday. The description had made Libby cringe but ignoring it, she had asked if it was possible for Tina to work any extra hours. Immediately the cheerfulness was gone, and a pair of heavily mascaraed eyes had stared shrewdly back at her.

'Are you saying I'm not doing a good enough job?' she asked.

Frankly that was exactly what Libby was saying, but she quickly refuted the suggestion. 'Not at all, it's just that it's such a large house to keep on top of.'

'Would there be an increase in my wages?' Tina asked. 'Because I haven't had a pay rise since I started here last year, and what with the cost of living going up and up and my youngest getting married later this year, a rise would go a long way to helping me out.'

'I'm afraid that would be for Miss Ambrose to decide,' she had said cautiously.

Catching sight of Libby now as she came towards the kitchen with the upright Hoover, Tina shouted above its noise that she'd done upstairs and had given the bedrooms a bit of spit and polish. Which Libby interpreted as a squirt with Mr Sheen and a flick of the duster.

'Is that working properly?' Libby asked. She couldn't help but notice that the Hoover didn't seem to be picking up very much.

'What's that, love?' Tina bellowed.

Libby pointed to the on/off switch on the Hoover and Tina stamped her foot against it, rendering the machine silent.

'I was just wondering if it's working as it should,' Libby said.

'Seems all right to me,' Tina answered with a shrug.

Libby let it go, deciding to check later on the Hoover herself. 'I'm off to the shops,' she said. 'Mrs Judd and Miss Ambrose are in the garden. Are you okay to come in on Thursday?'

Tina laughed. 'I might have something of a sore head, but I'll do my best.'

'Sore head?' repeated Libby.

'It's the Royal Wedding tomorrow and I'll be glued to the telly, and then there's the bash in the village afterwards. Sounds like it's going to be a right old knees-up. Are you going to come down and join in?'

Not wanting to appear standoffish, Libby said, 'I think it might be a bit too much for my great-aunt.'

'You should come down on your own later in the evening, there's going to be a disco. Might do you good to cut loose and have a bit of fun with some folk your own age.'

'It's certainly something to think about,' Libby said with a forced smile.

'Anyway,' said Tina raising her voice above the Hoover as she started it up again, 'another ten minutes and I'll be finished here.'

Behind the wheel of her campervan, and with the windows open to let in some cooler air, Libby slowly trundled the rattling vehicle down the drive and thought of Tina's suggestion that she should join in with the village jamboree to celebrate the Royal Wedding. Nothing would entice her to go, not when it would only be a cruel reminder of what she should have been doing this coming Saturday, walking up the aisle to marry Marcus.

In the last few days many of her friends had been in touch by telephone, Libby having given them the number before leaving London. They had wanted to know when she would be back, but for now she had no idea. The main news they had for her was that Marcus had finally got round to cancelling the wedding. Apparently, he had told people that Libby had abandoned him, which was true, but he hadn't said why.

Her friends were furious on her behalf at his behaviour and expressed their surprise at how calm she sounded. But she could honestly say she wasn't bothered; Marcus could do and say exactly as he wanted. For now, all she cared about was making life easier for Bess and to that end she had taken on the job of running the household, including doing the shopping, cooking and laundry, as well as sorting out the pantry and being on hand to provide plenty of tea and coffee for Steve while he fixed the attic floor. She had yet to make a start on redecorating, having decided that could wait for now.

Something else she had undertaken to do was to ring her mother every day with an update on Bess. 'You do care about Bess, don't you?' Libby had asked her when her mother seemed more concerned about receiving an apology for the way Libby had spoken to her.

'What sort of a question is that?' Mum had fired back. 'Of course I do.'

It was too big a conversation to get into right then and Libby had let it go.

Driving into the centre of the village Libby saw that preparations were well under way for tomorrow's celebrations. Shopfronts and cottages were festooned with red, white and blue bunting and hanging baskets filled with flowers from the same colour palette. The white railings around the pond and the war memorial had also been decorated and the pub was dripping in bunting and flags and pictures of Prince Charles and Lady Diana. It was, despite the connotations for Libby, a gay and cheerful sight.

She parked the van outside the baker's shop and went inside, the bell tinkling merrily as she opened and closed the door. She bought a large white split-tin loaf and a small cob loaf. From there she went to the butcher for some chicken breasts for supper that evening. She planned to cook them in an orange tarragon sauce, but with a light hand when it came to the amount of cream used.

She then passed the greengrocer's – with so much produce grown at Larkspur House she had no need to buy anything from there – and went further on to the delicatessen for some olive oil, Parmesan cheese, some Parma ham and a packet of risotto rice for tomorrow's supper.

Shopping basket in hand, she was on her way back to the van when a car drew alongside her and came to a stop: it was Daniel.

He leant over the gear stick and wound down the window. 'How's your great-aunt?' he asked.

'Still under strict orders from me to rest,' she said. 'How are you settling in at the new surgery?' She knew from when they'd last spoken on the phone that yesterday had been his first day.

'Pretty well,' he replied.

'That's good.'

There didn't seem anything else to say and when a car drove up behind Daniel's and pipped its horn because the driver couldn't pass owing to a bus on the other side of the road, he said, 'I seem to be blocking the road, I'd better go.'

Then just as he was about to wind up the window an impulse seized hold of Libby. 'If you're not busy this evening, I don't suppose—' Her words broke off as she realised Daniel had just said the very same thing.

'Go on,' she said with a smile.

'No, you go first.'

'I was going to ask if you would like to join us for supper. I know Bess and Elfrida would enjoy your company. It won't be anything special, just a bit of chicken and some strawberries for dessert from the garden.'

'It sounds a lot more appealing than the microwave meal-for-one I had in mind to eat.'

Another pip of the horn had Libby saying, 'Come at six-thirty, if that's not too early.'

'I'll be there.'

After he'd driven off, and before returning to her van, she went back to the butcher's shop to buy some more chicken.

*

Such was the pervasive warmth of the evening, they were still sitting outside long after dusk had fallen and the last of the birds had chirruped before retiring for the night. Moths fluttered around the candles on the table and above their heads in the star-pricked sky bats swooped in their now-you-see-me-now-you-don't fashion.

Listening to the music playing on the gramophone, Elfrida was glad that Libby had invited Daniel to join them tonight. His presence added a pleasingly male dimension to their number, something which Elfrida had always enjoyed. And after the scare Bess had given them a week ago, there was something to be said for having a doctor handily amongst them.

Even though it was a huge relief to know that so long as Bess followed to the letter the medical advice she had been given, she would be all right, Elfrida couldn't shake off the terrible memory of that moment in the drawing room when Bess had dropped the tea tray and collapsed. Nor could she forget the fear that had consumed her at the hospital when she'd thought she might lose her dearest old friend. It was an emotion she didn't want to dwell on, it was just too painful. Better instead to enjoy this beautiful night and be grateful for these moments they could share together while reminiscing about times gone by as they listened to the music.

The old gramophone had made a surprising appearance after they'd finished supper, when Daniel had said that he had never heard one play before. With Libby's help, Elfrida had dug out the antiquated device from the bottom of the china cupboard in the dining room, along with a selection of 78-rpm records and a tin of needles she still had. They had brought everything out to the garden and placing the gramophone on the table, Elfrida had selected a Cole Porter record – 'Let's Do It' – inserted a needle, and turned the handle, just as she'd done a thousand times before. After the obligatory crackles and hisses, the music had started and at once she had been flooded with a host of memories. She had seen from the faraway expression on Bess's face that the same was true for her.

Since Libby had brought down the trunk from the attic and effectively opened a Pandora's box, the past had insinuated its way into the present for Elfrida. Perhaps because she had more important things on her mind with worrying about Bess, Libby had lost interest in the project of sorting through the old photographs, but often late at night when everyone else was asleep in bed, Elfrida would delve into the trunk and step back in time to feel closer to all those she had loved and lost.

Now that 'Let's Do It' had come to an end, and with Libby and Daniel hunting through the collection of records in their tattered paper sleeves, Elfrida asked them to select one and place it on the gramophone.

Watching Libby carefully remove the Cole Porter record and replace it with another and then turn the handle, the voice of Al Bowlly singing 'Love is the Sweetest Thing' reached out in the stillness of the garden, wrapping Elfrida in its poignant embrace. With a small sigh, she closed her eyes and heard a voice from the past whisper to her that all that mattered in life was love; the giving of it and the receiving of it. Nothing was more important.

Chapter Twenty

October 1940
Larkspur House, Suffolk
Elfrida

I had been dreaming of Nikolai, of his lips brushing against my cheek as he whispered how much he loved me, when I woke with a start to the sound of crying. Loud insistent crying.

It had never occurred to me that such a small being could make such an almighty racket. I rolled over to look at the luminous hands of my bedside clock and saw that it was three-thirty. It had been the same time last night when the infant had woken to be fed. And the night before that. If nothing else, the little blighter was as regular as a Swiss cuckoo clock.

Closing my eyes, I tried to block out the din and sleep again, to slip back into the dream and be with Nikolai once more.

But the baby's cries, so persistent, yet at the same time so plaintive, continued and sleep was to be denied. For the both of us.

Wondering why the child hadn't been shushed by being fed or whatever else one did to soothe a squalling baby, I contemplated going to investigate, but decided against it. It wasn't my place and besides, I suspected that Bess would already be putting on her dressing gown and slippers to put her more maternal instinct than mine to good use.

The baby had arrived two months ago, nine days earlier than

its due date, and had taken us somewhat by surprise. The midwife had scarcely had time to wash her hands and put on her apron before the nipper made his appearance into the world with a bawling wail.

'He certainly has a fine pair of lungs on him,' the woman had said as she cleaned the boy up and handed him over to the exhausted mother who stared in bewilderment at the red-faced bundle as though she didn't know what it was or what to do with it.

'You'll soon get the hang of it,' the midwife, all breezy efficiency, encouraged the girl. 'Most new mothers feel out of their depth at first, but nature has a way of stepping in and guiding you with a steady hand.'

An hour later and I was showing the midwife out and then it was just me and Bess left to help Alice cope with being a mother.

Much against her wishes, nineteen-year-old Alice Pearce had been evacuated from London and sent to Finchley Green to escape the bombing the city was now enduring. We had been told to expect two evacuee children, a brother and a sister, but instead it was Alice who arrived with a cardboard suitcase, a ration book and gas mask, and a hugely swelling abdomen.

It was now just over a year ago since Neville Chamberlain had announced to the country that Britain was at war with Germany. In the months that followed, life at Larkspur House underwent a dramatic change. Iris, the housemaid, had left to go and work in a munitions factory and Riddles, my beloved cook who had been with me since I was a child, had retired and moved away to live with her niece.

Bess's husband, along with dozens of men from the village, had been called up to go and fight. Amos had been amongst the thousands of Allied troops who had been evacuated from Dunkirk in June of this year. It had been a desperately worrying time with Bess and me reading the newspaper reports and listening to the wireless for the latest news of the evacuation by the fleet of ships and small boats that had carried out the rescue expedition. On his safe return, Amos was given a couple of weeks' leave and then summoned for duty. All we knew of his whereabouts now was that he was at a training camp somewhere on the south coast preparing to go and fight again. The same was true for Alice's husband, Wilfred.

At the age of forty-three Mallory had been considered too old to be called up but had been given a posting in London at the War Office.

'I'm a boring old desk-Johnny,' he complained to me. 'I'd make a better Land Army girl, don't you think?'

Personally, I was glad his age made him exempt from fighting, although being in London didn't mean he was out of harm's way. Not if the Luftwaffe kept up its ruthless reign of terror on the city.

His beautiful Lake Como house – Villa Lucia – had been seized by the Italians who, in June, had announced they too were now at war with Britain and France. Mallory had confessed to me that his extravagant spending for the last twenty-odd years had caught up with him and he was reduced to letting his beloved home, March Bank in Oxfordshire, to a couple from London who wanted to stay there for as long as the war went on.

To make his financial situation worse still, Mallory had kept too much of his money in Italy to avoid paying excessive taxes here, but now he couldn't access the bank account. He was convinced Mussolini would simply help himself to every last lire of it. If only he'd been more sensible and put it over the border in Switzerland, as Nikolai had advised him to do.

As far away from me as he was in America, Nikolai was a constant presence in my life. He frequently sent parcels of food – tins of ham and salmon and peaches and bars of chocolate – and just as often he wrote long and beautifully composed letters. Page after page, he poured out his heart to me and I drank in his every expression of love. Many a time he swore that he was going to divorce his wife and to hell with the consequences. *I won't let her hold me to ransom all my life!* he wrote. I immediately replied, saying he mustn't do anything rash, that neither of us wanted his wife's suicide, or even an attempt to take her own life, on our conscience. *Didn't you tell me that love is all that matters,* I wrote, *that nothing was more important? Then let that be enough for us, I beg of you.*

The most poignant letters he ever penned were those which referred to his unspeakable sorrow at the loss of our child. My heart broke for him. For me too.

The memory of that dreadful day and how it resulted in a miscarriage still haunted me. Never more so than now with a baby in the house. The nightmares had just begun to lessen when Marjorie Spiller, the local billeting officer, arrived on our doorstep with Alice Pearce.

'No, no, no!' I told her firmly. 'This simply won't do at all. I signed up for two children, not a pregnant woman. I'm sorry, but this is out of the question.'

Enjoying her so-called position of authority a little too much, Marjorie informed me that I should be grateful that my house wasn't being requisitioned. She put a tick against something on her clipboard and told Alice to be sure to hand over her ration book to me. Once Marjorie had gone and realising how rude I'd been to this poor girl who looked as though Larkspur House was the last place on earth she wanted to be, I took her suitcase and called out to Bess to come and meet our evacuee.

It had taken the three of us a while to adjust to the unexpected situation. It had probably been harder for Alice as she'd clearly missed her friends and family back in the East End of London, but before long she'd succumbed to Bess taking her under her wing and began helping around the house. None of the heavy work, not in her condition, but she'd proved a dab hand in the kitchen with Bess, learning how to make jam from the autumn raspberries picked in the kitchen garden as well as bottle up the surplus of runner beans in brine.

The garden had initially been a strange and incomprehensible place to her. 'You mean this is all yours?' she'd said when I'd taken her outside to show her round. The wonder in her voice had bordered on alarm, as though we might encounter grizzly bears lurking in the shrubbery. Her trepidation soon changed when I showed her how to dig up some late potatoes in the kitchen garden and the last of the carrots. Her face had been a picture when she'd unearthed her very first potato from the soil and she'd held it in her hands as though she'd just dug up buried treasure. With all the excitement of a child, she had begged for that potato to be hers for supper that evening.

The crying had stopped now, the house perfectly silent. But finding myself still unable to sleep, and seeing that it was now four-thirty and not yet light, I decided I would make an early start on the day.

Downstairs, I added some precious coal to the Rayburn and made myself a cup of hideously weak tea – Bess ruled the roost when it came to eking out our rations and woe betide me if I was too heavy-handed with the butter or sugar. I took my tea through to the dining room which was where I liked to work. We had no need of the large table for entertaining these days and so I put it to good use as a desk, where I could lay out my papers and notebooks and where they wouldn't be touched.

Not surprisingly my garden design work had dwindled with the war. Lambert Chase in Northampton had been requisitioned, as had Strickland Hall in Buckinghamshire and Gillingham Court in Kent. I had been kept on a retainer basis for some years by the owners and the work had generated a steady flow of income, but that was gone now.

Only yesterday my sister had written with the news that

Tilbrook Hall was to be requisitioned and used as a hospital and a camp for POWs. So that too was a source of income that was gone.

Things were so tight it was as well I had only Bess and Alfie's wages to find these days. Alfie, who looked younger than his sixteen years, had fooled no one at the call-up centre in Bury St Edmunds when he'd tried to claim that he was eighteen and therefore old enough to fight. Privately, and with no Amos to help me in the garden, I was glad the lad had been turned down as I desperately needed his assistance, especially as we were all digging for victory now. The surplus of fruit and vegetables we produced was sold in the shop in the village. There was also a fair bit of bartering that went on, but perhaps the less said about that the better.

Possibly out of consideration for my financial situation, Prudence's husband had persuaded her to relinquish her joint ownership of Larkspur House. I had no idea how he had convinced my sister that she should do this, but he had the arrangement legally drawn up so I would have the security of knowing my home was my own. I would forever be grateful to George for this act of kindness on his part.

Sipping my tea, I thought of Prudence's letter and pushing away the planting plans I was supposed to be working on for Bourne Park in Hertfordshire, I decided to reply to her, if only to get the task over and done with. She'd written a stream of grumbles about how unfair life was and how *obviously* the war was being hopelessly mismanaged. Her husband, she claimed, would soon sort out the mess if he was given the chance. Too many young men were being put at needless risk as, in her view, the Air Ministry *obviously* didn't know how to run a tea party, never mind manage the affairs of the RAF. Everything was so *obvious* to her. Churchill came in for a share of her vexation, with her referring to him as that 'corpulent, cigar-smoking buffoon' who had *obviously* only become the prime minister because Chamberlain was a weak fool and Lord Halifax had been too scared to take on the responsibility of the job.

Nikolai had shared with me in his letters how worried he was for some of his old friends who had left Russia during the revolution and moved to Austria and Germany for safety, only then to find that because they were Jewish, they were at even greater risk. Nikolai had urged them to leave while they still could, but they had believed that their status as doctors and wealthy businessmen would protect them. Even when Kristallnacht happened in November of 1938, they saw themselves as shielded. But now, according to Nikolai's letters, they realised their mistake and lived in fear of what might happen next as every day more of their rights were taken away.

Hunting through my papers for Prudence's letter, I was distracted by the last one Nikolai had sent me and which I had yet to add to the rest. I kept his letters in the chest of drawers in my bedroom and sometimes, late at night when I couldn't sleep, I would re-read them, just to feel closer to him. Some, though, I just couldn't read again; they were too painful, too strong a reminder of what we'd lost. Of what might have been.

I put Nikolai's most recent letter to one side and returned my attention to the one I should write to my sister.

Dear Prudence, I began, *I'm sorry to read of your woes, but . . .*

But what? I pondered. *Pull yourself together and accept that we all have to make sacrifices for the greater good.*

Or: *What do you have to complain about when you have the house in Mayfair to live in, or the place in Scotland where you could hunker down and pretend there isn't a war raging across Europe?*

I sighed and took another sip of my tea, willing myself to think better of my sister.

I was saved from putting pen further to paper, by Bess appearing in the doorway. 'Presumably the baby woke you?' she said.

I nodded. 'He's a vocal little chap, isn't he, and tenacious with it.'

'In the end I went to see if I could help.'

'Of course you did,' I said with a smile. 'Alice is lucky to have you on hand.'

'I don't know about that. Shall I make us some porridge?' she asked.

'Do we have enough?'

'I'll make it stretch, don't worry.'

'You're a wonder, Bess, truly you are.' It was on the tip of my tongue to add, *what would I do without you?* But I didn't. The last time I'd uttered the words Bess had worked herself up into a fearful tizzy of apologetic guilt, declaring it would have been better for me if I had never met her because it was all her fault that I had lost my baby, for which she could never forgive herself.

No matter how vehemently I repeatedly attempted to disabuse her of this conviction, she refused to budge and continued to blame herself.

But then I carried my own share of guilt. Had I guessed the predicament in which Bess had found herself, that that vile man Michael O'Halligan had raped her, I would have done all I could to find a better solution than the one she'd devised for herself. And one I knew she regretted.

We had our fair share of secrets, Bess and I, but there was one that weighed so heavily on us both we neither could bring ourselves to talk about it. It was always there though, hanging over us like a large black cloud. My only hope was that the passing of time would eventually lift that cloud from our lives.

Chapter Twenty-One

July 1981
Larkspur House, Suffolk

Bess was not happy. Not happy at all.

'That girl has wreaked havoc in my pantry,' she said, emerging from the pantry into the laundry room. 'I can't find a damned thing.'

Elfrida was washing her hands at the sink and on the draining board was that morning's harvest from the kitchen garden – strawberries, redcurrants, cherries, tomatoes, peas, runner beans, new potatoes, bunches of herbs, and a cucumber along with a butterhead lettuce. It should have been a sight that had Bess rolling up her sleeves and putting everything to good use, but Libby had banned her from so much as making a drink and it was driving her round the bend with boredom and frustration.

'Language,' said Elfrida, drying her hands now. 'And if I'm not mistaken, I believe *that girl*, for our own good, is on a mission to cleanse us of our bad ways.'

'But I like my bad ways. God help me, I even like your bad ways. I don't want things to change. I certainly don't want my pantry rearranged. Or the dresser stripped of everything that was useful. Doesn't it bother you?'

'No. What bothers me far more is you not doing as you're told.

Now come and sit down in the kitchen where I'll make you a cup of tea before we watch the wedding.'

Bess puffed out her cheeks with exasperation. 'I'm perfectly capable of boiling a kettle myself,' she snapped.

'Really? Yet you couldn't find what you were looking for in the pantry?'

'Please don't be clever with me. Or imply I'm losing my marbles. Not when I'm trying to make a point.'

'Which is?'

'That you and Libby are treating me with kid gloves, and I really don't like it. The way you both look at me it's as if you think I'm about to drop dead any minute. Do you have any idea how unnerving that is? How would you feel if you were in my shoes? And how would you like it if Libby was rearranging your greenhouse or digging up your precious garden?'

'I'd chase her away with a broom and hosepipe!'

'Well then.'

'Well then, nothing. I'm not the one with angina, you are. So let's have no more of your petulant nonsense, or . . . or I'll have to take a broom and hosepipe to you!'

'I'd like to see you try.'

'Don't tempt me.'

'If I could interrupt this happy little spat, everything's ready in the drawing room. I've put the television from your bedroom in there, Bess. Perhaps you'd like to go and sit down now?'

They both turned round to see Libby standing in the doorway of the scullery.

'Do I have any choice in the matter?' muttered Bess.

'Do as she says or she'll send you to your room without any-thing to eat,' said Elfrida.

'The same goes for you too, Elfrida. Do as you're told, or no lunchtime snacks for either of you. Go on, off you go.'

'What about all this I've just brought in from the garden?'

said Elfrida, indicating the trug of fruit and vegetables on the draining board.

'I'll see to that.'

'In that case, we'll have two coffees and a couple of chocolate digestives, and make it snappy,' said Elfrida. 'Come on, Bess, let's go and make ourselves comfortable.'

With a weary sigh of resignation, Bess did as she was told. In the drawing room, she sat down in her usual wingback chair which Libby had moved so that she would have a perfect view of the small television now positioned on a table some eight feet away. They used to have a proper-sized set in this room but after it stopped working it had never been replaced, so if there was anything Bess wanted to watch, like *Crossroads*, *Take the High Road*, or *Dallas*, all of which Elfrida dismissed as rubbish, she did so upstairs in the privacy of her bedroom.

'Don't be too cross with Libby,' said Elfrida, 'she genuinely means well. I think it would be better for us to give in graciously and acknowledge our appreciation of her help.'

'You're right, I know, but it's just so maddening constantly being told to take it easy.'

'That's because we've never been very good at it; we've always gone at life full tilt. No such thing as half measures for us.'

'But now,' said Bess, 'life is to be rationed for me, portioned out in measly doses.'

Elfrida looked at her, her unwavering gaze as familiar to Bess as her own. 'A few adjustments here and there, that's all, we'll soon get the hang of it.'

'But I feel such a fraud doing nothing when I actually feel so well. Better, in fact, than I have in a while.'

'That's thanks to the medication you're taking and Libby's censure of you. So let's keep it that way, shall we?'

Bess frowned, knowing that Elfrida was right. But oh, goodness, it was so hard doing nothing!

Then, as if they'd said all that needed saying on the subject, they both turned to look at the television screen and the scene from the Mall in London. A BBC commentator was now standing amongst a group of Pearly Kings and Queens. Behind them was a large crowd of people waving flags and wearing patriotic hats of red, white and blue as they waited eagerly for a sighting of the royal carriages leaving the palace.

'Takes one back to the Coronation, doesn't it?' said Elfrida as a group of revellers struck up with an enthusiastic rendition of 'Land of Hope and Glory'. 'If there's one thing we British can be relied upon, it's to put on a decent show of pomp.'

'Do you suppose they'll be happy?' asked Bess, remembering the excitement of watching the Coronation on their first television set in the summer of 1953. At the time it hadn't seemed possible that they could be watching such an important moment in history unfold before their very eyes. She'd felt as though she'd actually attended the grand occasion.

'Who?'

'Charles and Diana.'

'Oh, I dare say they'll muddle through.'

'There's a lot to muddle through, though, isn't there? All that royal protocol and smiling and handshaking and posing for the cameras, it must be extremely tiresome.'

'I expect they'll both be glad to have today behind them so they can escape the attention of the press.'

'She seems so young. I wonder if she slept a wink last night.'

'Did you the night before you married Amos?'

'Not really.'

'My memory of your wedding was how nervous you looked.'

Bess could still recall just how nervous she'd been. Worried to death about consummating the marriage, she'd been terrified that she might not be able to let Amos touch her, that the very act of making love would make her physically ill. Her other fear was that he'd guess that he wasn't her first. In her nightdress in bed with him, she'd squeezed her eyes shut and willed her body to relax, to forget all about Michael O'Halligan and how he had violated her. Afterwards, and full of awkward embarrassment, Amos had apologised that it had been over so quickly, but she'd kissed him and said it was perfect.

In time they were both more at ease in bed together and she was able to give more of herself to her husband. She knew it was wrong, but she had initially seen lovemaking as a duty rather than an act of passion. But gradually that changed, and for the better. For Amos there was always the hope that sex would result in the creation of a child. But it never had.

*

'After the fuss that's been made of the dress,' observed Elfrida, 'all I can say is that it looks like it could do with a jolly good iron.'

'Imagine the weight of all that silk taffeta,' murmured Bess.

As the BBC's Tom Fleming kept up a steady commentary, Lady Diana, minutes away from becoming Princess Diana, was slowly climbing the steps of St Paul's with Earl Spencer at her side and where inside the cathedral three and a half thousand guests awaited them. The poor man appeared so frail, thought Libby, as if Diana was the one supporting him and not the other way round. There was no denying the affection they held for each other and it brought an unexpected lump to Libby's throat as she thought of her own father and how sad she'd been when planning her wedding that he wasn't alive to walk her up the aisle. To her mother's chagrin, Libby had said that because nobody could replace her father she had intended to break with tradition and would approach the altar alone.

'Earl Spencer looks so proud and happy for his daughter, doesn't he?' said Libby, passing round a plate of smoked salmon and cream cheese sandwiches, along with another of vol au vents and cocktail sausages she'd cooked in a sticky marinade of brown sugar and Worcestershire sauce.

'For a man who had a stroke and was in a coma not so long ago, I'd say he looks remarkably chipper,' said Elfrida, helping herself to a sandwich and a couple of sausages. 'Any more champagne going?'

'Of course,' said Libby.

'Am I not allowed a tiny amount so I can toast the happy couple?' asked Bess.

'Just a drop,' conceded Libby. She felt so torn when it came to her great-aunt. On the one hand she wanted to let her be happy and be left to do everything she always had, but on the other, she badly wanted to wrap her in cotton wool and keep her safe. But a small amount of champagne wouldn't hurt, would it, she told herself – it was a special occasion?

By the time she'd poured the champagne and helped herself to something to eat, Lady Diana and Earl Spencer had completed the seemingly endless walk up the aisle and now the radiant twenty-year-old bride stood beside Prince Charles who was decked out in his full dress naval commander uniform. They certainly made a striking couple, but then she supposed most brides and grooms did.

'Do you think Marcus is watching this?' asked Elfrida.

'Good grief!' tutted Bess. 'Could you be any more insensitive?'

'That's okay,' said Libby. 'It's a fair enough question. My guess is no, he'll be giving it a miss.'

'We could have done the same,' said Elfrida.

'Certainly not,' said Libby, keeping to herself that had she been on her own in London she would have probably avoided switching on the television, but being here with Bess and Elfrida it didn't seem such an ordeal. 'After all,' she added with forced brightness, 'it's billed as the wedding of the century and when I'm your age I want to be able to say I saw it happen.'

Out in the hall the telephone rang.

'Just leave it,' said Bess with a frown.

But the phone kept on ringing.

And ringing.

'Shall I go and answer it?' suggested Libby.

'No, I'll go,' said Elfrida, 'you're the one who wants to remember this big occasion in your dotage.'

Elfrida picked up the telephone receiver, wondering who on earth it could be. Surely the world and his wife would be glued to their television sets? Personally, she would sooner be in the garden than stuck inside.

'Hello,' she said in her most authoritative voice, the one she used when she wanted to cut short an unwanted caller. Occasionally she would be bothered by some garden club committee person asking to arrange a visit. 'Absolutely not,' Elfrida would bark down the phone, 'I don't open the garden anymore.' Her other tactic would be to say the caller had the wrong number and then leave the telephone off the hook.

'Elfrida?'

She recognised the voice straight away. A voice that could be even more imperious than her own.

'Hello, Prudence. You're still alive, then?'

A sharp intake of rattly breath followed by a spluttered cough had Elfrida removing the receiver from her ear. She waited for Prudence's riposte.

'Very much alive,' came the reply, 'despite you doubtless sticking pins into a voodoo doll to bring about my early demise.'

'I assure you I can find better ways to amuse myself than playing with voodoo dolls. Now let me guess why you've gone to so much trouble to ring me when we haven't spoken for . . . oh . . . what is it, five months?'

'Six months, as well you know.'

'Ah yes, I remember now, it was the day Libby and Marcus announced their engagement. What can I do for you, then? Other than listen to your delight at the wedding being called off. You never thought Libby was good enough for your precious grandson, did you, so you must be like the cat who got the cream.'

'Don't be such a hypocrite. From day one you were chafing at the bit to ruin things between them. You said that Marcus wasn't good enough for Libby.'

'An opinion which has now been proven to be entirely correct,' Elfrida asserted.

When, and out of the blue, Libby had told Bess and Elfrida that she had some amazing news, neither of them had expected her to announce that she was going out with a wonderful man who just happened to be Elfrida's great-nephew.

'*Marcus!*' both Elfrida and Bess had cried in surprise.

'Yes!' she'd laughed. 'We couldn't believe it when we realised there was a connection between us. Honestly, you couldn't make it up!'

In the face of the girl's obvious delight, they'd had their work cut out to keep their reservations to themselves. But Libby was clearly smitten, and they didn't have the heart to burst her bubble of happiness. While Bess had been prepared to give Marcus the benefit of the doubt, Elfrida had regarded the relationship as a mismatch from the word go. But whatever concerns they'd had, they had kept them to themselves. As difficult as it was in life, one often had to learn a lesson the hard way; the mistake had to be lived through in order for it to be recognised as such. Now Libby had learnt that lesson.

At the sound of a disagreeably wheezy cough in her ear,

Elfrida pictured Prudence in her Mayfair house where she had lived for the last fifteen years after handing over the keys of Tilbrook Hall to her youngest son, James. Faced with spiralling running costs, and death duties from when his father died, James and his wife, Cora, had turned the place into a hotel aimed at those wanting to experience a country house-style environment with fishing and shooting on tap. Much to Elfrida's surprise, in the five years they'd been running the place as a hotel they had so far made a reasonable success of it. Their son, Marcus, had shown no inclination to join the family business and had hightailed it off to London to work in a City bank. It was at Tilbrook Hall where Libby and Marcus's wedding reception had been set to take place.

'And don't you just love to be proved right?' sniped Prudence.

'Not always. But I really don't understand why you seem so put out. I'd have thought you'd be cock-a-hoop to be rid of Libby.'

'I'll grant you that I may have queried her suitability; after all, she and Marcus are not exactly from the same stock, are they, but I didn't dislike the girl.'

'Are you referring to stock cubes or cattle stock?'

'Stop trying to goad me, you know full well I'm talking about class and social position. My grandson comes from a different social class to Libby and by rights should have been marrying a girl from his own background, but because he said Libby made him happy, I accepted the situation.'

'How very generous of you. You speak as though it was your decision who Marcus should marry.'

'I wish it had been. But he was always easily led as a child and much too headstrong. I blame his mother for not taking a firmer hand with him. She spoilt him rotten.'

Elfrida could agree on that latter point, but before her sister embarked on a long rant of complaints about her daughter-in-law, of whom she had never really approved, Elfrida said, 'Well, it's been lovely having this catch-up, Prudence, but surely wouldn't you rather be watching the future king of England marry his sweet blushing bride?'

Her question was met with a scoff of derision. 'Quite frankly I couldn't stomach it. Everyone knows this marriage billed as a fairy-tale wedding is no such thing.'

'When you say "everyone", who exactly do you mean?'

'It's well known in certain circles that it's far from a love match, that it's merely to produce a son and heir.'

Knowing as she did that Prudence's circle of friends might very well make her privy to royal gossip, Elfrida let the remark go. She was more concerned about ending the conversation. But she had one more question for her sister, something she wanted to make sure of. She wouldn't have put it past Marcus to lie to his grandmother. 'You do know the reason Libby refused to marry Marcus, don't you?'

'That's why I've rung you.'

'What, to ask me why the wedding is off?'

'No, I know the reason: her name is Selina.'

'I suppose as his grandmother you're going to make excuses for Marcus sleeping with Libby's best friend, aren't you?'

'Far from it. I'm very disappointed in him, he's behaved dis-gracefully. But the purpose of my call is to let you know that I heard this morning that there is still going to be a wedding on Saturday; Marcus is going to marry Selina. I thought you'd want to know so you can warn Libby. She is there with you, isn't she?'

It wasn't often Prudence could shock her, but in this instance she had. 'Yes,' said Elfrida, 'Libby has been with us for a while now.'

'I can't say I'm terribly impressed with the swift turnaround in bride, but the young of today behave so differently compared to our generation. For them it's self, self, self and scant regard for what others might think. They lack all sense of decorum and social graces. You were the same, actually, when I come to think of it. You never cared whose feelings you trampled on. Particularly when it came to mine. I've never forgiven you for that.'

'Well, thank God you're above holding a grudge,' muttered Elfrida.

The irony was lost on Prudence and after she'd given another wheezy cough, she abruptly ended the call.

Elfrida put the receiver down and thought how wrong her sister was. More to the point, she knew that Prudence had been referring very specifically to a time in their lives when Elfrida had tried her best to protect her sister's feelings. It had sadly led to Prudence holding a grudge against her for very many years.

It was why they seldom spoke, and why Libby's engagement to Marcus had not been greeted with universal delight.

Chapter Twenty-Two

May 1946
Tilbrook Hall, Norfolk
Elfrida

It was so hard to feel sorry for my sister, or even imagine that somewhere in that cold heart of hers there lurked a tender spot that could feel pain. Not once had she shown remorse for anything she had said or done, nor had she revealed the slightest hint of vulnerability.

I was astute enough to understand that Prudence had built herself an unassailable fortress and placed her emotions at the centre of it. Nobody could be as insensitive or as hard-hearted as she portrayed herself without going to considerable effort to appear that way. I knew of course why she did it. Yet it didn't make it any easier to accept or forgive her rigid refusal to apologise or show compassion.

But in the spring of that year, twelve months after Nazi Germany was defeated, that fortress of hers very nearly came tumbling down when her eldest and most beloved son, William, was found dead. A young under gardener had discovered William's body hanging from a tree in the bluebell woods of Tilbrook Hall.

I was staying at Tilbrook, along with Bess, to continue my work in putting right the extensive damage that had been inflicted on the garden as a result of the house and grounds having been requisitioned for use as a hospital and POW camp. Many of my old clients were in the same position, restoring their beautiful homes and gardens to their former glory, and I was as busy as I'd ever been.

The lad who had found William had tried to take down the body from the tree himself, thinking he might be able to save William's life, and had been distraught when he'd been unable to do so. He'd come running to me where I was working in the peony borders to break the news. He was in such a state of shock he was scarcely able to get the words out. When I finally understood what he was telling me, I sent him to find the head gardener and a ladder while I flew like the wind up the lawn to the house to find George. Not until William had been taken down from the tree and carried inside did I want his mother to know what had happened. Under no circumstances did I want Prudence to see her favourite son's body dangling from a tree branch. No mother should ever suffer the torment of such a sight.

But that was exactly the sight George and I encountered when we hurried behind the young under gardener and head gardener carrying a ladder on his shoulder. It was an image I knew I would never erase from my memory and I doubted William's father would either. For me it was all too nightmarishly reminiscent of my brother's death when I was a child. I was the one who had found Bobby and I had never forgotten the contorted shape of his body and the blood pooling out from beneath him on the flagstones.

George carried William's body back up to the house and that was when Prudence looked out of an upstairs window and saw us. Initially she must have thought that her son had met with an accident and was merely unable to walk, but as we drew nearer, some instinct must have told her that William would never walk again.

We hadn't made it as far as the stone steps to the house when

Prudence was upon us and screaming. I don't think I had ever heard a noise like it. It came from a place deep inside her and maybe it was a scream for more than just her son. A wild primeval cry of tortured anguish for the brother we had lost, and for our parents, for whom she had never allowed herself to grieve.

In that moment as she threw herself onto her dead son, my heart broke for my sister. How would she ever recover from this?

The answer to that lay in her adamant refusal to accept that William had taken his own life. 'Never!' she cried. 'He would never do that!' She claimed it had to have been an accident, that he'd been climbing the tree and had slipped. He'd done it many a time as a child, she insisted. She repeated it so often I think she came to believe it as the truth and could deny all the evidence to the contrary. The doctor who examined William was a fool, she said. The police were fools too, and the official verdict of the inquest was a travesty, she later claimed. When George, distraught with grief himself, lost his temper with her and shouted that he had been the one to remove the rope from around William's neck, she accused him of lying.

'For what purpose?' he bellowed. 'Why would I fabricate such a thing?'

No suicide note was ever found, but had he left one I was convinced Prudence would have found a way to dispute its authenticity. Her mind had become so closed, we none of us could penetrate the walls she'd erected around herself. The walls of her fortress were deeper and higher than ever before and within that place of safety she could console herself with her own version of what must have happened.

For my part, I was pretty sure I knew why my nephew had killed himself. He had always been a sensitive young man and had felt things keenly. His experience of serving in the RAF as a Spitfire pilot in the final years of the war had left its mark on him. He'd seen too many of his fellow pilots die, men the same age as him, some even younger. When the war was over his mother could not have been prouder of him and the more she referred to him as a hero, the more he protested he was no such thing. He became withdrawn, rarely socialised and seldom left Tilbrook Hall. When I was working there, I often saw him wandering the woods. On one occasion I asked if he would like some company and to my surprise he said yes. He was silent for most of the time until finally he said, 'Don't you ever wonder what it's all for?'

'What in particular?' I asked him.

'Life,' he said morosely. 'Why do we bother with it when we know it's only going to end with death?'

Before I could answer him, he said, 'Mother doesn't understand the first thing about me. She thinks I'm a marvellous hero who acted with admirable courage while serving king and country. But half the time I was terrified out of my wits. I reached the point that when I climbed into the cockpit, I hoped it was my turn to die. I wanted the exhaustion and fear to be over.'

My heart had gone out to him. 'I wish I could say something that would convince you that what you experienced was only natural, but I doubt you'd believe me.'

He said nothing more until we were returning to the house. 'Will you promise not to tell Mother what I said? She needs to live in her own reality.'

I knew how true that was and so I smiled and patted his arm. 'My lips are sealed. But if you ever need to talk to someone, you know where I am.'

The secret he asked me to keep was just another to add to the many I already kept.

Of all the secrets I kept, Nikolai was the one I held closest to my heart. Not surprisingly, I hadn't seen him for the duration of the war. In 1943 he enlisted in the US Navy to serve in a non-combat role in what was known as a Construction Battalion. He hated being classified as too old to fight, but he served in the Pacific theatre and was there when General MacArthur waded ashore on the Philippine island of Leyte in October 1944.

He had planned to come over to Europe last autumn, but a week before he was due to cross the Atlantic, on the pretext of visiting his bank in Switzerland, he collapsed with a burst appendix. Reading between the lines of the letters he'd sent me since then, I could tell that he had yet to make a full recovery.

My old friend Dorothea was still sporadically in touch and last month she had written one of her lengthy letters, full of gossipy tidbits. The primary purpose of her letter was to say that she had married again – she was now onto her third husband and was living in Boston. *What can I say?* she wrote. *I'm either a glutton for punishment, or a hopeless romantic.*

She went on to tell me that she'd been invited to the opening in New York of the Grand Gala on Fifth Avenue, the latest addition to the Gala Imperial chain of hotels.

It was a very grand occasion, the crème de la crème had put on their finest glittery finery and turned out by the barrel-load for the ostentatious occasion. There was as much poor taste on display as there was champagne pouring from the heavens. You wouldn't believe the amount of caviar being passed around, enough to fill every bathtub in the hotel no doubt! Okay, that's a slight exaggeration, but you get my drift; let's just say there was no shortage of gilded razzamatazz or expense spared.

Naturally the man of the moment was Count Nikolai Demidov, who has now taken over the running of the business since his papa died last year. Funny to think that the family came to the good ol' US of A with barely two cents to its aristocratic name (another exaggeration, I know, but it makes for a better story!). Now here is Nikolai as rich as Croesus, just as the Demidovs once were in Russia before the revolution, I guess.

Although to look at Nikolai, you'd think he did only have a couple of cents in the pocket of his immaculate tux. Sure, he smiled for the cameras and when he mixed with the guests, he put on a regular show, but more than once I caught an expression on his face that I could only describe as haunted. When the smile slipped from his handsome face, I saw a man as if weighed down by the worries of the world. He looked haggard. Perhaps even ill. But then who wouldn't be with a wife as neurotic as his?

The rumours are rife about their marriage, that they make each other miserable, that she drinks and is in and out of clinics for her nerves, and that he seeks his pleasure elsewhere. But then who doesn't these days?

My guess is they don't make each other that miserable as if they did, they'd simply do what the rest of us do and seek a divorce. I'd say their marriage is a convenient sham to disguise the fact that Nikolai's taste runs in the direction of his own kind. If you know what I mean. But as I always say, each to his or her own. What harm a little spice or variety?

It was laughable what Dorothea was suggesting, but then she had no idea what Nikolai and I were to each other. All I had ever told her was that we had occasionally encountered one another through mutual friends and that I had found him good company, despite his propensity for aloofness.

But one thing that Dorothea's letter had confirmed was my concern that Nikolai was not being honest with me about the state of his health, and that had me instantly putting pen to paper and asking him outright what was wrong with him.

We might not be man and wife in the eyes of the church or the law, and we might not even spend that much time together, but we could not have felt closer had we spent every minute of every day of every week with one another. I cared for him in a way I had never cared for a man before, or was ever likely to for any other man. Nikolai was a part of my life and I was quite content to go on as we were, physically separated by a vast ocean but mentally bound by something that was fathoms deeper.

Well-intentioned friends were constantly setting me up with some man or other who they thought would make an ideal husband, or at least a man with whom I could have fun. Once in a while I went along with the latter category of man, because the truth was, I wasn't nun-material, nor inclined to live the life of a hermit. And I didn't believe for one minute that a virile man like Nikolai would be living the life of a celibate monk, of course he would be seeking his pleasure where he could. Sex and love were two different things entirely and I could easily separate the two. If that was me creating my own reality, then I could live with it.

We all needed to create our own reality at times, which was what my sister had done in order to survive the death of her son; but it resulted in her wearing a mask of hate behind which she hid her grief. She hated anyone who refused to accept her version of William's death. She hated her husband George for his weakness, for breaking down on the day of the funeral, for openly sobbing and letting the side down. She hated James, her youngest son, for living when his brother did not. She particularly hated me for seeing her precious William dead before she did, as though I had robbed her of that right as a deliberate act of spite, rather than one of kindness. She wielded her arsenal of hatred like a lethal weapon, lunging with it at anyone who displeased her.

We did our best to support her while all the time dodging or absorbing the worst of her bitterness that life could be so unfair. But our support and sympathy only seemed to bring her simmering anger to a roiling boil. Sometimes I thought that was what she needed, to be provoked to the point that she would let go completely and every molten grief-fuelled emotion would gush out of her.

It was now November and six months had passed since William's death and I was once again back at Tilbrook Hall to resume work on the garden.

Prudence had lost all interest in returning the garden to its former glory, but George had taken on the mantle of overseeing the work. Perhaps he needed the distraction. Whatever the reason, and given how grateful I was to him for enabling me to own Larkspur House outright, I was happy to take instructions from him, especially so during this visit when he explained that he wanted me to come up with a new design for an area of the garden which he wanted to be in honour of William. He wanted it to be a memorial, a place where he and Prudence could sit quietly and feel closer to their son. I asked if he had any thoughts himself as to what he might like by way of design.

'No trees,' he said gruffly. 'That's my only stipulation.'

'Leave it with me,' I said, already picturing a circular pond with a fountain at its centre, a gravelled pathway with stone seats and all enclosed by a circular yew hedge to provide shelter and a sense of privacy and retreat. It would have a sense of restrained self-containment. There would be no flowers, nothing to distract the eye or detract from the tranquillity of the space.

Called away by one of the maids because he was needed on the telephone, George hurried off and I pressed on with the task in hand, that of digging in barrow loads of well-rotted manure which the under gardener was ferrying across the lawn to the Rose Avenue where I was planting a dozen wisteria.

Before my arrival, a metal framework providing a structure some thirty feet long had been installed along the Rose Walk and at regular ten feet intervals, I would plant the wisteria. In time the wisteria would grow up the structure and create a tunnel effect, at the end of which was a statue of Diana the Hunter. I supposed that the day might come when the Rose Walk might be renamed to become the Wisteria Walk.

I had the last of the planting done, just as the late afternoon autumnal light was fading, when Bess appeared to let me know that dinner was being served earlier that evening.

Mealtimes had been hard going at Tilbrook ever since William's death, the conversation often non-existent, just the sound of cutlery scraping on crockery and the ticking of the ormolu clock on the mantelpiece. It might have been better if James had been present, but these days he seldom visited. I could understand why: his mother barely had a good word for him; she constantly criticised him as though he were a young boy and not a grown man. Consequently, he kept his distance. He'd been in his brother's shadow when he'd been alive and even more so in death. He simply couldn't compete, so preferred to opt out, to live his life his own way. Who could blame him?

When we'd finished eating and George had escaped to the library to smoke a cigar, Prudence and I withdrew to the drawing room where the curtains had been drawn, the lamps switched on and a fire lit in readiness for us. It would take more than a log fire to take the chill off the atmosphere when alone with my sister, I thought, as the two of us sat down.

Watching Prudence stare grimly into the flickering flames of the fire, I decided to be brave. To venture into a place where I had never dared go before. *Why do so now?* was a good question, but an even better question was *why not?*

'Prudence,' I said, 'do you ever think of Bobby?'

Her head snapped round to look at me. 'No.'

'I don't believe you. How could you not? He was our brother and you loved him just as much as I did.'

'I don't think of him,' she reasserted.

'Why not?' I pressed.

My question caused her to return her gaze to the fire. For some time she sat perfectly immobile and completely silent.

'I think of him often,' I murmured. 'I sometimes wonder what he'd be like now, if somehow he could have found a way to be happy, or . . . at least at peace with himself and his place in the world. Don't you ever wonder that?'

'No,' she said flatly. 'There's no point. He would never have been happy.'

'We could have helped him.'

She turned to look at me. 'How? How could we have helped him to be happy if he wasn't prepared to help himself? What he did was . . . was so unforgivably selfish. He didn't think of anyone he left behind and how his death would affect us. It was the same with our parents. Did they give us a second thought when they went off on yet another plant-hunting expedition? *No!* They thought only of themselves and of discovering some rare plant that they could bring home and show off to all their friends at the Royal Horticultural Society. They cared more about bloody hydrangeas than they ever did about us!'

'I don't think that's true,' I said softly and in stark contrast to the strident vehemence of her accusation. 'In your heart you know they loved us. That's why their death hurts so much. The same with Bobby. Instead of grieving for them properly, you turned your love to hate so the pain wouldn't touch you. Do you ever think of what our parents must have suffered when their ship was torpedoed, the terror they must have gone through knowing they were going to drown in the Atlantic, never to see us again? Don't you think in those last moments they must have regretted setting off on that expedition?'

A flicker of emotion passed across Prudence's face, but she masked it by standing and going over to the fire. She tossed a large log into the grate and with a poker jabbed it viciously into place.

Remaining where she was, poker still in hand, she said, 'What precisely is the point you are trying to make?'

In for a penny, in for a pound, I thought. 'It's time, Prudence, to accept that we're all flawed and that we all make mistakes and misjudgements. More importantly, we are who we are, and not what others want us to be. Bobby was the way he was and killed himself because he wished he wasn't made the way he was. William hanged himself because he was depressed. He simply couldn't live up to the expectations put on him. He needed—'

'*No!*' she screamed. 'No, no, *NO!*' She suddenly raised the poker and brought it down hard onto a side table, sending a lamp flying. She lashed out again with the poker, this time sweeping a large glass vase and a collection of framed photographs from another table. Consumed by a demented rage, she smashed at anything within range, screaming and screaming.

Genuinely terrified, I leapt to my feet and tried to take the poker from her, but she lifted it up and with an even louder shriek, she brought it down on top of my left arm which instinctively I'd raised to protect my head. The shock and searing pain caused me to lose my balance and just as she was about to bring the poker down on me again, the door burst open and in came George, with Bess right behind him.

Chapter Twenty-Three

July 1981
Larkspur House, Suffolk

Dusk was gathering and the warm air, gentled by the whisper of a breeze, was thrumming with activity. Gnats hovered in gauzy clouds, skylarks sang, and woodpigeons cooed, but the trilling of the nightingales from the coppice of trees was what Libby was really listening to. It was a sound to treasure because any day now the birds would be gone, leaving for their long journey to Africa where they would spend the winter. Many had probably already left.

Letting the soothing effect of her surroundings wash over her, Libby lay back and stared up at the sky. She had brought a cardigan with her for when the temperature dropped but lying here in this sheltered spot on the edge of the wheat field where the parched long grass had been warmed by the sun all day, she wasn't in the least bit cold. She stretched out her arms and legs and lay like a starfish, absorbing the heat from the sun-baked earth. It felt good. Better than good. Almost sensual. Like a lover's warm embrace.

Her thoughts stilled abruptly, and she closed her eyes. But her mind would not be stilled completely. How could it, after hearing that Marcus would now be marrying Selina?

Libby had to wonder if she had ever really known Marcus. Or Selina. If this was somebody else's life she would be rolling her eyes at the sheer crassness of a fiancé who could so easily switch brides at the eleventh hour. It took some incredibly brazen behaviour on the part of Marcus and Selina to do what they were doing. Did they hope that whoever now attended their wedding would think that it was all rather wonderfully romantic, that just in time the groom had realised who his true love was?

And what about the honeymoon? Presumably they would make good use of the hotel in Majorca which Libby had spent so long choosing. Why wouldn't they? Maybe Marcus was shameless enough to give Selina the engagement ring he had previously given Libby, and which had once belonged to his grandmother. Selina had certainly admired the sapphire and diamond ring when it had been on Libby's finger after Marcus had proposed to her. Had she been plotting all along to steal Marcus away from her? She would never know the answer and in truth she didn't need to know. It was difficult now to equate the Selina of today with the one that Libby had known before.

They had become instant and firm friends as flatmates while at secretarial college in Oxford, which was where Libby's mother had learnt to be a secretary and had subsequently deemed it perfect for her daughter. Sharing the bills, their clothes and make-up, as well as the ups and downs of their haphazard love-lives, they had been inseparable. They'd been like sisters and like all sisters, they'd occasionally had the odd tiff, usually over something trivial – a borrowed dress stained with red wine, the latest copy of *Cosmopolitan* dropped in the bath, or a newly bought lipstick that had gone astray. Trifling stuff that caused no more than a fleeting disagreement and was easily forgotten.

But the sharing – *stealing* – of a fiancé was a step too far in anyone's book. That could never be forgotten. Or forgiven.

Another jilted bride might rise to the challenge and show up at the wedding to cause a scene by leaping to her feet when the vicar asked if anyone knew of a reason why the marriage shouldn't go ahead, and yelling, '*It should have been me!*' But Libby would never do that, not when her natural inclination wasn't to cause a scene or make a fuss.

Growing up, she'd borne an excess of fuss and anger with Mum who could erupt with the most explosive of rages, but always behind closed doors. Her guiding principle was that there was no greater sin than to air one's dirty linen in public, and that no matter the sense of righteous anger, one had a duty to keep a tight lid on one's emotions for fear of letting the side down.

But far worse than all-out fury was her mother's silent rage, the portentous ticking of a bomb biding its time before going off. Dad used to lie low when Mum was in one of those moods, and when it was impossible to know what had annoyed her this time. If he could, he would slip away to the golf club, leaving Libby to deal with her mother. A natural peacemaker, Libby would try her hardest to coax her mother into a better mood, to deactivate the ticking bomb.

She had never been able to understand why her mother found it so difficult to be content; surely it took more effort to be miserable or angry? Whatever the reason for her mother's inability to enjoy life, it became important to Libby to please her in the hope that would make her happy.

When Dad died, Libby saw it as her responsibility to be the strong one, to be the support her grieving mother needed. It was what was expected of her. That's what Grandma Joan had told her.

'Now then, Libby,' she'd said, the morning of Dad's funeral, 'I want you to promise me something. Your mother is going to need you to be a big girl now. She won't have the strength to cope with you if you make a fuss about your daddy's passing. You're going to have to help her all you can. Do you think you can do that?'

Wanting to please her grandmother, and to prove that, aged twelve, she really was a big girl now, Libby had nodded solemnly. 'I promise I'll be very strong and do all I can to help.'

'Good girl, I knew you wouldn't let me down. Your father would be so proud of you, your grandfather too, God rest his soul.'

So there it was, the trajectory of Libby's life clearly mapped out for her, and being the good girl she was, she followed it to the letter. Which was why she wouldn't show up at the church in the village of Tilbrook on Saturday and cause a fuss. More importantly, she would not give Marcus and Selina, or anyone else for that matter, the satisfaction of seeing her losing her dignity.

Moral high ground.

Self-respect.

Self-preservation.

Stiff upper lip.

These were the things that had been drilled into her from a young age and now, ironically, she could see the value of what she'd been taught. Trying to score a point, or embarrass Marcus and Selina, would only lead to her being utterly humiliated.

She wondered how many guests were now invited to the wedding. No doubt her side of the guest list had been replaced with members of Selina's family. She almost wished that some of her friends would go, just so that they could report back to her.

It was strange, but though she had only been away a couple of weeks, her life in London now seemed alien to her, irrelevant even. As if it had all been for nothing. She had no desire to go back there, although she knew she would have to. It would be irresponsible of her to leave her flat empty for too long. She hoped that Selina, who had shared it with her, had by now removed her belongings from it.

Earlier that afternoon, when they'd been watching the Royal Wedding and Elfrida had come off the phone and rejoined them in the drawing room, both Bess and Libby had asked who she'd been talking to.

'I'll tell you later,' she'd said, helping herself to the bottle of champagne in the wine cooler and filling her glass. She'd downed the champagne in seconds flat, which should have warned Libby that something was wrong, but she'd let it go and returned her attention to the television screen.

It was later, after the happy couple had kissed on the balcony of Buckingham Palace and the crowd had roared with delight, that Elfrida had explained that it had been her sister, Prudence, who had telephoned. She had then explained why.

Picturing Marcus's grandmother in her Mayfair home dialling the number for Larkspur House, Libby wondered what the frail old woman really thought about Marcus's behaviour. No doubt she could justify it: he was, after all, her only grandson.

'What are you staring at, Marcus?' she had demanded of him the first time he'd taken Libby to meet her, only a few weeks into their relationship and when they still knew very little about each other. 'You're standing there gaping at me like a goldfish.'

Laughing, he'd kissed her cheek. 'I was just trying to work out if it was you or Elizabeth Taylor we'd come to have tea with!' he'd said.

'Oh, don't be so ridiculous,' she'd chortled, her gaunt and wrinkled face blushing with unabashed pleasure. It had been a ridiculous compliment to give because the object of Marcus's charm could not have looked less like the glamorous film star. Prudence was painfully thin, and her make-up only served to emphasise her hollowed-out cheeks and papery skin. She possessed none of Elfrida's naturally glowing good health.

It was only during the drive to visit Marcus's grandmother that Libby had made the connection that the woman she was about to meet was none other than Elfrida's sister, Prudence. Marcus had been equally surprised at the revelation, but to Libby it had seemed one of those extraordinary coincidences that added weight to the rightness of their relationship, as if they were destined to meet. Maybe destined to be together.

She had always been aware of the estrangement between Elfrida and Prudence, that something had happened between them years ago, but much like the rift between Libby's mother and Bess, she had simply accepted the situation. All families had their disagreements and skeletons they kept hidden in their cupboards; why should Marcus's be any different?

'All in the past and best to let sleeping dogs lie,' Bess had once said to Libby when she had asked why Elfrida and Prudence rarely spoke.

'Well, come along then,' Prudence had said to Libby after Marcus had introduced her and explained the extraordinary coincidence. 'Don't be shy, let me have a good look at Bess Judd's great-niece.'

Libby had stepped forward for inspection, reminded of being back at school when matron was checking to make sure the girls in her care had brushed their teeth and cleaned behind their ears to her satisfaction.

The hooded eyes had swept over her, and the scrutiny completed, she all but dismissed Libby, fixing her attention exclusively on her grandson, beckoning him to sit next to her on the sofa. It was as though Libby was no longer in the room. To his credit Marcus did his best to include her in the conversation, but really all Prudence wanted was his undivided attention. She lapped up his every word, especially when he complimented her on how well she was looking and was that a new dress she was wearing? It might have been then, because of the way he treated his grandmother so affectionately and with such reverence, that Libby had thought herself to be falling in love with him. Was there anything more endearing than a wildly attractive man going out of his way to make an elderly woman feel special?

After meeting Prudence, Libby made a visit to Larkspur House to tell Bess and Elfrida about Marcus and to whom he was related. Once they'd recovered from the surprise, they had expressed what she took to be a guarded response.

'So long as he treats you right and makes you happy,' Bess had said, 'that's all I'd ask of any boyfriend for you.'

Elfrida had remarked more ambiguously that life was full of coincidences, both good and bad.

The funny thing was that when Libby took Marcus with her on a subsequent visit, he didn't try charming Elfrida and Bess in the same way he'd charmed Prudence. If anything, he seemed wary of them both. But then, as he later explained, he'd been brought up to believe that Elfrida had done something unforgivably bad to his grandmother, which had resulted in them not being on speaking terms.

Most of his childhood had been spent at boarding school or at Tilbrook Hall during the holidays with Prudence and her husband. His father had worked for the diplomatic service and his job had taken him all over the world until he retired to run Tilbrook Hall as a country house hotel with his wife. Apparently, Prudence never forgave him for doing that. She saw it as a betrayal, a dishonouring of the family name.

It had been some time before Marcus introduced Libby to his parents up in Norfolk, as though as matriarch of the family it was only Prudence for whom Libby had to pass muster.

The old woman was certainly a force to be reckoned with and had very definite ideas on what constituted a proper marriage. Ideas which, once Marcus and Libby announced their engagement, she was only too keen to make known.

'A successful man needs the support of a loving and efficiently practical wife behind him,' she told Libby. 'I hope you understand how important your role is going to be if Marcus is to advance in his career in the City. He'll need to know he can count on you at all times.'

Not a word did she say about Libby being able to count on Marcus. It was always possible that she had known all along that he couldn't be relied upon. Maybe Selina would discover that too.

Nothing on earth would entice Libby to show up unexpectedly at the church on Saturday to cause a scene, but she'd be lying if she said she wasn't curious to observe Prudence's reaction to Selina saying the words 'I do.'

I do promise to lie and cheat.

I do promise to be the worst of friends.

I do promise to take what's not mine to take.

It was because of the longstanding estrangement between Prudence and Elfrida that Libby had reluctantly accepted that the two people she most wanted at her wedding would not be there. She had hoped that her marriage to Marcus might lead to a reconciliation between the two women, but Elfrida had claimed that it would be better if she stayed away, that Prudence would prefer it that way. Perhaps out of loyalty to Elfrida, Bess had then said she would stay away too. Libby had wheedled for all she was worth to try and make them change their minds, but they wouldn't budge. 'Weddings are for the young,' Bess said. 'You don't want a couple of old things like us there.'

'But Prudence will be there, and she's older than you both.'

'Well, she's Marcus's grandmother and rules the roost when it comes to that family,' Bess said. 'Now let's have no more talk about it. Just be sure to save us some wedding cake and we'll enjoy looking at your photographs when they're available.'

Opening her eyes and realising that it was almost dark, and the temperature had now dropped, Libby sat up and pulled on her cardigan. Bats were circling overhead and, in the distance, drifting across the fields, she could hear music. The party celebrating the Royal Wedding on the village green was obviously in full swing.

She ought to go back up to the house before darkness was complete, but she wasn't ready yet to face Bess and Elfrida's unspoken sympathy over the latest news that Prudence had shared with them.

'Do you suppose I should go and look for her?' Bess suggested. 'Maybe keep her company?'

Standing on the terrace and peering into the dwindling light, Bess was anxious. On the face of it, Libby had taken the news well about Marcus marrying Selina, and her wanting to spend time alone was perfectly understandable, but Bess would rather have the girl close by where she could watch over her.

At her side, whisky tumbler in hand, Elfrida tutted. 'If you think for one minute that I'm going to let you go stumbling about the garden in the dark, I have news for you!'

'I'm quite capable of finding my way around with the aid of a torch,' said Bess. Goodness, she was tired of all this mollycoddling and being told what she could and could not do!

'I'm sure you are, but why don't you stop fretting about Libby and come inside?' Elfrida said. 'There's something I want to show you.'

'What is it?'

Elfrida drained her glass. 'Come in and I'll show you.'

Reluctantly leaving her post waiting for Libby to come back from wherever she'd gone, Bess followed Elfrida inside to the drawing room where, laid out on a side table and illuminated by the soft light from a lamp, was a black and white photograph. Elfrida picked it up and passed it to her.

It was the last photograph ever to be taken of Amos, and seeing it after all this time caused Bess's heart to swell with loving pride for the selfless and courageous man her husband had been.

Chapter Twenty-Four

March 1947
Larkspur House, Suffolk
Bess

Four months had passed since our catastrophic visit to Tilbrook Hall in Norfolk when Prudence had gone berserk and attacked Elfrida with a poker. Elfrida had tried to play down how badly hurt she was, but because she allowed me to drive us home, something she rarely did despite having taught me to drive many years ago, I knew that she must have been in considerable pain. Without a thought for her sister's welfare, Prudence had given instructions that we were to leave that very night and that we were not welcome to return ever again. Privately I was glad as I never looked forward to our visits, not when they were such a disturbing reminder of what that monster Michael O'Halligan had done to me there.

It was not until we were back at Larkspur House, a little after midnight, and I had ignored Elfrida's insistence that I should go straight home to Amos, that she reluctantly allowed me to check her over, just to put my mind at rest that Prudence hadn't caused her any real harm. The vivid welt that the poker had made on her arm as she'd tried to defend herself made me wince and I knew that come the morning it would look even worse. Very gently I ran my hands over her arm to make sure there were no broken bones, but what were clearly broken, and caused by Prudence before George could prise the poker away from her, were two fingers on Elfrida's right hand. I strapped them up, just as I'd been taught in the first-aid lessons I'd attended during the war, but I advised her to see a doctor in the morning. Of course, she refused to do any such thing.

When I went home and told Amos what had happened, that Elfrida had tried to encourage Prudence to confront her grief, not just for William, but for their parents and beloved brother, he had shaken his head. 'Elfrida should have left well alone.'

'She was trying to help her sister understand the harm she is causing herself by not grieving properly.'

'But who's to say what's the proper way? I still say Elfrida should have left her sister be. Some things just shouldn't be said.'

For the sake of accord I left it at that. After all, throughout our marriage I'd kept many things unsaid in an attempt to protect myself. And my husband's love for me.

I was thinking about concealment that March morning, as I shivered with cold and stared through the iced-up kitchen window at our back garden that was hidden beneath a deep blanket of snow. At breakfast Amos had quipped that the snow was so deep we could hide a body out there and nobody would know. Not until there was a thaw. It was a comment that sent a chill running through me.

Ever since the middle of January the country had been at the mercy of the weather. For the last six weeks easterly winds had brought drifting snow and Arctic temperatures. There were reports of villages cut off and the RAF having to drop food supplies for people as well as animals. Trains and lorries struggled to transport the necessary coal to the power stations and some days we were without electricity. Even though the war was over, strict rationing was still in place and the morale of the nation was once again at a low. Amos and I had run out of logs for the fire and with no coal available, and after an evening of listening to our Bakelite wireless, we went to bed most nights in our overcoats, our hats and gloves too.

It was worse for Elfrida. Bedecked with icicles hanging from the roof and the guttering, Larkspur House resembled a frozen mausoleum and with her being all alone and fending for herself, I worried that she might literally die from the glacial cold. At least I had Amos to cling to for warmth when we were in bed. When the weather permitted, and no matter that Elfrida had told what remained of the household staff, including me, that we were not to put ourselves at risk, I trekked through the snow to go and see her. Sometimes Amos came with me, just for something to do, and because he worried that I might end up buried in a fresh fall of snow. He was completely at a loose end with no gardening work, so he welcomed the distraction. He and a few other men from the village tried to keep the roads and pavements clear of snow, but it was no more than a futile attempt to hold back the relentless tide.

Today we planned to go into the village in the hope that there might be some food available to buy. By rights we should have gone first thing that morning, but Amos had gone next door to our elderly neighbours, Edie and Walter, to chop up some old furniture for them. They too had run out of coal and logs and so had decided they might just as well burn an old bookcase and a table rather than freeze to death. I wondered if we might also be forced to do the same thing. Thinking of all the furniture at Larkspur House, maybe I should suggest to Elfrida that Amos take an axe to anything that wasn't precious to her.

It really didn't seem possible that this was how we now lived. When I thought of all the grand houses I'd stayed in with Elfrida, of the times we'd spent on the Riviera and Lake Como, and the hardship we'd faced and overcome during the war, was this how it would end for us: frozen to death in our own homes?

By the time we made it to the shops, there were very few people about, and very little on the shelves to buy. We made do with what we could – a tin of pilchards, three ounces of bacon and two ounces of sugar and two ounces of tea – and then promptly bumped into Elfrida. We hardly recognised each other, covered as we were from head to toe in our many layers of outer clothing. Elfrida was wearing a badly knitted balaclava and much to my surprise, she was holding a camera in her gloved hands, its strap hooked around her neck.

'I thought it was high time I took some photographs to record this extraordinary weather,' she said. 'I've just been taking some pictures of the children playing with a sledge on the iced-over pond. Why don't the pair of you strike a pose for me?'

Amos wasn't keen, but Elfrida was in no mood for taking no for an answer. 'For the love of God, Amos Judd,' she snapped at him, 'will you stop frowning and put your arm around Bess!'

'Just the one,' he muttered grumpily when Elfrida finally looked up from the Box Brownie and turned the handle ready to take another picture. He was about to take my arm and move us on when we heard a cry – the startled cry of a child.

Where there had been four children playing on the pond, there were now only three.

In a flash we surged forwards, the compacted snow crunching beneath our feet. I'd only taken a few steps when I stumbled and abandoning my shopping basket, I scrambled to my feet and pressed on. Amos was well ahead of me with Elfrida just a few paces behind him. I heard him call out to the three children who were in the middle of the pond and where, just a few yards from them, there was now a hole with the sledge half sticking out,

'Don't move until I tell you to,' Amos shouted in a loud commanding voice.

The children turned to look at him and I saw the fear in their faces.

'You must listen to me very carefully,' he instructed, his voice again full of authority and with not a trace of panic to it. Frighten the children any more than they already were, and I knew it could prove fatal. 'I want you to get down on the ice as slowly and as low as you can. That's it,' he encouraged them, 'on your hands and knees. Now start crawling towards us. Slowly! No sudden movements. That's it, keep going, you're doing well.'

As Elfrida and I waited for the terrified children to reach the edge of the pond, Amos skirted further round it and, throwing off his cumbersome overcoat, he stepped onto the surface of the ice. Doing the same as the children, he carefully lowered himself to his hands and knees and started crawling towards the hole in search of their missing friend.

With my heart in my mouth, I watched him inch as close as he dared so he could pull out the sledge and peer down into the black water. It was as he leant forwards that there was a horrifying cracking sound, and just as the last of the three children had made it to safety, the ice gave way beneath Amos. I let out a scream and hardly thinking what I was doing, I stepped onto the ice, but Elfrida yanked on my arm and pulled me back. I fought her off, yelling that I had to help Amos, but she held me firmly. She wasn't the only one stopping me. Donald and Bridget who ran the post office were there now, as were Geoffrey and his assistant Lennie from the grocer's shop. All of them were preventing me from doing what I had to do; I had to save my husband!

For what felt an eternity, we stood in agonising silence waiting for Amos's head to emerge through the cracked surface of the ice. But it didn't.

*

Amos's body, along with that of Billy Owens, the ten-year-old boy he'd tried to rescue, wasn't found until a week later when the weather finally thawed, and the ice melted.

His funeral took place in a heavy downpour of rain and gusting winds. Everyone from the village came to pay their respects. To my surprise, even my sister came with her husband, and Nancy as well. The girl was dressed in a chocolate brown single-breasted coat with a small net-trimmed beret and appeared much older than her twenty years with her scarlet lipstick and eyelashes thickly layered with mascara.

With Elfrida by my side, I'd never known pain like it as I sat in the front pew of the church with Amos's coffin a scant few feet away from me. All I could think was that I should have been a better wife. A wife who should have been more honest with her husband. A wife who should have been able to save him.

When the service was over and the mourners were gathered in the village hall and I was wishing I could escape to be on my own, I overheard my sister talking to the parents of Billy Owen. What she said filled me with rage and my face flaming and bile rising to my throat, I grabbed her roughly by the arm and propelled her towards the cloakroom area. Confident we were alone, I launched myself at her.

'How dare you tell those grieving parents that it was a shame Amos hadn't acted faster to save their son!' For good measure, I slapped her face hard.

She reeled back from me, but instead of the contrite expression I expected, she stared at me with cool defiance. 'I only said what everyone else must be thinking.'

'He died trying to save their son!' I cried. 'Do you think for one moment that pathetic husband of yours would have done any better? He didn't even fight for his country!'

'His poor eyesight meant he couldn't sign up, as well you know,' she retaliated. 'He did his bit by staying home and making a success of his business so there would be jobs for soldiers when they came home.'

The bile in my throat had reached my mouth now and it was venomous with hatred for my sister who had abused our relationship. I had given her the one thing she had so badly wanted – a child – and in return she had poisoned the love that had once existed between us.

God forgive me, but I now understood why Prudence had attacked Elfrida: the poor woman had been pushed too far. Just as now I was. My anger fuelled by grief, I was suddenly consumed with the need to puncture Joan's self-satisfaction and the perfection of her world where nothing ever went wrong for her. There she stood with her perfectly coiffured hair and perfectly manicured nails and her ludicrously ostentatious full-length mink coat and small turban-style hat decorated with black ribbon flowers which looked quite out of place at a village funeral, and I couldn't stop myself from doing the one thing I had promised myself I would never do and which I knew would shatter her perfect world. I did it because it was the cruellest thing I could do to her, to pay her back for criticising Amos, and for the hundreds of petty slights she had inflicted on me all these years, and which I had tried so very hard not to resent. For denying me time with Nancy, for begrudging me a few photos of her, and for not allowing me to play a bigger part in her life.

So I told Joan the truth, that I had been raped by a lowly footman and Nancy was the result of his violation of me. It was almost as though I wanted to make her hate the daughter of whom she was so proud, so I could claim her as my own and love her as I'd always wanted to.

But, of course, it was much too late for that.

Chapter Twenty-Five

July 1981
Larkspur House, Suffolk

'Sorry, but I won't be in today, I . . . I must have caught some kind of a tummy bug yesterday.'

'Is that so?' responded Elfrida in a deliberately loud voice, knowing that the woman was no more suffering from a stomach bug than she was. Tina had a hangover, pure and simple, and that was why she wasn't coming in to clean today.

Her voice louder still, Elfrida barked down the line, 'I hope you'll be feeling much better very soon. Goodbye!'

Perhaps it was wrong of her to enjoy the thought that she was adding to Tina's woes by raising her voice, but there again, if the woman fancied a day off because she had over-indulged at the village beano on the green last night, then Elfrida had no sympathy for her. People today had no backbone. When she thought of all the many hangovers and ailments she had worked through, she had no patience with lightweights. She would be the last person to deprive anyone of a high old time, but if there was a job to be done, then duty should come first.

Replacing the telephone receiver, Elfrida was shocked at how like her sister she suddenly sounded. Her sweeping condemnation was uncomfortably reminiscent of Prudence decrying the young while on the phone yesterday – *for them it's self, self, self* – and the

242

realisation did not sit well with her. She gave herself a mental rapping of the knuckles.

But when one really got down to it, didn't everyone put themselves first, even if they dressed it up with a veneer of altruism? It wasn't just a sense of duty and a strong work ethic that had driven Elfrida to work so hard for her many clients in the past, but the desire to earn enough money to keep her home, and equally important, to retain Bess as her companion, her very constant companion.

Bess and Larkspur House were the two constants in her life that had combined to be the most powerful of driving forces. God bless her, when times had been tough financially, Bess had foregone her wages. Somehow, they had muddled through those bleak weeks and months when money was in such short supply, and then just as soon as things picked up, Elfrida always rewarded Bess. Which was only right. Would anyone else have stood by Elfrida in the way Bess had, or put up with her? She doubted it.

Still standing in the hallway in front of the telephone table, she looked around her at the threadbare rug on the wooden floor, at the oak panelling to the walls, the stonework to the fireplace that hadn't been used in many a year, the arched oak front door with the deep-set stone mullioned windows either side of it, the exposed oak beams in the ceiling and the oak staircase that led up to the spacious galleried landing.

In her mind's eye, she pictured the ghosts of all those she had loved and lost standing on the galleried landing looking down on her – her parents, her dearest brother Bobby, Mallory, Dorothea, Ivan and, of course, Nikolai. What times they'd had!

Could her sister Prudence say the same? she mused. Probably not. Much like Nancy, she was one of those people who just couldn't allow herself to appreciate what she had. Forgiveness was as alien to her as was an open mind and that had been why for more than twenty years, she had refused to speak to Elfrida. It was only after her husband, George, had died, that she relented sufficiently to accept and thank Elfrida for her condolences. Even so, it was not a sudden opening of the floodgates that would lead to a reconciliation. That was still a long way off. If indeed it would ever happen.

Shaking herself out of her meandering thoughts, Elfrida wondered how Bess and Libby were getting on upstairs. During breakfast Libby had suggested she and Bess sort out the linen room together.

'Oh, so I'm finally allowed to do something, am I?' Bess had muttered.

'You're helping in an advisory capacity only,' said Libby.

As for Elfrida, she had work to do in the garden. The roses and sweet peas needed deadheading, the clematis feeding, the tomatoes and cucumbers in the glasshouse needed a good watering and a feed, and then there were the strawberries to be picked and there was no end of weeding to do. Hopefully Andrew would be here later to mow the lawns.

Steve was also due later to put the finishing touches to the repaired attic floor and he'd said he'd then sort out the brickwork path where Elfrida had missed her footing. She could have asked Andrew to do the job for her, but that would take him away from helping her with the garden.

Elfrida had promoted Steve from 'mere builder' to 'quite a find'. He was meticulously tidy and extremely reliable and more importantly, knew exactly what he was doing and didn't charge over the odds. Which was more than could be said for some of the builders who had rolled up here in the past in the hope that they could fleece Elfrida.

They had Daniel to thank for Steve and she rather hoped they might see more of the young doctor. Not in an official capacity, but more as a friend for Libby while she was here. At a time like this, when the girl's world had been turned upside down, friends that could be relied upon were invaluable. And who knew, if given time, where that friendship might lead them?

That was the thing about relationships, one never knew where they would lead, or where they would end up. Or indeed what part a good friend would play in one's life. Elfrida's old friend, Dorothea, had been one of those who had been on the periphery of her life, but had at various times played a central role.

Once more, the ghosts of all those Elfrida had loved and lost appeared before her, in particular Nikolai, and with a rare wave of nostalgic longing, she succumbed to mourning for what might have been if—

If what?

If they'd never met?

If he hadn't been married?

If Elfrida hadn't had such a wretchedly guilty conscience and forbade him from divorcing his wife for fear of what the woman might do?

Ironically, Nikolai's wife – *his so-called fragile wife* – had outlived him by many years. She had even remarried, as reported to Elfrida by Dorothea, and that news had certainly rubbed salt into the painful wound of her grief.

Chapter Twenty-Six

September 1952
New York and Boston
Elfrida

In the last ten years, and since setting up home in Boston, my old friend Dorothea had discovered the joy of gardening and was heavily involved in her local garden club which was part of the Garden Club of America. When she had first proposed the idea that I should give a series of talks to the GCA, my initial reaction was to decline the offer, and swiftly so. I had never given a lecture before and saw no reason to start now.

But then I thought of Nikolai and that if I accepted the invitation, it might provide the means for us to see each other again. We'd managed to snatch some time together only a few months previously when he'd been in London trying to seal the deal on a new hotel to add to his extensive portfolio. His visit coincided with the death of King George VI and the subsequent news that Princess Elizabeth was to be queen. Disappointingly the deal fell through, but Nikolai shrugged off the setback, saying it just meant he would have to make a return trip which would give him the opportunity of seeing me again.

In haste, and before responding to Dorothea's letter and invitation to speak to the GCA, I wrote to Nikolai. A telegram duly arrived from Nikolai with the words, *Dearest Elfrida, come as soon as you can, I shall be waiting for you!*

So the trip was decided upon and all was soon arranged, giving me three months to prepare what I would speak about. Knowing that Norah Lindsay had made the same trip and delivered a series of well-received talks to the GCA, I felt I had to do my absolute best, if only to honour the hallowed footsteps in which I was following. The news of Norah's death in the summer of 1948 hit me hard. I'd heard rumours that she was unwell, but I'd had no idea how ill she must have been. I had been far from an intimate of hers, but from childhood I had regarded her as my heroine and mentor; I had learnt so much from her. She had also been a connection to my parents and her death meant that another tie to the past had been cut.

Naturally Bess was to accompany me to the States. Since Amos's death she had moved back in with me at Larkspur House and we could almost convince ourselves that it was just like old times for us. It wasn't, of course; we both missed Amos terribly.

Obviously, Bess missed her husband in a very different way than I did, but I missed his terseness and no-nonsense approach to some of my more ambitious projects. He had been an undemonstrative, quietly spoken man who, even now, five years after his tragic death, I still expected to see in my garden. The place didn't seem the same without him. I missed his expertise and especially his passion when it came to growing sweet peas. Every summer he would produce the most exquisitely fragrant blooms on perfectly straight stems. Often when he'd finished work for the day, I would find him in the kitchen garden fussing over the canes of sweet peas, deadheading and picking the best flowers for Bess to put in vases to be dotted around the house. I would always associate sweet peas with Amos. As I would always associate French tarragon with Nikolai. The herb's fragrance never failed to remind me of that first evening we'd spent together on the Riviera at his cousin's villa.

For the duration of my trip to America, Dorothea had invited me to stay with her at her home in Chestnut Hill, an area to the west of Boston, but I had politely turned down the invitation on the basis that I was a shocking houseguest and didn't want to put her to any trouble. The truth was, Nikolai had arranged for Bess and me to stay at the Gala Imperial in the centre of town. We were to be his guests and there would be no question of us paying for our suites.

I'd had a profitable couple of years and so I pulled out all the stops so we could travel first class across the Atlantic on board the *Queen Elizabeth* which had undergone a refit after being used as a troopship during the war.

'If we're going to die as we sail across the Atlantic to New York, we might as well do it in style,' I'd joked with Bess. Which had made her scold me for my flippancy. It was a defence mechanism, my way of not thinking about my parents who had died while on board the *Lusitania*.

My excitement at seeing Nikolai again had grown exponentially with each day of the crossing and so when we docked in Manhattan, I barely gave the extraordinary skyscrapers and Statue of Liberty a second glance: I was too busy peering into the distance to catch a glimpse of Nikolai.

When I did set eyes on him, I was shocked by the change in him. Admittedly we were both in our fifties now – I was fifty-one and Nikolai was fifty-four – but, compared to the last time I'd seen him in London, there was a gauntness to his face, and he had lost weight. His lustrous hair had long since been flecked with silver, but now the threads of silver outnumbered the black. There were deep lines etched around his mouth and at the corners of his eyes. Oh, those beautiful eyes, so dark and mysteriously mesmerising! Yet as much as he had altered, he was still Nikolai – still *my* Nikolai – and he was no less attractive.

He drove us straight to the Gala Imperial where he personally checked us in as his VIP guests, then for the sake of appearances, left us to be shown to our suites so we could freshen up and settle in for our overnight stay before journeying on to Boston. Within the hour he was tapping lightly on the door of my luxurious suite and taking me in his arms.

It was extraordinary how easily we slipped into the rapturous rhythm of how we had always made love, as if we'd never been apart. How could that be? What was it about our love that had survived the years and distance between us?

Afterwards, as we took a bath together and were drinking champagne, I asked him to be honest with me about the state of his health.

'I'm fine,' he said, 'why do you ask?'

'Tell me the truth,' I said, ignoring his question.

'It's nothing much. I have a stomach ulcer for which I'm having treatment.'

That explained the weight loss, I thought. 'Anything else?'

'My blood pressure's a little high, but then I blame that on the thought of seeing you again. God knows what the sight of you in this bath is doing to it right now.' He grinned wolfishly and leant forwards and untied my hair so that it fell to my shoulders and into the water. I dropped down beneath the surface of the water and emerged as though reborn to see him smiling even more.

'You look just like the mermaid I fell in love with on the Riviera.'

'A mermaid who is thirty years older!'

'Not a day older in my eyes.'

'Then your eyesight needs checking,' I said.

'I like it just the way it is.'

I sensed he was relieved to move on from the subject of his health and such was my delight at seeing him again, I let it go. What precious time we were able to spend together during my lecture tour, I didn't want to waste on nagging him. Nor did I want to raise the subject of what happened the last time we were in

Italy together. But I longed to do so, to clear from my mind the worry that gnawed at me that the memory of what happened wasn't a contributing factor to his poor state of health. He was a man of conscience after all.

When I did finally refer to it, a few days later in Boston when once again we were in bed together, he silenced me with a kiss. 'We swore we'd never torture ourselves with talking about that,' he said sternly. 'It's in the past and can never be undone. You have to let it go.'

But what neither of us could let go of entirely, was the baby we had lost. Nikolai in particular often referred to the child we had created, musing on what he or she would have been like and the age they would now be had things not gone so disastrously wrong. Every year he would mark the anniversary of our loss with a special letter and a bouquet of flowers sent to Larkspur House. Our son or daughter would have been thirteen this summer.

To my amazement the series of talks I gave was so well received that the good ladies of each club I spoke to impressed upon me that not only should I return, but they all now wanted to visit my garden, as well as the many I'd helped create.

All in all, the trip was a resounding success. For having secured my services as a speaker, Dorothea was consequently held in greater esteem amongst her peers, which she found highly amusing. Bess had thoroughly enjoyed herself sightseeing with Ivan – the dear man had taken time off from running the restaurant in New York which he now owned – and I had managed to spend some precious time with Nikolai. And all the while maintaining the secrecy of our relationship.

Or so I thought.

It was after my last talk and when Dorothea took me home with her to see her garden, which was richly aglow with autumnal colour, that we sat down to enjoy our first cocktail of the day and she took me completely by surprise by announcing that she knew my guilty secret.

'What secret?' I replied nonchalantly. *Which secret* was what I really wanted to say, but surely Dorothea couldn't know the worst secret, the one Nikolai had said we were never to torture ourselves with? I looked at her closely, trying to read her face for some giveaway sign, but all I saw was my old friend smiling back at me with her customary effervescent charm. She had grown pleasantly plump with the passing of years and possessed a beautiful complexion that put mine to shame. The outfit she was wearing was impeccably cut to suit her perfectly and around her neck was a double strand of pearls.

'No need to be coy with me, Elfrida,' she said. 'I'm talking about you and Nikolai. Oh, don't look like that, I've suspected for ages that there was *something* going on between the two of you. You staying at Nikolai's hotel in Boston rather than with me told me all I needed to know.'

I tried to intervene, to say it was all nonsense, but there was no stopping her.

'It was Nikolai who really gave the game away,' she continued, 'when I ran into him last month while visiting New York. There was just a look, a *spark*, in his eye when I told him that you were doing me a huge favour by coming to speak to the members of the Garden Club of America. He asked if the talks were open to anyone, and I teased him that perhaps he was thinking of getting into the garden business now. To which he said, "Ah, if only I had the time." I then offered to send him the itinerary for your speaking engagements and he said that he'd try to surprise you by showing up unexpectedly.' She took a sip of her Manhattan and smiled. 'Of course, I knew very well that none of this was news to him and that he'd be seeing you in secret anyway.'

'Goodness,' I said, 'what a lot of thought you've given this.'

'I'm right, though, aren't I?'

'What makes you so certain that you are?'

'That *spark* in Nikolai's eye and his studied insouciance just didn't add up. Plus, I'd had my suspicions back when I attended the opening night of his hotel in New York.'

'But you said in your letter when you wrote about that night that you thought he might be more interested in men than women.'

'Oh, that was a ruse, to see if you would rise to the bait and defend Nikolai's honour. The very fact that you ignored my comment in your reply made me suspect you even more.'

I saw no reason to keep up the pretence any longer and confessed all, if only to be sure Dorothea hadn't voiced her theory to anybody else.

'Good God, of course I haven't!' she exclaimed. 'Why on earth would you think I would?'

Because, my dear Dorothea, you are an inveterate gossip.'

She smiled. 'You do me a great injustice. But in this instance, I am not guilty of the crime of discussing you with anybody else.'

Relieved, I took a sip of my drink.

'But why on earth haven't you and Nikolai dispensed with the secrecy and married?' Dorothea then asked.

'Because of his wife. Every time he tries to convince her that staying together only makes them both miserable, she threatens to kill herself.'

'A pity she didn't carry out the threat years ago and have done with it,' Dorothea muttered.

'I never wanted Nikolai to have that on his conscience, or on my own for that matter. There's also my very strong belief, being as pragmatic as I am, that I don't think we would ever be truly compatible as man and wife. I would never want to leave Larkspur House; it's been my *raison d'être* my whole life. Everything I've done has been to keep it as my home.'

'That's a hell of a price to pay,' Dorothea said. 'Giving your heart and soul to a house and garden.'

'But it *is* my heart and soul, that's the point. I would be utterly miserable if I had to give it up.'

'Are you telling me that what you've had with Nikolai, just occasional crumbs of each other, has been enough?' Dorothea's expression was incredulous.

I smiled. 'This way Nikolai sees only the best of me. For starters he doesn't see how hideously selfish I am. As for the rest of my faults, just ask Bess. She probably knows me better than anyone. I'm demanding and stubborn and forever wanting my own way. I'm a nightmare to live with.'

Dorothea frowned. 'I take issue with you about you being self-ish. I'd say you were the opposite. If you were selfish, you'd have made Nikolai divorce his wife no matter what and then made him live in England with you. Instead, you've been principled and self-sacrificing.'

I laughed and downed the rest of my cocktail. 'I don't think having an affair with a married man can be classed as principled.'

'Oh, don't be so pious, you're making me feel quite bilious.'

We both laughed, and leaving the comfort of our chairs, we took another turn around the garden to better enjoy the sight of the Japanese maples in all their autumnal glory.

It was when I was taking my leave to return to the hotel in town to meet up with Bess, that I swore Dorothea to continued secrecy about Nikolai and me.

She tutted. 'I've already told you that I haven't and won't breathe a word of it to anyone.'

The next day, and now back in New York, Bess and I were driven to the pier where the *Queen Elizabeth* was docked. Nikolai and Ivan had already gone ahead and were waiting on board along with many others seeing off friends and family. Everywhere we looked there was some kind of noisy *bon voyage* party going on in the cabins and spilling out onto the corridors.

When Bess and I had pushed our way through the crowds on deck, I found my stateroom was adorned with so many flowers it resembled a florist's shop. The scent of so many roses, carnations, lilies and freesias in the confined space made me feel quite lightheaded.

The flowers were, of course, a gift from Nikolai, who appeared perfectly at home, his jacket off and his tie loosened, and looking for all the world like he was about to travel across the Atlantic with me. For a moment I wondered how I would react if he said that was exactly what he was doing, that he was leaving his wife to be with me in England.

Assailed by myriad emotions I watched him ease the cork out of a bottle of champagne, while at his side Ivan unwrapped a tray of blinis and caviar which he'd made specially for us.

'If a thing is worth doing, it's worth doing well,' Nikolai said, handing me a glass and then one to Bess.

For all our efforts to enjoy the moment of farewell that so many others were doing, there was a hollow ring to our little gathering. After we'd drunk our fill and eaten as much of the blinis as we could force down, and as discreet as he always was, Ivan suggested he accompany Bess to her stateroom next door.

Alone, Nikolai took me in his arms. 'You have no idea what your visit has meant to me,' he said. 'Will you come again?'

'If Dorothea and the good ladies of the Garden Club of America have their way, I might well do.'

'But not of your own accord?'

'What a ridiculous question,' I said, kissing him gently on his cheek. 'But a good cover story is no bad thing.'

'Then there's nothing else for it, I shall definitely have to acquire a hotel in London, or the right piece of land on which to build one. I'm determined to do it.'

'Maybe it's just not to be,' I murmured.

'Don't say that.'

We clung to each other until the ship's horn sounded, warning all those who weren't travelling to disembark. His tie now precisely knotted and his jacket back on, Nikolai kissed me one more time and went to find Ivan.

Outside on deck, and crammed against the rail, as the ship's engines thudded beneath us and we began to move, Bess and I waved to Nikolai and Ivan down on the pier.

I don't think I'd ever experienced a sadder farewell and I was consumed with the desire to launch myself over the side of the ship to be with Nikolai.

As though sensing the urge, Bess placed a hand on mine as it gripped the rail. She said nothing; she didn't need to.

Chapter Twenty-Seven

July 1981
Larkspur House, Suffolk

'There now,' said Libby, 'I call that a job well done, don't you?'

Bess surveyed the orderly shelves of bed sheets, pillowcases, towels and blankets and reluctantly had to agree that it did indeed look a lot better than it had earlier that morning. Not that she'd had that much to do with sorting out the linen room, Libby had seen to that by insisting she do nothing more than sit on a chair and say what should stay and what should go. It was, she had to admit, one of those tasks she had been meaning to do for a long time but had never got around to. There was always something else to do, something more pressing, or simply more enjoyable. But then the trouble with leaving things was that before too long, what was originally just a small task became an unsurmountable challenge. When that happened, it was easier to close the door on the problem and pretend it no longer existed.

Having witnessed Libby's fervent attack on the linen that had seen better days, Bess wondered if it was the girl's mission to work her way through the entire house in order to rid herself of Marcus's duplicity and downright cruelty. Heaven only knew it was exactly the type of thing Bess and Elfrida had done over the years to keep themselves from dwelling on their loss and heartache.

'A day's honest graft never killed anyone,' Elfrida used to say after spending from dawn till dusk doing the work of at least two men half her age. 'But misery will,' Bess would finish for her. 'Never let misery over the threshold,' was another of their oft-repeated sayings.

'You've done an excellent job, Libby,' Bess said, making an effort to sound grateful, not wanting to dampen the girl's enthusiasm. But observing the mess that was now spread over the landing she couldn't help but wish that Libby had stuck to sorting through Elfrida's photographs and notebooks in the trunk that was still in the drawing room. The project to archive everything for posterity had apparently been abandoned in favour of more physical labour. She had even raised the subject of doing some decorating. Undeniably, the place could do with sprucing up, but Bess couldn't see Elfrida agreeing to that. There again, Bess had been wrong about Elfrida allowing Libby to snoop through the contents of that trunk. Wrong too about allowing Steve to put right the damaged attic floor.

Looking at the piles of discarded items that hadn't seen the light of day since goodness knows when – eiderdowns and threadbare candlewick bedspreads, half a dozen discoloured pillows, bundles of patched and darned flannelette sheets and several pairs of full-length faded curtains – Bess had to wonder why on earth any of it had been kept. She certainly couldn't remember when she'd last made up a bed with any of the eiderdowns which were badly split and leaking feathers. The ominously stained pillows smelt none too fresh and, as Libby had said, nobody in their right mind would want to sleep with one. 'Barring Marcus that is,' she'd added, 'because he'd clearly sleep with anyone and anything if given the chance.'

It was a particularly caustic remark from Libby and Bess feared there might be an awful lot more of that bitterness simmering away inside the girl. She had every right to feel bitter, but it wasn't a healthy emotion, not if it was left to fester. Allow it houseroom in one's heart and it was highly corrosive, with the potential to deplete one's energy as well as cause irreparable harm.

'Shall we have a bonfire to get rid of all this unwanted stuff?' asked Libby.

'The stink would be horrible,' said Bess, thinking of all the feathers.

'In that case I'll take it to the dump.'

From the floor above them came a voice. 'I could save you the bother by taking it there myself.'

Bess joined Libby at the banister and together they peered up to the top floor of the house where Steve was on a pair of stepladders painting the woodwork around the new loft hatch he'd installed.

'Are you sure about that?' replied Libby. 'We wouldn't want to put you to any bother.'

'It's no bother, I'm going there anyway when I've finished here.'

'In that case we accept your offer with gratitude,' said Bess.

'If there's anything else you need getting rid of, just let me know and I'll take that as well.'

'That's very kind of you,' said Bess as Libby scooped up an armful of pillows. 'How about another cup of tea?'

'That would be grand, Mrs Judd, thanks.'

'A slice of cake too?'

'Now you're spoiling me. Carry on like this and I might never leave here!'

'Which would be no bad thing, given what needs doing,' muttered Libby, adding another pillow to her load. When it dropped to the floor, Bess stooped to picked it up, only to be admonished with a tut from Libby. 'Oh, no you don't,' she said. 'Put that down. No carrying allowed.'

'It's only a pillow,' Bess protested.

'A pillow first and then what, a heavy bundle of towels and sheets?'

With a sigh of frustration Bess did as she was told and followed Libby down the stairs. The nursing staff at the hospital had said that she should give herself time to adjust to the medication she had to take, but they hadn't said anything about being a prisoner in her own home! She would give it another couple of days, then she would have to take a firmer line with Libby. Fussing over her was probably the girl's way of helping and pushing Marcus from her mind, but it really couldn't go on.

They were in the hall and Libby was throwing what she'd carried downstairs onto the floor when the telephone rang. 'I'll answer it,' she said, 'it'll probably be another of my friends having heard about Marcus and Selina marrying.'

There had already been two such calls that morning, so Bess left Libby to it and went to put the kettle on. She could at least do that!

*

Her hand wrapped around the telephone receiver as if squeezing the life out of it, Libby listened in disbelief to the voice in her ear. It had been the last voice on earth she'd expected to hear.

'You see, don't you, it was meant to be? It really was,' Selina said.

'Why?'

'Why what?'

'Why are you doing this, Selina?'

'What? Speaking to you?'

'Yes. I imagined that after our last conversation we'd said all we were ever going to say. You made your position very clear on the matter. Basically, you wanted what I had, and you took it.'

'What I said then was in the heat of the moment.'

'I don't remember it that way. I recall you were very cool at the time. Icy cool, in fact.'

'Granted I may have been a little offhand with you, but we were both being defensive. I acknowledge that Marcus and I could have gone about things differently, but we didn't, so we just have to accept that.'

The fingers of Libby's right hand played with the coiled cord of the phone. 'How marvellous it must be to live in your world where everything is so simple. Now if you don't mind, I have better things to do than—'

'But I haven't told you the reason for my ringing you.'

'You mean there's something more you want to do than rub my nose in you marrying Marcus in two days' time?'

'I don't want to rub your nose in anything, but there's something I want you to hear from me and no one else. I thought it only fair that I should be the one to break the news to you.'

'*Fair?*' repeated Libby. 'Oh, that's a good one! Suddenly you're concerned about being *fair*. What's happened, did you wake up this morning with a conscience?'

'Libby, please don't be like that.'

'Like what?'

'So determined to hold a grudge. Holding a grudge against someone is like drinking poison in the hope the other person will die.'

Libby let out a short bitter laugh that even to her ears sounded borderline hysterical. 'And where did you learn such a nugget of sickening wisdom?'

'It was actually from the vicar who's going to marry us on Saturday. Marcus and I have gone to great lengths to explain ourselves to him, we didn't want there to be, well, you know . . . any awkwardness or misunderstanding of the situation.'

'Perish the thought that there would be any misunderstanding over which bride Marcus will be marrying. But if I were you, I'd cling on tight to him between now and Saturday, just in case he changes his mind in the next forty-eight hours and decides to marry somebody else.'

'He won't do that. Not now.'

Libby let out another cheerless laugh. 'I wouldn't bet on that.'

'I'm serious.'

'As am I.'

'But what you don't know is that I'm pregnant, we're going to have a baby.'

The admission hit Libby with all the force of a sledgehammer, and it took her the longest moment to find the right response. 'Well, isn't that nice for you both?' she murmured.

'It is,' said Selina. 'Marcus is delighted.'

Libby thought of the last exchange she'd had with Marcus when he'd initially tried to convince her to forgive him so they could marry, and then how he'd turned on her. Nothing he'd said about Selina had indicated that he'd be delighted at the prospect of becoming a father with her. 'He wasn't surprised at you being pregnant?' asked Libby. 'Or shocked?'

Selina gave a trilling little laugh. 'We were both taken by surprise.'

'How very careless of you both,' Libby said, not giving a damn how nasty she sounded. 'How many weeks are you?'

'Ten.'

'*Ten!*' As the word exploded out of her, Libby suddenly saw it all too clearly. 'You did this deliberately, didn't you, Selina? Getting pregnant was your way of guaranteeing Marcus would marry you.'

'Oh, Libby, this is what happens to a person who is consumed by bitterness and the inability to forgive, you become blinded by hatred. You can't see any good in anything, only bad.'

'I'm not blinded by hatred, and I'm certainly not blind to what's going on, I can see through you perfectly. Which leaves me with nothing else to say other than I hope you and Marcus will be very happy together, you certainly deserve each other. Goodbye.'

She put down the receiver, not with a furious bang, but with a determined calmness and took a deep breath, filling her lungs with cleansing oxygen, then letting it out slowly. From upstairs she heard the distant sound of whistling and, remembering that Steve was up there, she hoped he hadn't caught any of what she'd said to Selina. Had she sounded bitter, full of blind hatred?

But what if she did? Wouldn't anyone in her shoes?

She took another deep breath, at the same time trying to decide, as she'd done before, whose betrayal hurt her more: Marcus's or Selina's. Whatever Selina claimed, Libby was certain that getting pregnant had been deliberate on her part. That silly trilling laugh when she'd said *we were both taken by surprise* had been too forced, too false. Marcus may well have been surprised, but Libby doubted Selina had been. If Marcus had been out for some fun with Selina and a more adventurous sex life, then having a baby would have been the last thing on his mind. But now he was trapped. Which served him right!

With a sigh, Libby finally moved from where she had been standing for the last ten minutes – minutes that now felt like days – and went through to the kitchen.

*

One look at the grim set of Libby's face and Bess knew something was wrong.

'Who was that on the telephone?' she asked, putting down the knife she had just used to cut a slice of cake for Steve.

'It was Selina.'

'Good heavens, what did she want?'

'Apparently she thought it only fair to let me know that she's pregnant.'

Bess was appalled. 'The wretched girl has no shame. But I suppose that explains why the wedding is going ahead on Saturday.'

'Yes,' said Libby matter-of-factly. 'Shall I take Steve's tea and cake up for him?'

Recognising that Libby had just brought a swift end to the conversation, that it had to be too painful to discuss any further, Bess nodded and handed her the tray. But she couldn't stop herself from saying, 'It will pass, Libby. I promise you that one day the pain will be gone, and you'll be loved and cherished by somebody far more worthy of you than Marcus was.'

When Libby had gone, and without another word, Bess stood in front of the kitchen sink thinking that she could happily ring Marcus and take him to task for his inexcusable behaviour. She wasn't normally vindictive, but after what he and Selina had done, she could readily make an exception with those two. She hoped the wedding on Saturday would be a disaster. That anything that could go wrong, would.

Having poured herself a cup of tea, she drank it while listening to the familiar hum of the old refrigerator, and wondered what it was about weddings that so often made them a catalyst for trouble. Especially family trouble.

Chapter Twenty-Eight

September 1952
Larkspur House, Suffolk
Bess

Nancy showed up out of the blue a fortnight before her wedding and a few days after Elfrida and I returned from our trip to America. It was a Sunday and the first I knew of her visit was when I cycled home from church to see a black Ford Prefect parked alongside Elfrida's Austin 16 on the drive.

Wondering whose car it was, I put my bicycle away and made my way round to the back of the house to let myself in. I had my hand poised to open the door when I heard raised voices coming from the terrace. Following the path round to the garden, I saw Elfrida and Nancy engaged in what was plainly a heated discussion. Neither was aware of my presence as I drew near.

'My whole life has been a lie!' she cried. 'None of it was true! Everyone has lied to me! Even my own mother!'

My breath snatched from me and my heart clattering inside my chest, I knew in an instant what Nancy was referring to. But how did she know? Had my sister finally decided it was time to be honest? But why? And why hadn't Joan warned me what she was going to do?

Elfrida saw me first and I approached nervously, desperately grappling to think what I could possibly say to Nancy that would help. Every time I had ever pictured the moment when she discovered the truth of her birth, I had clung to the most optimistic of hopes that she would throw her arms around me and say, *'I knew! I always knew you were my real mother!'*

But as Nancy became aware that it was no longer just her and Elfrida on the terrace, and she turned around to see me, her expression was so dreadful, so full of loathing, I actually took a step back. Had I been any closer, the white heat of her furious revulsion might have scorched me. I had never seen such a manifestation of pure blistering anger and it rendered me speechless. So I did the sensible thing, I waited for her to speak, for her to condemn me. At the same time, I cursed my sister for what she'd done.

But it soon became clear that I had jumped to the wrong conclusion.

'Now, Bess,' said Elfrida, in the placating tone I knew all too well. It was the one she used when she felt the need to apologise for doing something she knew would vex me, such as leaving her filthy gardening gloves on the draining board, or traipsing across the kitchen floor in her muddy gumboots after I'd just cleaned it. 'I'm afraid,' she went on, 'the cat is finally out of the bag.'

Nancy rounded on her. 'How dare you be so flippant!'

I had to agree, but again I knew it was Elfrida's way of trying to defuse an explosive situation.

Finding my voice, I said, 'Nancy, what has your mother told you?'

'Lies! Nothing but lies all my life. You've all lied to me. *You* especially!'

I made a small tentative move towards her, yet she was having none of it. With tears filling her eyes, she raised her hands as though to push me away. 'Don't,' she said. 'Not another step. Not until I've made sense of what Elfrida has just told me.'

A warning bell went off inside my head. 'What do you mean what Elfrida has just told you?' I asked.

'What the hell do you think? That the woman I've been led to believe is my mother is no such thing, but you are. *You!*'

I shot Elfrida a fierce look. 'How could you?' I hissed at her.

I had never seen her act in a cowardly manner before, but she couldn't meet my eye and picking up the trug that was on the cast-iron table between us, she said, 'I think I'd better leave you two to sort this out on your own.' She scooted away at top speed, as well she might. How dare she break the promise she'd made to me, that she would never breathe a word of this? Why then had she done just that and, to of all people, Nancy?

'Why don't we sit down?' I suggested anxiously. Even if Nancy didn't feel the need to sit down, I certainly did. I felt quite light-headed and my stomach was churning queasily just as it had on board the *Queen Elizabeth* during the journey back across the Atlantic.

Selecting the chair furthest from me, as if taking a tactical stance, Nancy sat bolt upright. 'Well?' she said when I was also seated.

'I'm not sure there's anything I can say that will lessen the shock for you, other than to tell you that I've always loved you and wanted only the best for you.'

Nancy snorted at that. A gesture that was very much at odds with her elegant appearance. She had slimmed down even more since I'd last seen her and as a young woman who always favoured the latest fashion, she was perfectly turned out today in a calf-length full-skirted dress with a cropped jacket, and judging by the upright stiffness of her bearing, I guessed that her waist was drawn in by a formidably tight girdle or corset.

'That's right,' she said, 'you loved me so much you gave me away to your sister when I was born.'

Worried just how much of the truth Elfrida had shared,

I summoned my courage. 'Would you tell me exactly what Elfrida told you?'

'She said that to avoid the shame of being an unmarried mother you dumped me on to your sister.'

'I didn't dump you, and I don't suppose for one second that Elfrida referred to my actions in the way you just did. It wasn't like that. I was twenty years of age when I was expecting you and I had no idea how I would cope looking after you on my own, especially if I had to give up my job. On top of that, there was the shame of being unmarried, the stigma would have been awful, not just for me, but for you too. But there was my sister desperate for a child and unable to conceive, and so it seemed the perfect solution for us both.'

'*A perfect solution*,' Nancy repeated with heavy irony. 'I was nothing but a shameful parcel to be passed around, wasn't I?'

'No!' I said vehemently. 'That wasn't how it was. You were a gift. A gift of love which I was able to give to Joan and Dudley.'

I hated myself for the gloss I was putting on my words, because there had been times when I'd definitely not regarded the baby growing inside me as a gift. But under no circumstances did I want Nancy ever to know the true origins of her creation. Yes, I had cruelly blurted out the truth to Joan to hurt her, but never again would I utter those words.

'Please believe me,' I continued, 'I wouldn't have given you to my sister if I didn't know she and Dudley would give you everything that I couldn't. With them you had loving parents who adored you and who couldn't do more to make you happy. I couldn't have done that alone. How could I have carried on working for Elfrida to support myself as well as take good care of you?'

Nancy fixed her gaze on mine, her eyes glassy with coldness. 'That sounds like you put working for Elfrida before me.' There was no doubting the hostility in her voice, or the superior look she was giving me which, no doubt, had been learnt from my sister, Joan.

God help me for yet another lie I was about to tell, but I went ahead with it anyway. 'No,' I said, 'I put you first. I wanted you to have the best possible start in life. And you did, didn't you?'

When Nancy didn't respond, I tried another tack. 'What would you have done in my shoes?'

'We're not talking about me,' she said flatly. 'We're talking about you. Did anyone ever plan to tell me the truth?'

'That would have been up to your mother and father.'

'How can you call them that when they're not my mother and father?'

'Easily, because that's who they are, and they always will be. Listen to me, Nancy, you are the same person you were yesterday, as are your parents. Nothing has changed.'

She gave me a chilling look. 'Everything's changed. And what do I tell my fiancé? Oh, sorry, darling, but you're marrying a bastard.'

I winced at the word and the brutal way Nancy used it. 'You must never use that word about yourself,' I said sternly. 'And why should you tell David anything about this conversation we're having? Why not keep it to yourself?'

'Because honesty is important. It's what a marriage should be based on, not a sham of lies and deceit.'

I thought of all the things I had kept from my own husband, for his good as much as mine. 'It's love that's important, Nancy,' I said. 'That's all that matters, and doing things for the right reason.'

Pursing her lips, she stared at me hard. Perhaps she was now viewing me with fresh eyes, trying to see me as her mother and not as an aunt who had been kept on the periphery of her childhood.

While it was true I had not always wanted her while she had been in my womb, handing her over to my sister and her husband had been far more distressing than I had imagined. A strong maternal bond had instantaneously made itself known the minute she was born, and I had suddenly wanted to back out of the agreement I had with Joan. Then later, and while my womb was contracting after the birth and my breasts were filling with milk, I had desperately wanted to snatch the child out of Joan's cradling arms and claim her as my own. But I had fought the urge and travelled home to Larkspur House determined to be satisfied with being Nancy's aunt.

When Nancy had been a small, pliable child that had been the hardest thing to do, but then as she'd grown and become thoroughly spoilt, I had found it easier to distance myself from her. I'd loved her unconditionally as an aunt should – and as a mother should – but that love was tested as the years went by when her head was filled with the mistaken belief that she was better than others. Full of pride, she held in disdain all those she considered inferior.

I felt that disdain aimed at me now, that I, Bess Judd, a mere housekeeper and companion, could possibly be the woman who had given birth to her. I felt sorry for her that her young mind had been shaped in so ugly a fashion.

Just as I was going to suggest that what we both needed was a drink, Nancy asked the questions which I most dreaded. 'Who is my real father, then,' she demanded, 'and why couldn't you marry him? Did he already have a wife, or was he merely some passing ship in the night who took your fancy?'

'He was a passing ship,' I said without hesitating. 'I'm sorry I can't give you any more information than that.'

Her eyes widened. 'But you must at least know his name? Or were you so casual with your favours that you didn't bother with the niceties?'

How cruelly censorious she sounded. 'It was a one-off,' I said. 'I never saw him again.'

'Did Uncle Amos know about me?'

I shook my head. 'No. I made a promise to my sister that I would never say anything to anyone.'

'You obviously told Elfrida.'

'She was the only one. I made a pact with Joan and Dudley that this would be our secret and that to all intents and purposes, you were their child from the day you were born. They put their names as parents on the birth certificate.'

Nancy blinked. 'Lies upon lies.'

'Yes,' I said quietly.

'Which means I have to live with those lies or expose you all for your deceit.'

'That, of course, is your choice. But would it help you in any way? Would it make you feel less upset at what you now know?'

Without answering me, she stared off across the garden, then suddenly jerked her head back to look at me again. 'Do you want to know why I came here today?'

I nodded.

'I came to find out the real reason you'd turned down the invitation to attend my wedding.' She gave a mirthless laugh. 'It's ironic that I came with such good intentions only to uncover a web of lies and learn that nothing about my life is genuine.'

The honest answer to the question she'd come here to ask me was that Joan had written to say that I was not to attend, that my presence would be unwelcome. In the five years since Amos's funeral, we had barely spoken and exchanged only a handful of letters. I had tried many times to extend an olive branch in the hope we could put that awful day behind us, but Joan was determined to let it drive an even bigger wedge between us. When I had received the wedding invitation, I had hoped that a reconciliation was on the cards, but then the following day a letter from Joan arrived making it plain that the invitation had been sent by Nancy and that I was to make my excuses and stay away.

'What do you mean by the real reason I turned down the invitation?' I asked.

'That you would miss the wedding because you would be away. I felt it had to be more than that, particularly as you and . . . Mother have hardly spoken to each other in a long time. I stupidly thought I could bridge the gap between the two of you.'

It pained me to hear her pause before using the word 'mother', but I supposed it was only natural, given what she now knew. 'That was a kind thought on your part,' I said, 'in coming here with that purpose.'

She scoffed at that.

In the silence that followed, she unfastened her handbag and pulled out a packet of cigarettes and lit one with a lighter. I abhorred smoking and I was disappointed to see that Nancy had acquired the habit. While she drew in deeply on the cigarette and then exhaled just as deeply, and snapped her handbag shut, I asked what had prompted the conversation that must have taken place between herself and Elfrida before I appeared.

'I told her that I knew. That I knew everything, and it was time for some honesty.'

Confused, I said, 'I don't understand. What did you know?'

'That it had always been Elfrida with her constant interfering who had been so divisive and turned you away from your own sister. That it was Elfrida who had stopped you from being a proper aunt to me, and that it was her fault that you weren't coming to my wedding.'

'And you said all that to her?'

'No. I'd only got as far as saying that I knew the truth and didn't want any more pretence or lies and she said she couldn't agree more and then said something about it being high time that it was out in the open about you being my mother. She even said she was glad I was taking it so well.'

I put a hand to my face and inwardly groaned. Elfrida had got the wrong end of the stick! But as upset and as furious as I was with her, all I really cared about was whether Nancy would ever forgive the deception that had been played on her.

Chapter Twenty-Nine

A recurring dream that Libby often had when she was anxious or upset was of being lost. Sometimes she was lost while driving a car and would find herself repeatedly negotiating the same maze of unknown streets. Other times she was on a bike and it was dark and raining and she would suddenly find herself cycling the wrong way along a busy dual carriageway and unable to find an exit road.

That was the dream that woke her this morning. For a moment she lay very still on her back, forcing her eyes to remain open so that sleep wouldn't reclaim her and once again she would be pedalling like mad, trying to dodge oncoming cars, their horns blaring angrily at her, their headlights blinding her.

There was no need to analyse why this dream had surfaced; given her emotional state for the last couple of weeks, the surprise was that it had waited until now to plague her and not before. But today was special, in that it was Saturday, 1 August and should have been the best day of her life: her wedding day. Now it would forever be remembered as the day she didn't marry Marcus and he took Selina to be his lawfully wedded wife.

Last night Bess and Elfrida had gone to great lengths to keep the atmosphere cheerful. Elfrida had even played the piano after supper and the combination of her hitting plenty of wrong notes through lack of practice and the piano being hopelessly out of tune had made them all laugh. They had then played several games of canasta, followed by a round of rummy until Bess threw in her hand of cards because she had caught Elfrida cheating. It had been an unexpectedly fun evening and Libby had gone to bed not only a little tipsy from one too many nightcaps which Elfrida had insisted she drink, but immensely grateful to the two women who were trying so hard to jolly her along.

Of course, it was impossible to put Marcus completely from her mind, not after Selina's phone call to inform Libby that she was pregnant. Every time Libby thought of that conversation, a tangle of knots tightened inside her. She had tried to tell herself that she didn't give a damn that Marcus and Selina's sordid affair had resulted in a child. So what! Their lives would no longer touch hers, so why should she care? Except their lives probably would touch. Mutual friends would doubtless guarantee – intentionally or otherwise – that Libby was kept abreast of their latest news.

There was also the small matter of Libby having looked into the not-so-distant future and imagined herself as a mother with a baby to love. Now she felt as though the rug of life had been snatched from beneath her feet and she was, at the age of twenty-seven, destined to be a barren old spinster.

That, she told herself firmly, was a sure sign that she was in danger of wallowing in self-pity. Which was not allowed! Flinging off the striped flannelette sheet and woollen blanket, she propelled herself to her feet. This was a day for *doing*, not *dwelling*. She needed to be active. Lolling around dwelling on what could have been would do her no good. She needed something positive to do, another room to sort out, perhaps.

Yesterday she had mended the broken clothes airer in the kitchen, then she'd tackled the scullery and boot room, clearing the shelves and cupboards of accumulated 'this will come in handy one day' useless junk.

Bringing order to chaos was as good a way as any for Libby to keep her mind busy. She had tackled Elfrida about redecorating and to her amazement, and Bess's too, she had agreed to let Libby update the bedroom she was currently sleeping in. 'If you do a good enough job, I might let you give my brother's old room a refresh.' Libby knew that the room hadn't exactly been kept as a shrine to Elfrida's dead brother, but nor had it been used in a very long time. But then these days, other than Libby, Larkspur House didn't have any houseguests. Not only was it a surprise that Elfrida had said what she had, but Libby took it as an honour.

She did have something positive to look forward to, and that was an evening out on Monday. Conscious that she was driving her great-aunt crazy with her constant vigilance, she had decided to ring Daniel and ask if she was overreacting. She had felt guilty ringing him for his professional advice, but the last time he'd been here he'd said she could call him any time she wanted.

'If I hadn't meant it,' he'd said when she'd apologised for bothering him, 'why else would I have given you my telephone number?' By the end of the conversation, he had helped to put her mind at rest. He had then suggested they maybe meet for a drink.

'Only *maybe*?' she'd said.

He'd laughed. 'I was choosing my words with too much care. Blame it on being out of practice.'

'When were you thinking?'

'I'm busy over the weekend, but how about Monday evening next week? Maybe we could have a bite to eat?'

'There's that word *maybe* again,' she'd commented.

'Okay, I'm going to scrub it from my vocabulary. I'll *definitely* pick you up Monday evening at seven-thirty and we'll *definitely* go for a drink and something to eat.'

'And I shall *definitely* be waiting here for you.'

After she'd rung off, she'd wondered about him saying that he was out of practice. Out of practice for what? Asking a friend to go for a drink, or asking a girl to go on a date?

By the time Libby was dressed and downstairs, and after registering what a beautifully sunny morning it was and that bad weather was unlikely to ruin things over in Norfolk for Marcus and Selina, she had decided how she was going to distract herself for the day.

Finding Bess and Elfrida in the kitchen already eating their breakfast, she told them what she wanted to do, and with Bess's help, if she were willing.

'Well,' said Elfrida, 'I for one am wholeheartedly glad that you're taking a break from ruthlessly stripping us bare of our possessions and returning your attention to sifting through my life's work, as you so grandly referred to it. What say you, Bess?'

'Oh, I'm being asked, am I, and not being told what to do?'

'Don't be churlish, Bess. You know perfectly well we're coddling you because we love you dearly.'

'I've never been coddled in my life and if this is what it feels like, you can keep it!'

'Temper, temper,' Elfrida said with a shake of her head, as if rebuking a naughty child.

'I'd really value your help,' tried Libby in a more amenable voice, 'and I promise not to tell you what to do anymore.'

'That,' said Bess, 'is a promise I shall hold you to.'

Putting the trunk onto a rug so as not to scratch the wooden floors, Libby dragged it through to the dining room where they would use the large oak refectory table to lay things out on, and in date order. She didn't doubt the challenge that lay ahead, though.

Nor did Bess, it seemed. 'I hope this will be worth the effort,' she remarked as Libby began placing pieces of paper along the length of the table. On each one she had written a decade: 1910, 1920, 1930, 1940 right up to 1970. 'I doubt there'll be anything from the last decade, as to my mind there wasn't anything particularly memorable to record from those years. But then who knows with Elfrida? You're being very thorough, aren't you?'

'I'm just trying to be as methodical as I can,' Libby said.

'Well, that much is obvious from the way you've been determined to put us in order here.'

Libby glanced anxiously back at her great-aunt. 'I'm sorry if I've overstepped the mark.'

A ghost of a smile softened Bess's expression. 'I know your heart is in the right place, and that's all that matters.'

'Am I forgiven for fussing over you as well? I know I've gone on at times, but as Daniel said, it's all about finding the right balance: care without instilling fear or frustration in the patient.'

Bess pulled a face. 'I'd sooner be regarded as *me* rather than just a patient.' Then with a small smile, she added, 'I'm glad you're going out with Daniel on Monday.'

Libby smiled too. 'So long as you're not reading too much into it.'

'I shan't read anything into it, my dear, so long as you don't rule out the chance of falling in love again, when the time is right. And one day, it will be right, because there'll come a time when Marcus and Selina will no longer dominate your thoughts. This whole painful episode will be behind you and you'll have made a wonderful new life for yourself.'

Libby wanted to believe Bess, but it felt more likely that she would sprout wings and fly to the moon before she fell in love again. 'Is there any reason why you never found love again after your husband died?' she asked.

'No special reason,' answered Bess, moving a chair to sit down on it. 'It just didn't happen, and I suppose I didn't need to. My life with Elfrida was fulfilling enough as it was. Don't forget I was a lot older than you are.'

Libby sat down too. 'Even so, it must have been hard losing him. What I'm going through can't compare to what you must have experienced.'

'Loss is loss, Libby. Heartache is heartache. There's no point comparing or thinking in terms of degrees of hurt and pain. What you're feeling now is just as valid as anything I ever experienced, which is why I know you'll soon be able to put it behind you. You really will.'

Libby smiled. 'Being here with you and Elfrida is helping me to do that. I don't know what I would have done without you both.'

'You would have coped, but I'm glad you turned to us when you needed help. But before you know it, you'll be back on your feet and having fun with all your friends in London again.'

'Are you trying to get rid of me?'

'Not at all. You're welcome to stay with us for as long as you want. And it works both ways; having you here is good for us, even if we grumble about you seemingly dismantling the house brick by brick. But, and this is important, I wouldn't want you to think that you couldn't leave.'

'What do you mean?'

'I don't want you thinking that because I've had this little health scare, I'm suddenly your responsibility.'

'I don't see it that way. I care about you more than anyone else in the world, so it feels perfectly natural to want to look out for you.'

'Which I do appreciate. Now come on, all this chuntering won't bath the baby, so let's make a start sorting out these photographs.'

Doing as Bess said, Libby delved into the trunk and picked a photo at random. It was of a man wearing what appeared to be a pair of tartan trousers and a beret perched jauntily on his head. He was sporting an impressive moustache that had more than a hint of Salvador Dali about it. 'Who's this?' she asked.

Putting on her reading glasses, Bess smiled. 'That's Mallory Vaughan.'

'Was he at a fancy dress party?'

Bess laughed. 'No, God bless him, he went through a phase of always wearing tartan trews.' She turned the photograph over but there was nothing written on the back. 'It must have been taken before the war,' she said, 'as he shaved off the moustache once he was assigned to the War Office. In the circumstances he felt he needed to present himself with a touch more gravitas.'

'Yes,' said Libby, amused. 'I would imagine it might be hard to be taken seriously with a set of whiskers as ritzy as that.'

'The war changed us all and in so many ways,' Bess said, still staring at the photograph.

'You and Elfrida rarely speak of that time,' said Libby, 'whereas Mum and Grandma used to talk about it a lot, about the rationing, the blackouts and the endless dreariness of it all.'

'Again, that's an example of how we all deal with hardship differently. Some people dwell on things while others try to forget them. Elfrida and I have always preferred to look to the future, perhaps in the hope that it would be less painful than some of what's gone before.'

Libby frowned. 'Would you rather we didn't do this? I'd hate to upset you by dredging up things you'd sooner not remember.'

'Oh, I think it's a bit late for that, and if I'm really honest, the past has been on my mind for a while now. I think it was something to do with you marrying Marcus, it made me conscious of the passing of time. One minute you were a little girl playing in the orchard here and the next you were a fully grown woman planning your wedding day.'

'Since it's the past we're dealing with,' said Libby, remembering with fondness her childhood holidays here, 'can I ask you something?'

'That sounds ominous.'

'I don't mean it to be, but will you tell me the real reason you and Mum don't get on?'

Bess lowered her glasses and looked at Libby. 'What do you mean, the *real* reason?'

'Well, in the past you've been a little dismissive when I've asked why the two of you don't get on; you've said that it's all water under the bridge. But it isn't, is it? Because if that were true, you'd have patched things up a long time ago. When Gran was alive she never said anything bad about you, but she never said anything good about you either.'

'Oh, sisters can be very silly, even when they're old enough to know better.'

'Did you have a serious falling-out at some stage?'

'Not as such. More of a . . . a distance that developed between us. It happens in families, particularly when family members live very different lives, and one disapproves of the other. I'm afraid my sister never approved of my working here. The truth is, she didn't really approve of Elfrida.'

'Why?'

'Joan didn't know how to handle Elfrida, so it was easier to look down on her, and me for working for someone who was so different.'

'Although worlds apart, you make her sound just like Elfrida's sister, Prudence.'

'I hate to speak badly of your grandmother, but she really did have a lot in common with Prudence, in that she was a terrible snob. Which in turn rubbed off onto your mother.'

'But not me?'

Bess smiled. 'No, thank goodness. I think your father had a lot to do with that.'

'I think the way you and Elfrida have lived is marvellous and something to be proud of. I wish I were half as unconventional.'

'You're more unconventional than you think you are. Look how you gave up the job you hated in order to run your own catering business.'

'A business I've effectively chucked away because of Selina.'

'Which gives you the opportunity to start a new catering business or to do something different. What you mustn't do, Libby, is let anyone ever tell you something is out of your reach. It's all for the taking.'

Libby thought of how she had allowed her mother to limit what she wanted to do with her life. Or was she making excuses for herself? Shouldn't she have been braver and done what she really wanted to do as a teenager, which was to go to horticultural college? But instead, and to keep the peace with her mother, she had cast aside that dream.

Deciding to give this some more thought later, Libby reached into the trunk for a bundle of photographs held together with string. Untying the knot, she found the photos were all clearly labelled on the back: *Lambert Chase, Northamptonshire 1948*. Passing them to Bess to add to the 1940s section, she delved into the trunk again. This time she pulled out a random selection of photographs. The one on the top showed a young woman with a baby in her arms. The back of the photograph was blank and held no clue as to who the woman was.

'Who's this?' she asked, handing Bess the photo. 'Is it Gran with Mum when she was a baby? Or maybe you?'

Adjusting her spectacles, Bess said, 'Good heavens no, that was Alice Pearce, our evacuee during the war. She was one of the many pregnant women who were evacuated out of London. She was a lovely girl and really took to living here once she got over the shock of being in the country.'

'What happened to her?'

'I don't know. After the war we lost touch with her.'

The following photographs were of gardens at various stages of creation. They were all labelled on the back, with the dates helpfully added. With the photographs fanned out in front of them and determining that if the job was worth doing it was worth doing properly, Libby suggested they make a list of the gardens featured in the pictures.

Bess offered to do that, and they soon settled into a steady rhythm and were making good progress. It was only when Libby's stomach began to rumble that she checked her watch to see what time it was and realised that it was not only long since past lunchtime, but by now Marcus and Selina would have exchanged their vows.

Libby was about to say something when there was a sharp rap on the open window and Elfrida peered in.

'I'm gasping out here,' she exclaimed. 'Who's for a cocktail? Or better still, how about a Bloody Mary to give us some vim and pep. Bess, I'll mix you a Virgin Mary to keep you on the straight and narrow.'

*

With a pitcher of extra-strong Bloody Mary and a vodka-free version for Bess, and a picnic lunch which Libby had put together, they sat in the orchard in a haze of deliciously lazy contentment.

The intense heat of the midday sun had given way to a pleasant warmth that was teeming with butterflies, bees and hoverflies drinking in the nectar from the wildflowers growing all around them in the long grass. It was one of those perfect moments when all was well in the world. When, thought Elfrida, that in spite of all the pain and sorrow the world could throw at one, a moment like this could wipe the slate clean.

Raising her glass to her lips, Elfrida took a long and satisfying swallow, savouring the spicy flavour and the generous amount of vodka she'd poured into the pitcher. *Not bad*, she told herself, topping up the glass. Not bad at all.

The only person who had ever made a better Bloody Mary than she did had been Nikolai. His way of making it was to dip the rim of the glass into lime juice followed by celery salt. He only ever drank Russian vodka, nothing else would do in his opinion. 'Why compromise when you can have the best?' he would say.

She had pointed out to him that he'd compromised all his life. As had she. But then came the day when they decided they would compromise no more.

Chapter Thirty

June 1953
Larkspur House, Suffolk
Elfrida

It was some years since I had thrown a party, certainly not on the scale to which Larkspur House had once played host, but with Mallory's fifty-fifth birthday coinciding by a few days with the coronation of Queen Elizabeth, I decided it was time for a grand celebration. A fancy dress party, no less, with a Kings and Queens theme.

The invitations had been sent out in plenty of time for guests to organise their costumes and while I would have liked the night to be a surprise for Mallory, I knew he would prefer to know about it well in advance so he could be sure to out-dress everybody else. Not a word would he divulge to me of his costume, and likewise I was keeping my own under wraps. Bess was the only one who knew what I would be wearing and that was because she was making it, as well as a costume for herself.

It was a sign of the times that while for many households having a cook had always been regarded as a necessity, it had now sadly become something of a luxury. Bess had been the one to point out to me that with the way my finances were going, I could either have her, plus a cook and a housemaid, or her and a full-time gardener and an under gardener. Obviously, I had no difficulty in making my choice, not when Bess offered to claim the kitchen as her new domain and where she could reign supreme.

We still had a woman from the village to come in to clean four days a week, and Bess did her bit too, but I was aware that while the garden had never looked better and had recently featured in *House & Garden* and *Gardening Illustrated*, the house no longer bore the shine it once did. The William Morris wallpaper which had been chosen by my parents was, for the most part, in reasonably good order, but it was coming away from the walls in some of the bedrooms. Many of the curtains were faded by the sun and the bathrooms were not as up to date as they could be, not compared to some of the houses I stayed in when working on clients' gardens. There was no getting away from it, I was guilty of neglecting the house.

Undaunted, I planned to decorate it from top to bottom with flowers for the night of the party and to use candles which gave a softer and more forgiving illumination than that of electric light. I'd ordered in extra vases and as many candelabra and candles as could be had, but far from impressed with my ingenuity, Bess tutted and said we'd better warn the local fire brigade as doubtless we'd have the house up in flames before we'd even sung Happy Birthday to Mallory.

Bess had offered to take on the job of planning the menu for the big night as well as rounding up a number of girls from the village to act as waitresses. I had proposed that we could pay for outside help, but she dismissed the idea out of hand, saying she was quite capable of rustling up a bit of party food.

Mallory insisted on making a contribution to the party by booking a jazz band from London for the night, as well as organising crates of champagne to be delivered to the house. His much-depleted finances had taken an unexpected turn for the better following the death of an elderly and much-loved relative who had left him a townhouse in Mayfair and a sizeable art collection, most of which Mallory had sold, keeping just a couple of Impressionist paintings. In the aftermath of the war, he'd tried to reclaim Villa Lucia, but despite producing the deeds for the Lake Como property, his right to ownership was rejected by the authorities. It was blatantly unfair, as was the disappearance of his money from his Italian bank account, but Mallory had accepted that he was fighting a losing battle and had walked away.

'When you're up against state-run corruption,' he'd said, 'there's nothing for it but to throw in the towel.' He vowed though never to visit Italy again. I had made the same vow, but for a very different reason.

The morning of the party dawned and gave the promise of a spectacularly glorious day of sunshine. I had expected Mallory to arrive the day before, but he'd telephoned to say there'd been a change of plan and he'd be with me in time for luncheon today.

When his Lagonda appeared on the drive it had just turned midday and I was in the front garden filling a bucket with lilac blooms with which to decorate the house. I was leaving the early flowering peonies until later, along with the forget-me-nots, wallflowers, bearded irises, ranunculus, scabious, and the last of the late-flowering tulips.

Going over to greet Mallory as he parked in front of the coach house, I saw that he wasn't alone: he had a passenger. For a moment I didn't trust my eyes. Surely, I was imagining it? But as if my body had overruled my disbelief, I found myself moving at speed towards the car, to where the passenger door was now opening.

We had our arms around one another before either of us had uttered a word and then we were kissing and laughing and I think I might even have cried, or maybe we both did, I don't know.

When Nikolai and I finally let go of each other, Mallory

demanded a kiss as his reward for engineering the surprise. I obliged but said he deserved a thump for keeping such a colossal secret from me.

As we carried the luggage to the front door, questions tumbled from my lips. 'When did you arrive, Nikolai? . . . How long are you staying? . . . Why didn't you tell me you were coming? . . . Why are you here in England . . .?'

I was babbling like a lunatic and both Nikolai and Mallory were laughing at me. At the noise we were making, Bess appeared in the hall. The smile on her face, accompanied by a complete lack of astonishment, told me that she had been expecting Nikolai.

'You!' I cried. 'You were in on this surprise as well!'

She smirked. 'I couldn't possibly comment.'

'*Traitor!*' I hissed. It now made sense why she had been fretting about the state of my bedroom, that it needed a good spring clean.

'Ivan sends his regards, Bess,' said Nikolai, 'and buried deep in my luggage there's a gift for you from him.'

'How kind,' she said, her cheeks flushing a delicate shade of pink. 'Now might I suggest you all go and sit on the terrace while I finish making lunch? There's an open bottle of champagne waiting for you in the ice bucket and some cheese straws just out of the oven.'

We had only been sitting on the terrace for a few minutes when it became clear that Nikolai was restless and in no mood for relaxing with a drink. He'd only taken a couple of mouthfuls of champagne before he was on his feet and asking me to show him round the garden.

'Off you go, you happy little love birds,' Mallory said with an extravagant wave of his hand. 'I know when to keep my distance. But if you return from canoodling in the shrubbery and find me half sozzled because I've drunk this bottle dry, you'll have only yourselves to blame.'

'One bottle wouldn't touch the sides with you, dear man,' I teased, kissing his cheek and then setting off arm in arm with Nikolai.

Given how long we'd been lovers, it was extraordinary that this was the first time Nikolai had visited me here at Larkspur House. Our trysts had always been conducted elsewhere and in strict secrecy, but at last here he was. It was the strangest thing though, but with the house and Mallory behind us, as we reached the end of the Long Walk and I guided Nikolai to the left so we could pass through the archway in the yew hedge, I suddenly felt shy. This was very much my kingdom and I had spoken of it so frequently to Nikolai, I wanted him to understand why it was so important to me. I had never sought anyone's approval before, it was anathema to me, but as we strolled at leisure, his long strides shortened to match mine, I needed him to appreciate all that I had achieved here. This was my life's work and if it fell short of his expectations in some way I would be devastated.

We'd gone as far as the circular Hydrangea Haven when he indicated the carved oak bench. 'Let's sit for a while,' he said.

Once we were settled, I explained why this area of the garden was so important to me, that I'd created it to honour my parents.

'What do you think of the garden?' I asked eventually, and with a certain amount of trepidation.

He closed his eyes briefly. 'I think,' he said, breathing in deeply and expanding his chest as he filled his lungs, 'that being here is the nearest to being in heaven anyone could ever feel.'

'Do you mean that?' I asked.

'Since when have I said something I didn't mean, and since when did you seek another person's approbation?'

'But you're not just any old person, Nikolai, your opinion has always mattered to me. Whether I cared to admit it or not,' I added with a smile.

He returned my smile but contained within it I caught a wistfulness and it caused me to put aside my delight at seeing him again and to study him objectively. Nine months had passed since I last saw him during my trip to America and superficially, he didn't appear to have changed in that time. However, it bothered me that he didn't look any healthier. As slight as it was, there was a discernible sallow hue to his complexion and beneath his eyes the skin seemed looser and bruised as though he hadn't slept well in a very long time. There was also a careful way in which he held himself, as though he might be in pain.

I was about to question him on his health, namely whether the medical care he'd been receiving last year had resolved the issue of the stomach ulcer he'd told me about – a subject I had frequently touched on when I wrote to him, but which he had consistently glossed over – when he reached for my hand.

'I have something to tell you,' he said.

Hearing the solemnity in his voice, I instantly feared the worst and gripped his hand.

'My wife has finally agreed to a divorce.'

'Goodness,' I murmured, thankful that he hadn't confirmed my fear that he was suffering from some terrible illness. 'After all this time, what made her do that?'

'I offered her money. Lots of it. Along with a sizeable share of the business.'

'How do you feel about that?'

'Relieved. I should have given her the lot years ago and walked away.'

I thought of Mallory and what he had said about his villa in Italy and the money he'd been swindled out of, that it had been easier to walk away. 'But you've worked so hard to accomplish what you have.'

He shrugged. 'It's only money.'

'Says the man who has plenty to spare,' I said lightly.

'I'd have sooner been a pauper and free than a wealthy man in a cage.'

'We're all in a cage of some sort,' I said, 'and invariably of our own making.'

'I don't see any bars around you?'

'Don't be fooled. My stubborn determination to keep my home has been my cage all these years. It's a gilded cage, I'll grant you,' I said, glancing around at the lush new growth of the hydrangea mopheads and the emerging flowers. Cool and tranquil, this area of the garden was where I felt most connected to the beauty of what I'd created. It was where all the hard work and sacrifices I'd made for the greater part of my life felt worth it. If it were possible, this would be where I'd want to be laid to rest.

'So,' I ventured cautiously, 'suddenly your wife isn't as fragile as she's made out all these years?'

'Tenacious might be a more appropriate word to use.'

I could think of plenty of other words to describe the woman – selfish, twisted, unhinged, deranged, self-absorbed, dishonest, spiteful, manipulative, devious, and all-out plain malicious, forcing her husband to stay in a loveless marriage by emotionally blackmailing him with the threat of killing herself. What husband would ever want that on his conscience?

'She's played me for a fool,' Nikolai said bitterly.

'No, you're an honourable man who did the right thing.'

'I'm not honourable; I've been unfaithful to my wife for the whole of our marriage.'

'But only because you weren't happy.'

'And because of that I've compromised my integrity, as well as yours. The worst of it is, you and I could have spent our lives so differently. We could have been married. We . . . still could,' he said, 'if you'd have me?'

When I didn't say anything, he said, 'Does the idea appal you very much?'

'*No!*' I exclaimed. 'Not at all. But I'd be lying if I said the idea doesn't frighten me.'

'*You?* Frightened? Never! You've never been afraid of anything in your life.'

I smiled. 'That's not entirely true, my lack of funds has on many an occasion scared me. And Bess can be quite terrifying when she chooses to be.'

He smiled at that. 'I'll let you into a secret; you've terrified me since the day we met.'

'Really? How so?'

'From the moment I met you on the terrace of Mallory's villa on the Riviera I've been in a constant state of alarm, with my heart and emotions thoroughly ambushed. God knows I tried to resist you, but it just wasn't possible.'

'I think that's the nicest thing you've ever said to me,' I responded, leaning into him and resting my head against his shoulder.

'Which is all very well, but I sense you're prevaricating and refusing to answer my question.'

Gently easing my head away from his shoulder, he stood up, then slipped down onto one knee directly in front of me. 'Elfrida Ambrose, we have been bound together all these years in a way that few couples could ever be. Will you, my darling, when my divorce is finalised, marry me?'

I stared into his eyes and saw our past in those pools of sultry darkness, all the fun and love we'd shared, the heartache and so much more too. I tried to look deeper into those eyes, to see our future. What would it be like? How would we live? And where? And would Nikolai still love me when he saw more than just the best bits of me? How could we ever make marriage work?

Was it fear holding me back as I felt myself hesitating? But as Nikolai had just said, since when had I ever really been scared of anything?

'Yes,' I said quietly. And then more loudly and with genuine conviction. 'Yes, Nikolai, I will marry you!'

I don't know who was the more surprised at my reply, Nikolai or me.

'No more compromising,' he said, before kissing me on my lips. 'Those days are behind us.'

Chapter Thirty-One

August 1981
Larkspur House, Suffolk

'I suppose they're married, then?'

'I suppose they are,' said Bess in answer to Nancy's question. 'We certainly haven't heard anything to the contrary.'

'Is Libby very upset?'

What do you think? Bess wanted to say but being snippy with Nancy would serve no purpose. 'More so than the poor girl's letting on,' she said.

'And how are you?'

The question shouldn't have surprised Bess, but it did. She couldn't recall Nancy ever directly enquiring about her health before. 'I'm feeling a lot better, thank you,' she said. 'Libby and Elfrida have had me practically under house arrest and banned from doing anything more strenuous than filling the kettle.'

'But you're okay?'

'As good as new,' Bess said, again surprised at Nancy's apparent concern.

'Libby said you had all sorts of medication to take and tests which you must do.'

'The tests will be to make sure I'm taking the right dosage. All perfectly straightforward, so I'm told.' Then assuming it was Libby who Nancy wanted to speak to, she said, 'I'm afraid Libby's in the shower at the moment and then she's driving me to church. Shall I ask her to call you back when we're home?'

Last night Bess had voiced her desire to go to church this morning and Libby had immediately offered to drive her there and stay for the service as well. Then at breakfast Elfrida had declared herself in dire need of some communing with the good Lord. 'I've a good mind to put him right on a few matters,' she'd said. 'It's about time somebody did.'

With her usual attendance at Morning Service hijacked and turned into a major outing, it was decided that Family Service would be preferable. That's if they ever made it! With Libby upstairs in the shower and Elfrida in the greenhouse, it seemed increasingly unlikely they'd make it to St Jude's before Evensong.

'Are you still there?' demanded the voice in her ear. 'Were you listening to what I just said?'

Oh dear, thought Bess, without even trying she had annoyed Nancy. 'I'm sorry, I was . . . I was distracted by Elfrida calling to me,' she lied. 'What did you just say?'

'I was saying what a devious little vixen that Selina has proved to be by getting herself pregnant so Marcus would have to do the right thing.'

'I think we can safely say Libby has had a lucky escape from having either of those two in her life,' Bess said. She waited for Nancy, given her previous stance, to defend Marcus by laying all the blame on Selina. But she didn't.

'Sometimes we never really know who to trust or rely on, do we?' she said.

'No,' Bess responded with as much care as she could place into that one small word. Rather than add to it and risk saying the wrong thing, she waited for Nancy to speak again. The wait seemed to go on for an interminable length of time.

When Nancy did speak, Bess could hardly believe what she was hearing.

'This isn't easy for me to say,' Nancy began, 'but I want you to know that I'm glad Libby has been with you while this sorry mess has gone on. I never said it all those years ago, but it was a relief for me that when her father died, she was with you. She was better off with you than with anyone else.'

As though walking a tightrope and scared of the slightest wrong word sending her crashing, Bess said, 'I appreciate you saying that, Nancy; it means a lot to me.' She remembered all too well the day when she had been given the task of telling Libby her father was dead. The poor girl had been sent to stay at Larkspur House so that Nancy wouldn't have to deal with Libby at the same time as coping with her husband in the final days of his illness.

'You've always believed that I'm too hard on Libby, haven't you?' said Nancy. 'But I treated her the way I did so that she would be able to cope with the knocks life will inevitably throw at her. If I had been treated similarly as a child, I might have coped better myself. Instead . . .' She paused. 'Instead I was indulged and overly protected and that didn't prepare me for how cruel life can be. But then you've always known that, haven't you? You never approved of the way your sister spoiled me.'

Bess was stunned into silence. Of all the conversations she and Nancy had ever had, this was the most revealing, and perhaps the most crucial. It gave her hope that there might now be a chance to put things right between them. With that in mind, she put forward a tentative suggestion.

'You did what?'

'You heard me perfectly well,' said Bess, without turning around to look at Elfrida who was seated in the rear of the campervan.

'What I heard seemed so improbable I had to make sure my

ears weren't playing tricks on me. What on earth possessed you to invite Nancy to stay?'

'It does sound highly unlikely.'

This last comment was from Libby.

Bess had deliberately waited until they were on their way to church before telling them what she'd done, as she hadn't wanted to delay their setting off for the village any more than it already was. After she'd finished the call with Nancy, Elfrida had come in from the garden and announced that she should smarten herself up. When she reappeared downstairs in a cloud of Joy perfume, she was wearing a pretty floral dress which hadn't seen the light of day in many a year and had tied her hair up with tortoiseshell combs. Around her neck was a silk scarf and her gardening boots had been exchanged for a pair of ivory-coloured peep-toe shoes. Hanging from her wrist was a crocodile-skin handbag.

'Very nice, dear,' Bess had said. 'Clearly you're out to make an impression this morning.'

'Aren't I always?'

'No,' said Bess, 'you're behaving completely out of character because normally your default setting is not giving a damn what anybody thinks.'

'You know best, Bess,' Elfrida had said with a smile.

Thinking that Elfrida wasn't the only one to be acting out of character, Bess said, 'I invited Nancy to stay with us because she sounded different on the telephone. More conciliatory than usual. So I seized the nettle and extended an olive branch.'

Elfrida clicked her tongue. 'Do try not to overdo the horticultural metaphors, won't you?'

Now Bess did turn around to look at Elfrida. 'I know I should have asked you first whether or not she could stay for a few days, but I just thought it might—'

'What, tip us all over the edge?'

'There's no need to be silly. I'm hoping it might help smooth things out between us. It could be a turning point. That's if we can behave.'

'You mean if *I* behave.'

'That would certainly be a step in the right direction.'

Elfrida humphed. But Libby said, 'Let's hope you're right and it is a turning point. When is she coming?'

'Tomorrow.'

'*Tomorrow!*' squawked Elfrida. 'Good God, in that case we'd all better get down on our knees in church and pray extra damned hard for—'

'Deliverance?' suggested Bess.

'No, for there to be sufficient alcohol in the house to numb the senses for the duration of her stay.'

'That's no way to speak about Libby's mother,' warned Bess.

Libby laughed. 'I'm with Elfrida, we'll need something to take the edge off things.'

'There speaks the voice of common sense. But Bess, you'll just have to make do with your tablets as there'll be no hard liquor for you.'

*

When the service had finally drawn to its conclusion, a moment that didn't come soon enough for Elfrida, she abandoned Bess and Libby to the solicitous vicar who said he'd heard that Bess had been unwell and was eager to know how she was now. Not concerned enough to make a house call, then? And how had he heard that Bess was unwell? Had some busybody at the doctor's surgery been gossiping in the village about Bess? Or maybe Tina had been tittle-tattling?

No doubt there'd be tongues wagging as a result of Elfrida's appearance here at St Jude's this morning. She was, after all, the strange eccentric woman with whom Bess lived. The woman who

rarely attended church but whose parents had a special memorial plaque on the west wall of the building. The then vicar, the
Reverend Eustace Bingham, who had carried out the memorial
service for Cecily and Charles Ambrose, had been a good friend
of the family and that was why he'd made sure Bobby was buried
here. Had Bobby's death been declared a suicide, and not a terrible
accident, his remains would have been unceremoniously dumped
God knows where. Taking his own life would have been seen
as a sin, an affront to God, and that was on top of Bobby's even
greater sin in the eyes of the Church.

It was to her brother's grave that she now went, which was
why she had decided to come here today with Bess and Libby. She
had dreamt of Bobby last night, of the two of them as children.
They were with Prudence and their parents and were sitting
dutifully in the front pew of the church while the vicar delivered
his Christmas morning homily. Afterwards, they had emerged
from the church to find it was snowing and they had thrown
snowballs at each other while Prudence looked on, tutting at
them for their rowdy behaviour.

'It's a graveyard,' she told them, suddenly now a prim and
proper middle-aged woman while they were still children.
'A place for the dead, not a place for high jinks. Now go back
inside the church and ask for forgiveness.' Elfrida and Bobby's
response had been to pelt her with snowballs and then run away
before she could catch hold of them.

It had been one of those strange dreams that felt so real it had
the power to linger and leave Elfrida with the sensation that it
meant something, that it contained a message. But what?

On her way to find Bobby's grave, she passed the grave of
Bess's husband, neat as a pin, and where before the service, Bess
had placed a bunch of sweet peas in a vase which she'd hastily
filled with fresh water from the nearby tap.

Moving along the path and skirting round the back of the

church, she came to where Bobby had been laid to rest. Just as she knew it would be, it was as well cared for as Amos's plot. Bess never said that she tended it, but Elfrida knew that she did.

That was Bess all over, quietly getting on with doing the right thing. Which was why the dear old thing had invited Nancy to stay. Full credit to Bess that she had held on all this time to the hope that one day the past could be righted; and who knew, maybe it could actually happen.

Elfrida stared at her brother's grave and waited to feel something, some kind of small connection with Bobby. But she didn't. She never did; which was why she seldom came. He was no more here than she was the Queen of Sheba. If he was anywhere, he was at Larkspur House where he'd been so happy as a boy. And he had been a happy child, always quick to play some game or other with her, to invent some story of them being pirates sailing across the high seas to find treasure in some far-off land. He would write plays for them to act out in front of their parents when they returned from whatever expedition they'd been on. He had such a cheerful and engaging personality, even when so young. Everyone had adored him.

Especially Elfrida and Prudence. They'd missed him badly when he went away to school. They were not so fortunate with their education and had to make do with a battle-axe of a governess who swore on more than one occasion that she would beat Elfrida with a stick if she didn't concentrate on her lessons. But all Elfrida wanted to do was be outside in the fresh air, on her hands and knees in the flowerbeds. She hated being stuck in the schoolroom.

It was later when Bobby returned home after his first term away at Cambridge that he seemed altered. The joy had somehow gone out of him and was replaced with a serious and more anxious manner. Then, during another time he was home, he brought a friend with him, a fellow student from his college. He was very good-looking and very suave and sophisticated, and Elfrida disliked him on sight. Again, Bobby seemed much changed and told Elfrida to leave him alone, that he wasn't interested in spending any time with her playing some silly game. Hurt by what felt like his rejection of her, Elfrida took to spying on him and his friend.

She should never have done that; it was wrong, and it was something she had regretted all her life. What she saw that evening in the woods confused her at that young age and peering out from behind her hiding place, she'd tried to make sense of it. Why was Bobby's friend pressing him against the trunk of the large beech tree and why were they kissing each other? That wasn't right, surely? When the friend started to unbutton his trousers, Elfrida acted on instinct – she had to save her brother from this horrible friend who was going to do something awful to him.

'Stop it!' she shouted at the top of her voice, jumping out from her hiding place. 'Let my brother go!'

The look on Bobby's face was not what she was expecting. She had thought he would be grateful that she had come to his rescue, but he looked anything but thankful. His expression was one she had never seen before: it was a mixture of guilty shame and angry shock. What made it worse was that his friend just looked straight at Elfrida and laughed. His laughter chased her all the way back to the house and she could still hear it that night when she lay in bed unable to sleep.

Early the next morning Bobby came to her room and told her that he and his friend had been playing a game, a game that she had to promise she would never tell anyone about. She promised all too readily but begged him to make his friend leave.

Less than a week later Bobby opened his bedroom window and fell to his death, and Elfrida knew it was her fault. If only she hadn't followed him and his friend. If only she hadn't felt

300

so hurt by his rejection. Which wasn't rejection at all. He was merely growing out of boyhood and becoming a man.

Bending down so she was kneeling on the grass, and although she didn't believe he was present and could hear her, Elfrida laid a hand gently on the grave. 'I'm so sorry, Bobby,' she murmured. 'Sorrier than I could ever say. I wish you were here to say you forgive me.'

It was the oddest thing, but she could have sworn she felt a small pulse beneath her hand. Her reaction was to snatch her hand away, but then, and because it had felt so real, she returned her hand to the same spot. But this time there was nothing. It had been nothing but a figment of her imagination, she told herself. She was behaving like a stupid old woman who should know better.

But try as she might, and for the rest of the day, she could not shake off the feeling that what she'd experienced had been real. That in asking Bobby for forgiveness, he had given it to her.

That night in bed and unable to sleep, her mind kept playing over what had happened in the churchyard. She had never been remotely convinced by the concept of a greater being, of an omnipotent god who looked down from on high and effectively played chess with people's lives and then expected to be thanked for his trouble.

But Nikolai had been. He had claimed that he'd sooner have faith as his insurance policy than live with nothing. The last thing he ever gave Elfrida was the silver Russian icon his grandmother had given him when he'd been a boy. She had always kept it on the dressing table in her bedroom. Being solid silver, it was undoubtedly quite valuable but even if the bailiffs were banging at the front door, she would never part with it. Before giving it to her, Nikolai had had it engraved on the back. The words had been written in Russian, which of course he'd had to translate for her – *To Elfrida, the love of my life. For all eternity we shall be together. Forever yours, Nikolai.*

He'd given it to her the day he'd proposed to her and when she'd agreed to marry him. But the wedding had never happened. They never got to plan how they would make their marriage work. In fact, Nikolai stayed married to his wife right to the end.

Chapter Thirty-Two

June 1953
Larkspur House, Suffolk
Elfrida

Three days after Mallory's birthday party, Nikolai left for London. He was stopping there for a night before travelling on to the French Riviera where he would check on the refurbishment of a hotel he'd recently acquired. In its heyday, before the war, it had been a majestic watering hole where the rich and famous had stayed, but its grandeur had been destroyed by the Germans when they moved into Nice in 1943 and used the hotel as a base for SS officers whose job it was to search the city for Jews and despatch them to the death camps.

Ten years later and Nikolai was determined to return the hotel – now named The Gala Azure – to its former glory and at the same time provide a garden area within the grounds that would honour the many Jews of the city whose lives had been lost at the hands of the Nazis. He had asked me to create the garden and I had, of course, agreed. Our plan was for me to travel with Bess to Nice in a week's time to meet Nikolai there so I could begin work on a suitable design. I would also visit other gardens in the area, not so much for inspiration – I had plenty of that myself – but I wanted to be sure that the garden I made for Nikolai would be unique, that it would be in a class of its own.

I had been designing gardens all my life and never once doubted my capabilities but accepting this commission for Nikolai made me anxious to create the very best garden I could. It would, I believed, be the single most important garden I would ever design.

Yet that wasn't the only thing that was causing me to be anxious. While Nikolai had been at Larkspur House, I had been very aware that he was not as well as he'd tried to make out. More than once I caught him grimacing with pain, particularly after he'd eaten. His appetite was vastly diminished as was his taste for alcohol. Where once he would have knocked back shot glass after shot glass of vodka without blinking an eye, now he drank very little, saying his doctor advised against it.

'It will pass,' he would say when I asked if there was anything I could do. It was the nearest I ever saw him come to losing his temper when one evening I pressed him too hard to be honest with me about his health, and to see a doctor while he was still in England. 'Just leave it, will you?' he snapped. 'If there was anything seriously wrong, I would tell you!'

I didn't believe him and after he'd left for London, I asked Mallory for his opinion. I tackled him while he was upstairs trying ineptly to pack before he set off for home.

'Well, of course he's ill!' Mallory said as though I was being particularly dense. 'The man's a shadow of his former self, anyone with eyes in their head can see that.'

'I wouldn't go so far as to say that,' I said, perversely wanting to defend Nikolai. 'Besides, we've all changed, we're all older now.'

'Rubbish, you're as fit and as energetic as you ever were and doubtless you'll outlive the whole bally lot of us. But face it, darling, Nikolai is far more ill than he's letting on.'

'Then we must insist he sees a doctor before he returns to America.'

'I already suggested that to him when we motored over to see you and he flatly refused. He says he trusts the doctor he's in the care of back in the States.'

'Then his doctor must be some kind of snake oil salesman because whatever he's doing for Nikolai is not enough.'

Patting my arm, his expression suddenly grave, Mallory said, 'If I were you, I wouldn't delay your marriage to him. When he's divorced, make haste to the altar and enjoy the time you'll have together.'

'Good God!' I exploded. 'There's no need to be so overly dramatic.'

'There is every need. If you love Nikolai, and I know you do, for once in your life put this bloody house to one side and devote yourself to something more important!'

'*Bloody house*,' I repeated, stunned at both Mallory's description of my beloved home and the swerve of his accusation. 'Is that how you see it?'

'Yes! It's been a millstone around your neck for too long. You've worked tirelessly to maintain it and while I grant you it's fed your soul all these years, it will also, if you let it, sap your soul until its very last drop. And for what?'

I goggled at him in ever deepening shock, my mouth working open and shut in the manner of a goldfish, but with nothing coming out of it.

'Darling Freddie,' he said, 'you need to learn when to walk away from something that is a burden to you. That's what I had to do with my villa in Italy. I knew I couldn't win the fight against the people who claimed I had no ownership of it, so I let it go.'

'Easy for you to do that when you still had March Bank to love,' I said, miraculously finding my voice.

'But you could have a new house and garden to love, something that wouldn't make you its slave. And that home could be with Nikolai. Just think how marvellous that would be.'

Tears filled my eyes, and my throat clenched with emotion

as I mumbled something about him not understanding a damn thing.

'I understand what drives you only too well,' he said more gently. 'Now promise me you'll think hard about what I've said.'

'No!' I told him. 'I shan't!'

He'd smiled. 'You are truly the dearest person in the world to me, and the most stubborn and defiant and absolutely the most bloody-minded woman I know.'

'And ditto to all of the above to you too.'

'But you love me anyway. What's more, when you've thought about what I've said, you'll accept that I'm right. Now don't just stand there, give me a hand with my packing. You know how hopeless I am at folding shirts.'

Relieved that he'd brought an end to his so-called advice, I took the scrunched-up dress shirt from his hands. 'How on earth do you manage these days without a valet?'

'I have no idea,' he said good-humouredly. 'But we all have to make sacrifices in these tiresomely modern times. I can't tell you how much I miss George. He was the best valet a man could have, and I mourn the day he retired.'

I smiled, wanting so much for the unpleasantness of our exchange to be behind us. 'I'll know for sure the world has gone to hell in a handcart when you no longer have a butler organising your life at March Bank. I'm just surprised you didn't bring Bennett with you.'

'Don't think I didn't ask him if he'd would care to accompany me, but he opted instead to visit his sick mother in Eastbourne.'

After lunch, which we ate in the garden, Bess and I waved Mallory off. As he drove down the drive, pipping the horn of his Lagonda as he went, Bess put her arm around me. 'It's going to feel very quiet round here for a few days, isn't it?' she remarked.

'Yes,' I said.

'But at least we have a trip to the Riviera to look forward to,' she said. 'Perhaps we should start thinking about which outfits you'd like me to press and put ready to pack?'

'I'll leave you to decide,' I murmured absently. Picking out clothes was the last thing on my mind after everything Mallory had said.

For the next two days while Bess organised our trip to the South of France, I threw myself into creating a new border in the garden. I stripped away an area of turf and wielded my spade like a thing possessed. While I dug, I kept thinking of what Mallory had said about Larkspur House being a millstone around my neck.

How could I abandon it the way Mallory advised me to?

I couldn't do it. It was my enchanted place. It was, in a strange way, my child, a child whom I could never give up. I had lost one baby, how dare Mallory think I could lose this one as well? Moreover, if anyone had a right to ask me to surrender Larkspur House, it was Nikolai and he hadn't. Not a word had he ever said about me doing such a heart-wrenching thing.

With a houseful of guests for Mallory's birthday party there had been no time for Nikolai and me to discuss how our combined future would actually work.

'I trust us both to find a way,' he'd said. ' I have every confidence in our ability to build a life together. It might be unconventional, but I know we'll make it happen.'

The only two people who knew that Nikolai had proposed to me and that I had accepted were Bess and Mallory. Our affair was to continue as our secret until Nikolai was divorced. He didn't want his wife to know he planned to marry again so soon for fear of her having a fit of jealous petulance and changing her mind about their divorce. Or she might be smarter than that and raise the stakes in terms of the financial settlement – her pound of flesh – which she saw as her due. I couldn't really blame her.

Why not grab what she could when it was there to be grabbed? If the woman had any sense, she would demand whatever she believed Nikolai would hand over to be free of her.

But then that would mean I would be the cause of him losing yet more of his fortune, and I didn't want that. Hadn't he lost enough when he and his family fled Russia before the revolution?

The day before we were due to leave for London and then take the boat train down to Dover the following morning to catch the ferry to Le Havre, the telephone rang. I rushed to answer it in the hall, expecting it to be Nikolai. He always rang at six o'clock in the evening. As one of the most punctual people I knew, I was surprised to see the time was actually six forty-five. I was all set to tease him for being tardy, when I heard a voice in my ear which I didn't expect to hear. It was a woman's voice, and the line was so crackly, I could barely hear what she was saying.

I shook the receiver in my hand in the vain hope it would somehow help to clear the line. It seemed to work.

'Elfrida, is that you?'

'Yes! How lovely to hear from you, Dorothea, how the devil are you? And how's that garden of yours?'

'Oh my God, you haven't heard, have you?'

'Heard what?'

'It's Nikolai.'

Again, the line was full of crackling static, and I raised my voice so Dorothea could hear me. 'What about Nikolai?' I asked.

There was a long pause during which a chill of unease trickled through me. 'What about Nikolai?' I repeated.

'I'm so desperately sorry to be the one to tell you this, Elfrida, but he's . . . he's dead.'

'*No!*' I cried.

'I wish it weren't true, my dear, but it is. It's been on the news here for the last few hours that the wealthy hotelier

Nikolai Demidov died last night in Nice. Apparently it was a per-forated ulcer and—'

'*No!*' I cried again. 'He can't have died. I would have known. I would have *felt* something.'

Ignoring my protestations, Dorothea said, 'Is somebody with you there? You shouldn't be alone at a time like this.'

I couldn't answer her. I had no words. Tears streamed down my face, and I dropped the telephone receiver, letting it bang against the wall. My legs giving way, I sank to the floor and sobbed uncontrollably. Nikolai, the love of my life, was dead.

Chapter Thirty-Three

August 1981

Larkspur House, Suffolk

'Good God, do we really have to go to all this trouble?'

'Elfrida, as far as I can see it's been no trouble to you whatsoever,' said Bess from the sink where she was scrubbing potatoes. 'You've been out in the garden all morning.'

'Ho, ho, do I detect touchiness in the lower orders?'

From where she was rolling out a circle of pastry for a quiche Lorraine, Libby laughed at Elfrida. 'Carry on with that kind of talk and the lower orders may well rise up and put you against the wall and throw rotten eggs at you.'

'I'm game if you are!' chortled Elfrida as, just then, came the sound of the Hoover starting up in the hall accompanied by Tina singing Sheena Easton's '9 to 5' at the top of her surprisingly tuneful voice.

Earlier, when she'd been helping Libby to prepare the guest room for Nancy, Tina had sung a medley of songs starting with Bonnie Tyler's 'It's a Heartache' before slipping into a snatch of Shirley Bassey and 'Big Spender' and ending with Abba's 'Dancing Queen'. With no false modesty she'd told Libby that she'd missed her true vocation, that she could have been a professional singer.

'I would have given Bonnie Tyler a real run for her money,' she'd said. 'I'd just left school and was all set to be on *Opportunity*

Knocks and then wham, the door of opportunity was slammed in my face when I found I was pregnant with our Gary. But hey, as the great Frank Sinatra sang, *that's life.*' She had then burst into song again, singing that you could be riding high in April and shot down in May, and then something about finding yourself flat on your face and picking yourself up to get back in the race.

'That's the thing,' she'd said when she appeared to run out of lyrics, 'life's never what you think it's going to be. I didn't think I'd be cleaning for a living, but here I am, duster in one hand and can of Mr Sheen in the other. And you know what, there's bugger all point in moaning about it.'

Fine sentiments indeed, Libby was forced to agree as she continued rolling out the pastry while wondering if Tina in her not-so-subtle way was giving her a kick up the backside. *Time to move on, girl, no point in wasting any energy on regret!*

'When is Nancy due?' asked Elfrida, going back to the scullery to wash her hands, Bess having made it clear she wasn't welcome to do that at the kitchen sink.

Glancing at her watch, Libby called to her, 'In about forty-five minutes.'

'Time enough for you to smarten yourself up, Elfrida,' added Bess.

'I'll do no such thing!' came the shouted response. 'Her ladyship can take me as I am.'

'You're a fine one to call her your ladyship!' retaliated Bess. Then, and more quietly to Libby: 'I do hope she's going to behave.'

'She'll be fine. You know what she's like, she enjoys winding you up and—' Before Libby could finish what she was going to say, and without them noticing that the noise of the Hoover had stopped, Tina appeared in the doorway of the kitchen.

'That's me done for the day,' she announced.

Wiping her hands on her apron, Bess went over to the dresser to fetch Tina's wages. Tina took the money from her and pushed it into her jeans pocket. 'I'll see you the day after tomorrow, then.'

'Thank you for your extra help today,' Libby said. 'That was very good of you.'

'That's okay. I hope your mum enjoys her stay with you. Oh, and by the way, I had a bit of an accident in the dining room, I knocked some of those photos off the table and the Hoover nearly sucked them up. That new bag you put in has given it a fierce new lease of life! I tried to straighten them out, but . . . well . . . sorry and all that.'

While Bess saw Tina to the front door, Libby went into the dining room to assess the damage. She'd stayed up late last night putting letters and garden notebooks into date order as well as sorting through every last photograph. She'd unearthed a small treasure trove of fascinating photos, each one showing Elfrida with a strikingly handsome man. There were no dates on the back of the photographs but judging from the clothes worn by Elfrida and her good-looking companion, they must have been taken over a period of time.

The pictures that stuck out most for Libby included one of a young and very beautiful Elfrida. Wearing a fetching 1920s flapper dress, its fringed hem resting just below her knees, she looked like one of those exquisite silent screen actresses – all large expressive eyes with a perfect cupid-bow mouth and a body as delicate as a china doll. She was made to appear even smaller by the distinguished-looking man at her side who towered over her. Whereas there was a gaiety about Elfrida as she posed for the camera, the man had a contemplative expression on his face as he stared seriously back at whoever had taken the picture. He looked very correct in his well-fitting tailcoat and white scarf around his neck. Very formal. Very proper.

Another photo showed Elfrida and the man informally dressed, perhaps daringly so, in bathing suits on a beach. Elfrida's long wavy hair was draped around her shoulders and reached down as far as her tiny waist. She looked so young, almost ethereal compared to the powerfully built man sitting next to her.

Another photo, possibly taken in the 1930s – Elfrida was wearing wide-legged trousers and a matching kimono style top while her companion was in light-coloured flannel trousers, a shirt with the sleeves rolled up and a cravat at his neck – showed them in a garden with a panoramic view of a lake and mountain scene beyond. The man had an arm around Elfrida and there was no mistaking the adoration on their faces as they looked at each other, as though completely unaware of whoever was taking the picture.

The photo Libby found the most amusing was one of an older Elfrida looking very regal as Cleopatra, complete with heavily made-up eyes. Once again, the tall handsome man was at her side with his arm around her and he was dressed in a frock coat and breeches and large buckles on his shoes. Libby guessed they must have been at a fancy dress party.

There was no guesswork required in concluding that they made a very arresting couple and must have been lovers. As soon as a suitable moment arose, probably after her mother's visit, Libby planned to ask Elfrida who the man was. Could it be Nikolai, the man whose name she had been muttering in her sleep after her fall in the garden?

It had always puzzled Libby why Elfrida had never married and when she had once raised the subject with Bess, the answer had been along the lines that there had never been a man alive who could have put up with Elfrida on a permanent basis.

To her relief, there was no scene of devastation in the dining room as she had dreaded there would be after Tina's admission that she'd had a *bit of an accident* – all she found were a couple of badly crumpled photographs. *Small mercies*, Libby thought.

She very much hoped there would be further small mercies during her mother's stay. Was it too much to hope that Bess was right, and that Mum really was in a more conciliatory frame of mind? More likely the moment would have passed, and she would be her customary old self, taking offence for no real reason and going on the attack.

Not for the first time Libby wondered what made her mother so bitter and hard done by. Had there been a great disappointment in her life when she'd been young? Had she had her heart broken and never truly recovered from it?

Who knew? But it was a warning to Libby that she mustn't let what Marcus and Selina had done turn her into a carbon copy of her mother.

*

By the time Nancy arrived all was ready, and they were able to greet her with a calmness that belied the true state of their anxiety.

This was the first time Nancy had ever stayed at Larkspur House. In the past she had always turned down any invitation to stop the night, limiting her visits to no more than a few hours. Bess had never pushed it; instead she had been only too grateful that Libby had been allowed to stay. That had been down to Libby's father. He had been more than happy for his daughter to spend part of her summer holidays with them, and Nancy could hardly say no without causing David to ask awkward questions.

Bess had suggested that Libby should show her mother upstairs to her bedroom so she could settle in. Libby had given her the room she had previously been staying in, because it had one of the best views of the Long Walk, and had moved her things into a smaller room at the front of the house.

It was an example of them all bending over backwards to make Nancy's visit as harmonious as they could. For her part, Nancy seemed her usual self – complaining about the lack of consideration from other road users and that the journey had given her a headache. Poor Nancy, she could always find something to grumble about.

Pushing this negative thought from her mind, Bess reminded herself that the only thing that mattered was that Nancy was here. It had to be a step in the right direction.

Elfrida had put forward the theory that Bess's health scare may well have sharpened Nancy's focus and prompted her finally to let bygones be bygones. If true, it was a sad state of affairs that it had taken an illness to draw them closer, but Bess was prepared to accept the chance of a truce on any terms Nancy chose.

Having put the kettle on to make Nancy a cup of restorative tea, Bess searched through the dresser drawer for the first-aid box where they kept the paracetamol and aspirin. Nothing was where it should be since Libby had set about tidying the place, but Bess left the grumbling to Elfrida on that score. Libby's efforts to bring order to the chaos served to emphasise just how badly the situation had been allowed to slide in recent years. Bess couldn't remember exactly when it had begun; it wasn't as though it was a conscious decision, more a case of running out of steam to do what used to take no effort at all.

Pulling open the other drawer, and after delving under some tea towels, Bess found what she was looking for. She'd just prised the lid off the first-aid box when Elfrida's voice from behind her made her start.

'You're not thinking of taking an aspirin, are you?'

'Of course I'm not,' Bess said, noting that Elfrida had changed out of her scruffy gardening clothes. 'The tablets are for Nancy; she said she has a headache.'

'We'll probably all have one by day's end. Now don't you think you should compliment me on making such a fine effort to smarten myself up?'

'You don't think you've rather overdone it, do you?' Bess replied, taking in the emerald green kaftan with gold trim, the collection of bangles on both arms, and the *pièce de résistance*, a gold turban. On her feet were a pair of espadrilles revealing ten very badly varnished toenails in scarlet.

Elfrida laughed. 'I was going for my Gloria Swanson in *Sunset Boulevard* attire.'

'I think we can safely say you've easily accomplished that,' said Bess, going over to the kettle which was now boiling.

'Perfect! Which calls for a glass of sherry at the very least. Well, not for you, Bess, you'll have to settle for tea, or a glass of lemon barley water.'

By the time Libby and Nancy reappeared, the tea was ready to be poured and Elfrida had knocked back a schooner of sherry and was refilling her glass. 'Just to steady the old ship as we sail into choppy waters,' she muttered *sotto voce* to Bess. Then to their guest, she was all smiles and bonhomie.

'Nancy, my dear,' she said in a theatrically exaggerated voice, 'how simply splendid that you're going to be with us for a couple of days.'

Nancy looked as though she might make a run for it. 'It's good of you to have me,' she said stiffly.

'It's our pleasure,' enthused Elfrida. 'Now come along, let's make ourselves comfortable in the garden. Libby, be a dear and bring the tea tray, will you, we don't want Bess taxing herself by carrying it.' And as if to ensure that Nancy couldn't make a run for it, Bess watched Elfrida do something she had never done before, she slipped her arm through Nancy's and led her outside.

Left alone in the kitchen with Libby, Bess shook her head in disbelief. 'Good God,' she said, filling a glass with water for Nancy, 'whatever's got into Elfrida?'

'I think that's what is called in the business, a command performance.'

'And some. How did your mother seem when you were upstairs with her?'

'Subdued.'

Which was never a word one associated with Nancy, thought Bess as they went out to the garden where the other two women were seated at the table beneath the pergola – one ramrod straight in a cerise two-piece suit and the other looking as cool as a very green cucumber with a gold topknot. In that moment Bess didn't think she could love Elfrida more for doing what she was for her and Libby's sakes.

Passing Nancy the glass of water and the packets of paracetamol and aspirin, she said, 'I didn't know which you'd prefer, so I brought you both.'

'Thank you.'

'It was probably the stuffy heat in the car while you were driving here,' said Bess helpfully.

'And the glare of the sun in your eyes,' added Libby, as she poured their tea.

'Or simply the trepidation of coming here again?' suggested Elfrida.

Bess cleared her throat warningly but Elfrida ignored her.

'After all, it's never been your favourite place to visit, has it?'

Nancy looked up from the two paracetamol tablets in her hand and stared at Elfrida. 'You always did favour blunt truth over polite falsehoods, didn't you, and no matter the consequences?'

'I suppose it is rather my stock-in-trade. So were you dreading coming here?'

'Would you blame me if I were?'

'Gracious no. But I do think we're beyond all that now, aren't we?'

'Is life always so black and white for you?'

'I could ask the very same thing of you.'

Giving Nancy her tea, Libby said, 'Please, wouldn't it be lovely if we could just sit here and be nice to one another? Is that too much to ask?'

'Libby, my dear girl,' said Elfrida, 'your mother and I *are* being nice to each other. Don't you agree, Nancy?'

'I'd like to think so,' Nancy said.

'And dare I suggest that the reason you're here is to build a bridge and put—'

'Elfrida,' implored Bess, 'don't say any more, please, just drink your tea and let Nancy relax.'

'As you wish.'

In the awkward silence that followed, Bess looked across the table, not at Nancy, she didn't dare do that, but at Libby, who was sitting back in her seat and frowning.

'Is this when you finally tell me why there has always been a rift between you three?' the girl asked, turning to each of them in turn.

Nobody answered her.

The silence was unbearable for Bess and as it lengthened the warmth of the midday sun suddenly felt uncomfortably oppressive.

'Nothing to say, any of you?' asked Libby when still nobody said anything.

Bess did now risk a glance in Nancy's direction, silently beseeching her not to feel angrily defensive. Although she had every right to feel just that. 'Perhaps this isn't the right moment,' Bess murmured.

Nancy slowly turned her gaze towards Bess. There was torment in her eyes, genuine distress, and Bess longed to put her arms around her daughter and take that pain away from her. To give Nancy the love Bess had never been allowed to give as her mother. Not since the day she was born.

'Maybe this *is* the right moment,' Nancy said quietly. 'But only if I can explain things in my own way. And without anyone interrupting me.'

She pointedly aimed this last comment at Elfrida, who gave a cursory nod of agreement.

Chapter Thirty-Four

Nancy

I was what people these days would call an archetypal fifties housewife, and while I know the term is used to demean women like me, I was proud of my status as Mrs David Mortimer. I saw no shame in being a wife who was devoted to the care of her husband.

I sound as though I'm justifying myself, and I'm not. Why should I? I loved my husband and wanted to do everything I could to make our marriage a happy one. I wanted everything about our union to be perfect, for him to love me as much as I loved him.

When I started work as his secretary, he was older than me by nine years and recently widowed. From day one I could see that he needed somebody to organise him, someone to ease the burden of his grief by ensuring everything in his professional life ran smoothly. His previous secretary had been very slipshod in my opinion, having left the filing in disarray. Frankly, there was no system, just files and documents shoved in drawers and cupboards any old how. There was no order. No organisation.

Within six weeks of starting work at the law firm, I had everything running like clockwork and Mr Mortimer – it would be some time before I referred to him as David – complimented me on my efficiency. Basking in the glow of his praise, and the smile he gave me, I felt the first stirrings of attraction for him. Until that moment I had been so preoccupied with finding my feet in my new job, I had not regarded the man I worked for as anything more than one of the senior partners. In the weeks and months that followed, I saw the shroud of grief he'd been carrying for his dead wife gradually slip from his shoulders and then one morning I arrived for work and found a bouquet of flowers on my desk. There was a note attached to it:

Thank you for bringing a sense of order and happiness into my life again.

David

I could barely meet his eye when I went through to his office with that morning's mail and to take the first dictation of the day. Sitting down, my pencil poised over my notepad, I thanked him for the flowers. Somewhat clumsily I added that there had been no need to thank me for doing my job, not when working for him was such a pleasure.

Brushing aside my comment, he said, 'I'd like to thank you properly by taking you out for dinner one evening. If you think it wouldn't be too improper to have dinner with me?'

At all times, whether inside or outside the office, David behaved with impeccable correctness. Ours wasn't the most romantic of courtships, but then neither of us viewed life through rose-tinted spectacles. Certainty, appreciation and honesty; they were the qualities that were important to us. I met a few of his friends and they all said I was good for David, that I had helped him to recover from the death of his wife. Their marriage had not produced any children and I was secretly pleased about that, it simplified matters.

Fifteen months after David had left those flowers on my desk,

I embarked on married life with him in a beautiful mock-Tudor detached house overlooking the golf course. Out of deference to me, David had sold the house he'd shared with his first wife and bought somewhere new, and grander, for us to live. I appreciated that gesture on his part enormously and I threw myself into taking care of our wonderful new home, organising decorators, curtain makers and carpet fitters. A woman came in three times a week to clean, and I watched her like a hawk to be sure she did a thorough job. Sometimes I wondered if it wouldn't be quicker to do the work myself.

My job – now I was no longer David's secretary – was to provide the perfect sanctuary for my husband when he came home after a busy day at work. I delighted in having everything just so with the evening meal prepared, a gin and tonic already poured for David the moment he put his key in the lock of the front door, my hair brushed, and my make-up reapplied, and perfume dabbed behind my ears and on my wrists. I wanted David to walk into a perfect house and to be greeted by a happy and contented wife.

To be as perfectly presented as I could be, every Monday and Friday afternoon I went to the hairdresser and had my hair shampooed and set so I would be impeccably turned out for any entertaining we would be doing, or to which we'd been invited. Our circle of friends was largely based around the golf course where the menfolk played. One or two of the wives had taken lessons at the club, but it didn't interest me. I preferred playing bridge and was regularly told I had a mind that was well-suited to the game. I had, as I discovered, the capacity to recall every card put down during and after a game. A photographic memory, according to one partner with whom I played.

My memory served me well in other respects too. I never forgot a name or face, a birthday or a special occasion, or some interesting little fact that I had gleaned while in conversation with one of my husband's work colleagues or clients. The art of small talk was impressing upon the other person that there was nobody one would rather be talking to. Such was the power of my memory that without any effort on my part, I could store those little facts away inside my head, as though storing them neatly in a filing cabinet, and retrieve them when the situation required. My husband was very proud of this skill of mine and joked that where once I had been his wonderfully efficient secretary, I was now his wonderfully efficient wife.

Elfrida once said of my ability to remember things as well as I did that it was a pity I used it to tot up perceived grievances or slights so I could use it against a person at a later date. As always with Elfrida, the barb was sharp and precisely aimed. But her accusation wasn't correct. The only grievance I held was against those who had genuinely hurt me, particularly those who had deceived me.

The reason I wanted my life with David to be perfect was to make up for the awful lies I had been told. I had found out just weeks before my marriage, during a visit to Larkspur House, that I had been duped in the worst possible way. Quite inadvertently I stumbled upon the knowledge that I was Bess's illegitimate daughter. The discovery filled me with a rage I could barely contain or control and after Bess had tried to whitewash the truth, to make the deceit seem less terrible, by saying she had been unable to keep me when I was born so had given me to her sister and husband, I tore home in the car to my parents in Tunbridge Wells to have it out with them.

Except they weren't my parents; they were strangers to me. They were lying conspirators who had robbed me of my very identity. I was nothing. Nothing about me was real. I didn't really exist.

Bess must have telephoned to warn them what had happened

because when I arrived, the woman who I had thought was my mother was crying, and the man who had pretended he was my father was trying to comfort her. I launched myself at them, screaming that I hated them, and Bess, that there was nothing they could say or do that would make up for what they'd done.

'I'll never trust you again or believe a single word you ever utter!' I shouted before getting into my car and driving at breakneck speed to my flat in London.

I didn't speak to them for a week. David noticed a change in me, but I couldn't bring myself to tell him the reason why. How could I tell him I wasn't who he thought I was, that I was a bastard? An unwanted and shameful child who had been conveniently passed off onto another couple. If David knew the sordid truth, he wouldn't marry me. So I lied to him. I said it was pre-wedding nerves and there was nothing to worry about. But I could see he was worried, that concern for me was playing on his mind. Perhaps he thought I was about to back out of the wedding.

In the end I telephoned my parents, but only because I needed them to play their part.

'Don't think for a moment that I've forgiven you,' I said, 'I never will. But you'll come to my wedding and being the experts you are at the art of deception, you'll pretend that everything is perfectly normal between us. Do you understand?'

I heard the pitiful relief and gratitude in my mother's voice when she said she understood.

Would anyone blame me for reacting the way I did, or for how badly I wanted to pay back those who had lied so brazenly to me and without a thought as to how I might feel?

Was it any wonder that I then spent most of my energy striving for perfection, to atone for all that ugly imperfection that had gone before? Was it any wonder that it drained me and made me so miserable? Every day was such an uphill struggle and no one, absolutely no one knew the pain I was in.

But on I went, striving ever harder to be the perfect wife. And subsequently a perfect mother. Some days I thought I'd achieved it and other days I just wanted to shut myself away, draw the curtains, and descend into that black hole of nothingness. There had been so many times when I considered alcohol to dull the pain, but instead, and because I was a mother and knew I had to be sensible, I went to the doctor to ask for some tranquillisers. There was no harm in that, surely? I knew several wives at the golf club who confided in me that popping a few tablets every day made them feel so much better and more able to cope.

I didn't tell David about my visit to the doctor, and I kept that brown bottle of life-improving pills hidden from him. But the pills didn't improve my life. Far from it. They made me feel as though my every sense had been dulled, and maybe that's what they were meant to do, but it wasn't what I wanted. I wanted clarity, not yet more opaqueness and deception in my life. I swapped and changed between countless variations of pills prescribed to me by a revolving door of GPs. Sometimes I lost track of what I was taking and mixed up the new prescriptions with the old, resulting in my being at the mercy of intense mood swings.

By this time Libby was eleven, and for her own good as much as mine, I was adamant that she should go away to school. We had reached an awkward stage when I could do nothing right in her eyes, and she could do nothing right in mine. It was better all round that she was given the space to stretch her wings, leaving me to concentrate on running the home and maintaining the level of perfection I needed to mask the ugliness of who I was, and which taunted me at the slightest provocation.

As a child I had adored my mother, or the woman I had assumed was my mother, but once I knew the truth, things were never the same between us. How could they be? How could

I trust her and the man I had regarded as my father when they had kept the truth from me for so long? The deep affection and admiration I had held for them was forever damaged. But there was no denying their love for Libby when she was born, and our relationship did recover slightly when I became a mother myself. If only because, and as David pointed out to me, a grandmother was an extra pair of hands when it came to looking after a child.

Libby's arrival into the world two years after David and I were married was not the happy event I had thought it would be. My labour went on for over thirty-six hours and in the end a doctor had impatiently dismissed the midwife and all but ripped the baby out of me. I lost a lot of blood and remained in hospital for three weeks, during which time I was too ill to see to my newborn child. I'd had no intention of breastfeeding, which was just as well as I developed mastitis and when I was eventually allowed home, I found that David had arranged for my mother to come and stay to help with the baby.

Under normal circumstances I would have put my foot down and claimed I didn't need my mother's help, but I was too weak to complain. All I wanted was to sleep and to be left alone. My nerve endings jangled every time I heard the baby cry and I veered from tearful frustration that I couldn't make her stop, to fury that she refused to sleep. I became convinced that the child only cried for my benefit, that when she was in her grandmother's arms, or her father's, she was as good as gold. She was, I believed, doing it deliberately, just to prove how useless I was.

'Oh, it's just the dreaded baby blues,' friends told me when they heard that I was feeling a bit low, 'it'll soon pass. Second time around is always better.'

The thought of going through all that again horrified me, and I insisted that David and I slept in separate beds. From that point everything in my life began to be segregated, nothing was to overlap or impinge, and as a result I started to feel more in control again. I resumed aspects of my life from before I gave birth – twice-weekly visits to the hairdresser, games of bridge, even the occasional dinner party. All this was made possible by my mother and the daughter of my cleaner who would babysit. It was on these terms that I found a level of contentment as a mother. Everyone told me what a perfect baby I had. Complete strangers would lean into the pram and declare Libby the bonniest little thing they'd ever seen. 'You must be so proud of her,' they'd say. To which I would always reply, 'Of course.'

If I were to be completely honest, I was jealous of the attention Libby drew. Throughout my childhood I had been doted on and constantly told how clever and beautiful I was. Which was yet another falsehood as I learnt one day at school, when I was about fifteen, and I overheard a group of girls sniggering about the fat girl in the class. It took me a few seconds to realise that it was me they were talking about. I was mortified. At home that evening, I looked in the mirror and instead of seeing the girl I had always thought I was, I saw a lumbering, heavily set teenager staring back at me; one who had a pudgy face, with spots. An ugly deluded girl. That's who I was. I vowed then to lose weight.

It wasn't easy; Mother kept forcing all the things I liked to eat onto me. 'But these cream slices are your favourite,' she would say, 'I made them specially for you. Go on, just one won't hurt, will it?'

It became a battle between us, my resistance to her smothering persuasion. It was as though she loved me more when I enjoyed what she cooked for me. But the sniggering at school fuelled my determination to lose weight and I did just that, much to my mother's consternation. As the pounds were shed from my body, she swore I was going to make myself ill. In her eyes, the more I ate the healthier I was. She too had gained weight with the passing of years, as had my father.

Dieting for me then became a way of life which I accepted. I did not want to be the fat girl other girls made fun of. I wanted to be like one of the popular slim girls with long slender legs and pert breasts. I could hope for it all I wanted, it was never going to happen; there was nothing slender or pert about me.

By the time I left school and went on to secretarial college I had grown taller and lost nearly three stone. I was not a catwalk beauty, but I was happy to be called statuesque. It sounded regal and possessed of a sense of purpose. And I did have a sense of purpose. I wanted a husband. I wanted a man to adore me as my parents adored me. There were a few boyfriends I dated, but they only wanted one thing and I wasn't prepared to give that. Mother had drilled into me that I was not to throw myself away on the first boy who showed any interest; I was to hold back until the night of my wedding.

At school I had been aware that a lot of the other girls came from a different background to mine. Their fathers didn't buy second-hand cars from my father, for instance. One or two of the girls were driven to school by a chauffeur and they revelled in the shabbiness of their uniforms, viewing a rip or a patched-up hole, or a battered straw boater as a mark of honour. Whereas I kept my uniform pristine, because I knew how much it had cost my parents. My shoes were always polished, usually by my mother, and my socks were as white as snow and never hung round my ankles.

I was secretly envious of the girls with their cutglass accents who swaggered about the school as though they didn't give a hoot, but I didn't dare follow their example for fear of upsetting my parents. They paid so much money for me to attend this exclusive school and I didn't want to let them down. I knew I didn't really fit in, and not just because I was a day girl and not a boarder, but I saw it as a learning exercise. I would be like those girls one day. I would watch them and learn from them. That was the reason my parents had wanted me to attend such a posh school. 'It will open doors for you,' my father would say, 'it'll give you the advantages we never had.'

The only other person I knew who belonged to that world of upper-class folk and who possessed such a careless sense of entitlement was Elfrida. Bess had worked for Elfrida since forever and once in a while we would visit Larkspur House to see my aunt – or the woman I thought was my aunt. I never enjoyed the visits because I sensed my parents' awkwardness being around Elfrida. They said she was a thoroughly disreputable woman who didn't have a moral bone in her body. 'Mired in scandal,' Mother would mutter darkly about her, 'and unfortunately Bess is tainted by association.'

On one occasion when I was quite young – and long before I knew what *'mired in scandal'* and *'tainted by association'* meant – we were driving home after a visit to Larkspur House, and I commented how kind Aunt Bess always was to me and that she seemed so very friendly. Mother said I wasn't to be fooled by her sister's apparent kindness. She then went on to say that Bess had a strange condition that made her tell lies and I was to promise that I would never believe anything my aunt told me. 'She can't help it, it's an illness she has,' Mother said. 'She makes things up to make herself feel important. So we just have to humour her.'

As intrigued as I was by this revelation, I promised that if my aunt ever said anything odd, I would tell my parents about it.

I was also warned that the woman my aunt worked for wasn't to be trusted either. Elfrida told even worse lies than Bess did, and this, so my parents claimed, was one of the reasons they didn't like to associate with Aunt Bess too much.

Years later, when I was planning my wedding, Mother said that we'd better not send an invitation to my aunt. 'She might let the side down and besides, she never goes anywhere without Elfrida, and we certainly don't want her as a guest.'

To this day I'll never really know what made me do it, but I sent Bess a wedding invitation anyway. Perhaps it was out of pity for the poor woman. She had always remembered my birthday and never failed to send me generous Christmas presents. She also sent me postcards whenever she was away travelling with Elfrida.

When I confessed about the invitation I had posted to Bess, Mother hit the roof and demanded to know why I had defied her. I was surprised by her reaction. I had thought it would be a good thing to do. After all, Bess was her sister and my aunt. My only aunt.

A fortnight later and Bess wrote a polite card saying that she was very sorry, but she wouldn't be able to attend the wedding. She gave no reason and maybe that was what irked me most. What could be more important than coming to my wedding? I'd have thought she would have leapt at the chance to be there on my big day. I was used to getting my own way and perversely I particularly wanted my own way in this matter. It was *my* wedding after all! With only a few weeks to go before I would be married, I drove to Larkspur House, never knowing that for the rest of my life I would wish I'd never made that journey.

Chapter Thirty-Five

August 1981
Larkspur House, Suffolk

When Nancy finally fell quiet, Libby's head was a dangerous powder keg of emotions and questions.

There was so much to take in and in order to process what she'd just heard, and better understand it, she wanted to be anywhere but sitting here. Walking away seemed the safest thing to do because what compassion she had for her mother was curdled with its polar opposite, and Libby was frightened what might emerge from her mouth if she did speak. Not a word of sympathy had her mother expressed for Bess, for the difficult decision she had made all those years ago, and what she had so clearly been denied as a result.

But Libby couldn't walk away, not without saying something. 'Mum,' she said, 'I don't understand you. You hated it when you found out that you'd been deceived, and yet you did the same to me, you withheld the truth about Bess being my grandmother. How could you do that?'

Her mother looked at her apprehensively. 'Would your relationship have been any different if you'd known the truth?' she asked.

'That's not the point!' Libby snapped. 'You denied me, and Bess, the proper relationship we should have had.'

'I couldn't tell you the truth, it would have brought everything crashing down. Don't you understand that? And did I ever stop you from seeing Bess? Did I?'

'You didn't exactly go out of your way to encourage me to spend more time with her. You always made it feel as though it were a privilege that could be withdrawn with one click of your fingers.'

'That's not true. You spent most of your summer holidays here every year.'

'Only because Dad was all for it,' Libby fired back, 'and if you're honest you preferred not having me around. Bess was convenient to you, then, wasn't she? She offered you a place where I could be dumped so you didn't have to be bothered with me. Just as you dumped me at boarding school! Everything's always been about you, hasn't it?'

'But you loved it here, Libby,' her mother objected. 'You even told me that you wished you could live here for ever with Bess and Elfrida.'

'And why the hell do you think that was?'

Her mother flinched and it was a moment before she answered. 'Because I was a dreadful mother,' she said faintly. 'Because Bess and Elfrida made you happy and I couldn't. I couldn't give you what you needed. I've always known that and how do you think that makes me feel, knowing that I've been such a bad mother?' Stifling a sob, she covered her face with her hands and the only sound to be heard was the cooing of a dove in a nearby tree.

'Libby darling, I think after all that your mother has just shared with us, a moment of calm reflection might be in order. Why don't I make us a fresh pot of tea?'

Libby had been so focused on her mother she had scarcely been aware of Bess and Elfrida around the table. Now she looked at Bess, and anger was once again the emotion that was determined to have its way. Another cup of tea just wasn't going to patch things up all nice and neatly! 'Why didn't you ever tell me the truth?' Libby demanded.

'I wanted to,' Bess said, 'of course I did, but I'd promised Joan and your mother that I wouldn't. It was their place to share the secret with you, not mine. I had to respect that.'

'And you,' Libby said, switching her gaze to Elfrida, 'did you never feel I should know the truth?'

'I didn't agree with the deception, but out of respect for Bess, I held my tongue.'

Libby contemplated the three women before her. The three women who had deceived her. 'So out of respect for my mother's wishes,' she said tightly, 'nobody thought of me and how I might like to know who my real grandmother was?'

'My sister was always your grandmother,' said Bess. 'Nothing should ever make you think differently.'

'But how could you accept that? Why settle for less when it was your right to have more?' Libby knew it was unkind of her, but she felt let down by Bess.

'Bess accepted what she did because I gave her no choice in the matter,' said her mother. 'I made it clear when you were a baby that if she ever breathed a word of the truth, she would never see you.'

Libby drew in her breath sharply. 'What a truly vindictive thing to do.'

'I'm not proud of what I did. I did it because—'

'It was the only way you could pay Bess back for giving you away when you were born,' cut in Libby. 'Is that it?'

With tears filling her eyes, her mother nodded. Again, she covered her face with her hands. 'I'm so sorry. I'm so very sorry. I knew it was wrong, but I couldn't stop myself. I wanted everyone else to feel just a fraction of the pain I'd felt. I hated how easily and happily others could live their lives, never knowing a moment's disappointment, never knowing what it felt to be an outsider. All my life I've been on the outside looking in, waiting for someone to invite me in, to be a part of their lives.'

At the misery in her mother's voice, Libby wanted so much to feel sorry for her, but she just couldn't bring that emotion to the surface. 'But you had Dad,' she said. 'He loved you.'

'You're right, and yet I couldn't really trust his love. I lived in fear of him discovering that he'd married a fraud, that I had no right to be his wife.'

'Why did you see yourself as a fraud?'

'I wasn't the person I had grown up thinking I was. My parents weren't who I thought they were, none of it was real and the stigma of being a . . . bastard made me feel as though I could never belong.'

'Nancy, didn't you ever tell your husband that Bess was actually your real mother?'

Her hands twisting at a handkerchief she'd pulled out from the sleeve of her jacket, her make-up ruined from her tears, Nancy looked at Elfrida.

'Of course I didn't. David would have been horrified if I had told him that the woman who gave birth to me didn't even know the name of the man who got her pregnant. That kind of thing didn't happen in the circles in which we moved.'

'I think you'd be surprised by how much it goes on,' said Elfrida.

'But Dad loved you, Mum. You should have trusted him to understand.'

'He loved the woman he thought he'd married,' her mother said. 'Not the ugly woman who existed beneath the perfectly polished exterior. How could I ever show him the real me? He would have been appalled at that person.'

'But real love means you love unconditionally.'

Her mother shook her head. 'No such thing exists. We fall

in love with the person we've created in our imagination, the person we want them to be, with all sorts of conditions attached.'

'What a cynical view of love.'

'But it's true. Wouldn't you two agree?'

Libby expected a swift and adamant denial from Bess and Elfrida and was surprised when Elfrida said, 'I believe this may well be a first, but I agree with you, Nancy. Many years ago, there was a man I genuinely loved but I didn't want him to see the whole of me – the real me. I preferred for him to know what I was prepared to share with him. Just the best bits.'

'Bess?'

'I'm sorry, Libby, but I didn't share everything with my husband Amos for fear of what he might think.'

'Are you saying you didn't tell him about Mum being your child?'

'I didn't. I couldn't bear the thought of him thinking badly of me, that there had been anyone before him. It was a different time back then and he was very old-fashioned in many ways. But what you need to understand, Libby, is that the longer you keep a secret, the harder it becomes to share it. In the end it just seems better to keep quiet.'

Which begged the question, thought Libby, why, after all these years, had her mother broken her silence? What had triggered that?

With her shock and upset now subsiding, Libby was forced to acknowledge that her reaction to her mother's confession had been selfish. She had acted in the very same way she had accused her mother of behaving, and that realisation sickened her.

Taking in the haunted expression on her mother's face, Libby found herself beginning to comprehend the hurt her mother must have carried for so much of her life. It had shaped her and was probably the driving force behind all her actions. Had she so hated what had been done to her and in turn grown to hate herself? And if that were true, how could she have ever been kind to those around her?

'Don't look at me like that,' her mother said in a defensively tight voice. 'You have every right to hate me even more than you already did, but please don't judge me. You can only do that if you've walked in my shoes.'

'Mum, I might hate a lot of the things you've said and done, but I don't hate you. I never have.'

As though that didn't satisfy her, her mother glanced across the table. 'Elfrida, you've never liked or approved of me, have you?'

'I'll admit I've disliked the things you've said and done, just as Libby has, and that's because I know how much it's hurt Bess. But really a lot of the blame lies with Joan and Dudley. They should have behaved more honourably to Bess. After all, she gave them the one thing they wanted above all else: a child.'

'I'm sure we don't need to apportion blame,' murmured Bess. 'The important thing, Libby, is that you now know the truth, and I for one desperately hope you can find it in your heart to forgive us all for the deception we've inflicted on you. We each had our reasons for keeping quiet.' Very slowly, she pushed back her chair and rose to her feet. 'And I don't care what any of you think, I'm going to make a fresh pot of tea.' She picked up the pot. 'Elfrida, perhaps you'd come and help me.'

Elfrida looked at her blankly and then, as if the penny had dropped that Bess was being diplomatic and giving Libby some time alone with her mother, she stood up.

*

It was once they were safely inside the kitchen and out of earshot that Elfrida said, 'I must say, Nancy did herself proud out there, finally finding the courage to be honest. Not just with Libby and you, but with herself. She's to be applauded for that. Maybe now she can allow herself to be happy.'

Turning around from the sink where she was filling the kettle, and where on the nearby worktop their lunch waited to be cooked, Bess said, 'It breaks my heart to know how unhappy she's always been. It must have been dreadful for her when she'd been a child and realised at school that she was an outsider. Children can be so cruel to one another.'

'That was Joan and Dudley's doing; they should never have sent her to that school and they certainly shouldn't have spoilt her.'

The kettle now put to boil, Bess faced Elfrida with a stern expression on her face. 'Elfrida,' she said, 'you have to promise me something.'

'What?'

'That you will never reveal who Nancy's father was. You must never *ever* do that. Do you promise?'

'Now why on earth are you asking such a thing? You know full well I promised you years ago I wouldn't do that.'

'You promised you'd never let on to Nancy that I was her birth mother, but you did.'

'But only because of a misunderstanding; I didn't mean to.'

'Well, it did happen, and I don't want another slip-up to happen. Libby is inevitably going to ask me who Nancy's father was, and doubtless she'll ask you as well. She'll keep on digging until she's satisfied. Look what she's been like with all those old photographs she dragged down from the attic. But that man's name must never be mentioned, or how I ended up pregnant. We haven't come this far for Nancy now to discover that awful part of her story.'

Elfrida went over to her and took Bess's hands in hers. 'I may have broken a few promises along the way, dearest Bess, but that is one I shall never break. You, Nikolai, Ivan, Mallory and

I vowed together that we would take the secret to our graves, and I fully intend to do just that.'

'And you're sure there's nothing in any of those garden notebooks that Libby has yet to look through that might give us away?'

'Trust me, she'll find nothing because there is nothing.'

Chapter Thirty-Six

October 1938
Villa Lucia, Lake Como
Elfrida

It was the day after Bess had confided in me what Michael O'Halligan had done to her that he showed up at Villa Lucia.

I was still reeling with shock at what Bess had borne so bravely, both at the time of her ordeal and afterwards. I was furious with myself that I had never guessed at her secret, and disappointed too that she had never confided in me until now. Had I seemed so unapproachable to her? For all my own misgivings, I had to applaud the sacrifice she had made in handing over the baby to her sister. But then how could she have truly loved the child when it had been created in so brutal a way?

In my own situation, the child I was carrying had been conceived through the act of love – somewhat careless love it had to be said, but love nonetheless. Which made the months ahead for me all the more precarious. My every instinct was that I wanted this child, that I would not be parted from it. But where did Nikolai fit in to the equation and how could I live with the consequences? Good friends would stand by me, but many would desert and shun me for having a child out of wedlock. Commissions for my garden design work would dry up and without a decent income I could lose Larkspur House. It was a depressingly bleak prospect.

Common sense dictated that I should tell Nikolai of my predicament straight away, as soon as he and Ivan returned in the morning from Switzerland, and that I should of course marry him. I had tried to imagine that scenario, of us combining two very different lives and at the same time living with the guilt of what that course of action might do to his first wife. I just couldn't see it working.

I knew, though, that I couldn't keep the baby from Nikolai, that to deny him the pleasure of knowing he was a father would be an unforgivable act of treachery on my part. I knew in my bones as well, that asking Bess and Amos to care for the child as though it were their own wouldn't work either. I would be too interfering and too insistent on how things should be done.

For most of that day I had worked hard in the garden digging and planting along with Giovanni and his son, Giacomo, and it was as good a way I knew as any to stop me from worrying about the future. Now though, as Bess and I sat on the terrace eating our evening meal while across the lake, the last of the setting sun's rays gilded Bellagio with a burnished coppery glow, we heard a voice calling from across the lawn.

My first thought was that it was Nikolai and Ivan back earlier than planned, but then when the voice called out again – *Buonasera!* – and we turned to see who it was, I knew I was mistaken. The frozen look of horror on Bess's face, and the clatter of her knife and fork dropping from her hands, told me that she recognised who it was, even though he was some distance away.

'It's *him*!'

I could hear the panicky fear in her voice. 'Who?' I asked.

'Michael O'Halligan,' she whispered, the colour draining from her face.

'Well now, isn't this a *bella* sight to behold?' the man drawled in a lilting Irish accent when he drew near. 'Two beautiful English ladies enjoying the magnificent view.'

'Leave this to me,' I said, putting a restraining hand on Bess's arm and rising from my seat. I had been told many a time that my authoritative bearing belied my lack of stature and I knew as never before that I had to put it to good use now. 'How the devil did you get through the gates?' I demanded.

'Begging you kindly,' he said in a mocking tone, 'but two well-disposed gardeners on their way home after a day's toil let me in. I told them I was an old friend of one of the guests currently staying here and that she would be bound to give me a warm welcome.'

'You're no friend,' said Bess, now also on her feet. 'And a welcome is the last thing you'll ever be given. Now please just go.'

The scoundrel actually had the temerity to wink at her. 'Oh, Bess,' he said with a laugh, 'how very grand you sound, but come on, don't be a spoilsport. Not when you and I once had such a memorable night of passion together. Do you know, if I close my eyes, I can picture you in my arms all over again.'

'That's enough!' I said. 'I know exactly who you are, Mr O'Halligan, and what you did to Bess that night at Tilbrook Hall, and if you don't leave in the next two minutes, I shall call the police.'

He laughed again. A loathsome laugh of goading. 'I can see where you learnt your grand fighting talk, Bess, straight from the mouth of her snooty ladyship here. Now the thing is, ladies, I have a mind to stay and keep you company for a while as I have some important business to discuss with you. Shall we sit down?'

Without waiting for either Bess or me to respond, he made himself comfortable on one of the cast-iron chairs. Neither Bess nor I joined him. We stood resolutely together, side by side.

'I can't imagine for one second what sort of business you think we would be remotely interested in discussing with you,' I said.

He picked up the bottle of wine that was on the table and took an uncouth swig from it. 'And that's why I'm going to lay it all out for you,' he said, wiping the back of his hand across his mouth. 'I'll even make it nice and easy so there'll be no difficulty in you grasping the arrangement we're going to have. You see, I know all about you, Miss High-and-Mighty Elfrida Ambrose and a certain Count who goes by the name of Nikolai Demidov and with whom you are conducting an affair. Oh yes,' he said, wagging a finger at me, 'you've been careful, but not careful enough. An evening of grappa in a bar with the locals and easy as anything I had teased out the story of the wealthy Russian gentleman and the beautiful English rose who was his mistress. You see, Italians love the romance of an affair, especially a *secret* affair.'

'I've never heard so much nonsense in all my life,' I said, fighting hard to disguise my trepidation. 'You're clearly out of your mind or drunk on your own self-importance. I've asked you once very politely to leave, now I'm asking you again. Please go.'

He leant back in the chair and let his gaze trail over me in a very disagreeable manner. I knew it was a deliberate act on his part to unsettle me, but I wasn't going to be intimidated.

'Your type,' he said, lifting the bottle to his mouth again and drinking thirstily from it, 'always thinks you can boss the lower orders about, don't you? But let me assure you, I'm not leaving until you've given me what I want.'

'Which is?'

'Money, of course. Money to buy my silence. Give me what I want, and your secret will remain safe with me.'

'What a ridiculously stupid man you are,' I said, 'there is no secret affair going on between me and the Count.'

I saw the flash of anger blaze in his eyes then and he brought both his fists down hard on the table. 'Don't lie to me!' he roared.

At my side, Bess started, and despite my own increasing alarm at the situation, and knowing we were completely alone and without help, I was determined not to show a scrap of fear. Bullies like Michael O'Halligan enjoyed scaring women; it made them feel superior and powerful. But he was not going to frighten me. Nor was he going to blackmail me. Pay him once and he'd only keep coming back for more until the well was dry. So I went on the attack, using the information Bess had given me after she'd confessed to what had happened to her at the hands of this vile man.

'Bess told me all about you bumping into her in Menaggio,' I said, 'and how you boasted about the employer for whom you now worked, a wealthy American industrialist currently holidaying here at the lake. I wonder how he would feel knowing that he has a rapist working for him? I can't imagine that he'd keep you on if he knew the truth about you, do you?'

'That's where you're wrong,' O'Halligan said with a patronising laugh while idly crossing one leg over the other. 'I have enough dirt on my current employer to keep me in the style I've become accustomed to for as long as I want. Let's just say I help in facilitating some of his less than savoury liaisons. Especially the younger ones.'

Realising I'd lost the one trump card I had, it was my turn to affect a dismissive laugh. 'What a thoroughly repugnant man you are.'

'I've never claimed to be a saint, whereas the likes of you,' he jabbed a finger in the air in my direction, 'always like to make out you're so much better than everybody else.'

'How very unpleasant it must be to be you, Mr O'Halligan, and to be burdened by such a cumbersome chip on your shoulder.'

'Oh, it's not so bad, you know, I tolerate myself. But I do not tolerate women who try to take me for a fool.'

'If it's respect you want,' I said with contempt, 'trust me when I say you go about it entirely the wrong way.'

His eyes narrowed at that and after taking another long swig of wine, he shook his head. 'I really wouldn't cross me if I were you, not when I know that you're here all alone. Not when I could snap you like a twig with my bare hands and then do exactly what I wanted with you. Actually, come to think of it' – once more he ran his gaze over me – 'a little fun before we get down to business might be quite pleasant. How about it?'

As revolted as I was by his disgusting suggestion, I fought hard not to react to it and wondered instead how he knew that Bess and I were alone. Had the flow of grappa in a bar in town helped to loosen tongues and he'd learned of Nikolai's movements, and also those of Mallory that way? Yet how to get rid of him? Other than to give him what he wanted. But we had precious few lire in the villa; everything we needed to buy from the local shops was on account and Mallory saw to it that the bills were settled each week. All I could realistically offer him was something from my jewellery collection; not that I had that much with me, just a few bits and pieces I wore in the evenings when I dressed up for Nikolai's benefit.

While my brain was turning all this over, I was conscious that Bess had been as quiet and as still as a broken clock, but now she stepped towards our uninvited guest.

'If you have any sense, you'd go now,' she said. 'Count Demidov and his valet will be here any minute and I wouldn't rate your chances against either of them, let alone the two of them combined. They won't take kindly to a pathetic bully like you who picks on defenceless women.'

Rising slowly to his feet, he stepped towards Bess and sneered down at her. 'The way I heard it they're not due back until tomorrow.'

'Then you heard wrong; there's been a change of plan.'

'Nobody tells me that I'm wrong. Not ever.' He glanced over to me. 'Now, Miss Ambrose, how about we go inside this lovely villa and find what cash you can lay hands on, along with a trinket or two of jewellery, and then I'll be on my way. How does that sound?'

'It sounds like a very bad idea,' said Bess. 'Because whatever we give you it won't be enough, will it?'

'But it'll do for starters. Let's call it a first instalment until we have things better established. I'll even take a traveller's cheque if it helps.'

'Fine,' I said, turning to go inside the house. 'If that's what it takes to be free of your odious company, then so be it.'

'No, miss!' cried Bess. 'You can't give in to him! You mustn't!'

'Oh, but Bess, I disagree,' O'Halligan said. 'Finally your employer has seen sense. I knew she wouldn't let me down, not when she has so much to lose.'

I didn't really know what I was doing, only that I didn't want this vile man's presence at Villa Lucia for a moment longer than was necessary, and that if handing over a pearl necklace and a traveller's cheque would get rid of him, then I'd do so. Once he was gone, I would have to think of something longer term to be rid of him.

I was at the top of the short flight of stone steps that led to the villa when he grabbed me from behind and twisting my arm, shoved me roughly against a large stone urn. His face just inches from mine, his breath hot and foul, the pupils of his eyes fully dilated, I tried to free myself from his strong gasp, but he just laughed and held me all the harder. 'I want you to know that I'll be watching you closely when we go inside, so don't go thinking you can pull some kind of clever stunt on—'

His words stopped abruptly and from behind him, a flash of movement caught my eye and simultaneously there was the sound of a thwack. I felt the thwack too as his body bumped heavily against mine and then fell away. For a moment he simply stared at me as though in confusion, then he was toppling backwards down the stone steps until he landed at the bottom. In front of me stood Bess and in her right hand was the wine bottle from the table and there was what looked like blood splashed down her dress, but which was in fact red wine.

As if frozen in time, we stared at each other, then we moved as one down the steps to the body sprawled on the paved ground and where there was now a puddle of blood forming around O'Halligan's head. A haunting feeling of déjà vu came over me as I recalled the horror of finding my brother's body beneath his open bedroom window. But whereas Bobby's eyes had been closed, O'Halligan's were open and staring up at the darkening sky above him, looking for all the world like he was counting the stars that were now just beginning to show. When a strange gurgling sound came out of his mouth, Bess dropped the wine bottle and it shattered on impact with the ground. Her hands flew to her face and she let out a cry.

I bent down beside O'Halligan and placed my fingers to the side of his neck. When I didn't find a pulse, I then tried his wrist. But still I couldn't find a pulse. Blood was now coming out of his mouth and nose and his eyeballs hadn't moved; they continued to stare glassily up at the sky.

'He's not . . . he's not dead, is he?' asked Bess, her voice quivering.

On my knees now, I tried again to find a pulse, I put a hand to his chest to feel for a heartbeat, but there was nothing.

'Quite dead,' I said.

'He can't be . . . I didn't mean to kill him . . . I just wanted to hurt him . . . to make him stop. I was scared what he might do to you and . . .' Her words fell away as she began to cry.

I stood up and put my arms around her. 'Bess,' I said, 'it was an accident. A terrible accident. Now you have to pull yourself together because we have to decide what we're going to do.'

'What can we do?' she asked through her sobs. 'I killed him. I'm a murderer . . . I'll be hanged!'

She began to shake uncontrollably, and I feared she might collapse unless I could calm her down. I led her back to the table and chairs and pushed her into a seat. Kneeling in front of her and holding her chin in my hands, I lifted her face up so she was forced to look into my eyes. 'Listen to me, Bess, you're not a murderer and you're not going to be hanged. I won't let that happen. Do you understand?'

Her sobbing stilled and she gave a shuddery nod. 'But what are we going to do?' She glanced over my shoulder to where O'Halligan lay.

I held her face in my hands more firmly, again forcing her to look at me. 'We're going to get rid of the body and pretend that nothing untoward happened here this evening.'

She stared at me as though I were mad. And perhaps I was, but I was thinking fast, doing my damnedest to find a way out of the nightmare in which we found ourselves.

'How are we going to get rid of the body?' she asked. 'And we can't pretend he was never here, the gardeners know he came. He spoke to them.'

'If we're ever asked, we shall say he paid us a visit and then left. That's our story and that's what we will always say. Yes?'

'But he's dead, miss, and all because of me. If it hadn't been for me, he would never have come here.'

'Well, he did, and he was a thoroughly nasty piece of work who got what he deserved.'

'But shouldn't we call the police and say what happened? If we explain everything they might understand. They might take pity on me and be lenient.' Her hands were trembling on her lap and her eyes were filled with tears. 'I'll tell them the truth, that it was an accident, that I only meant to hurt him so he wouldn't blackmail you.'

'No,' I said as sternly as I could. 'We can't involve the police because Nikolai will then be dragged into this. It would be an awful scandal for him. For Mallory too. We have to sort this out ourselves.'

She swallowed. 'So what are we going to do?'

I ran through several options in my head. Burying the body was my first thought and then planting a tree or something equally permanent over it. My next thought was the lake. Could we get the body down the hillside and then into a boat and dump it in the middle of the lake, weighing it down with rocks beforehand? Both options would involve a good deal of effort, but my preferred option had the potential to be a lot easier. But I would need Bess's help, I didn't think I could do it on my own. In fact, I knew I couldn't.

I told Bess what we were going to do, and she reluctantly agreed to it.

It was now pitch black but with our eyes accustomed to the darkness, we began the monumental task of moving O'Halligan's dead weight of a body from the terrace and down the sloping lawn, around the side of the villa and to the front lawn where the disused well was located. With my hands under his armpits, I bore the heaviest weight of him, and Bess held his ankles. Puffing and panting, we shuffled our way in the darkness. The moon was still low in the sky and was of little use in guiding us in the blackness, but eventually we made it to our destination.

The next part of our grisly challenge was to shift the slab that covered the well in order, ironically, to make it safe from anyone accidentally falling down the shaft. The slab was so heavy it took all our strength just to move it a couple of inches. But on we went, the macabre sound of the concrete slab grating on our nerves as we gained another inch, followed by another, and another.

'Just one more push,' I gasped when we were at the critical stage of the hole being large enough to accommodate O'Halligan's body.

It was then that I felt something tightening and then twisting in the lower part of my abdomen. I straightened up and took a deep breath. Muscle strain, I told myself. That was all.

'What is it?' asked Bess. 'What's wrong?'

'Nothing,' I replied, but then I caught my breath as the tightening made itself felt once more, and this time much more painfully. Suddenly feeling lightheaded and as if I were swaying, I rested my elbows on the top of the well and leaning forwards, my chest touching the brickwork, I squeezed my eyes shut to block out the pain, hoping against all hope that this wasn't what I feared it was. But when I felt a warm wetness between my legs, I knew the worst.

I had always prided myself on my strength and ability to cope with anything that was thrown at me. I viewed weakness as something to be overcome at all costs. Being vulnerable and at the mercy of my emotions was not my style. But right now, I was powerless to stem the flow of tears at what was happening to me. I wanted to tell myself that losing the baby was for the best, but I couldn't. I had wanted this baby. I had wanted Nikolai's child, to have that part of him for the rest of my life. Now it was draining out of me, leaving me bereft. It didn't make sense that I could feel that emotion so soon when I had only suspected for a short while that I was pregnant. Yet as irrational as it was, it was wholly real, and I let out a howl of intense sadness.

At my side, Bess let out a cry too. '*No!*' she cried. 'Tell me it isn't so! Not that! Not the baby!'

But we both knew that it was. Our act of evil, our plotting to cover up O'Halligan's death, had rewarded us with a punishing blow that neither of us would ever forget, or forgive ourselves for.

It was when I had slid to the ground and was on my knees, and with Bess cradling me in her arms and trying to offer comfort, that we saw the flash of car headlamps down by the gates. Seconds later, we saw the shape of a man getting out of a car and opening the metal gates and then waiting for the car to pass through, before closing them again and climbing back in. The curving nature of the drive meant that the headlamps swept over the front lawn and for a moment we – and our crime – were bathed in the brightest of lights. The car then came to an abrupt stop and the two occupants came running towards us.

I don't really recall what happened next, I was too distraught to take it all in, but what I do know is that I was lifted off the ground and carried inside the house.

I woke in the night to find Nikolai watching over me. With the light from the moon streaming in through the unshuttered windows, he was sitting bolt upright in a chair beside the bed. He looked as ghastly as I felt, and seeing that I was awake, he snapped forwards.

'Why didn't you tell me about the baby?' he asked. His voice sounded weirdly muffled and far away, as though my ears were full of water.

'I didn't know for sure,' I said. 'Not until you'd left for Lugano.'

He leant even closer to me and touched my cheek tenderly with his hand. 'I'm so sorry,' he said.

The sadness in his voice was unbearable. 'So am I,' I said, turning to kiss the palm of his hand and wishing I could fight my way through the dense fog that seemed to have engulfed my senses and was weighing me down. I tried to move, to sit up in the hope that might clear my head, but Nikolai stopped me.

'The doctor gave you something to sleep,' he said, 'so it would be better if—'

'Doctor?' I repeated as a warning bell began to ring very faintly in my befuddled brain. 'What doctor?'

'A very discreet doctor. There'll be no record of his visit.'

Something in Nikolai's reply made another warning bell ring. This one was much louder. And then I knew why, and a bolt of alarm shot through me. 'O'Halligan!' I exclaimed, almost launching myself out of bed.

'Ssh, my darling, it's all been taken care of. Bess explained what happened and Ivan and I have dealt with it. There's nothing to worry about, everything's going to be all right. Now go back to sleep.'

Amazingly, thanks to whatever the doctor had given me, I did sleep.

Chapter Thirty-Seven

August 1981
Larkspur House, Suffolk

It wasn't until almost seven o'clock that evening that Libby remembered she had agreed to go out for a meal with Daniel.

Given the emotionally draining day they'd had it seemed more appropriate to put him off, but both Bess and Elfrida had been quick to urge Libby to spend the evening with Daniel as arranged. Libby's mother wasn't quite so enthusiastic. She hadn't actually uttered the words, 'How can you think of going out when I'm here?' but the look she'd given Libby when she'd come downstairs after hurriedly swapping her jeans for a dress and sprayed perfume on as well as a hastily applied dash of make-up, had said it all the same. The tight-lipped expression on her face bore all the signs of the Nancy of old, the hard-done-by Nancy, the Nancy who imagined she was being slighted yet again.

The pub Daniel had booked for them was a twenty-minute drive from Finchley Green and was as picturesque as it was quaint. Half-timbered and beautifully thatched and painted in traditional Suffolk pink, it was tucked away down a narrow lane. Surrounded by willow trees, it had a delightful fairy-tale quality that made Libby think of Hansel and Gretel coming across a gingerbread house in the middle of a forest.

Inside, it was just as charming, with uneven stone floors, a couple of fireplaces and rough-hewn oak beams. Shiny copper pots and pans, horse brasses and old sepia photographs of Shire horses ploughing fields covered every conceivable inch of wall space, including the blackened beams. Ordering their drinks at the bar and their food from the chalkboard menu, Libby observed two old boys playing dominoes in a nook to the right of the largest of the fireplaces. There wasn't a fire burning, not when it was such a warm summer's evening, but there was plenty of smoke being produced by the domino players who were sucking hard on their pipes. Watching them through the cloud of thick blue pipe-smoke, Libby had the feeling of stepping back in time.

It was, she thought now as she and Daniel went outside to the beer garden to find a table, precisely what she had done when she'd left London and fled to Larkspur House. She had wanted to escape to the past of her childhood where deception and betrayal couldn't touch her.

How wrong she'd been!

Now she'd discovered that Marcus and Selina were not the only ones who had deceived her. Mum, Bess and Elfrida had done so too. What shocked her most was that her mother had behaved so cruelly to Bess, and for so long. How could anyone do that? Why couldn't she have understood the situation from Bess's standpoint? Why only hers?

So many lies, so many secrets, thought Libby. Would there be any more hidden skeletons to come crashing out of the cupboards? she wondered.

'I suppose we could sit here in silence for the evening like an old married couple, if you'd prefer, but it might be nice to exchange a word or two.'

Libby looked up from her untouched glass of wine, appalled that in brooding over her mother she had been ignoring Daniel. 'I'm so sorry,' she said, 'I was miles away, lost in thought.'

'I was beginning to worry that maybe you were regretting coming here with me this evening,' he said.

'Absolutely not. It's just been one of those days.'

'Care to share it with me? Or I could send you to sleep with some of the medical cases I dealt with today which include a urinary infection, a fungal rash, and a broken toe. All in a day's work,' he said with a wry smile.

Libby had promised herself before getting into Daniel's car that she wouldn't ruin the evening by talking about the day's events. That by relaxing and enjoying a change of scene with him the rising sense of outrage she felt at her mother's treatment of Bess would be quelled. It didn't seem to be working though.

'Is it your great-aunt?' Daniel asked. 'Has she had an angina attack today?'

Libby debated with herself how to answer his question. She could simply lie, as it seemed others found it so easy to do, or she could be honest and explain why she was being less than sparkling company. At the look of genuine concern on Daniel's face, she decided he deserved her honesty.

'Funny you should ask after Bess,' she said, her hands fidgeting with her wineglass, turning it clockwise, then anticlockwise, 'because I was told today that she's not my great-aunt, but is actually my grandmother, just as, ironically, you thought she was the day the attic floor gave way.'

His hazel eyes fixed on hers, Daniel contemplated her for a few seconds. 'And is that a bad thing?'

She shook her head. 'Not at all. But it's wrong that I've been deliberately kept in ignorance of the truth by my mother. To put it bluntly, it was her secret weapon, and she was determined to use it on the two people it most affected: Bess and me. And the more I think about that, the more I feel unable to forgive her for being so selfish and spiteful. I'm sorry if that makes me sound as heartless as she's behaved, but it's how I feel.'

'Hey,' he said, 'don't be so hard on yourself. It's clearly a big deal to you when you've always been so close to Bess. But may I offer you some advice?'

'What,' she said with a frown, 'that I try and see things from my mother's point of view?'

The smile he gave her immediately made her feel guilty at the crabbiness of her reply.

'No,' he said. 'My advice is that you should stop spinning that wineglass around and drink its contents.'

Libby smiled too. 'I'll bet you tell all your patients that, don't you?'

'Never fails.' He raised his glass of beer and waited for her to do likewise. When they'd tapped their glasses together and Libby had taken a good glug of her wine, he said, 'If you thought it would help, you could tell me the whole story. Or as much of it as you feel comfortable with sharing.'

Her mother might hate the idea of Libby revealing the truth of her birth, but she didn't care. She wasn't going to live her life ruled by secrets and lies. If there was one thing she valued more than anything, it was honesty. Her mother's example proved beyond doubt that deceit had a detrimental effect on a person and Libby wasn't going to make the same mistake.

She had only got as far as explaining about her mother's visit when a waitress appeared with their meal.

When the woman had gone, Daniel passed Libby the salt and pepper and bottle of malt vinegar. 'I hope you weren't hoping for a slap-up gourmet dinner in a smart restaurant with candles and pretentious waiters gliding about the place and looking down their noses at us,' he said.

'Chicken in the basket suits me perfectly,' she replied, and meaning it. 'I can't remember when I last had a meal like this in such a lovely pub. Marcus always favoured fancier food over pub grub. How did you find it? It's a hidden gem well off the beaten track.'

'A patient in my new surgery told me about it. Don't laugh, but I came on Saturday to suss it out, just to make sure it would be okay for you.'

Thinking how thoughtful it was that he'd gone to so much trouble, she said, 'You needn't have worried, it's great.'

He shrugged. 'I wanted it to be right for you, knowing that you're something of an expert when it comes to cooking. This is my small way of thanking you for feeding me so well at Larkspur House.'

'I love to cook and Elfrida loves to have an audience, so you must definitely come again. But maybe after my mother has gone.'

'I'd like that.' Splashing vinegar onto his chips, then adding a sprinkling of salt, he looked up at her. 'So come on, continue where you left off before our meal arrived.'

Libby ate a chip which was deliciously crisp and salty on the outside and pillowy light on the inside. 'Are you sure you want me to?'

'I wouldn't have asked if I didn't, and if I'm honest, I'm curious to know the story. But, if you'd rather not, I understand. Family stuff isn't always that easy to share.'

'There's no need to tiptoe around me,' she said with a smile. 'I'm not going to do anything embarrassing like burst into tears and cause a scene.'

'But I might.'

She laughed, then took another sip of her wine, followed by a mouthful of tasty chicken, and then proceeded to give a condensed version of the day's revelations. She tried hard not to sound too censorious but was conscious that she was coming across as lacking in compassion towards her mother. Checking herself, she finished by saying, 'I don't think my mother has ever been truly happy, not since the day she realised she was a figure of fun at school for being overweight. If her mother – Joan, the woman who brought her up – hadn't been so possessive of her, or so determined to turn her into something she should never have been, things might have been different.'

'That might well be true, but at some point in our lives we all have to take responsibility for ourselves, and for our actions. Do you think that's what your mother is now trying to do?'

Libby considered this. 'I hadn't thought of it like that, perhaps you're right. She did admit that shortly before her mother – *Joan* – died, Joan said she needed to put things right with Bess, while she still could. Apparently, she regretted that she had never done that herself. But to me that puts my mother in an even worse light, that she couldn't bring herself to do what Joan had urged her to do.'

'But she has now. Bess's collapse, right there in front of her, probably sharpened her focus. After keeping a secret of that magnitude for so long, it must have taken an incredible amount of courage to let go of it finally.'

'You're beginning to sound like my mother's biggest advocate,' Libby said light-heartedly.

'It's easy to be objective when there's no personal involvement, and as a doctor that's one of the challenges we face, how to keep an open and objective mind.'

'The challenge for me is to overcome how much it hurts knowing that she treated Bess so badly. And what if Bess had died and I had never known the truth while she was alive?'

Taking a long and thoughtful swallow of his beer, Daniel said, 'Does it really make that much of a difference to you whether Bess is your great-aunt or your grandmother? She's the same person today as she was yesterday, as are you.'

'Mum said the same thing,' Libby answered. 'But somehow,' she added with a smile, 'it sounds more reasonable coming from you.'

'That'll be on account of my effortless charm, and not forgetting my inexhaustible supply of modesty.'

'Well, that goes without saying,' she said, thinking that at last she really was beginning to relax and enjoy the evening.

'One thing I don't understand,' she said, when she'd finished her chicken and had eaten the last of her chips, 'is why, even when she knew about Marcus cheating on me, Mum was initially so intent on my marrying him. After the miserable life she's had, why did she want me to marry a man I'd never be able to trust and who would make me so unhappy?'

'Did you ask her that?'

'I did, and I'm afraid her answer made me incredibly angry. She claimed she wanted me settled with somebody who was financially secure and who would give me status in life. She even went so far as to say being married to Marcus would stop me from demeaning myself by working as little more than a waitress. She said Bess had made the mistake of turning herself into a drudge for Elfrida and I was doing the same serving food to wealthy City types.' Taking a breath, Libby paused to pick up her wineglass and drink from it.

For a while Daniel said nothing, but after he'd finished eating, he said, 'What do you think your father would have made of all this?'

Libby was so surprised by the question, she nearly lost control of the wine in her mouth. Managing to avoid spluttering it across the table, it then went down the wrong way. Daniel was quick to offer a pat on the back.

'I'm okay,' she croaked, sounding like a strangled Donald Duck. Ignoring her, he gave her back a firm thump and miraculously the obstruction in her throat shifted.

Her eyes watering, she said, 'The next time you ask me such a loaded question would you warn me, please?'

'I'm sorry. And sorry too if I walloped you too hard.'

'You're stronger than you look,' she quipped.

'Full of surprises, that's me.'

Aren't you just? she thought. 'And surprisingly intuitive,' she said. 'You went straight for the jugular by asking about my father.'

'Again, sorry for that. Blame it on a terrifying matron in the hospital where I was a registrar; she laid down the law when it came to listening closely to a patient and asking the unexpected, as often the answer would be remarkably helpful when it came to making a diagnosis.'

'Well, the answer to your question is that my father would have been horrified. He always had my best interests at heart. Which was why he encouraged my visits to Larkspur House; he knew I loved being there and that I benefitted enormously from Bess and Elfrida's company.'

'Did he know the truth about your mother and the source of her unhappiness?'

Libby shook her head. 'From what Mum says, she would have sooner died than open up to him.'

'What a shame. But then I suppose it was different then – being illegitimate used to carry such a weight of stigma. It still does for many people.'

'You're right, I know.'

'And in a quick change of subject,' he said, 'how about another glass of wine?'

He was on his feet before she'd even replied and watching him go back inside the pub, she observed the busy beer garden. All the tables were occupied and judging from the rising levels of convivial chatter and laughter everyone appeared to be having an enjoyable evening out, as though they didn't have a care in the world.

But appearances could be deceiving. Who knew what heart-ache anyone here had experienced? Nobody went through life without being touched by some traumatic event or other. Nobody was immune from loss or suffering, and yet somehow it could be overcome.

Which made Libby think of Daniel. To her shame she had been so fixated on her own problems, she hadn't asked him how he was, or how his divorce was going. The realisation was deeply unsettling, and she vowed to make amends. For the rest of the evening, she would stop going on about herself and would instead concentrate on getting to know Daniel better. Because he was genuinely someone whom she would like to know a lot better.

Turning around in her seat to look at the beer garden from a different angle, she was rewarded with a spectacular sight. The sun was sinking like a fireball in the vast sky, scorching it with trails of blazing orangey hues. She rarely saw sunsets as beautiful as this in London and not for the first time she wondered how on earth she could ever go back.

Well, that was a stupid question because she knew in her heart she wasn't going back, not permanently. When she did return, it would be to sell her flat and pack up her life there. She had yet to have the conversation with Bess and Elfrida, but she was hoping that she could stay with them while she found somewhere to live here in Suffolk, and hopefully not too far away.

It wasn't just one thing that had brought her to this conclusion, but Bess's health scare was certainly part of her thinking. It had given her cause to reflect on what the future might hold for Bess. Her angina would always have to be managed and Libby didn't want Elfrida to be solely responsible for Bess's well-being, and since Libby had no desire to live and work in London any more, moving close by seemed entirely the right thing to do. And hadn't Bess spoken of Libby making a wonderful new life for herself? Where better to put down roots than near Larkspur House, where she had always been happy?

There was another reason why she had begun to think that she could make this area her new home, and it was as a direct result of sorting through Elfrida's fascinating collection of photographs. Admiring the beautiful gardens Elfrida had created had sown a seed of an idea in Libby's head and she wanted to discuss it with Elfrida before taking it any further.

More immediately she knew that she had to put things right with her mother. And to a degree with Bess. She was ashamed of the way she had effectively accused Bess of being complicit in keeping the truth from her. She should never have done that. It had been judgemental of her and was another instance of her replicating something her mother would do. She must not on any account end up repeating the pattern of behaviour that had gone before. She had to be the one to break the mould. Wouldn't that be what her father would want her to do?

The thought of her father made her think of Daniel's question, which had been like an arrow straight to her heart. He had been dead for so long, yet she still cherished every memory she had of him.

Turning around to face the table, she saw Daniel advancing with their drinks. Caught as he was in the radiance of the setting sun, it struck Libby as it had before that he was an eye-catchingly good-looking man. She wasn't alone in thinking so, as two women sitting at the nearest table nudged each other as he approached.

Dressed in faded Levi's and a navy-blue polo shirt, the luminous light was doing all sorts of lovely things to his hair, giving it an attractive coppery warmth. She had noticed much the same thing that day at Larkspur House when they'd been leaning against the fence while enjoying the view of the meadow.

When he drew level with Libby and placed their drinks on the table, she saw the two women exchange another look, as if clocking her and thinking how lucky she was. *And perhaps I am*, she thought with a smile.

'What's that smile for?' Daniel asked when he sat down. 'Not that I'm complaining. You have a great smile.'

She felt herself blush at the compliment, and then noticed

that his face had changed colour too, as if he hadn't meant to say what he had. 'I was thinking what a beautiful evening it was,' she said, 'and how lucky I am to be here.'

'Funnily enough, I was just thinking much the same thing,' he said.

*

Bess let out a weary sigh. It had been a long and very tiring day and supper had been an exceptionally awkward affair.

The three of them – Bess, Elfrida and Nancy – had resembled strangers sitting around the table in the garden, politely passing food to one another, and not really knowing what to say, even though there was so very much to be said. But the rulebook by which they had previously coexisted had suddenly been ripped up and they were like actors on a stage who hadn't been given a script. It was a relief when Elfrida announced she needed to do some watering, despite it almost being dark, and Nancy said she would like a bath and an early night. It was obvious they needed to escape from each other.

Alone in the kitchen and making a start on the washing up, Bess might have expected to be filled with the need to celebrate what had been a truly momentous day, something for which she had waited so long. But rejoicing was not uppermost in her mind. What she did feel was an abiding sense of loss. It was as though she was grieving for all the time she had missed out on as Nancy's mother.

Was it possible that Nancy now regretted her actions all these years? She hadn't said as much, and maybe she never would. Really all that was important was that they could now be happy around each other. To do that they needed to put the past to rest and hopefully today they had made a start on doing just that.

But Bess knew better than anyone that it wasn't possible to

put the past entirely to rest. There were some things which just couldn't be forgotten or forgiven.

Deciding to leave the washing up until later, she ripped off her rubber gloves and went through to the dining room to look at the photographs still laid out on the table.

Chapter Thirty-Eight

October 1938
Villa Lucia, Lake Como
Bess

I woke in the morning to the shock of finding Ivan asleep in a chair by the side of my bed. Sitting bolt upright and clutching the bedclothes to me as though defending my honour and horrified at what Amos would think, a far greater shock hit me when I remembered the events of the night before. My last and abiding memory of the night was that I had been hysterical – literally out of my mind with disbelief at what I had done – and had been given a strong sedative by a strange man to calm me.

What had possessed me to do such a dreadful thing?

Even as I asked myself the question, I knew exactly what had seized hold of my senses when I'd grabbed the wine bottle from the table. I'd wanted to hurt O'Halligan as much as he'd hurt me. I'd wanted to wipe that sneering cocksure smile off his face. I'd wanted him gone. Gone from my life forever and the memory of what he'd done to me gone too. In short, I'd wanted revenge, to even the score by giving in to the blinding rage I felt and killing him.

But the second I'd heard his head smash against the paved terrace, I had regretted succumbing to such a base emotion. I'd become no better than he'd been, and I deserved whatever punishment would be my fate. I would be hanged. I *should* be hanged. I pictured my body dangling from a noose and it made a distraught whimper escape from my lips. At that Ivan stirred and his eyelids flicked open, making me clasp the bedclothes even more tightly to my chest.

'How are you feeling?' he asked, rubbing the sleep from his eyes and straightening his back from where he'd been slumped in the chair.

'Terrible,' I said. 'How long have you been there?'

'Most of the night,' he replied. 'And Nikolai has done the same with Elfrida.'

To my shame it was only then that another memory returned to me and I recalled what had happened to Elfrida. With not a thought to any impropriety, I flung back the bedclothes and hurled myself to my feet, realising as I did that I was fully dressed and in what I'd worn yesterday. 'I must go to her!' I cried.

'There's no hurry,' Ivan said, quickly rising from the chair and standing between me and the door.

'Out of my way,' I said.

'All in good time. For now, you should stay in bed and rest some more.'

'I don't need to rest. I have to make sure Elfrida is all right.'

Despite my insistence, Ivan refused to budge, his burly, broad-shouldered body remaining resolutely where it was, a solid wall barring my way. He then led me firmly by the arm back to the bed.

'Please,' I tried one more time. 'Let me go to Elfrida, just to put my mind at rest. I won't disturb her if she's still sleeping. But I need to know that she's all right . . . and that the baby is all right.'

He looked at me and I saw at once the awful truth in his expression. 'I'm sorry,' he said with a slow shake of his head, 'but she lost the baby, that was why we sent for a doctor.'

At his words, my body went slack, and I began to weep. 'It's all my fault,' I wailed. 'How will she ever forgive me? And the Count too?'

As my weeping increased, Ivan held me in his firm grasp again. 'No,' he said, 'you must not torture yourself with these thoughts. It was simply not meant to be. Elfrida and Nikolai will recover from this and maybe God will grant them another child.'

'But *I* won't recover from this!' I cried. 'Not ever!' Such was my anguish I fell against him and sobbed. He held me close, his strong hands pressing firmly into my back and shoulders.

When the worst of my torment was spent and my tears ran dry, I stepped away from Ivan and after promising that I wouldn't bother Elfrida, I begged to be allowed to go to the bathroom to change out of my dress which was grubby and stained with blood and red wine. He reluctantly agreed and said he'd wait for me downstairs.

Once I was dressed in clean clothes and had tidied up my face and hair, I kept to my promise and passed Elfrida's room without going in. I listened at the door for a few seconds, but there was no sound from within.

Downstairs in the kitchen I was greeted by the smell of freshly brewing coffee and the sight of Ivan beating eggs.

'You need to eat,' he said gruffly, 'so please don't tell me you're not hungry. Sit while I cook you an omelette.'

I did as he said. He poured me a cup of coffee, and then in silence I watched him cook the eggs in two pans side by side, adding sliced mushrooms, grated Parmesan and chopped parsley and salt and pepper before sliding the omelettes onto plates and placing them on the table.

'Eat,' he said. 'Then we talk.'

I had never felt less like eating, but Ivan's gaze was so fiercely stern, once more I found myself doing as he said. I was, I knew, totally in his hands because just as I had made Elfrida complicit in my crime, so too were Nikolai and Ivan.

We ate in a jarring silence, the only sound the scraping of our cutlery on the plates. With the tiled floor and high ceiling, the noise was magnified and set me even more on edge. In that moment I hated Villa Lucia and never wanted to see it again as long as I lived. All I wanted was to be back at home in Finchley Green, sitting at the small table in my own kitchen with Amos smoking his pipe and me thinking that I was the luckiest of women to be married to such a kind and gentle man. A man I didn't deserve. A man with whom I had never been truly honest and never would be. Especially not now.

'Good,' said Ivan, breaking into my thoughts. 'You have eaten it all.'

I looked at my plate and saw to my surprise that it was empty. I had indeed managed to eat what he had cooked for me. He removed the plates and placed them in the sink, then returned to the table with the coffee pot and refilled our cups.

'Now,' he said, 'it is time to talk.'

My stomach suddenly churned, and I feared the omelette I'd just eaten might not stay down. 'Tell me everything,' I said.

He nodded and proceeded to do just that, saying that while Nikolai had carried Elfrida inside and put her to bed and called for a doctor, I had been coherent enough to explain to Ivan my history with O'Halligan and that he had come to the villa to blackmail Elfrida about her relationship with Nikolai.

'Once we understood what had happened,' Ivan continued, 'and while we waited for the doctor to arrive, Nikolai and I dealt with the body.'

'Did you put it down the well as Elfrida and I were trying to do?'

'Yes. But first we stripped it to reduce the risk of it being identified.'

I shuddered at the thought of the pair of them doing that, picturing them in the darkness carrying out the gruesome task.

'And so today we will have a bonfire to burn the clothes we removed, and the man's passport which was in his jacket pocket. There will be no trace of him here.'

'But Giacomo and Giovani let him in at the gates,' I pointed out. 'They will know that he was here.'

'That is unfortunate, but not too much of a problem. If you are ever asked, and I don't think you will be, you and Elfrida must say he came and said hello and then left. You must never say anything different. Do you understand?'

'Yes,' I said.

'I wish you had told me the truth about him. If I had known what he had done to you, I would have ended it right there.'

'I'm sorry,' I murmured as a fresh wave of guilt swept over me, 'but I couldn't.'

Ivan really had been so very kind to me that day in Menaggio when I'd fainted at the shock of seeing O'Halligan again. Coming to, and while Ivan had summoned a waiter to fetch me a glass of water, O'Halligan had pressed upon him that he was an old friend of mine and currently visiting the lake with his employer. He'd sounded so sickeningly charming and convincing and once I was strong enough to stand, I insisted Ivan took me back to the villa.

'I knew you were hiding something,' Ivan said now, 'but I just assumed he was someone for whom you once had feelings, so to respect your privacy I said nothing.'

I could have wept all over again at his consideration. Which I didn't deserve. I had brought nothing but disaster on us all.

'What about Mallory?' I asked. 'Do we need to tell him what we've done . . . that we've put a dead body in the—' But my words were cut off by a violent sob and I couldn't finish the question.

'It would be better if we did not implicate Mallory in what

has happened, but we need to ensure that he never opens up the well, that it stays disused. Nikolai will explain the situation and impress upon him that this secret remains between the five of us.'

My lips quivered and I buried my head in my hands, appalled at what I had done, that I had incriminated so many people into keeping such a dreadful secret.

'Wouldn't it be better for everyone if I went to the police and confessed my crime?' I asked when I felt brave enough to look up at Ivan.

'It's too late for that. What's done is done and we must live with our actions. You must remember, Nikolai and I, and Mallory, have killed before.'

My jaw dropped at his admission but before I could say anything, he explained. 'We were soldiers in the war, and we were trained to kill the enemy. This man who came here with evil on his mind was your enemy. He became our enemy too and now he is no more.' Ivan's matter-of-fact tone then softened. 'He did a terrible thing to you, Bess, and he has paid the price. You are free of him. You must go back to England and be with your husband and live your life as though none of this ever happened.'

He made it all sound so reasonable and so very plausible.

A week later and with Nikolai and Ivan staying on at the villa with Mallory, who had now returned to the lake from Milan, Elfrida and I set off on the long journey home. We had wanted to leave before then, but Nikolai wouldn't hear of it; he wanted to be sure Elfrida was well enough to travel before parting with her. As for me, I could hardly bring myself to look anyone in the eye. I was wracked with guilt.

'I'm a murderer twice over,' I said to Elfrida one day. 'I killed Michael O'Halligan and your child.'

She was furious with me for saying that. 'Both deaths were accidents,' she said, 'and from now on we will never discuss it again. We do not take this home with us; it stays here in Italy.'

I wanted so badly to believe that it could be as simple as that, that we could leave the nightmare behind us at Villa Lucia.

*

It was years later, in 1968, at about the time that Jackie Kennedy married Aristotle Onassis, that Mallory shared some grisly news with us. A friend of his had been staying in Lake Como at Grand Hotel Villa Serbelloni in Bellagio and had been intrigued by a conversation he'd overheard between two waiters during dinner about some skeletons having been found at the bottom of a well in the garden of a villa.

Intrigued to know more, Mallory's friend had learnt that the villa in question was none other than Villa Lucia where, before the war, he had been a frequent guest. After several owners, the latest had decided to investigate the disused well and had made the macabre discovery.

The conclusion reached was that the bodies were of German soldiers and had been put there by local partisans after Italy declared war on Germany. Two of the skeletons had bullet holes in the back of their heads and the other had a cracked skull. Nobody, it seemed, much cared who the men had been, according to what Mallory's friend was told, and just as soon as it could be arranged, the bodies would be despatched to Germany and that would be that.

For weeks after hearing this I suffered terrifying nightmares of being trapped at the bottom of a well with three rotting corpses. It was another bad dream to add to the many I already suffered.

Chapter Thirty-Nine

August 1981
Larkspur House, Suffolk

Elfrida had gone off to do some watering in the glasshouse to give Bess and Nancy some time on their own and, if she were truthful, to give herself a break. She wholeheartedly applauded Nancy's honesty, but the baring of her soul had had a depleting effect on them all.

While much of what she'd shared explained why Nancy had been the person she was, it didn't magically exonerate her of the harm she had inflicted on those who she should have loved. Actions always spoke louder than words and only when there had been a complete sea change in Nancy's behaviour towards Bess would Elfrida be capable of forgiving her. Bess seemed happy enough to do so, but Nancy probably had some work to do when it came to earning her daughter's forgiveness.

In the pale light cast from the kerosene lamp, and having fed and watered the tomato plants, Elfrida now set about securing the trusses of the beef tomatoes to ensure they didn't droop or snap off under the weight. Working steadily along the row of plants, she wondered if Libby was back yet. She hoped not. If the girl had any sense, she'd wouldn't cut short her evening, she'd stay out with Daniel for as long as possible. Whether Libby and Daniel ever became more than friends wasn't important; for now they should just enjoy each other's company. Sometimes all you needed was a good friend in life. Elfrida had been blessed with some wonderful friends, but none better than Bess and Mallory. Dear Mallory, what times they'd enjoyed together!

His death in the winter of 1972 had been a sad loss for anyone who had known him, but especially so for Elfrida. His funeral service had taken place in the small Norman church within walking distance of his beloved March Bank and had been packed to the rafters. Being one of his oldest friends, Elfrida had been asked to give the eulogy and several times while addressing the congregation she'd had to stop to compose herself.

Afterwards, and in the bitingly cold blustery wind, everyone had made the short journey on foot to March Bank. The house had been no warmer inside because the ongoing miners' strike had led to the country being without electricity for much of each day and with no coal for the fireplaces, the guests had huddled together for warmth. But there had at least been copious amounts of champagne to drink from Mallory's well-stocked wine cellar. That had been one of his last wishes, that the contents of his cellar were to be fully enjoyed to chase away the threat of any miserable faces.

That winter had been one of the gloomiest Elfrida had ever experienced. With the striking miners holding out for more pay and the country on a three-day working week and the power off for hours at a time, many an evening she and Bess sat in the kitchen swaddled in woollen blankets eating their cold supper by candlelight. Nothing could shift her melancholy. Not even when she was told what Mallory had left her in his will.

But as great as the impact of Mallory's passing had been, it hadn't compared to what she'd experienced when Nikolai had died. For a long time afterwards, Elfrida had blamed herself for his death, for not insisting he stay in England and see a doctor. She had known he was unwell and that he was making light of how ill he was, and yet she had let him go. Less than a year later, Dorothea had contacted Elfrida with the news that Nikolai's supposedly grief-stricken widow had just married an oil tycoon from Texas. 'Not so fragile as she'd always made out,' Dorothea had remarked. 'Tough as old boots, in fact.' Still grieving for Nikolai, Elfrida had wept angry tears for what might have been. Bess was such a comfort to her through those times, but then she always had been.

It was hard to pinpoint exactly when their roles had changed from the days when as a young girl Bess had come to Larkspur House to work as Elfrida's lady's maid, to what they were now. A lifetime together and they were as equal as two peas in a pod. Yes, there had been obvious milestone events which had bound them in ways they could never have predicted, but it went deeper than that. Much deeper. They were friends and sisters all rolled into one. Certainly, Bess had been a better sister than Prudence had ever been to Elfrida.

With nothing else to do in the glasshouse, she switched on her torch, turned off the kerosene lamp and ventured back out to the garden. She had only taken a few steps when the light from the torch began to flicker, a sure sign the batteries were about to die. Knowing the garden as well as she did, she had no cause to worry, moreover Steve had made a beautiful job of relaying the brickwork path that had been so hazardous.

As she approached the house, and with the curtains undrawn, she saw Bess in the lamplit dining room. She was sitting at the table and Elfrida didn't need to ask what she was doing there: she was looking at the photographs she and Libby had spent so much time sorting through.

Seeing Bess so engrossed, Elfrida recalled the day when she'd banished the hoard of photographs to the attic. It had been after Mallory's death and when she couldn't bear to have the past so close at hand. Many of the photos had been stored in boxes or envelopes, but some had been put into proper albums. From these she had removed the photos and thrown away the albums. She had been tempted to light a bonfire and burn the lot, but something had stopped her. She couldn't say what exactly, other than giving in to an uncharacteristic streak of sentimentality, but while Bess was at church, she had gathered everything together, including her old notebooks which she had occasionally used as personal diaries, and ferried it all up to the attic and shoved it into a trunk. Out of sight, out of mind.

If only.

Now inside the house, she washed her hands in the scullery, and helping herself to what was left in the wine bottle on the countertop, she went to join Bess in the dining room.

But the lamps were extinguished and there was no sign of Bess. Switching the lamps back on, Elfrida's gaze travelled the length and breadth of her past laid out before her until it settled on a black and white photograph of her and Nikolai. She picked up the photograph and smiled at the sight of her dressed as Cleopatra and Nikolai as Peter the Great. That was the weekend of Mallory's birthday party and not long before Nikolai died.

She returned the photograph to where she'd found it, then moved to her left, to the far end of the table where the oldest photographs had been placed. It was here that she found herself as a child with her long hair in ringlets and dressed in a pinafore dress and sitting on Prudence's lap, her sister's arms wrapped protectively around her. Bobby was standing behind with Mama and Papa either side of him. The picture had been taken in the garden with the house behind them and as formal and as stiffly posed as they were, there was no doubting the happiness that radiated out from their faces as they stared back at whoever had taken the photo.

Which made it all the sadder that their happiness as a family had been so short-lived, crushed by the loss of Mama and

Papa and dearest Bobby. If they hadn't died in the way they had perhaps things might have been different between Prudence and Elfrida later in life.

The thought stayed with her long after she'd heard Libby returning from her evening out and long after she'd said good-night to Bess. It took her an age to fall asleep as she couldn't stop thinking about her sister. Prudence was there again in her thoughts when she woke in the morning. Followed swiftly by Nancy.

*

'All I'm saying is that if someone as intransigent as Nancy can come here and say she's sorry for the way she's behaved all these years, then there's no reason why Prudence and I can't forgive each other.'

'*Ssh!* Don't speak that way about Nancy. Not when we've come so far.'

'She's hardly likely to hear me when she's in the garden with Libby.'

'Even so,' said Bess with a frown, 'you need to break the habit of being so . . . so negative about her. Something you might like to think about before speaking to your sister if you do intend to try and make peace with her. If you treat her as you always have, you won't get anywhere.'

Elfrida smiled. 'Rest assured, I will take it upon myself to be the model of agreeableness and with not a critical thought in my head.'

Bess threw her a look. 'I'd pay good money to see that.'

'Oh, ye of little faith.'

'And when do you propose making this visit?'

'That has yet to be decided. But once Nancy has gone, I shall put things in motion.'

'She says she wants to leave this afternoon.'

They both turned in their seats to look through the window to where Nancy and Libby were sitting on the terrace. They had been talking now for the best part of an hour, having gone out there at midday with a tray of coffee and shortbread biscuits. Libby had specifically asked for some time alone with her mother and Elfrida had been only too happy to accommodate that wish. It gave her the chance to have the conversation she was now having with Bess.

They were in the dining room and Elfrida had just gone to great lengths to prove to Bess that there was nothing incriminating on the table. There were no photographs of her with Nancy as a child that might have given away Bess's true relationship to her, not that that mattered now the truth was out, but more importantly, the notebooks, which she had been most concerned about, and which they'd both now flicked through, had revealed nothing about Michael O'Halligan.

Bringing the conversation back to why they were sitting here together, Elfrida said, 'So do you accept that our secret is quite safe and that no one will ever know what happened that night at Villa Lucia?'

Bess turned away from the window to face Elfrida. 'I'm not sure that I will ever lose the fear of being found out.'

'That's never going to happen. And really you should have put more trust in me. Why on earth would I have written anything about that odious man? Or taken a photograph of him?'

'It sounds ridiculous, I know,' Bess said, 'but you often took group shots of the gardeners you worked with when creating a garden, and occasionally other members of the household staff appeared too, and I just had this awful feeling that he would have somehow insinuated his way into a photograph.'

'You're right, that is ridiculous, because even if he had, he would have been nothing but an anonymous character amongst a hundred other anonymous faces whom nobody would ever ask about. I'm afraid, dearest Bess, you've allowed your guilty conscience to make the most improbable of scenarios seem scarily credible. But you've more than paid your dues for what we did, and after all this time you really must stop feeling so guilty. What good does it do?'

'It's because of Nancy I can't let go of the guilt. She's a constant reminder of him.'

'Then focus on the good that came out of his existence. Without him there'd be no Nancy and no Libby. And isn't Libby the best thing that ever happened to you? If God had been that furious with you, would he have given you Libby, the greatest blessing of your life?'

Bess clicked her tongue. 'For somebody who doesn't believe in God, you have no shame in using him to your advantage, do you?'

Elfrida smiled. 'None whatsoever. But Libby is a blessing. I've enjoyed having her here with us; she's been a breath of fresh air. And as painful as it's been for her, Marcus being out of her life is going to be the best thing all round for her. Again, it's an example of something good coming out of something bad.'

Elfrida picked up one of the notebooks in front of her. 'You know, I never once wrote anything about Nikolai in any of these books.'

'Why not?'

'What we had was sacred. It was for us only. It mattered, therefore it was private.' She shrugged. 'Everything else was just amusing frippery and fair game.'

'From what I've read, you wrote some quite scathing things about some of your clients who had more money than taste. And then there's the risqué stuff about a few of the men you slept with. What are you going to tell Libby when she reads that?'

Elfrida chuckled. 'She's a grown-up, I'm sure she can handle it.'

'Or we could just throw the notebooks away to save your blushes, hers too.'

'I think you're talking about your own blushes, Bess. I've done nothing of which I'm ashamed. And anyway, now that these notebooks have seen the light of day again, I want Libby to do what she said at the outset. I'd like her to put together a proper record of the gardens I created and how I went about it.'

'You've changed your tune! What happened to the gardens speaking for themselves and you having everything about them inside your head?'

'No, no, you misunderstand me, it's not for my benefit; it's for Libby's. Oh, hello, things must be going well out there.'

Through the window they saw Nancy and Libby embracing each other, and if Elfrida wasn't mistaken, they were both crying and smiling all at the same time.

'I think,' observed Elfrida, 'we can safely say things are moving in the right direction. Now how about I make some lunch for us all?'

'You?'

'Don't look like that, I'm perfectly capable of making a few cheese and pickle sandwiches.'

Bess tutted. 'As am I.'

'In that case let's compromise and make them together? And while we do that, I'll tell you what I have in mind for Libby. I think you'll approve.'

Later that afternoon and despite them encouraging her to stay for another day, Nancy stuck to her plan and put her overnight bag into the boot of her car. They gathered around her in an awkward semicircle, doing their best to adjust to the new dynamics between them. Always an advocate of spontaneity, Elfrida leaned in and before Nancy could resist, she quickly planted a kiss on the woman's cheek. 'You must come again,' she said, 'don't be a stranger to us now.' Poor Nancy, she looked too shocked to respond, other than to fiddle with her car keys.

Standing aside so Bess and Libby could make their farewells, Elfrida looked on, thinking that was exactly what Nancy was to them now: a stranger. But hopefully that meant they could start afresh with a clean slate. All those old prejudices, slights and grudges had to be left in the past, just as Elfrida hoped she might be able to do with Prudence. It was the longest of shots, but since when had Elfrida ever been afraid to take a punt? Even on what appeared to be a thoroughly lost cause. Yet that was what she had thought about Nancy, that there was no chance of there ever being a reconciliation.

They had just waved Nancy off when Elfrida could hear the telephone ringing from inside the house. It was the second call in the last hour. Previously it had been the doctor's surgery in touch with Bess to say that the results on her latest blood tests were in and she was required to go back to see the doctor so that her medication could be readjusted accordingly. The doctor had told Bess that there was nothing to worry about, all was well, which was music to Elfrida's ears.

Unlike the awful blast of a hacking cough when she picked up the telephone receiver in the hall.

'Elfrida, is that you?' demanded her sister.

'This is a coincidence,' Elfrida said, 'I've been thinking of you.'

'Playing with that voodoo doll of me again?'

'Not at all. But would you believe me when I say I was going to ring you?'

'Is that so?'

'But before I say why, you go first and say why you've called. Is it something to do with Marcus?'

Another rattling cough hurtled down the line. Then: 'No, nothing to do with that wretch of a boy and that ghastly creature he's married. I don't know what he was thinking when he cheated on Libby with that trollop. She has no shame and a distinct lack of class. Can you believe she was so drunk at the reception she was sick in the garden? Outrageous behaviour!'

'Oh dear,' said Elfrida, suppressing the urge to revel in a moment of gleeful schadenfreude. 'Even by my low standards, that's very poor form.'

'But enough of that, the reason I've telephoned you is to ask you to do something for me. Of course, I quite expect you to be churlish and say no, but if you could take a moment to consider my request, I'd be grateful.'

Intrigued, and still thinking of the coincidence of her sister ringing, Elfrida said, 'Come on then, don't beat about the bush, just say what it is you want me to do.'

When Prudence did so, Elfrida had no hesitation in agreeing to do what her sister wanted. It seemed they had both, quite independently, decided it was time to bury the hatchet.

Chapter Forty

It was the first week of September and the softly undulating fields of wheat to the right of them were golden in the bright morning sunshine. To their left, the crops had already been harvested, leaving the remaining stubble poking through the rich Norfolk earth while fat round bales of wheat lay warming in the sun.

They'd set off after breakfast and aimed to arrive by eleven. Libby had expected to feel apprehensive about the trip, but she didn't. Last night Bess had said that nobody would blame her if she wanted to back out of the expedition to Tilbrook Hall; after all, it couldn't be easy returning to where her wedding reception should have taken place. But Libby didn't plan to linger, just long enough to drop off Elfrida and Bess. Besides, if anyone should feel nervous, it would be Marcus's parents. If she encountered them, Libby was fully prepared to be the bigger person, to give the impression that there were no hard feelings on her part. She would hold her head up high and then she'd probably trip over because she wasn't looking where she was going! *Pride before a fall*, she heard her mother say.

In the weeks since her mother's visit to Larkspur House, there had been a definite improvement in their behaviour towards cach other. They were both trying hard to find the new rhythm to their relationship. Libby was doing her best to be more patient and understanding and in turn her mother was learning to be less defensively aggrieved and less critical. It wasn't easy. Occasionally, while talking on the phone, they would lapse into their old ways, but the good thing was that they both recognised what they were doing and stepped back so the disagreement didn't escalate. It was progress.

And progress had been made with Bess. With exactly the right dosage of medicine now prescribed for her, both Libby and Elfrida had more confidence in her claims that she was feeling so much better. Nonetheless, they continued to keep an eye on her just in case she overdid it and had a relapse. Thankfully she seemed to have learnt her lesson and understood that the less physical strain she put on herself, the more like her old self she felt. It was a matter of retraining her mindset, so Daniel said. Which was something Libby was having to do as well, clearing out all the 'what ifs' and 'what might have beens' from her thinking and focusing on what came next for her.

She had expected to feel a raft of emotions when she'd gone down to London last week to put her flat on the market to sell, but she hadn't. When she'd turned the key in the lock and stepped inside after so many weeks away, she had waited to be hit by a wave of sad regret, but she'd felt utterly detached from it. Her overriding response was one of relief that the flat, now tainted forever by memories of Marcus and Selina, was devoid of anything that belonged to her so-called friend, other than a pair of wrinkled tights inside the drum of the washing machine. There was nothing of Marcus either. No stray shirts, socks or toothbrush.

In reality, she had been away from the place for so little time, not even two months, yet it felt longer. Long enough for it not to feel like home. The estate agent with whom she'd placed the flat had said he'd have no trouble in shifting it, and yesterday he'd been as good as his word and rang with the news that an offer had been made. Next week, and with her mother's help, Libby would start the job of packing up and putting her things into storage until she had found somewhere new to live.

Much to everybody's surprise, Mum was now talking about moving house. 'Maybe, like you, I need a fresh start,' she'd said when she'd met Libby for lunch in London last week.

'Do you have anywhere in mind?' Libby had asked her.

'I'm wondering about Richmond so I can be closer to town, but without being in the thick of it. It would be lovely to go to the theatre more regularly and attend art exhibitions. A woman in my bridge circle moved there and says she'd wished she'd done it years ago. Your father was never really interested in those things, for him being on the doorstep of a golf course was all he really cared about.'

'He cared about you, Mum,' Libby had said gently.

'I suppose he did in his own way,' Mum had said. 'I don't think I made it terribly easy for him.'

'Perhaps not, but I'm sure he would have understood if you'd given him the chance.'

'Life is full of lost chances,' her mother had said with a sigh.

'It's also full of lots of new opportunities,' Libby had asserted, 'as you and I are both discovering.'

When she had then asked why her mother hadn't felt the urge to move before now, her mother had admitted that change didn't come naturally to her. The very fact that she had expressed this obvious trait about herself was a good sign. Fear of change perhaps partially explained why it had taken her so long to reach the decision she had to try and make amends for all the years of bitter resentment she had clung to. It took courage to admit one had made a mistake and just as much courage to change, and Libby didn't doubt the challenges her mother would face if she did take the plunge and move to Richmond. But it might just be the new beginning she needed, just as Libby was facing her own fresh start.

In the days she'd been in London she'd hooked up with her friends and at their insistence they'd had a night out in lieu of the arranged hen party. They had called it her Lucky Escape party and once the drinks had flowed, they had brought her up to date with what gossip they knew about Marcus and Selina. They'd cheerfully reported that the happy couple had had a massive row during the honeymoon and had been arguing since they were home. It was Gemma who seemed to know the most because her brother played squash with Marcus. Libby didn't care that she was as guilty as her friends for relishing this nugget of news. Why should she pretend otherwise? Marcus and Selina deserved to make each other miserable. It was just a shame there would be a child caught in the crossfire of their conflict.

As the evening had worn on, Libby had told her friends about her plans to move to Suffolk and the career change she was embarking on. And then, and because she'd had too much to drink by this stage, she'd told them about Daniel. In a rush of voices, they'd clamoured to know more, making her regret saying anything. But the truth was, deep down she had wanted to tell them, not in the hope that it would somehow reach Marcus and Selina's ears, but to see how it felt to talk about Daniel, to hear the words out loud. She'd made it clear though that since he wasn't yet divorced and she was in no state to be considering a new relationship, friendship was all that was on the cards. It was, she stressed, the sensible approach.

Her words had been met with cries of *'BORING!'* from her friends. Their advice was to take a risk and have some fun.

Libby knew what Elfrida would say, that a life devoid of risk was a very dull life indeed.

'Can a person say they've truly lived if they haven't thrown caution to the wind and taken an unexpected path or stepped into the unknown?'

This had been something Elfrida had written in one of her notebooks, along with so many other thought-provoking observations. Many of her handwritten notes had revealed a woman who hadn't given a damn about the risks she took. There was little sign of regret either, not even when it came to the occasional flings she had experienced, all of which had tended to be brief and with no real emotional attachment involved.

There were some great one-liners in the books too, about people Elfrida had met at house parties, or clients for whom she'd worked. The sharp-tongued comment Libby liked most was of a client she plainly detested. *The ghastly woman has all the charisma of a turnip and the ability to liven up a room the moment she leaves it.*

Libby might well have been intimidated by Elfrida's younger self, but to have witnessed such a force of nature would have been something to behold.

Curiosity about Elfrida's romantic (and not so romantic) antics had compelled Libby to ask if there hadn't ever been a man who was special enough for Elfrida to marry. She'd been thinking of the handsome man who had featured in a number of the photographs she'd collated and who she now knew had been called Nikolai. Intrigued, Libby had wanted to know more about him, but Elfrida had told her very firmly not to be so inquisitive. Then she'd said: 'Now if you could stop ferreting about in my long-ago love life, you might hear something to your advantage.'

That was when, in the kitchen garden with the sun beating down while Libby was filling a trug with globe artichokes for supper, and Elfrida was picking runner beans, the old lady made her an offer to which she couldn't say no. It was a dream come true and pre-empted anything Libby had had in mind to discuss with Elfrida, about her applying to do a diploma in horticulture and garden design.

'You're under no obligation to say yes,' Elfrida had explained, 'but personally I believe it's one of my finest ideas. Bess thinks so too. You see, I'd like to pass on my knowledge to you. I'm not saying I'm the best teacher in the world, but I've trained up enough young under gardeners in my time to know what's what. As my protégée, you won't end up with a bit of paper proclaiming you a fully qualified horticulturist, but by the time I've finished with you, you'll be streets ahead of anyone who goes to some fancy college. Actual on-the-ground dirty-hands experience is what you need, not book learning. I never studied a book in my life, I learnt everything I know from looking, listening, and doing. And you've been doing that ever since you were a young child and came to stay with us here.'

Libby had been so stunned she had nearly sliced her finger off with the sharp knife she'd been using on the artichokes. 'But why? Why would you do that for me?'

'Oh, for heaven's sake! Do I have to spell it out for you?'

Smiling, Libby had said, 'Yes, I rather think you should.'

'It's because I'm inordinately fond of you, dear girl, and I truly believe you have the makings of a fine gardener. If your mother hadn't shunted you off to secretarial college to follow in her hideously mundane footsteps, who knows what you might have achieved.'

'That was my fault as much as anything,' Libby had said in defence of her mother. 'I just went along with Mum's wishes because I hated seeing her so angry, particularly when I knew I was the cause of it. What really made her go ballistic was when I said I thought you had the perfect life doing what you loved most.'

Elfrida had chuckled. 'Yes, that would have infuriated poor old Nancy. But you were never the direct cause of any of her anger. You know that now, don't you?'

Libby had said that she did, and then Elfrida had gone on to say that she and Bess had already discussed how they thought things could work if Libby accepted the offer. Libby couldn't find a single reason why she shouldn't agree to be Elfrida's protégée, and so from that day on, her future was set on a new and exciting course.

At the sound of Elfrida in the front of the car saying, 'Can this Swedish contraption not go any faster?' Libby turned away from the passing scenery and caught Daniel's amused gaze in the rear-view mirror.

'It can,' he said to Elfrida, 'but if you don't mind, I'll stick to the speed restriction.'

'Take no notice of her, Daniel,' said Bess. 'Her ladyship has never understood the concept of a speed limit.'

'Not true,' Elfrida remonstrated, 'I just didn't ever think they applied to me.'

'As with so much in life,' muttered Bess, leaning through to the front and rustling a bag of sweets. 'Barley sugar, anyone?'

Elfrida shook her head. 'You know I can't stand those sweets; didn't you bring anything else?'

'What about a saucer of milk for that acid tongue of yours?'

'I think it's you who needs the saucer of milk, Bess.'

Ignoring the comment, she offered the bag to Daniel.

'Not for me, Mrs Judd,' he said politely, once again catching Libby's eye in the mirror, causing her to bite on her lower lip to stop herself from laughing. The situation just seemed so incongruous. When Dr Daniel Matthews had first visited Larkspur House to check on a patient, never in his wildest dreams could he have imagined that he would end up being roped in to act as their chauffeur for the day.

Last weekend, and when Libby had returned from London, Elfrida had informed her that she had invited Daniel to join them for supper that evening. It was while they were enjoying an aperitif on the terrace that Elfrida had asked Daniel if he was busy the following Saturday, and if not, would he like to join them on a day trip to Norfolk? By the time they'd sat down to eat it had all been decided, they would set off as early as possible on Saturday morning and Daniel would drive them in his Volvo estate on the basis it might be a little more comfortable than Libby's campervan. Then, and while Bess and Elfrida were at Tilbrook Hall, Libby and Daniel would drive on to the coast and enjoy a day at the beach.

'If I didn't know better,' Libby had said to him much later that evening when they'd taken a torch to go for a walk across the meadows in the hope of hearing the last of the nightingales singing, 'that had probably been Elfrida's cunning plan all along, to trick you into being our driver for the day.'

'Very likely,' he'd said, 'but I really don't mind. It'll be fun. I can't remember the last time I went to the beach. I'll have to dig out my bucket and spade,' he'd added with a smile. 'That's if you don't mind my company for the day?'

She'd looked at him, surprised. 'Why would I mind?'

Without answering her question, he'd said, 'Just so long as you don't.'

'I don't, far from it.'

'That's good.'

She had wanted to say that there was no need to be so wary with her, but then wondered if he was being as careful as he was to put a protective barrier around his own feelings.

They hadn't heard any nightingales singing that night, but there had been, as corny as it sounded, a song in Libby's heart when they'd followed the beam of light from the torch and retraced their steps across the meadows. She was just thinking about her friends in London who'd urged her to take a risk with Daniel and have some fun, when she'd felt his hand reach for hers. He didn't say anything, and nor did she, there didn't seem to be any need.

'Everything all right in the back there?' he asked now.

'Yes, thank you,' replied Libby with a smile.

'Mrs Judd?'

'Perfectly fine, thank you, Daniel. And as I've told you before, please call me Bess.'

*

Perfectly fine was not an entirely accurate description of how Bess felt. The truth was she had never liked visiting Tilbrook Hall, even less so after O'Halligan's violation of her, but she was determined to hide any unease she felt. If only because she didn't want to set her heart racing with anxiety. Not that she feared a 'funny turn' as she now knew exactly what to do. It still amazed her that one small tablet placed under her tongue could have such an immediate effect. The wonders of science!

She knew, though, that she had to be careful and accept that she couldn't do as much as she once had, and while initially that had driven her to distraction, she had come to terms with it. As extreme as it sounded, she could even be grateful for being ill because it had finally brought her and Nancy closer. Nancy had confessed that it had been the shock of seeing Bess collapse and be rushed to hospital in an ambulance that had caused her to realise that she had to put things right while she still could. Bess didn't underestimate how difficult that must have been for Nancy, to put aside a lifetime's worth of ill-feeling.

But the biggest joy for Bess was hearing Libby call her Grandma. It shouldn't make any difference to their relationship, but the gift Nancy had given her was the gift she had craved for so long. It meant that she felt liberated, free to be her true self around Libby – her *granddaughter*.

And knowing how uplifting it felt to be on good terms with

Nancy, Bess hoped that today's visit to Tilbrook Hall would bring about the reconciliation Elfrida sought with her sister, Prudence.

When the trip had first been proposed, Bess had said she would prefer not to go, but Elfrida had begged her to accompany her. 'I know why you'd rather not come,' she'd said, 'but how can I go without you? You have to be by my side, just like in the old days, and who knows, maybe together we can slay a few dragons. Not that I'm calling Prudence a dragon,' she'd added with a mischievous wink.

Bess kept telling herself that her reluctance to return to Tilbrook Hall was irrational, it was just a house, no more than bricks and mortar. O'Halligan wasn't there. He couldn't hurt her again. The only thing that could was the memory of what he'd done. It wasn't as if she'd never been back since O'Halligan had assaulted her, she had gone there frequently with Elfrida for her work. But somehow she had blocked that night from her mind during those visits by keeping herself extra busy. It was only once Prudence had gone berserk and banned Elfrida from ever crossing the threshold again that the visits had stopped, and to Bess's relief. That had been in the spring of 1946, and they hadn't been back since, which was why this was such a momentous journey for them both.

Up ahead on the road and where the tarmac shimmered in the bright sunshine, Bess saw a sign indicating they were now only five miles from the village of Tilbrook. None of what she saw out of the window was familiar to her. On both sides of the road there were housing estates, then a series of dilapidated warehouses, a petrol station, and a reclamation yard. A mile further on and once again they were flanked by open countryside where the fields had been ploughed. Rooks high up in the trees looked down on the turned earth that was baking in the sun. Bess had no memory of ever driving along this road.

'Do you recognise anything, Elfrida?' she asked, leaning forward.

'Not a thing,' Elfrida responded. 'It's an alien country to me.'

Daniel laughed. 'Isn't that what all Suffolk people say about Norfolk?'

'I think you'll find we say an awful lot worse. But I don't doubt it's a two-way street and the good people of Norfolk have plenty to say about us.'

*

For once it appeared that Prudence Lassiter, who had never been short of anything to say to, or about, Elfrida, was remarkably taciturn. Maybe the shock of seeing one another after so long had rendered her lost for words.

Elfrida had never dwelt on the loss of her youth or the slow inexorable decline to which her body surrendered itself, she had simply acquiesced to the inevitability of it in the same way she accepted the changing seasons; but the change in her sister's appearance was a jolt.

Yet as shockingly frail and diminished as she looked, Prudence was immaculately dressed in a black woollen dress with a white Peter Pan collar set off by a diamond brooch and a string of pearls. The dress had doubtless fitted her perfectly at some point, but now it was too big for her bony frame – the sleeves gaped to reveal wrists that were as thin as twigs, the skin loose and papery.

Her stockinged legs were just as thin, and on her feet she wore black patent court shoes with an unfeasibly high heel. Her make-up had been applied too heavily and the sight of caked foundation, smudged mascara, over-rouged cheeks and too much lipstick saddened Elfrida.

The saddest sight though was the wispy thinness of Prudence's pure white hair. It had been set and dried into a rigid transparent bonnet by a clever hairdresser, but it had the unfortunate effect of making the sight of that baby-pink scalp even more painfully obvious. Elfrida had to resist putting a hand to her own hair, plaited as it was in a long thick silver rope.

She too had chosen what to wear today with care, but in her case, it was to eschew her customary gardening clothes for a lightweight summer dress with a matching bolero jacket and a pair of sandals. Her legs were bare, which no doubt Prudence would think was beyond the pale and breached every rule in the etiquette book.

They were sitting in Prudence's ground-floor suite of rooms overlooking a small private area of the gardens that was bordered by an ugly wooden fence. The fence, so Prudence had explained, was to keep the PGs – paying guests – at bay. When she had reluctantly handed over Tilbrook Hall to her son, James, it had been on the understanding that she was to have her own private quarters which were to be kept exclusively for her personal use. Her visits were infrequent now, she'd told Elfrida, due to the effort it took to travel up from London.

When Daniel had driven through the stone pillars of the entrance and approached Tilbrook Hall, Elfrida's first thought was that the long driveway was in need of repair. The house itself, as large and solid as it was, was a shadow of its former grandeur. It looked like a weary old giant weighed down by the worries of the world. Where once the honey-coloured stone walls had glowed proudly in the sunlight, today they were mottled with discoloured water stains and goodness knows what else. Taking in the shabbiness of the edifice, Elfrida was reminded of her first impressions of Venice as a young naïve girl when she'd gone there with Dorothea. She had expected to be surrounded by exquisite perfection but had found a city that was crumbling and decaying. It wasn't long though before she had been seduced by the city's inimitable charm.

But there was nothing charming about Tilbrook Hall to her mind. She was amazed that people actually paid to stay here. When they'd entered the hotel reception area, Elfrida had remembered it when it had been a grand entrance hall with a log fire burning, even on the warmest of days. Back then it had been a cold house at the best of times, and today, despite the bland music playing in the background and the smartly dressed woman behind the desk smiling when they introduced themselves, the place was as bleakly welcoming as a graveyard. Horror of horrors, Elfrida had gone over to admire a large flower display on a table only to discover the flowers were artificial.

They had been shown through to the guests' lounge – the very room where Prudence had attacked Elfrida with a poker – while someone was despatched to inform Mrs Lassiter that her visitors had arrived. Another call had been put through to James and his wife, Cora, which was Libby and Daniel's cue to leave and drive on to the coast. Libby had said that she had no desire to hang around and make Marcus's parents feel any more awkward than they probably already felt. After all, it wasn't their fault Marcus had done what he had. As it turned out, they'd had to go out but were expected back in due course. Elfrida hoped so. She had always had a soft spot for James when he'd been a boy. His mother had not given him the love he deserved, giving it all instead to his brother, William, who could do no wrong in Prudence's eyes.

Now, and drinking coffee brought to them by a young waitress, Elfrida and Prudence sat in silence facing a pair of open French doors. On the paved area directly in front of the doors, a robin flew down and looked in at them. Elfrida wished a plate of biscuits had been provided with the coffee so she could throw a few crumbs to the bird. As if sensing there was nothing on offer, the robin flew off and Prudence put down her finished coffee cup.

'I feel like a prisoner when I'm here,' she said bluntly. 'All that's missing is a watch tower to make me feel even more captive in this miserable patch of garden.'

'There are worse prison cells,' Elfrida commented, secretly thinking she would feel the same, hemmed in all sides. Trapped.

'You always did take a more contrary view,' Prudence said, twisting her head to look at her. 'But then that was your modus operandi. I must say, you look well. Better than I—' Her words were cut short by a hacking cough that wrenched at Elfrida's chest in sympathy. When it had passed, Prudence said, 'I've had three bouts of pneumonia in as many years and the doctors say it's a miracle I'm still here.'

'I'm sorry.'

'What, that I'm still alive?'

Elfrida smiled. 'No, that you've been so unwell. You should have let me know.'

'Why, so you could revel in what a hideous old crone I've become?'

'Heavens, what a cheery soul you are!'

'It's true. Just look at me. I'm nothing but a bag of bones.'

'But a bag of bones that is impressively turned out.'

Prudence scoffed at that. 'Nothing fits me these days and who do I see that would appreciate what I wear? Nobody dresses up anymore, not the way we used to.' She glanced at Elfrida's bare legs as if this alone proved her point.

'Nothing stays the same,' said Elfrida, 'and maybe that's a good thing. Think how boring life would be if it did.'

'How can you say that when your life hasn't changed at all? You're still at Larkspur House and you still have Bess loyally by your side.'

'But I've changed. I'm not the person I was. How could I be?' Receiving no reply from Prudence, she put her finished coffee cup and saucer on the table between them and bent down to her handbag. From it she retrieved an envelope and took out the photograph she'd brought with her. It was the one of Prudence, Elfrida and Bobby with their parents. Offering it to her sister, she said, 'I thought you might like to see this.'

Wordlessly and without expression, Prudence took the photograph and studied it.

'We look so happy in the picture, don't we?' ventured Elfrida.

'For a brief time we were.'

'Better to have had that than nothing.'

'Is that what you really believe?'

'Yes. Life. Love. Happiness. It's all fleeting. Here today, gone tomorrow.'

Her caked, made-up face wreathed in a contorted pout of displeasure, Prudence passed the photograph back to Elfrida. 'It seems so pointless. Why bother?'

'Because those snatches of good times always make up for the bad. You and I have both experienced heartbreaking loss, the kind no one should ever suffer, but we did and we survived it.'

'What have you lost?' There was withering resentment in Prudence's voice, as if whatever Elfrida may have lost didn't count.

'You don't know the half of what I've been through, so let's not make this a competition for who has suffered the most. Have you never stopped to think how I might feel about losing our brother, Bobby, and how that's haunted me since the day he died?'

Prudence's lips quivered and then she pursed them tightly. Elfrida decided to press on. This was a day for being courageous, for acknowledging mistakes had been made on both sides, but also for accepting it wasn't too late to say sorry and make amends. Wasn't that why Prudence had invited her here in the first place? To that end, Elfrida was going to tell her sister something she had never told anyone before.

'Before we discuss William and the reason I'm here,' she began, 'I want you to know why Bobby's death mattered so much to me. It's because it was my fault that he killed himself.' She then shared with Prudence what she had done as a child, how she had followed their brother and his friend into the copse, and what she had seen. 'So you see, if I hadn't been so jealous of him always wanting to be with his college friend and not me, he wouldn't have committed suicide.'

From behind the smudged mascara Prudence's eyes narrowed. 'As always, you're quite wrong.'

'I'm not, Prudence. You might not like the idea of it, but I swear to you that's what happened.'

'Just for once in your life will you not contradict me or assume you know what I'm thinking? I know you're wrong because it was me. *I* was the one who killed our brother as surely as I'd held a gun to his head. I found him and his friend together in Bobby's room in what would be called a compromising state of undress and position. Unlike you, I knew exactly what they were doing, and I told Bobby that I would tell Mama and Papa what he was like, that he was a filthy deviant. He begged me not to say anything and that he would never do it again. He kept his word because after his friend had left, he threw himself out of his bedroom window.'

Elfrida was shocked. It had never occurred to her that Prudence might have witnessed something similar to what she had. 'Why did you never say anything?'

'Why didn't you?'

'Guilt,' said Elfrida. 'I couldn't bear to admit that I was to blame.'

'And how have you coped with that?'

'I think it's partly what made me the person I became, someone who believes in letting others live the way they want to and never judging them.'

'But that's not dealing with the guilt, is it?'

'It wasn't easy, but as the years went by, I reasoned that it could have been anyone who caught Bobby in, as you called it, a compromising position, and he may well have reacted in the same way.'

After a long pause, and choosing her words with extreme care, Elfrida said, 'It's the saddest thing when somebody feels they can't live up to the expectations others have of them. That was true of William. He was hailed a hero for what he did in the war, but it wasn't how he saw himself, was it? The war damaged him in ways the rest of us never fully appreciated and with no one he felt able to turn to, tragically he took his own life to end his suffering.'

It felt like an age before Prudence responded. 'I should have realised what he was going through, but I didn't. I just didn't see the signs. Or maybe I didn't want to. And then afterwards I behaved intolerably. I failed him in life, and in death.'

'Oh, Prudence, you were quite literally out of your mind with grief.'

'That's no excuse.'

'I think it is.'

'I turned into a monster and pushed you, and George, away. The poor man tried so hard to make me see sense, but I refused to listen. I'm surprised he stuck it out with me. Although I'm quite sure he frequently sought comfort elsewhere. One could hardly blame him for that.'

'That sounds very equitable of you.'

'I can be sometimes, you know.'

'You were certainly that when you signed over your share of Larkspur House to me. I've always been immensely grateful to you for that generous act on your part.'

'That was George's doing.'

'But you agreed to it, that's what counts.'

'If you say so.'

Smiling at her sister's reluctance to accept a compliment, she said, 'George was a thoroughly decent man. Do you miss him?'

'I do, actually. He's been gone for nearly ten years, but there's never a day when I don't think of him. But everyone's gone now from my life. Those from the old days, that is.'

'I miss my old friends too,' said Elfrida, 'especially Mallory.'

'What about that American woman you were so fond of, the one you met in Italy at our finishing school? Is she still alive?'

'Sadly not. Her family wrote to me several years ago to say she had passed away peacefully in her sleep.'

Prudence sighed. 'We have long since traversed the autumn of our days, now all that's left is the bleak loneliness of winter.'

'It needn't be like that.'

'You're lucky, you've had Bess at your side all this time. She could have joined us for coffee, I hope you told her that.'

'I made that quite clear to her, but she said she would rather go for a walk in the grounds, plus she felt you might prefer it to be just the two of us. Bess has always been very good at being discreet.'

'Having worked for you with your scandalously indiscreet behaviour, she'd have to be.'

Elfrida smiled at the sharpness of her sister's riposte; it made a refreshing change from the morose air of pessimism that had gone before. 'As you just pointed out,' she said, 'I've been lucky to count on Bess as both friend and confidante. I don't know what I would have done without her. Through the good and the bad times.'

'And how is Libby? Is she coping with the disappointment of being let down by Marcus?'

'All things considered, she's coping very well,' replied Elfrida, picturing Libby and Daniel hopefully now at the beach and enjoying themselves. She thought also of how much she was enjoying teaching Libby and imparting the wealth of knowledge she had amassed, from the time she had been a young child trailing around after the gardeners at Larkspur House and begging them to teach her what they knew. Transferring all that she had learnt to Libby would be her legacy. That and what she would one day pass on to the girl.

With no children of her own, to whom else could she leave Larkspur House when both she and Bess were no longer around? There was also what she had inherited from Mallory as well as Nikolai, and which she had wisely invested and managed to live off the interest. But there was no need to dwell on any of that; with any luck, wills and bequests were all a long way off.

For now, it was more important and much more pleasurable to focus on the present rather than the future. It had surprised her just how gratifying it was teaching Libby; she was such an eager student. They'd been studying some of her old garden designs from her notebooks and it had taken Elfrida right back to those long-ago days, with her recalling just how much she had loved taking on a new commission and turning what was often a blank canvas into something beautiful and lasting. Nothing else had given her so much satisfaction. She hoped that one day Libby would experience the same fulfilment.

Meanwhile, Bess was over the moon having Libby live with them for the foreseeable future, until, that was, she found somewhere to buy or rent. Bess and Elfrida had gone out of their way to make it clear to Libby that she was not to regard herself as their carer in any way, but if she wanted to make herself useful, just to give Bess a break, then that would be appreciated.

Of course, Libby had done a lot more than that. She'd been like a thing possessed redecorating two of the bedrooms, including Bobby's old room. She'd chosen some beautiful William Morris and Sanderson wallpaper, and while it had made Elfrida's eyes water at the price, she had to concede that the girl had a natural flair for interior design and had done a top-notch professional job.

'I'm sorry my grandson treated Libby the way he did,' said Prudence, breaking into Elfrida's thoughts. 'She didn't deserve that, and I told the wretched boy that myself. His parents are none too impressed either. They, and many of the guests, squirmed their way through the marriage service. As for the reception, it was the most excruciatingly awful occasion I've ever had the misfortune to endure. It was quite ghastly.'

'I'm sorry I missed it,' said Elfrida with a wry smile, 'but what's done is done, no point in raking over these things. Now what say you we go outside, and I tell you what I have in mind for William's memorial garden?'

'Don't you want to know why I've asked you to do this after all these years?' asked Prudence, as she struggled to her feet with a creak of bones.

'I was waiting for you to tell me in your own good time,' answered Elfrida. 'I may not have seen you for many a year, but I know you never liked to be rushed.'

'With the end currently in sight,' Prudence said with a tight smile, 'I believe a little rushing might be in order. James must think so too as he's responsible for making today happen. He's been nagging me for a while now to do something in his brother's memory here.'

Elfrida was pleased to hear that. James could so easily have held a grudge against his dead brother, but this proved he didn't. 'Why didn't James go ahead and arrange it himself?' she asked.

'To his credit, he wanted me to oversee the project. My last hurrah, I suppose.'

'And why exactly did you want *me* to come up with the design for you?'

Prudence tutted. 'Don't you dare start fishing for a compliment. You know perfectly well that with your personal connection it has to be you. Now pass me that walking stick over there in the corner and let's go outside while I still have the strength. I don't know how much you've seen of the grounds, but I shouldn't think for a minute that you'd approve. Much of what you created had to be turfed over to keep costs down. The cost of gardeners these days is prohibitively expensive.'

'I hope this isn't when you tell me you're not going to pay

my fee, Prudence.' At the startled expression on her sister's face, Elfrida said, 'I'm joking. Of course I'm not going to bill you. This is for you and William.'

And for all those we have loved and lost, she thought later when she and Prudence had made the long and very slow trek outside to where Elfrida had originally imagined a memorial garden for William when George had first discussed it with her.

The thought was still with her that evening when they arrived back at Larkspur House. At Libby's insistence, and while she rustled up a supper of Welsh rarebit and Daniel made cocktails for them, Elfrida and Bess were on the terrace watching the setting sun. It had been a tiring day and before long it became increasingly difficult for Elfrida to keep her eyes open. The instant they closed, it was as if a film began playing inside her head and she saw all those she had loved and lost coming into clear focus and then drifting away. But one face didn't drift away; it stayed firmly in focus and was as real to her as if he was right there with her. *'I'll never leave you,'* Nikolai said. *'Never. I'm with you until the end of time.'* Oh, how wonderful it was to hear the rich timbre of his voice and to see his sultry dark eyes looking into hers again!

But just as she was about to raise her hands to reach out to him, his handsome face blurred, and he vanished into the ether. The sudden sense of loss was so palpable, she snapped her eyes open as if to seek him out and bring him back. All she saw was Bess giving her an odd look, her brows drawn.

Embarrassed, Elfrida said, 'Dear me, I must have nodded off for a moment.'

'I thought you might have. I nodded off too for a few minutes. It must have been all that dragon slaying we did today.'

'How did your dragon slaying go?' Elfrida asked, sitting up straighter and shaking away the last trace of the dream.

'This might seem strange, but it was rather a let-down.'

'In what way?'

'I felt absolutely nothing while I was there, not a single flicker of emotion. I know it's a hotel now but the place seemed so different, it was as if I'd never been there before.'

'I know what you mean. The garden was unrecognisable to me.'

'Did that upset you?'

'Not at all. As I told Prudence, nothing stays the same, and nor should it.'

'It's good that you and your sister have made peace with each other after all this time. Do you know when you'll return to supervise the work to be carried out?'

'It will have to be soon as Prudence wants everything done yesterday and, to quote her own words, before she drops off her perch. I'm going to enlist Libby's help with the project; it will be a useful learning exercise for her.'

Bess frowned. 'You don't think that could be a touch insensitive, given the Marcus connection? It's still early days.'

'Oh, I think she'll cope.'

Just then a burst of laughter came from behind them, and they turned to see Libby and Daniel coming towards them with their supper and drinks. Her voice low, Elfrida said, 'That's your answer right there. And trust me, it's more than a day at the coast that's put that radiant glow on their faces.'

'I thought that too when we were driving back,' whispered Bess with a smile. 'But you must promise not to say anything,' she added. 'Do that and you could wreck everything.'

'I have no intention of wrecking anything. I want a happy-ever-after for Libby as much as you do.'

'Ladies,' announced Daniel when he drew level and placed the tray of drinks on the table in front of them, 'I bring you a special Daniel Matthews gimlet cocktail for your delectation!'

'And about time too, young man, I thought I was going to die of thirst out here!'

'Really, Elfrida,' rebuked Bess, 'you could show some proper gratitude.'

'Nonsense, Daniel's practically family now and knows me well enough to appreciate my funny little ways.' She took the glass Daniel offered her and met his eye, deliberately ignoring the tut from Bess and Libby's eyebrows that had shot up almost to her hairline at the word *family*. 'Am I right?'

'I'm quite at home with familial abuse,' he said, 'so please don't hold back on my account.'

*

Later, and after Bess and Elfrida had claimed they needed their beauty sleep, Daniel said he really ought to be going.

'There's no need to rush away,' Libby said, looking at him across the table in the flickering candlelight. 'Not unless you have an early start in the morning.'

He shook his head. 'No, no early start tomorrow, but I fear, as I've said once before, I could just get too comfortable being here.'

Libby smiled. 'I think that's how most people feel when they come here – they fall under the spell of the house and garden.'

'And now it's to be your home,' he said.

'Until I've found somewhere more permanent. But for now,' she added with a happy laugh, 'I feel like I've hit the jackpot – I've left London and am embarking on an exciting new phase in my life as Elfrida's protégée. I never dreamt she would come up with such an incredible idea; all I wanted from her was some advice!'

Daniel smiled back at Libby. 'I for one am very glad you're sticking around, as hopefully it means I'll be able to see a lot more of you.'

'Why *hopefully?*' she enquired. 'Why not *definitely?*'

In the pause that followed, Libby pondered her directness, and Daniel's apparent uncertainty.

'Can I be honest with you?' he asked.

'You mean you haven't been honest with me previously?'

'Yes and no.'

'Okay, tell me what you've been lying about. I've become quite adept at handling lies these last few months, so fire away.' As frank and as flippant as she sounded, Libby wondered if Daniel was about to break it to her that he and his wife had made it up and weren't going through with their divorce. But if that was the case, why had he just said he wanted to see more of her and why had he been so keen to hold her hand as they'd walked along the sandy stretch of beach at Hunstanton with the warm breeze blowing in off the sea? And why had he said how much he'd enjoyed spending the day with her? Had it all been—

'I haven't been completely truthful about my feelings for you,' he said, bringing her runaway thoughts to a crashing stop.

'Go on,' she said warily, 'what does that mean?'

'It means I've deliberately underplayed them to avoid the risk of ruining things between us. In so many ways it's too soon for you even to think of me as other than a friend right now, but . . . but I can't stop thinking how much I'd like it to be more than that between us.'

A flood of relief swept through Libby, which raised all sorts of questions about the extent of her own feelings for him. Was it right that she should experience an emotional connection to someone so soon after breaking up with Marcus?

Yet whatever the rights and wrongs, she couldn't deny that spending time with Daniel always had a positive effect on her. Just as being here at Larkspur House did. Wasn't that what she should think about rather than any textbook advice about avoiding the danger of a rebound relationship? Why not embrace the moment rather than rationalise it?

Aware that Daniel was looking expectantly at her, she said, 'I'd like us to be more than friends too.'

'But in a very slow and cautious way?' he suggested, the hesitancy now gone from his face and voice.

She nodded, but felt duty bound to flush out the last of her doubts. 'We get on so well, it would be a shame to lose that, wouldn't it?'

'It would,' he agreed. 'But it would be a bigger shame to lose out on the chance of something more.'

'Put so persuasively, how could I disagree?'

He looked her straight in the eye. 'So, what do you recommend we do to resolve things? And I'm talking about the immediate future, not some vague time in the future.'

At his teasing tone, she pressed an index finger to her top lip and tapped it as though giving his question her utmost deliberation. 'How about you move from that chair the other side of the table and sit closer to me?'

He rose smoothly from his chair and sat down in the one to her right. 'Now, seeing as you're the one with all the bright ideas,' he said, placing an elbow on the table and resting his chin on the upturned palm of his hand to look at her, 'what do we do next?'

'Well, we could sit here in the moonlight and enjoy the view of the garden, or . . .' She deliberately left the word hanging in the air between them.

'Or?' he repeated, staring even more intently at her.

He was so near now she could see the golden flecks in his amber eyes in the candlelight and for a split second she thought she could hear his heart thumping, but then she realised it was her own heart beating wildly as she felt herself falling headlong into the exquisite embrace of the moment. 'Or,' she murmured, 'we could make full use of the moonlight and enjoy our first kiss?'

His response was to put a hand lightly to her shoulder, before moving it to the nape of her neck and drawing her to him. The exact moment when their lips met in a deliciously soft and uncomplicated way an owl hooted, followed immediately by the call of another.

'Is that a good omen?' Daniel asked, barely moving his mouth away from hers. 'Owls serenading us?'

'The very best of omens,' she replied.

They kissed again, and for the longest time, each exquisite second filling Libby with the sensation of coming home. Of being exactly where she was meant to be.

Acknowledgements

This book came about because of my love of gardening and a moment of idle curiosity about garden designers, specifically trailblazing female garden designers like Gertrude Jekyll. After a little digging (*pun fully intended!*), I came across Norah Lindsay who led the most extraordinary life as a socialite and garden designer between the wars. As I delved deeper into her story, I was so inspired that the seed of an idea was sown (*there goes another pun!*) and before I knew it, I was putting together a cast of characters for a book.

While the life of Norah Lindsay inspired me, the characters of Elfrida and Bess and everything I put them through is down to me and my vivid imagination.

As always, I must thank my editor Kate Mills for helping to prune my manuscript into shape (*yes, there's another deliberate pun!*) and for the whole team at HQ Stories and my agent Jonathan Lloyd for their support and care.

If I didn't thank Mr Trevor Newell, he'd never speak to me again, so thank you, Trevor!

Finally, I'd like to thank and applaud all the amazing gardeners and garden designers who make our world a better place.